CHRISTOPHER EVANS ... South Wales. He has a B.Sc ... Certificate in Education fro ... moving to London in 1975 ... industry before becoming a full-time writer in 1979. He was recipient of an Arts Council grant in 1980 and is the author of three novels: *Capella's Golden Eyes* (1980), *The Insider* (1981), *In Limbo* (1985) and a guidebook, *Writing Science Fiction* (1988). He has recently completed his new novel *Chimeras*, and is about to start work on another.

ROBERT HOLDSTOCK was born in Kent, in 1948. He has degrees in Zoology and Medical Zoology and worked in Medical Research before becoming a freelance writer in 1975. His novels include *Eye Among the Blind* (1976), *Earthwind* (1977), *Necromancer* (1978) and *Where Time Winds Blow* (1981). More recently he has published a volume of short stories *In the Valley of the Statues*. He has written historical fantasies, as Christopher Carlsen (*The Berserker*) and a series of occult novels as Robert Faulcon (*Night Hunter*) as well as the novelisation of *The Emerald Forest*. *Mythago Wood* (1984), won the World Fantasy Award: its companion volume, *Lavondyss* has recently been published.

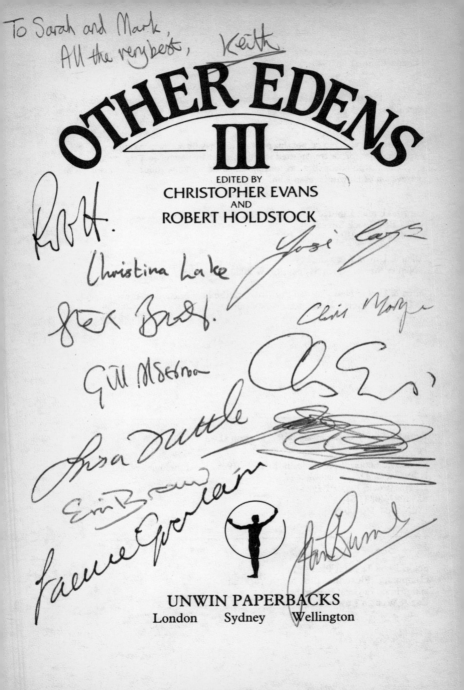

To Sarah and Mark,
All the very best, Keith

OTHER EDENS
III

EDITED BY
CHRISTOPHER EVANS
AND
ROBERT HOLDSTOCK

UNWIN PAPERBACKS
London   Sydney   Wellington

First published in paperback by Unwin Paperbacks, an imprint of Unwin
Hyman Limited, in 1989.

Unwin Hyman Limited
15–17 Broadwick Street
London W1V 1FP

Allen & Unwin Australia Pty Ltd
8 Napier Street, North Sydney, NSW 2060, Australia

Allen & Unwin New Zealand Ptd Ltd with the Port Nicholson Press
75 Ghuznee Street, Wellington, New Zealand

British Library Cataloguing in Publication Data

Other Edens 3.
1. Science fiction short stories in English, 1945 – – Anthologies
I. Evans, C. D. (Christopher D.), *1951–*
II. Holdstock, Robert, *1948–*
823'.0876'08 [FS]
ISBN 0-04-440400-X

Set in 10 on 11 point Plantin by
Computape (Pickering) Ltd, North Yorkshire
and printed in Great Britain by
Cox & Wyman Ltd, Reading

Contents

v

OTHER EDENS 3

Introduction

This third volume of *Other Edens* appears at a healthy time for science fiction and fantasy in Britain. When we originally proposed the idea for the anthology in 1986, we did not know what sort of response it would receive, although the prevailing wisdom maintained that there was no market in the UK for new short story collections. Since then, a variety of publishers have commissioned original anthologies, some of which should be appearing this year. In addition, an annual reprint collection of the best sf stories of the year has been inaugurated, incorporating critical articles surveying what's been happening in the field.

On the magazine front, there are similar signs of good health. The stalwart *Interzone* has now moved from quarterly to bimonthly publication, the first issue of a new magazine, *The Gate*, is about to appear, and other outlets such as *Fear* and *GM* magazine have begun to publish sf and fantasy regularly. All in all, it's a good time to be writing imaginative fiction in the UK.

Other Edens 3 contains a higher proportion of newer authors than previous volumes. Some have already published work in *Interzone* and elsewhere, others have novels forthcoming or in progress, others still have only recently begun to write seriously for publication. We believe that all have the potential to make their mark on the field over the next decade or so.

Once again, the stories we've assembled range from strongly science-based fiction to the wilder reaches of fantasy, continuing our policy of trying to make each collection as mixed as possible. One of the interesting things about responses to previous volumes is that readers are adamantly pro or con quite different stories. This is fine with us, since a principal aim of the series has been to show how *diverse* the field now is.

A few readers have also commented on the brevity of our introductions to each volume. In response, we can only say that this was deliberate and meant to reflect the fact that we have no particular agenda for the field, no fixed philosophy about what writers should be writing. Even well-intentioned literary ideologies have a habit of straightjacketing writers or condemning others out of hand for not following them. We believe that the best stories arise from inspiration and passion rather than ideology, and those in *Other Edens* are meant to reflect that ethos. To us, they simply demonstrate that new talent certainly is burgeoning in all areas of the field, offering continued proof that imaginative fiction remains an important tool for interpreting the modern world and our place in it.

One final point: the present vitality in the British sf and fantasy scene is due in no small part to the efforts of committed and enthusiastic editors at a number of UK publishing houses. Our particular thanks go again to Jane Johnson for backing us a third time; also thanks to Jim Burns for his splendid covers.

Christopher Evans and Robert Holdstock
London, April 1989

KEITH ROBERTS

The Grey Wethers

They had left the car where they always left it, on the grass verge by the two green-painted signs, to the Nature Reserve and to Adam's Grave. The Grave itself, the great Mound, lay high atop its hill, a notch cut, small with distance, into the dazzle of sky and wind. Opposite, the track climbed to the ridge, above which the land swooped into a great bowl, the long slope marked with tiny lateral furrows. Deeper ruts, crisscrossing, showed where the farm carts came; in winter they filled with iron-green glass that cracked and fractured, white, and sealed across again. Though the cracks still showed, like deep milk underneath the mud. Now, the March winds had dried the crests so that Dell hopscotched between, Mairead following, Skip bounding ahead, bounding as he bounded everywhere, lashing his shaggy white-tipped tail, spinning and crouching. And him no longer a pup, no longer a puppy dog at all but five years old, half as old as her.

Mairead held the gate that led on to the down, the long steel gate that would always jam against its post, have to be lifted to the latch. The wheel ruts curved beneath, fanned across the shoulder of the nearer hill to where the old fort gripped the crest, earth walls worn to nubs, to hollows in the grass. Best seen from farther off, the valley where the cars ran bright as insects; dark lines of bank and ditch, a slanting cap crowning the crest of down that butted, always butted, against the sailing sky.

Dell looked down around her feet, turned back to see the Grave that as ever climbed as she climbed, towering, staying level with her eyes. Here, so high, the grass was nibbled tiny, grass and the clover, worn by sheep, the thousands of munching years. Her father showed her once; 'Look, Dell,' he said, 'how small. Tiny, Dell, how small.' So she knelt close to the little land, the Fairy land that clothed the greater, and Time stopped for a while.

1

Between the hills the wind was hardly felt, though on the drive back from the coast it tugged and pulled the car. Dell sat content, Skip curled up close, knowing Mairead would stop as she always stopped, close to home where the hills sprawled ahead. Always the walk to the fort, her favourite walk though she could not say why, the fort where her mother drew and painted once, in summer. The wind that always blew rattled the paper edge against the board, made little white vibrations; while she sat cross-legged staring to the Grave, the grave where Adam lay ybounden, like the Bible, like in the song, on Wodnes Beorge, Walker's Hill. Her map proclaimed the words, with pride it seemed, in curling letters that themselves were old.

The girl turned, shoulders hunched, began to climb. The wind pushed instantly at her back, as she had known it must. Later she would turn to face it; open her mouth and let it enter, make her cold and clean. Her hands were in her pockets; one gripped the ball that all day long had made a hard lump in the anorak. She took it out and threw it, not strongly, for the wind would take it too, hurry it over and beyond the ridge of chalk. The shape of Skip, pursuing, seemed flattened to the ground, jinking as the ball caught tussocks. On the way back the ball would hang against the wind, dipping sudden to the gusts; but the dog would never miss. He would take it from the air each time with a sidelong leap and twist; snap of the jaws, as he took stormflies in the summer.

New-bought, the ball was yellow, acid-green; the mud quietened it, mud and the chalk, as Mairead quieted the colours on her palette with umber, raw sienna. To one side, always, the long squirl of cobalt, like a bright, unlikely worm. Cold, for the shadows; though there were few shadows now, in her paintings of suns and moons. The new phase obsessed her, so she had worked days, till the house was redolent of turpentine; the narrow, precious bottles, easy to upset. When her daughter bounded through, or Skip. Mairead would not complain; though the studio door was afterwards more firmly latched.

The scent of other bottles was more private. Dell sniffed them, cautious, vaguely curious. The gin was sharp and sweet together; the whiskey peppery, metallic. Each label bore a map, in blue and red and green. Mairead painted the maps; then the bottles themselves, lit gold and silver by the moons and suns, each burning in the liquid. Later she would lie back, on the sofa that itself was paint-splodged, and her breathing would become harsh. Her daughter would bring

2

her blankets; next day the canvases would be destroyed. Which was a waste and loss.

Dell turned finally at the crest; and the wind was a solid thing at last, pushing the breath back into her throat. On the road below, the cars still moved; light flared above the Grave, the dark, inverted notch cut from the sky. From here too she could see the farther scarp; long grey-green slope that was the true edge of the Downs. The road dropped to it, causewayed for part of its length; on the map the banking showed like caterpillar legs, sharp-pointed, outward-facing strokes. The hills showed too; brown lines that crowded close, like rucks in cloth. '*Wodnes Beorge*,' she said, liking the syllables. '*Wodnes Beorge*.' Then it seemed the words themselves were split, as the afternoon was split in fragments, bright planes through which Skip jumped, frozen each time as Time itself slowed down, like snapshots in a camera. '*Wod-nes Be-orge*,' she said. '*Wod-nes Be-orge*.' It was an incantation often used; the sounds the Old Men made. They had a taste like electricity.

Her mother was calling. Dell knew it was a question; but the wind took the syllables away, shredding them peel-thin. She shrugged and nodded. Beyond the Grave a blue cloudbank was forming, driving from the south. Beyond it, a thousand miles away, the sunlight shot in beams like searchlights, radiating. 'You can see the air,' she said. 'You can see the air.' She opened the anorak; the drawstring of the hood flogged round her face. If she stood on tiptoe, arms raised so, then surely she would lift up like a bird. She felt the grass light beneath her feet. Soon she would rise; or be bowled back the farther slope, to where trees thrust up like buttons on a cloth. But they of course were models, not real at all. Her father took her once to see such things; raised her to see small trains move, each no longer than her arm, past cottages and stations. While a man worked switches, lights came on in each tiny compartment. 'Look,' he said. 'Look at all the people, Dell.' She was inside already though, while gaints watched through glass, cloud-tall; there was no scale to things. 'I could fly,' she said, then as now. 'I could fly if I really tried.'

At her feet were molehills. They stretched for yards along the crest, back down the slope. Mole City, she called the place; because she had never seen so many. Each was conical, of fresh brown earth, though the track below was greyed by chalk; their shape echoed the great hill to the north, the hill with its circling stones. She touched the nearest with her foot. All things could be made to join, blend with each other.

3

Her mother read a piece once from a book. A man became an animal, turned to a sky star. She understood the words, though Mairead did not explain them. She closed the pages; and the man-thing trotted away, tossing its horns, across a field of grass.

'We'll go back now,' said the woman. Her body was thin and sharp; the wind was biting her.

'No,' said Dell. 'Let's stay.' Later though she too was glad to climb into the car.

'Were you all right?' said the other. 'Did it happen, on the hill?'

She shook her head. 'No,' she said. 'I didn't smell the lilacs.'

She took the ball from her pocket, offered it to Skip. He nosed at it, then her hand. But he wasn't interested now; it was only alive when he could chase it. 'You couldn't have done any drawing today,' she said. 'The paper would have blown away.'

She sat in her room, stared down through the one low window. The paint round the frame was cracked, yellowing a little. Though that did not trouble her; it had always been that way. Like the frayed rug, the ceiling that bulged down at one corner and was stained with damp. The house was old; as old, she sometimes thought, as the stones. Hilda, from school, had turned her nose up mightily, the one time she had been invited in. 'I don't know how you can *stand* it,' she said, pulling a face. '*My* mummy wouldn't, that's for sure.' The last was a new phrase, one she was proud of. Dell turned away, uninterested; though later she did show the other how she spelled her name. Dearbhla, the old way. It was on her birth certificate; Mairead let her keep it, along with other things, in a box beneath the bed. But Hilda was once more unimpressed. 'Fancy saying all that,' she said. 'It would sound like being sick.'

Dell shrugged. Hilda was a podgy little creature; blonde plaits that struck out stiffly, small cunning sideways-sliding eyes. She wondered vaguely why Mairead had called her in. 'You want some friends,' her mother had said, in a rare moment of expansiveness. 'Some company.' But she already had her friends.

She hunched her shoulders, arms linked round her knees. In front of the house, on a triangle of grass, was what they called the Playground; a climbing frame, a swing, a little roundabout. At one time you could sit on the slatted top and be whirled around, stand on the wooden running board that brushed the grass as it rotated. As she became giddy so the flower heads, dandelion and campion, became stars in a bright green sky. But the centre pivot broke, and nobody had fixed it. Michael would have, her father; only he had gone. Nobody came much now; just the older children sometimes, with their shouting and their trannies. She'd heard folk complain from time to time; but Dell was never troubled. To her the shouts seemed far off, like insect-buzzings heard through glass. Perhaps it was the Wethers, making a silence round themselves.

She raised her eyes. Beyond the Playground was the lane, slightly sunken between low earth banks. One way led to the Grave and the old fort; the other, past the school, went finally to the big hill and the stones. Opposite, behind a low hedge, were the Wethers, crouched in their narrow field. From the house you could nearly see them all; perhaps that was why Mairead had chosen it. Certainly she had painted them often enough, she never seemed to grow tired. It would be the bottles for a time, or suns and moons like now; drinking the gin, and sleeping on the sofa. Always though, she would go back. The Wethers called her, stone voices in the night. Dell heard them sometimes; only the voices themselves were silence. Silence that made shapes.

. From where she sat, she could see most of the flock; the huge ones, grey and flat, that were the great rams, the small ones snuggled at their sides. Once, they owned all Wiltshire; there was a notice by the hedge, close to the little stile, that told how it had been. *Fragments of a sarsen sheet once covering the county*. That was how the words went. *The holes seen on some were made by the roots of palm trees*. Though that was obviously wrong; no palm trees ever grew here. Then the machines had come, breaking them up, dragging them away, till only these few were left. After them had come the ploughs, changing the land for all time. Now only the Grave was safe; not even machines could climb as high as that.

She frowned. She had been puzzled when she first heard the word, perhaps a little scared; though now she was older she knew they were her friends. Dawns, and in the slow twilight of the Plain, they looked like sheep lying down; which was how they got their name. *Wether* from Old English; Old High German *Widar*, Old Norse *Vethr*, Gothic *Withrus*. The names were like the stones; you could sense the years inside them. She rushed to Mairead, proud of her discovery; so the Celt, to please her stalk-thin daughter, made another painting. She put the words around it, like a scroll of honour; then came the gin, to wash it all away. Like Inky Pinky Spider.

5

Dell hadn't cared. Some of the stones had faces on them, made of lichen; she sat on their backs and counted, over and again. You never reached the same total twice; but that was as it should be. Because the Wethers weren't the same. Michael told her; at night they ran about, if you saw them once, in one place, they wouldn't be there again. She knew it to be true. Mornings, when the mist lay milk-thick in the lane, the field was empty; the stone sheep were at play. She licked her lips, whispered the old words. *Withrus, Vethr, Widar, Wether*. If you knew the names of things, then you could call them. And they would come.

She was grateful to Michael for the learning of the words. Sometimes, even now, she wished he would come back.

She got up, stared a little longer at the blueing field. Mairead had gone straight to the studio when they got back; by now she would have lost track of time. She'd go down soon herself, make jam sandwiches for tea. Skip liked them; and they never seemed to spoil his proper meal. She'd walk him then, circle back to the field. Once inside the stile he was always quiet.

She dreamed that night; the same dream as before. The scent came first, like lilac; though that didn't really describe it at all. Rather, it was sharp and sweet together, like the gin; it left a taste in her mouth like metal. It didn't matter though, not when she was lying down.

Later, the lane filled with the machines. Their wheels were huge, with thick, slanting treads, and each had a tall black chimney. There was much clanking and fussing; the smoke they made was sharp and cindery, catching at the throat. They'd come for the Wethers, the last flock of all; but the Wethers would not be caught. Instead they came charging, fast across the field. Their stony hooves drowned all other sounds. Dell, waking, remembered the look their faces bore. She squealed with delight. Night was sectioned as the day had been; split into pieces.

Next morning was a school time; she could never tell beforehand whether Mairead would send her or no. On painting days, or when she drank her whiskey, she would as often as not forget; other times she would shout and wave her arms, scurry round the little kitchen that always smelled of cabbage. Its floor was of red, uneven brick; potato peelings spilled from the plastic bin beneath the sink. Dell would swallow lumpy porridge, half-warmed from the night before.

It lay heavy in her stomach, like a weight. She had never been very interested in food.

The school stood back a little from the lane. Like the cottage, it was built of old red bricks, with tall windows that from the outside always looked dark. Except at Christmas when she came back for the carols; they shone yellow then, like eyes. Their frames were green, with diamond shapes at top and bottom. The woodwork round the gables was painted green as well, with lines of wooden points Miss Chaston said were dags. Though to Dell they looked like little fences, hanging in the air. The week before, they'd been told to paint a picture of the place; only she became bored, began to paint the Wethers instead. Miss Chaston had frowned. 'Now, Dell,' she said, 'there aren't any rocks and pebbles in our playground; you know we always keep it tidy.'

Nobody knew, of course, where the sheep would rest. She almost shrugged, till she remembered it made Miss Chaston angry. She had called her to the front only the week before, made her stand on the little step beside her desk. She rolled up the sleeve of the floral smock she always wore in class, and made her hold her arm out. 'Remember, Dell,' she said, 'this hurts me as much as you.' She'd slapped her wrist then, ritually; and Dell had frowned. It didn't hurt at all; she wondered why the other bothered to do it.

She picked a brush up, smudged the stones out. Some of the paint ran down. She saw, without surprise, the face of a great sheep; a sheep with angry, slitted eyes. She smoothed the paint again, till the paper was all plain grey.

Mr Harwood took the class in the afternoon. He didn't teach them often; just when the mood was on him, as Miss Chaston muttered once. She stood aside, one foot thrust out, her wooden pointer to her throat to show her disapproval; only he never seemed to notice. He would make the class chant poetry, shout sometimes when they got it wrong; take down the dusty wooden shapes from the shelf above the blackboard, the cones and cubes and bricks, show how if you cut through them you got triangles and ovals. He was tall and stooping, smelling of tobacco; his hair was grey, hanging across his forehead, and there were leather patches on the elbows of his jacket. Dell liked him, vaguely. He never stood too close, like Miss Chaston when she was angry. She didn't like people who stood too close.

They'd gone on an outing the week before, to the big hill and the stones. She'd had to take a pound; Mairead muttered and complained, found a coin finally in her purse. The sandwiches Dell made herself, wrapping them in clingfilm. They'd used it on the cottage windows in the winter, to keep the cold out. Some was still there; in the studio it went brown from Mairead's cigarettes. She had wanted to take Skip on the coach, but it hadn't been allowed.

Mr Harwood had said he would test them. He began at once.

'Who put the stones there?'

'In the Bronze Age. Hundreds of years ago.'

'That's right. Why did they do it?'

'To make the crops grow strong.'

'Very good, Jane. How did they move the stones? Remember, some of them are very heavy.'

A chorus. 'Ropes and rollers!'

'That's right. With ropes and rollers.' The Head began to draw on the blackboard, carefully. After a time he seemed to forget the class. Whispers and gigglings, as the children lost attention; Miss Chaston looked round quickly, and they stopped.

As always, the chalk made little scraping sounds; small flecks fell to the wooden ledge below the board, collected there in drifts. Dell had read somewhere that was how chalk cliffs were made. She imagined the flecks, the little shells, dropping down through water. Sometimes they swirled, like snowflakes. Then the cliffs reared up. Like horn notes almost; the records Mairead played sometimes in the evenings. She told her the first horns were really that, made from heads of animals. The notion fascinated Dell. If you blew through one, the sound was the creature's voice; so it was still alive.

Mr Harwood sketched the rollers on which the stones had moved. He drew more, joined them in a band. 'What does this remind you of?'

'A tank!' That from the boys, with more enthusiasm.

'That's right. A tank. That's how they move, on tracks. They're just like rollers, really. Are any of your fathers in the Army?'

Miss Chaston drew a long, slow breath. He'd told her often enough he liked to relate lessons to modern things, things children could readily understand. But this was still her class; tanks didn't figure in her syllabus. He had no right, Headmaster or no. In any case she'd never really trusted bachelors. They didn't have the proper view of things.

He was talking now about the Site Museum. It was housed in the stable block of the old Manor. Harwood reflected vaguely that another trip should take in the house as well; more there for the children to relate to.

'Who founded the Museum?'

'Mr Keiller, sir!'

'The man who made the marmalade!'

At least the class remembered that. It had made them laugh.

'That's right. He became very rich; he bought up all the land around the stones.' Up to the outbreak of the War, English archaeology had still been in the hands of amateurs; at Sutton Hoo, a gardener found the shadow of a ship. Sites were protected now; but the museums could do little. Roads and towns still spread remorselessly; the professionals spent their time in hasty salvage.

The Head held up a photograph. The blades of the scissors seemed overlong, the looped handles jutted at an unaccustomed angle. Awkward to use, no doubt; but still an improvement on the old spring-loaded shears.

'What can you tell me about these?'

'Sir! Sir!' Again, an eager chorus.

He had been a barber-surgeon. A travelling man perhaps. Keiller found the bones, under the greatest of the fallen megaliths. The scissors were still there in the leather scrip; also a lancet, the coins that dated him. Edward the First, French copy of an English Stirling; though he wouldn't trouble the class with that. His own collection, such as it was, was private; relic of a former self, hardly to be recalled.

'The Middle Ages people were burying the stones. One fell on him as he was going by!' Children loved that sort of gory detail. He wondered what it really meant to them.

'Why were they burying the stones?'

'Devil worship, sir!'

Despite herself, the mistress flinched. That subject, likewise, was outside her scheme of things.

'Perhaps,' said Harwood mildly. 'Something made them do it, certainly. Perhaps they were afraid of the stones. We shall never know for sure. Like we don't know the name of the man who was killed. Maybe he was helping them.'

Dell was puzzled. Nobody should be afraid of the stones. They had faces on them; so they were like the Wethers. If they could be called as well, the world would shake. 'He was called Mansel,' she said.

Silence, in the room. Like the silence that came so often, round the stones.

9

'What, Dell? What did you say?'

'The man underneath. He had grey hair. His wife was dead. A mole grew, on her cheek. It spread all over. There was a big lump on her neck. The priest touched it and it came open. Then she died.' She didn't often speak that many words at once. Usually there was no need.

Mr Harwood was kind to her. Sometimes when he wanted her to do a painting he called her out from class. Wall Charts, he called them. He would always say the same. 'Dell, would you do me another Wall Chart?' He gave her books to copy from; butterflies and moths, the parts of a flower. The paintings were easy; the lettering was harder. She had to make it thin, or Miss Chaston would be angry. Lettering should be thin and wobbly, drawn with pens.

There was a long bench, in the room where they did the dancing and P.E. She used that; there was space to lay the paints out. She washed the brushes carefully each time, as her mother had taught. The paintings made the others jealous; or so she had been told. Though she didn't know the meaning of the word. It sounded spiky, boring; so she hadn't looked it up.

Hilda stuck a pin in her, in Needlework. She watched the blood spot well up on her arm. It was a beautiful crimson-red. 'I'll bring my sheep,' she said. 'They'll tromple you.' She wasn't angry; Miss Chaston, shouting, sounded a long way off.

There were skeletons in the little Museum. One was a dog. It poised on tiptoe in its tall glass case, as if it was dancing. The rest of the class pulled faces, made noises like being sick. Till Miss Chaston snapped at them, shooed them outside. Dell stared, elbows on the little ledge below the glass, chin in her hands. Skeletons had puzzled her when she was small; though of course she understood them now. They were like sketches of things. Mairead made sketches before she began to paint. Little squiggles, broad charcoal sweeps. Sometimes the paint didn't cover all the lines. They were like bones themselves then, showing through. She decided the dog had probably been like Skip.

There was a card at the bottom of the case. It said about Windmill Hill. She didn't know where that was; but it sounded a good place to be. Windmills creaked as they went round, like bones. Or the Wethers, straining to get up. After a long day in the sun.

*

10

The Head faced Miss Chaston mildly across the desk. The study was small and square, skirtings and cupboards painted the same dark green. The single window faced onto the lane; the thin frames ended in decorative chevrons. On the sill stood an arrangement of dried plants; teazel heads, sprays of Honesty culled from the teacher's garden. The evening was bright; the room, east-facing, shadowed. The silver membranes of the seed pods were like things glimpsed beneath the sea.

His attention had wandered. 'I'm sorry?' he said. He eyed his pipe rack, vaguely. He would have liked to light up; it would be his first of the day.

'The child is evil,' said the other stubbornly.

He considered. 'Evil' was a complex word; too complex, surely, for a little village school. 'Freda,' he said, 'don't you think that's coming it a bit strong?'

She turned away, paced to the window. Stood staring into the lane. He regarded her square back, the rigid set of her shoulders. A scent came from her; something evanescent, vague. Redolent somehow of the cottage in which she lived; lavender and beeswax, plain, no-nonsense soap. Old grates still black-leaded, the piano in the front with its dull brass candle holders. Music was her forte, as he discovered early on; the nineteenth century of course, Elgar at a pinch. Though she confided once she thought *Gerontius* a little florid. On Tuesday mornings, her harsh voice always echoed from the hall. 'Sing,' she would command, imperiously. 'Sing . . .' She struck the keys stiff-fingered, discovering square rhythms, while the school chanted dutifully of March winds, Polish grenadiers. She was, he had decided, a good teacher of children. And also of course his second in command; the school depended on her.

The slang had irritated her, as he had known it must. He suppressed a smile. Mr Kenworth, certainly, would not have used it. But then, Mr Kenworth would not have done a lot of things. The previous Head had run the school for close on thirty years; on occasions it was still, 'Mr Kenworth used to say . . . Mr Kenworth always believed . . .' Usually though, the thoughts were unvoiced. From loyalty to him, or to her calling. For whatever reason, she was conscientious; he was aware of it, and felt proper gratitude.

She swung back. 'Mr Harwood,' she said, 'something must be done.'

He considered again. He knew Dell's background of course; as

11

much, at least, as the papers in his desk revealed. Mother an alcoholic, father a wastrel and worse. She was withdrawn, remote; but that, under the circumstances, was only to be expected. He had encouraged her where he could, seemingly with no result; but that too was allowed for. Cause and effect seldom related directly; such hopes were for the young and keen. Or maybe the old and foolish. Aloud he said, 'She has a strong imagination.'

The teacher snorted; the only word to describe the sound she made. 'You heard her this afternoon,' she said. 'It was sheer wickedness.' She paused. 'She upsets my class,' she said. From her, surely, the ultimate condemnation.

He rubbed his face. The child had described, accurately enough, the onset of skin cancer. He doubted she had got that from her books; though of course all things were possible. He wondered if Freda Chaston had come across the notion of psychometry. Certainly the museum cases had been unlocked, part of the private arrangement he had made. The children, Dell among them, had handled artefacts; flints and arrowheads, sherds of dark red haematite. He dismissed no concept, however unseemly or bizarre; not at least until such time as it could be disproved.

He glanced at the register the other had laid on the desk, drew it toward him. Red ticks denoted absences; a line of them stretched out beside Dell's name. He turned the page. The line extended itself. A poor record, certainly; the worst in the school. Also, the child was scruffy; no denying that. Hair lank, unkempt, where the rest were primped, beribboned.

He frowned. Scruffy, but no more. After all, the Health Visitor came each term. With her bowl of disinfectant, her telltale metal comb . . . He felt a gust of something that was nearly anger. He had known shabby children before; it was no crime.

The teacher had begun to speak again. He cut across her. 'It's been hard for her mother,' he said. 'It's not an easy living.' Privately he had been impressed by Mairead's work, the odd time he had visited. He tried to call on the parents of all the children; or those at least who didn't come to meetings. She'd answered the door herself, in paint-daubed shirt and jeans, stared blankly; but at least he'd been invited in. Paintings were scattered round the little house. The brush strokes had an angry, dancing quality; the line work was tortured, wiry. He saw, again and again, studies of the Wethers; graffiti, gin-assisted. To Freda Chaston, graffiti were an affront; blemishes to

12

be hidden, smoothed away. Certainly not art; but he'd seen enough of the alternative. Women in designer smocks, modelling coy terracotta when the mood was on them.

The painter handed him a glass. It was a little stained about the rim. He took it gravely, said, 'Cork Distillers' best.' He smiled; but the smile was not returned. She was inscrutable as her daughter.

Miss Chaston was still speaking. He realized he had missed more evidence. Strange to meet closed minds, here in the vastness of the Plain. Maybe that was the reason for them though. The people huddled in their cottages, trained clematis up trellises; but the night still seeped between the cracks. 'I'll see her,' he said tiredly. 'I'll have a talk with her. It can all be sorted out; just give me a few days.' He knew of course the other's real opinion of him. 'Left wing do-gooder' was a phrase that flitted across his mind. 'Bleeding heart Liberal' was another, though he doubted she would approve. She polished brasswork in the little church, made more of her Arrangements; Sundays she changed hymm numbers, hammered out the tunes. The iron fist lay on the organ keys as well.

He realized he had misjudged her mood. She was shaking with barely concealed rage; while still the words came hissing. Disgrace brought to the village; the stranger, the Irishwoman, still living in their midst. A pagan probably, or even worse, a Catholic; the child disrupting classes, spreading her wicked lies. Something must be done, and done at once. The girl must be Taken into Care. She gave the words full emphasis, as if they needed capitals.

He was jolted to awareness. He'd seen the process once; a scandal best forgotten. Children clinging screaming to their mothers' clouts, condemned by the machineries of state; a state professing welfare as its goal. Logic, justification, might well change their shape; repression never. He said, 'I hardly think –'

She shouted him down. She'd made the school her life's work; she'd not stand by and see it thrown away. If he could do nothing, there were those who would.

He was on his feet at last. Hard to remember the last time he'd felt rage. Her comments had been noted. The welfare of the children and the school were his responsibility and his alone. He must ask her now to leave.

She backed off, startled by the change in him. Hurried out and slammed the door. The flustered footsteps receded, mixed it seemed with the echoes of his voice.

He sat back slowly, staring at the wall. He picked his pipe up, laid it down again. He wasn't seeing the study. There'd been another schoolroom once, a schoolroom many miles away. Grimed brick outside, a fire escape, the noise of traffic. To it they sent the hopeless, the inept, to kick their heels till the law declared them free. He'd made mistakes of course, mistakes in plenty; born of frustration, the estate to which he'd come. Till finally he realized the higher duty laid on him. They were good children; proud to be Bell Monitors, make tea for all his guests, the endless visitors foisted on him by the authorities. While the children pottered at their woodwork, splashed about with paints, fed pigeons on the narrow, spotted sills. Beyond, their minds were empty. Press them for more and they would break; they'd already broken once. Students were sent him, from the training college; do-gooders one and all, keen to attest vocation, notch up credit. After the first few he would accept no more; it took too long, after they had gone, to calm and reassure his Innocents. During which time the school became a Unit, finally to be rationalised away. They took the last few from him, into Care. The screaming started then; he wondered sometimes if it had ever stopped. Meanwhile, he'd been lucky with the new position. The offer came from the blue; maybe the state owed something for the years he'd spent.

He rose, shrugged himself into his coat. He picked the pipe up from the desk, tapped out the bowl. Next term would be his last; he'd been planning his retirement for some time, hadn't as yet got round to making it known. A pity; because he knew he could have helped the child. He could have helped by leaving her alone.

She had learned to recognise the Old Dream by its smell and taste. The smell was compounded of many things; spitting tallow of the dips they lit for Feast Days, harshness of sweat, sweetness of dung and straw from the byre where the animals were penned against the dark. As ever, her father featured in it; her First Father, she called him. She had taken the phrase from a poem, though she didn't fully understand it. Summers, she would run to him readily enough; at the merrymaking in the village, the village with its scattering of huts, their roofs mounded with turves till they seemed to be growing from the land itself. Or in the church with its bare stone floor, piled with the thanksgivings of Harvest Home; she'd huddle, sucking her thumb, while the priest droned on about Sin and Death. In winter, the priest's barn swollen with tithes, the grain on which the villagers dropped sweat, his temper grew less certain. He was vaguer then and grim, grim as the bears that sometimes plagued the place; through the long nights, days when the sky was green-grey and the sun never came. Then he would kill the pig they fed all year on scraps. The first cut made a leaf shape in the fat, glistening and yellow; it was only later, when the blade touched its life, that the animal woke from trance. The squealing was like needles in the ears; till it was cut off finally and her father appeared, encrimsoned, arms full of the entrails from which he squeezed the shit, in honour of God's Birthday.

She didn't like his smell. Not when he came too close. Also, his weight was on her; and there was pain. Though that was later; her mother in the earth, his need to be assuaged. She understood, dimly; nonetheless, she screamed. He broke her lips, impatiently; and she cried out again. Distant, like the sounds made by another; the Sheep heard though, and raised their heads. They nuzzled him, the whole flock, bonking and crashing as he fled along the lane. The bites they took from him were not bites from his body. His arms and legs moved jerkily, flicking from plane to plane.

Skip followed, barking. The ice on the puddles was thin, breaking where he touched it with his feet. She gripped herself low down, and watched. Her heart was lightened fractionally. The Wethers had promised an early spring; she would plant her wheat and cut it, carry in the sheaves. Brush the earth floors, call neighbours to the feast; she would be free. But Michael shook his head, smiled at the fantasy. 'That's not work for a girl,' he said. 'For a pretty girl like you . . .'

He was more gentle with her. The Sheep stood round and watched; but they made no move to interfere. 'It's just a game,' he whispered, over and again. 'A lovely, pretty game . . .' Next day though she felt unwell; open, and a little slack somehow. Till the blood ran sudden to her sock, a vivid, telltale streak; and she was surrounded once again by noise. Everyone, it seemed, was shouting; her teacher, Mr Kenworth, the whole world. She wished it hadn't happened in the class; it made her feel ashamed. She disliked the voices, clattering, white coats; they started the lilac-smell. She'd scratched herself on brambles; later she stepped in a puddle, so the dye came from her shoe. They wouldn't believe her though, wouldn't believe a word. She wanted to go home.

Michael was good to her, buying the dog, taking her to see the little trains. Skip he brought home one night in his coat, a tiny bundle of black and white over which she crowed and chortled, being small.

15

Though Mairead was less pleased. Her voice was wispy, cornstalk-thin; sharp finally in anger, at another mouth to feed. Which was unusual; her nature, once more open, had been undermined by stress. Dell lay huddled with the puppy, hearing the voices through the wall. Michael had the drink on him; it was a night for anger, breaking of things once precious. At breakfast she kept her eyes down, not wanting to see bruised faces. Later she sat astride the greatest of the Wethers, felt the coldness of it shift a little and move. She patted it, to make it be still. She loved her folk, the both of them, wanted no harm to come.

The house was unusually quiet, and the car had gone. Maiead had left odd times before, without announcing the fact; this time though she had taken her paintings. Also the rest of her things; the studio was empty, save for the suns and moons. Those she had cut through with a knife. Dell supposed the strain had become too much.

She was not vitally concerned. There was butter in the freezer, a sack of potatoes in the outhouse. Its stone walls were hung with cobwebs now; it looked friendly, not the sort of place where pigs might die. She would boil the potatoes and mash them, make puddles with the butter from which Skip would lap. She fed him, opening a tin; washed her face, and dressed herself for school.

Harwood was ill. He couldn't remember being sick in term time before; but there was no denying it. Neck glands swollen to grotesque proportions, till his face looked like a dumpling set amid rolls of fat, the hairs of his beard sticking out like individual silver wires. The fact must be reported; after which there would be quarantine, something his soul abhorred. But the children had to be protected. And Freda would cope of course; she would be in her element, she had been Acting Head times enough before. She would change the morning service, bring forward those hymns closest to her heart; all things would be bright and beautiful again.

The fever made him giddy; he half-fell, on the way back from the bathroom. Though the floating sensation was by no means unpleasant. Waiting for the doctor, his chin fell toward his chest. The dream that came was by no means to his taste. It seemed he took a spade, drove it into fresh green turf. Beneath were white worms; featureless and stubby, frozen into arabesques. He knew if he looked up, other worms would fill the sky. They would be black; his

16

Innocents drew them, when the students pushed too hard. Always the same, the dark worms and the pale; much better not to use the spade at all.

The downstairs bell was ringing. He tried to call, to say the door was open; but all that emerged was a croak. He sat up, struggled into a dressing gown. Doc Freeman was a good man; brusque, but reliable. And always on the dot. He wondered about the young girl he'd been troubled over. Maybe the doc would have the answer. He'd forgotten her name though. He opened the door, still fumbling with the cord of the dressing gown. 'Look at this,' he said. 'Twenty quid, on the drip-feed; and the elbow's going through already.'

He lay back, jolted by the hard springs of the ambulance. As ever, the thing was noisy and uncomfortable. He felt sorry for those genuinely sick, who had to travel in it. The driver used his siren; and he smiled. That would bring the neighbours out in force; if they weren't out already. '*The clinking bell gaed through the toon*,' he said; a line from a poem he hadn't thought about in years. Later, he fell into a doze.

Miss Chaston faced her class impassively, one foot as ever thrust a little forward. The children were quiet, unusually so for them; more then one glanced uneasily at the tall windows, where rain wept steadily from the cold grey sky.

'Pay attention please,' said the teacher. As badge of her new status she was wearing her best suit; neat, old-fashioned and dark. Her white blouse sported a froth of lace at the throat; tying the bow, she had been uncomfortably aware of how her neck was wattled and discoloured. She herself was not as young as she had been; for her too, in the new climate of things, retirement would shortly loom. What would happen to the school then, she didn't like to think.

She put the thought from her. Duty, after all, came first; and her responsibility was a heavy one. She had never believed in shielding children from the harsher aspects of life; on the other hand, there was need for caution. They showed so little, seemed at times uncaring; but their minds were still at their most impressionable. No telling what might result in later years from thoughtless errors now. In that at least she had agreed with her late Head; though in other matters they had been in less accord. Almost, she supposed one might say, at daggers drawn; though she instinctively disliked such violent metaphors.

'Mr Harwood,' she said carefully, 'was a very good man. He was caring and conscientious, and had all your interests very much at heart. I'm sure the news of his unexpected death was a great shock to you, as it was to us all. And that you will miss him.' She smiled; for her, a rare expression. 'Life, though, must go on,' she said. 'As the school must go on. This, after all, is what he would have wished. We all feel very sorry; but we must not let that affect our own lives, or our work. In particular, our work. That, also, is something he would have wanted.'

She paused, to let the effect of the words sink in. The children stared woodenly, unsure for the most part how they were supposed to respond.

The stocky woman consulted a typewritten sheet, began to read off names. 'Those of you attending the funeral will please be back at one o'clock sharp,' she said. 'The coach will be leaving promptly at one fifteen. You will assemble in the main hall; Alice and Moira will take charge of the wreath, to which you have all contributed. The rest of you will go to Mrs Leonard's class; she will look after you. Now, is that clear? Does anybody have any questions?'

Silence from the children. None of them, it seemed, wished to question either death or its appurtenances.

'Very well then,' said the teacher. She glanced at the wall clock. 'You may begin to pack your things. But quietly.' Her glance, travelling on, came to rest on the thin child in the centre of the front row of desks; the position to which she had been elevated when news of Harwood's illness reached the school. She was small for her years; face pointed, eyes dark-shadowed. It seemed a gust of wind might blow her away. For a moment, Freda Chaston felt a twinge of compassion; then something in her seemed to snap. 'Dell,' she said, 'what did I tell you yesterday? About your blouse and skirt?'

The girl was silent.

'They are filthy,' said the teacher deliberately. 'There are food stains all over them; and your collar is disgusting. You cannot have changed that garment for at least a week.'

A giggle from somewhere; she silenced it with a glance. 'You, of course, will not be attending the service,' she said. 'This evening, I shall come to see your mother. This whole thing has gone far enough. You may now dismiss.'

Dell sat thoughtfully for a moment. The fat, as Michael would have said, was in the fire. She sensed, dimly, what the phrase meant; though at times it still puzzled her slightly. After all, nobody threw

18

food away. To burn it was to feed the Devil; Mairead had dinned it into her often enough. She thought, in a moment of spite, that she would set Skip onto Miss Chaston when she arrived; but she knew it wouldn't work. He would cringe and back away, tail wagging furiously; he wasn't a fighting dog. Though she didn't blame him for that; she supposed it came from once being a stray. It was the same with dustbins; he could never resist them, no matter how well he was fed. She'd seen him round the back of the school once or twice; there had been trouble over that as well.

She squared her thin shoulders fractionally. If Skip couldn't help, there were others who would. She'd not give in tamely; after all, she wasn't Mairead's child for nothing. Or her father's.

The woman pushed cautiously at the low door. It yielded to her touch, creaking faintly; it seemed as ramshackle as the rest of the place. Beyond was a narrow, stone-flagged hall. She glanced back. The policemen had followed; behind them was the inevitable group of gawpers, craning and fidgeting. She tutted irritably. 'Wait here,' she said. 'I'll call you if I need you.' The older of the constables shrugged slightly; the other turned away toward the cars, herding the onlookers before him. 'Nothing's happening,' he said, 'there's nothing to see. Just go home, all of you. Come on, move along . . .'

The visitor stepped forward, wrinkling her nose with distaste. The cottage stank of dirt and stale greens; but the first encounter was important. Children were often uncooperative; sulky and recalcitrant, or worse. Old folk were easier in many ways; they usually followed orders, if enunciated clearly and concisely enough.

She had reached the kitchen. She frowned again at the sink loaded with crockery, the overflowing waste bin beneath. The crockery itself was chipped and old, no plate matching any other. These people had been little more than gypsies; she was surprised the Department had not been alerted before. Someone had slipped up badly; she could see already what the place could become. In the hands of a young couple, perhaps; folk with something to contribute to the country. At least the press hadn't got wind of the visit; busybodies were the bane of her life.

Something made her turn. Her back hair prickled slightly. A black and white mongrel had materialised from the shadows, stood watching her fixedly. She took a breath. 'Good boy,' she said, 'good dog. Where's your mistress?' She half stepped forward; and her heart

19

skipped a beat. The thing volleyed barks; but it was backing off already. It squatted in the corner of the room, its tail thumping nervously.

'Good boy,' she said again. She edged past, unlatched a second door. Beyond was a small room, bare-floored. The boards were spotted here and there; she saw a squashed paint tube, spoiled canvases stacked against the wall. The one old couch was similarly daubed; shreds of browning plastic hung across the window.

She turned her head. From upstairs somewhere came a sound. Dull, and intermittent. *Be-dop*, *be-dop*. She stood a moment then began to climb, placing her feet at the sides of the treads with care.

Dell had slept badly. They hadn't come yesterday; but she was sure she wouldn't be left in peace much longer. Who 'they' would be she didn't know; but they would mean no good to her, Miss Chaston would see to that. She wondered why the teacher hated her so much; after all, she had never done her any harm.

Perhaps they would take Skip away. She hugged him in the dark. 'I won't let them.' she whispered. 'I won't let them.' A tear formed suddenly, splashed onto her wrist. She hadn't cried when Mairead went, or Michael. Skip was special though.

She walked with him, first thing. Halfway to the Grave, or so she thought. The morning was warm but overcast; the sky was a sort of bleary blue. She was back by eight; she sat and watched the children trudge along the lane to school. Somehow she didn't want to be away from the house too long.

She had thought for a time she might barricade the door. She dragged the big chest of drawers part way to the hall; but it jammed irretrievably, there was no way she could move it further. She left it, went up to her room. Perhaps it was for the best. Mairead might come back first, or even Michael. They would protect her, she was sure of it.

She felt drained now. Helpless. She stared down at the Sheep. They were asleep though, she could always tell. They wouldn't wake till dark; if the people came then, it would be all right. But she knew they wouldn't wait.

She pulled the box from underneath the bed. In it were her treasures; the birth certificate, an old book with brown pictures of the Stones, Skip's first toy of all that was only a piece of knotted rag. And drawings, some by herself, the ones Mairead had said were best; though she was sure she could paint much better now. Finally she lifted out the first of her own Sheep. They lived in the box as well; the small ones, small enough to be picked up from the fields and carried home. She stroked their beautiful grey roundness, crooning; arranged them in circles then in lines, like armies come for battle. Once the dog pushed his head round the door, but she shooed him off. 'Go away, Skip,' she said. 'I'm busy.' She was wholly engrossed; she hadn't played this game for years.

She picked two of the Sheep up, one in either hand. They sniffed each other, cautiously; then they decided to fight. Their noses clashed together. *Be-dop*, *be-dop*, they went. Then again.

She looked up. A stranger was standing in the doorway. She was tall, very tall it seemed; she wore smart clothes of browny, greeny cloth and a bag was on her shoulder. When she saw the girl her face relaxed. 'Hello, Dell,' she said. 'I've been looking all over for you. You can put those dirty old stones away now; you're coming with me.' She hurried forward.

They heard the crashing from the stairs; and a cry, cut off as soon as uttered. They ran forward; and the leading constable checked. 'Jesus Christ,' he said. 'Jesus Christ . . .' For the visitor was no longer smart. She came on hands and knees, groping for the light through a world that was blind and warm and stinging. On her back, jigging triumphantly, a small shape. '*Be-dop*, *be-dop*,' it cried. 'Gee-up . . .' And each word was a blow.

They hauled Dell off. She dropped the stones, because her hands were slippy; she began to cry again, because she wanted them back. 'It wasn't me,' she said, 'it was the Sheep.' Then the world began to fade; and there was a smell of lilacs.

They had parked their car on the triangle of grass before the little cottage; the banked lane beyond was narrow, it would have impeded other traffic. Now he turned, hands on hips, to stare at the place. The dulled windows, bright FOR SALE sign on its pole beside the gate. He looked across again to the swing. A car tyre hung from one rusty chain; beside it the slatted roundabout tilted to the grass. 'A pity,' he said gently. 'They could be repaired. The house would need a lot of work; but it would be a fine place for the children.'

The woman tightened her grip on his arm. She said, 'I don't like the Stones.'

'Oh,' he said, 'the stones. They're rather fine, actually. There are only two patches of them left, the others are a little north of here.' He looked down at her, smiling. His hair was fair and curly, turning to grey; the plain white neckband showed a modest inch through the collar of his vest. 'Just think,' he said. 'The Wethers, almost in our garden. We could make a feature of it; show off, to all our friends.'

She wouldn't look at him. 'Please, John,' she said. 'I followed you in everything else. But not this. It wouldn't be right. Not for us.'

He stared a moment longer, quizzically. Then he reached across to grip her hand. 'It's all right,' he said, 'don't worry. We'd best be setting back now anyway.' He began to walk her, slowly, toward the rusty Ford.

THE GREY WETHERS
BRITISH NATIONAL GRID REFERENCE SU 144 673

J. D. GRESHAM

The New Mapper

The late afternoon sun was warm, even through the haze, and Merritt had rolled back her grey sleeves and tilted her face towards it. Feeling the heat on her forearms, she smiled, eyes closed in pure pleasure. Her shoulder ached from the weight of the map bag, and the leg which dragged when she was tired had troubled her for the last few miles.

Her smile faded as she looked around. The gentle rise and fall of the hills did nothing to soften the barren aspect of the land which stretched in uniform browns and yellows to the horizon. She glanced back the way she had come, seeing the same tedious combination of soil and patchy plant growth that she had been walking through for weeks since her arrival from the Sahel. The ache in her shoulder was matched by the longing she felt to see cultivated land again, a longing that had increased with every day's journey northwards. She needed to see signs of human habitation, instead of the interminable succession of ridges and slopes that sprawled like ungainly limbs around her.

She squinted across the valley to the west of the knoll where she was resting, glancing down once at the unrolled map on her knees, and screwing up her eyes again to look where the slightly darker ground showed her the line of the Old road. The trees had all gone, of course, merely a few withered stumps where there should have been a good few acres of copse skirting the hillside which hid the next village from view.

'Dunwick,' she said aloud, hoping that the sound of the name would stop her thinking about how tired she was. 'I wonder if you'll be there.'

She speculated briefly as to which would be the greater surprise: to find the village standing, whole and inhabited, or to find that it had completely disappeared. In the end, she decided that the latter would probably give her the bigger shock. She had found people in a village once, a religious community which had settled there, risking the tainted soil and poisoned water to preserve their freedom of belief. She had found it hard to believe that people would put such a value on freedom; she thought she understood it better now.

She looked down at the map again. It had been painstakingly drawn and coloured. She could see the faint correction marks in a couple of places, though an untrained eye would not have noticed them. She wondered vaguely who had made the copy; it was not a hand she recognised, certainly not one of those who had sat near her in the inadequate light of the map room. Her finger ran lightly along the brightly coloured roads, touched for a moment on a name, ran on, stopped on another, went back to the first.

Dunwick. Pronounced, probably, Dunnick. It was the names on the Old maps that had lured her away from the safe desk job, the assured credits, the hostel room that went with the post. Leaping up from the paper, they seemed to draw her into the Old creased paper, as if her feet were walking along the byways, taking her from village to village, past Public House and Telephone, the contours rising and falling around her. In the stuffy room, the rustle of paper and the occasional squeak of a map drawer being slid open the only sounds to disturb her, she strode across paper miles, shaking off the dusty air as she went, leaving the quietly-cleared throats for birdsong, the bent heads of her colleagues for the outlined hills.

She had made three applications before they would accept her as a New mapper, partly, she suspected, because Todd did not want to lose her from the group of copyists he had so carefully built up over the years. She had told him she was making her first application, and he had merely smiled at her, saying nothing. She did not mention the next one, which she made a year later, but he had spoken to her, just after they had sent her the second curt note of rejection.

'Don't wait a year this time. Get another application in at once.'

She had looked up at him as he stood over her desk, his fingers toying with the magnifying glass: Old, brass-handled, it was her pride and joy; she had spent nearly a month's credits to get it and for weeks afterwards she had half-starved.

'What's the point?'

'Just do it, Merritt. I know what I'm talking about.'

And seemingly he did, for this time there had been a much longer

24

interview, where the questions had been easy to answer, and where the face across the table had nodded sympathetically, instead of staring expressionlessly at her while she spoke.

There was the inevitable mention of her leg, but she was ready for this now, could list the sports she took part in (unwillingly, for she hated all games), her impeccable medical record, her part in the pioneering expedition to Cornwall three years earlier, the many field trips in southern Europe. The man opposite had listened and jotted a few notes, but she knew, suddenly, that it was all right, that they were going to say yes this time. She had not even minded his comments on her age and appearance. She knew what he meant when he talked of their advantages. She reported his words to Todd later, and he had thrown back his head and laughed.

'It's that bloody hair, Merritt. You always remind me of a Yorkshire terrier.'

When she looked blank, he had fetched an Old book with photos of the different breeds. She had looked at the photograph, trying to see what he meant.

'Mine doesn't flop all over my face like that.'

'The streaky colours . . .'

She had flicked through the pages in wonder. 'Were there really so many different types?' She thought of the vicious Yellows which roamed the edge of their Sahel settlement.

'Yes. There used to be special shows, and a big one in London every year.'

But he would not lend her the book, sending her off instead with a volume of place names that she had not seen before. She had hardly glanced at it before the New Mappers' Handbook appeared on her desk, mere hours after the letter of acceptance. She could remember her joy as she turned its stiff grey pages, reading at random the information and instructions that lay within it.

'Mappers are reminded that UNDER NO CIRCUMSTANCES may Map Credits be exchanged for alcohol.

'On arrival at a place of rest, Mappers must identify themselves and show their seal and badge.'

And later, more ominously, 'The Guild of Mappers will defray the cost of cremation, including transport, but will not undertake to make any payments to the deceased's dependents.'

Sitting now in the sunshine, it was hard to think of death, though she had already lived longer than many; she knew it was because she

25

could not be expected to give many more years to the Guild, or anyone else, that they had finally chosen her. And because, she thought, I am a bloody good mapper and they know it.

She picked up her heavy bag, adjusting the strap so that it hung slightly higher above her hip, and set her teeth for an instant as the left leg took her weight. A song was in her head, as she looked again at the green blob on the map, and she hummed it, then sang aloud as she headed for the Old road:

> The gypsy rover came over the hill,
> Down to the valley so shady.
> He whistled and sang, till the greenwoods rang,
> And he won the heart of a lady.

It was a song her mother used to sing, usually when her attention was fixed on some task in their tiny room. The first time she had consciously heard it, she had asked her mother where she had learnt it.

'What?' Roxanne's eyes had unglazed, focused on her daughter.

'The song. What is it?'

'Just a song. Granny used to sing it.'

'Is is an Old song?'

Roxanne's laugh was bitter. 'What songs are there now?'

'What's a greenwood?'

Her mother had sighed, picked up *The Old World In Colour*. How many months' credits had that cost her, Merritt thought now, remembering its hand-coloured pictures.

'Here. Look for yourself.'

The open pages showed trees in their full summer foliage. The child gazed at them in wonder.

'Wood,' she said suddenly. 'Like Granny's box.'

Grey and cracked, the Old box stood on the highest shelf in their room. It contained a few Old trinkets that Merritt was allowed to finger when she had been especially well-behaved.

'That's right.' Her mother glanced up at it too. 'They cut down the trees to make things like that.'

'Cut them down!' Merritt was agonised. 'But they were so beautiful.'

That bitter laugh again. 'They had so many, Merritt. They say you could walk all day through the forests of the North and never see another person.'

26

She could not grasp this, stared again at the bright-painted pictures, trying to imagine what it would be like to be inside the wood, walking under the trees.

'Like a green ceiling,' she said.

Roxanne nodded. 'Something like that. But moving – not solid.'

They looked at the book for a moment, trying to visualise the wood.

'And aren't there any now?'

'Who knows?' Her mother had turned away, was busy with a bowl of water. 'Perhaps in the North . . .'

The North. Even now, the word had a ring to it that made her shiver, though she had seen for herself on her field trips and on her travels as a mapper that it was far from being the land of her childhood imagination, and that it certainly did not contain the trees that the book had shown her. The chemical ravages that had laid the land bare and made it unhabitable for generations also made it nearly impossible to envisage the land as it had been, if *The Old World In Colour* was to be believed.

She remembered her mother's anger, which she was too young to understand.

'They didn't know what they had. And if they hadn't been so obsessed with the idea of nuclear attack, they would have seen what was coming.'

The Chemical Wars. Generations after, the words could bring a tremor of fear to a child who could neither imagine what they had meant, nor the world that had preceded them.

They made the adult tremble, too. Merritt rolled down her sleeves and looked west beyond the Old road, to where the hillsides groined in the distance. Her gaze flicked backwards and forwards across the landscape, occasionally dropping to the map and then up again. The contrast between land and paper jolted her; though she had confronted the same shock many times, she still could not accept that all the richness of the Old landscape had simply disappeared. And yet everything was as she had learnt to expect; the tree cover on the southern slopes had all gone, and yellow patches of spinygrass straggled across them. There was a dry stream-bed running through the valley. She found the name again: Tottlebrook. She ran her finger along the blue line and then looked up, imagining the grass and bushes that must have bordered it, the birds that had swooped and dipped over it, the fish that would have floated in the deeper pools. She followed it along the map to where the contours twisted it to the south and the woodland hid it. Lifting her head, she saw where it disappeared in a dab of green.

Of green.

She was on her feet, the glasses against her eyeballs.

'Jesus.'

She let the glasses fall, decided she needed to sit down; her legs were already giving beneath her. After a few moments, she picked up the glasses again and looked for a long time at the distant fold of the hills.

That is quite definitely green, she told herself. Her heart was thumping inside her chest; she felt the rise of bitter saliva in her throat, swallowed it down, sensed the clammy ooze of sweat on her forehead. She closed her eyes, breathed deeply. Inside her head, the bright spot of green leapt and shimmered.

She opened her eyes and looked down at the map. The woodland had once spread across both slopes and curved between the fields. But there was no reason that she could see for a patch to have remained.

She stood up again, the glasses clamped to her face, trying to see exactly where the green began. It appeared to spill out from between the hills along the stream-bed, stopping almost immediately, as if cut off by an invisible screen.

She fought down the excitment rising within her. All the old stories of New mappers who had discovered wonders poured into her head, making her gasp. I've found the first trees, she wanted to scream. A voice in her head was telling her she was mistaken, that she was imagining it, that it was a mirage, a trick of the light, but another voice, growing steadily louder, was singing the familiar words:

> *'He whistled and sang, till the greenwoods rang,*
> *And he won the heart of a lady.'*

She fumbled the glasses into their case, folded up the maps and adjusted the straps across her shoulders. She would go to the greenwoods.

It was almost dark when she came to the cleft in the hills and found herself beneath the first tree she had ever seen. She had not been mistaken, then. Even in the dimness, she could see the hint of green high above her. She tipped back her head and gazed up at the branches, which bent and thrust upwards. Looking ahead, she could see more, set widely apart at first, and then standing closer together, both frightening and inviting at the same time. She glanced back for a moment at the bare land behind her, then took a deep breath and a step forwards, edging between the boles that stood beyond the first, avoiding the temptation to strip off a glove and press her hand against the bark. Though she longed to feel the roughness under her fingers, she was too well-trained for that.

The woods were silent; she listened, heard nothing but her own footsteps crunching the ubiquitous stickyweed. She wanted to look more closely at the greenery, but there were no low branches, and every time she looked up it seemed that a little more light had gone and that the leaves were blackening above her. The sheer size of the trees amazed her, the solidity of the trunks in their upward sweep. She saw how the lines in the boles occasionally twisted, as if the tree had forced itself round in its urge to grow towards the sun. At school, they had taught her that plants sought the light, but at this moment the idea was suddenly real to her, as it had never been in her life spent among plants that rarely grew above waist-height. She wanted to examine each tree minutely, to see how they differed from each other; the variety in the trunks alone was staggering. In the morning, she said to herself, it will be easier. Especially if the sun shines again.

She decided to walk on until it was too dark to see safely, and then find a place to sleep. The idea of lying under the trees excited her, though there was a fine taut wire of fear jerking her legs forward too. It was strange to turn after she had been walking for about ten minutes up the valley, and to see nothing but the trees. She spun slowly, watched the woods rotate around her, until dizziness brought her back to her senses.

'Maybe in the North . . .' Roxanne had said. She wished her mother was beside her now, could see with her the curious shapes of the forked branches, which no picture could have adequately prepared her for.

Just as the light was almost gone, she came to the ruined house. It lay apart from the trees, close to the stream-bed. They must have been able to hear the water from inside the house, she thought. She saw that it must have stood quite high, noting where the crumbling stone rose at the corners: at least two storeys. She climbed carefully over the lowest wall, placing her foot, letting her weight press slowly, placing the next. Fragments of rotten roof timbers lay among the stinkbladder and the redfungus. Pieces of furniture, some with

29

decayed strips of material still adhering to them in places, peeped through.

Something rustled in the darkest corner; she stamped her foot and shouted and everything was still, apart from the drone of the nightflies. She pushed through the stickyweed which hung over the tumbled-down interior wall, finding a rusted upright box with a door, a huge hole eaten away round its handle.

No looters, she thought. I am the first. She had said this so many times since she had started her journeys as a mapper, and she had so often been wrong, but this time she was sure of it, so sure that she half-feared that she would find some yellowed bones under the weeds. She stepped cautiously over a tumble of cracked slates. But probably the inhabitants had gone away like everyone else, she thought. Probably they had walked and walked, thinking there was somewhere for them to go that would be safe, clean. Until they were too sick to go any further,

In the dark corner where the rustling had been she found the remains of a wooden case, the glass windows still largely intact. Behind the grey panes lay books. Her heart began to thump again, less insistently, but steadily. Tomorrow, she promised herself. She climbed back over the wall and made her way to the trees. She eased off her backpack and let everything fall to the ground. Massaging her shoulder gently, she looked up again. Dark sky showed through darker foliage. She remembered the conversation with Roxanne, as they had gazed at the picture.

'Like a green ceiling.'

'But moving.'

There was no perceptible movement, but there had been no wind that day, and even the evening breeze that had followed her up the valley had died away. She unrolled her sleeping bag, ate and drank a little, though she did not feel the need for either, and lay down, placing the nightmask over her face. The filter pressed lightly against her lips. Even after nearly three years as a mapper she still hated the time before sleep when the mask lay on her like a hand. In the early days she had sometimes woken to find she had torn it off in her sleep, before she learnt to secure it more carefully.

The trees were hard to make out through the thick lenses. She lay flat, looking upwards, trying to calm her heartbeat. The voices in her head began the argument she had been suppressing ever since she had seen the ruined house.

You could live here. Send your maps back without marking the trees. Finish this trip, go back to Sahel, check the results of the soil samples secretly. Do a few more trips, so no one would guess, and then say you want to retire. You're getting old; they'd be annoyed, but they wouldn't stop you. Then wait a few months, come back and live here under the trees. Grow roundroot and nugrain, keep a few fowls. So long as there was enough rain, you couldn't fail.

The other voice reminded her of why she shouldn't even think of it. She knew all the arguments against it well enough. It broke all the Guild rules. If they found her, she wouldn't be allowed to stay there, and there would be no return to Sahel. They would stop her credits, refuse her a room, banish her from the settlements. It would be, in effect, a death sentence. Though it was unlikely her route would be re-mapped, at least for the few years that probably remained to her, it was perfectly possible for a group of scientists to stray across what she already saw as her woods.

It was every mapper's dream – and nightmare: to find an untouched pocket of land, to live there, to keep it for themselves to enjoy as the finders. She supposed it must be possible to succeed, though she had only ever heard of the failures.

She would live under the beauty of the trees, surrounded by their green shade. She murmured the words of Roxanne's song; no matter that there was no gypsy rover, whatever he was, or that she was too old, even if there were one, to lose her heart to him. This could be mine, she thought. No one would tell me how to live here. It was an idea that both thrilled and terrified her. She rolled tighter into her bag and pushed her thoughts into the greyness of sleep.

In the morning light, she wondered how she had been fooled. The enamelled green threw its poisoned shimmer around her, giving a sickly sheen to her skin. She could taste the metallic tang from the bitter coating that had frozen the leaves, and even the trunks, into eternal summer. And yet not quite for ever, for as she stepped closer, she could see where the solid coating had crumbled in places, leaving little holes through which the sun filtered. She searched carefully for pieces which had fallen, and which the wind had not blown away. When she could not find one, she lobbed bits of rubble from the house up at the branches, until one or two small chunks fell. She sealed them in specimen bags, slipping them inside the map bag.

She wondered how great the contamination was. She burnt the

handling gloves as directed, rinsing her hands afterwards in the prickly decontam liquid from her backpack. She ought to head back down south to the nearest settlement for a medical; she had lain there all night inhaling the chemical air. Though she felt well enough now, she might start to feel the effects later of whatever poison it was that had been dropped from the sky to petrify the valley. Her heart sank at the thought of retracing her steps all that weary distance.

She shrugged on her backpack, hoisted the map bag to her shoulder, began to make her way back through the viridian reminder of the end of the Old world. The gypsy rover had brought more than a whistle and a song to these greenwoods, she thought grimly, trying not to look up at the motionless canopy above her. She followed the stream-bed to the edge of the solidified copse and then made for the knoll from where she had seen the valley the previous day.

Once back there, she sat down and opened her map bag. On her sketch map, she marked the extent of the pollution. In her notebook she wrote:

'Largescale poisoning by chemical(s) unknown; samples taken; New plant growth established.'

She snapped the notebook shut, looked at the Old map copy. Dunwick, she read. She had lost all of yesterday's desire to find the village. She scanned the barren landscape with distaste, until she found the line of the Old road. A vision of the woods was in her head and she pushed it out as she bent her head over the map. She was annoyed to see that the lines wobbled slightly, and that when she looked up to see where she must go first, there was a blur.

She stood up, felt her left leg take the weight. She turned her head in the direction she must go. As she took her first steps, she saw, faint but clear from the corner of her eye, the gleam of green.

ERIC BROWN

The Disciples of Apollo

'I'm sorry .. '
  'How long?'
  'At least six months, perhaps even as many as nine.'
  'How will I know when ... ?'
  'For two days beforehand you'll feel drowsy, lethargic ...'
  'And pain?'
  'I can assure you that your condition is quite painless.'
  'I suppose I should be thankful for small mercies.'
  'There is a retreat for sufferers of the Syndrome. Because of the highly unusual nature of the disease, you are advised to spend your final weeks there. Of course, you can go before then, if you wish. Your family will be able to visit you – '
  'I have no family.'
  'In that case Farrow Island might be perfect.'

Between the time of diagnosis and the actual realisation that he was going to die, Maitland passed through a period of disbelief. There is a difference between the intellectual knowledge of one's eventual end, and the sudden sentence of death. Grief came one morning when he awoke and knew that his awakenings were numbered, and as he watched the dawn he realised that soon the sun would rise without his continued presence to witness it; grief filled his chest with nausea and suffocated him, and he turned like a loner in a crowd for someone on whom he might unburden his anguish and regret. There was no one, and this compounded his pain. At times in the past Maitland had managed to convince himself that he could do without the usual human involvements that most people took for granted. Yet now, with the imminence of his extinction, he realised that no one could live – or die – without having shared in some experience of affection,

33

even love. He cursed himself for so aloofly denying down the years the inner voice that had cried out for human contact, cursed the coward in him that had shied from the trauma of new experience with the excuse that he had existed for so long without it . . . It came to him with the intensity of an inner scream that now it was too late. He had no chance of finding in six months that which had eluded him for a lifetime. He would die alone, as he had lived, and whereas to live alone was easy, he knew that to die alone, with so much guilt and remorse, and yearning for a somehow *altered* past, would be beyond endurance.

Then, however, he passed through this phase of anger and entered a period of passive resignation, and he saw his death as the inevitable consequence of a life lived as he had lived it. He would gain nothing from regret, he told himself; his former self was a stranger whose actions he had no way of changing. He could only accept his fate, and anticipate anything that might lie beyond. He recalled the doctor's recommendation, and made arrangements to leave.

In the following weeks Maitland said goodbye to his colleagues at the university, making the excuse that he was taking a short vacation. He sold his house and all his possessions, his books and his classical record collection. He felt a buoyant sense of relief when at last his house was empty. Since the diagnosis, he had been troubled at the thought of his material possessions remaining *in situ* after his death, mocking him; it was as if the acquisitions of a lifetime somehow circumscribed the parameters of his physical existence, and would bear mute testimony to his non-existence when he died.

Spring came and Maitland left the mainland on the ferry to Farrow Island. On the crossing he attempted to determine how many of his fellow passangers were also suffering from the Syndrome. As far as he knew there were no outward, physical symptoms of the disease – the physiological debilitation was taking place on a sequestered, cellular level. Nevertheless, Maitland convinced himself that at least a dozen other passengers, of the twenty or so aboard the ferry, were making their way to the hospice. Their despondent postures and sapped facial expressions spoke to him of moribund futures, bitter presents and only guilt and regret in retrospect. He realised, as the ferry approached the island, that they were mirror images of himself.

A car was awaiting him on the cobbled quayside of the small

fishing village. He was greeted by Dr Masters, the woman with whom he'd corresponded.

'Aren't we waiting for the others?' he asked as he climbed into the rear of the car.

'Others? The other passengers are Islanders.' Dr Masters regarded him with a smile. 'You are my only new resident this week.'

The hospice was a sixteenth-century mansion set in wooded parkland on a clifftop overlooking the straits. Dr Masters conducted him around the workshops and recreation rooms, the library and dining hall. She told him that the residents could take their meals in their rooms, if they wished, and that the recreational facilities and group therapy sessions were optional.

Maitland was thus reassured. The thirty or so residents he had seen so far in the mansion had about them a collective air of apathy, as if the fact of their ends had reached back and retroactively killed them in both body and in mind.

In contrast, Maitland had briefly glimpsed a few lone individuals in the grounds, striding out resolutely across the greensward, or posed in isolation on the windy clifftop. Maitland fancied that he detected something heroic in their lonely defiance in the face of death, and ultimately sad and tragic also.

As the weeks passed and Spring turned gradually to Summer, Maitland imposed his own routine on the identical days that stretched ahead to the time of his death in the New Year.

He would rise early and breakfast alone in the hall before setting out on a walk around the island that would often take him three or four hours. He would speak to no one, not because he wished to be rude or uncivil, but because no one ever spoke to him. He was a stranger on the island and therefore an 'inmate' up at the mansion, and the locals viewed the victims of the Syndrome with suspicion, sometimes even hostility.

He would take lunch to his room and eat it slowly, sometimes taking an hour to finish. Then he would sit by the window and read, or listen to the radio, until the gong announced the evening meal at seven.

This meal he did take with the other residents in the main hall, though he rarely joined in the conversation, which he found inane and self-pitying. There were constant debates about the reasons for the disease, and the only conclusion ever arrived at by the residents was that they were the chosen ones of their God, Apollo. These

35

people, in Maitland's opinion, were as irrational as the madmen who could no longer live with the thought of their deaths, and had to be removed to psychiatric units on the mainland.

One night, over coffee, Maitland decided that he had heard enough. He threw down his napkin and cleared his throat. The dozen residents at the table, the people Maitland considered to be the hard core of the hospice's strange religious movement, until now debating among themselves, fell silent and stared at him. They sensed his long-awaited contribution to the discussion.

'There is,' Maitland said, 'no *reason* for what we have. It's a freak, an accident, a cellular mutation. We are just as likely to be disciples of the Devil as we are to be the chosen ones of your God. In my opinion we are neither . . . '

Later, as he stood by the French windows and watched the sun fall behind the oaks across the river, he sensed someone beside him. 'But how can you continue, Mr Maitland? How do you manage to live from day to day if you believe in nothing?'

Maitland could not reply, and retired to his room. He often wondered the same thing himself.

Summer gave way to Autumn, and the sunsets beyond the stand of oak turned the golden leaves molten. Maitland struck up an acquaintance with a fellow resident, a retired major who bored him with stories of his army life. The only reason Maitland tolerated his company was because he played a passable game of chess, and they would spend the long Autumn afternoons in the library, intent on the chequered board between them. They rarely spoke; that is, they rarely *conversed*. Maitland tried to ignore the major's monologues, for he was contemplating – in contrast to the old soldier's full and eventful life – the arid years of his own brief existence, his time at university, both as a student and later as a lecturer, and the missed opportunities he told himself he did not regret, but which, of course, he did.

The major's going came about on the third week of their acquaintance. The old man had been complaining of headaches and tiredness for two days, and his concentration had often wandered from the game. Maitland suddenly realised what this meant, and he was unable to say whether he was shocked by the fact of the major's approaching death, or at the realisation, for the first time, that his own life too would end like this.

On the third day the major did not arrive, and Maitland sat alone by the window, his white pawn advanced to queen's four in futile anticipation of the challenge.

He took to playing chess against himself in the empty afternoons that followed the major's death. Winter came early that year, impinging on the territory that the calendar claimed still belonged to Autumn. Maitland found it too cold to enjoy his walks; the wind from the sea was bitter, and it often rained.

He appeared a lonely figure in the library, bent over the chessboard, apparently concentrating on the game but often, in reality, devising for himself an alternative set of events with which he wished he had filled his life. He repulsed all offers to challenge him, not with harsh or impolite words, but with a silent stare that frightened away would-be opponents with its freight of tragedy and regret.

One afternoon, during a storm that lashed and rattled the windows, Dr Masters joined Maitland in the library and tried to persuade him to take up her offer of group therapy, or at least counselling. They had experts who could . . .

He wanted to ask her if they had experts who could revise his past, give him the happiness he should have had long ago, but which had passed him by. He stopped himself before asking this, however. He knew that he had only himself to blame for the emptiness of his life.

Dr Masters said that she thought he should mix more with the other residents. Didn't he know that, even now, nothing was so important or rewarding as human relationships?

And Maitland replied that he needed nothing, and never had, of *human relationships*.

One week later he met Caroline.

He noticed her first one Sunday at the evening meal. She was at the far table by the blazing fire, and it was more than just her youth that set her apart from the other diners; she was *alive* in a way that none of the others were. Something in her manner, her movements, told Maitland that she could *not* be dying. Then he experienced a sudden stab of grief as he realised that her dynamism might be just a facade, an act to disguise her despair.

Later it came to him – with a sweeping sense of relief – that she was related to one of the residents and down here on a visit. Relatives came so infrequently – like the Islanders they saw the victims of the Syndrome as bizarre and freakish, as if the disease were some kind of curse, or could be transmitted – that it hadn't occurred to him that this was what she was, the daughter or granddaughter of one of the afflicted.

She excused herself from the table and Maitland watched her leave the room. Seconds later he saw her again through the window. She crossed the patio and ran across the greensward towards the clifftop. She wore moonboots, tight denims and a chunky red parka, and he guessed that she could be no more than twenty-five. Maitland had almost forgotten what it was like to feel such yearning, and to experience it now served only to remind him of his wasted years and the fact of his premature death.

In the morning, Maitland went for a long walk through the wind and the rain. He returned, showered and ate lunch in his room and, feeling refreshed and invigorated, went downstairs to the library and played himself at chess.

In the middle of the afternoon he sensed someone beside him. He turned and saw the young woman.

She smiled. She was dressed as she was last night, with the addition of a yellow ski-cap pulled down over her ears, and mittens. Evidently she too had just returned from a walk.

'Can I give you a game?' she asked, pointing at the board. Despite himself, Maitland smiled and began setting up the pieces.

They played for an hour with only the occasional comment, and then she looked up, directly at him, and said: 'You're not like the others. You've not given in . . .'

He wanted to tell her that he had surrendered long ago, that his resolution now in the face of death was nothing more than the cynicism that had fossilised his emotions years before.

Instead he smiled.

'I mean it,' she said, as she toppled her king in defeat. 'There's something about you . . .' She gestured. 'The other fools have given in, one way or another – gone stark staring mad or joined that crackpot cult . . .'

She mistook his cynicism for valour, seeing him through eyes of youthful enthusiasm, and Maitland hated himself for the charlatan he knew himself to be.

He felt a sudden sympathy, then, with the residents who had taken to religion, or madness, as protection against the inevitable. At least they had had full and worthwhile lives against which to measure the futility and horror of their deaths.

'Perhaps if you were in the position of these people, facing death, you might give in too. Don't belittle them – '

Something in her eyes made him stop.

She began collecting the scattered pieces, placing them in the wrong positions. 'But I am a resident here,' she said. 'Another game?'

They played all day, but Maitland gave little attention to the games. During the hours that followed he found himself intrigued by the young woman, who introduced herself as Caroline. He opened up, talked about himself for the first time in years. He wanted to turn the conversation around, to ask Caroline about herself, her life before the hospice but mainly her life since the diagnosis. Most of all Maitland wanted to know how she could remain so overtly optimistic with the knowledge of what was to come.

But she parried his questions and kept the conversation trivial, and Maitland was happy to join her in the exchange of banalities he would have found intolerable at any other time.

Over the next few weeks Maitland and Caroline sought each other's company as often as possible. They went on long walks around the island, and spoke guardedly of their respective pasts. Maitland was attracted to Caroline because of her courage, optimism and disregard for the proximity of her death; she perhaps was attracted to Maitland for what she saw as similar qualities. It hurt him to deceive her – he often wanted to tell her that you could not fear death if you had never really lived – but as time went by he became too attached to her to tell her the truth.

Their liaison, however, stopped short of physical intimacy, and it was as if this was a tacit agreement between them. For his part, Maitland could hardly conceive that intimacy might be possible, much less how he might react emotionally to something he was yet to experience. Perhaps fear prevented him acceding to the desires of his body, as if to consummate what he felt for Caroline would bring home to him how much he had come to delight in life of late, and consequently how much he had to lose.

As for Caroline . . . They talked all day, and often into the early hours, but never about their relationship. Maitland was still in ignorance as to her almost blind, at times even childish optimism.

For days now the wind and the freezing rain had promised worse to come, and then one quiet night, with only two weeks to go before Maitland died, snow fell.

In the morning he awoke to find a pearly radiance filling the room.

He dressed and drew aside the curtains and was dazzled by the brilliance of the white mantle.

He pulled on extra clothes with the enthusiasm of a child and met Caroline in the hall. They embraced, restricted by the bulkiness of their padding, and hurried outside hand in hand.

For as far as the eye could see, snow had covered the land with a perfect record of passage. They were the first residents abroad this morning, and they set off together away from the mansion. At one point, Maitland looked back at the building – its hard angles softened and upholstered in a thick, dazzling fleece – and he saw their footprints following them to their present position. He looked ahead at the virgin expanse of snow, and he shivered with what he told himself was nothing more than a sudden chill.

They walked through the woods and came out on the far side of the headland. They stood side by side and stared out across the shipping lanes, at the scimitar-shape of a tanker on the distant grey horizon. Then they moved towards the small pavilion where they often spent the afternoons, talking and staring out to sea.

As they made their way towards the open entrance of the small stone building, Caroline pulled away from him, then bent double and screamed into her mittens. Maitland looked from her to the pavilion, and saw with revulsion that during the night a resident had chosen it as a place in which to die.

They returned to the mansion and for the rest of the day and all through the night they remained in bed and made love. This set the pattern for the following week. They would take a brisk morning walk and then seek the refuge of bed and the bliss of each other's bodies, as if making up for the weeks of wasted opportunity. Caroline said nothing about the obvious fear the sight of the corpse had instilled in her – instead it was as if she were trying to exorcise from her mind the fact of her death with the positive catharsis of sex.

Maitland, at last, found what he knew to be love, and he passed through the fear of the inevitable with the knowledge that he might never have found happiness had it not been for his terminal illness. His only regret was that he had not found such happiness earlier.

One week later he felt himself going. On the morning of the first day he felt too drowsy to accompany Caroline on their ritual stroll through the snow. He made the effort, though, but something about his lethargy as they walked side by side communicated itself to Caroline, and she was silent.

In the afternoon they went to bed, but Maitland fell asleep beside her within seconds. In the morning he felt vaguely ill, nauseous. He tried to hide this from Caroline, but it was impossible. She dressed him and assisted him downstairs to the library, where they played chess. Often Maitland slipped into sleep, and he would awake with a start to see Caroline crying quietly to herself at the far end of the room.

On the morning of his last day, Maitland awoke before Caroline and forced himself out of bed. He dressed with difficulty, then kissed Caroline on the cheek and slipped quietly from the room so as not to wake her.

He walked through the woods to the pavilion overlooking the sea. Already he was tired, as if the short walk had exhausted him, and he hoped he would be asleep when it happened.

Caroline joined him not long after, as he guessed, and secretly hoped, she would. 'You should go back,' he told her, but he knew it was a token protest. 'You still have months to live . . .'

She ignored him; he sensed that she wanted to say something, but could not bring herself to do so without tears.

Later, for the first time, she mentioned the Syndrome.

'Years ago we wouldn't have known we were ill,' she whispered, her breath visible in the air. 'We would have . . . *gone*, suddenly, without all these months of –' And Maitland realised then that she was crying. 'Why?' she said at last. 'Why did they have to tell us?'

Maitland held her, shocked at her sudden capitulation. 'Modern medicine,' he said. 'They can diagnose it now. They know when it's going to happen. Given that knowledge, they have to inform the sufferer. Otherwise we could go at any time, anywhere, endangering others besides ourselves. There are many more of us now. The Syndrome has reached almost epidemic proportions.' He drew her to him affectionately. 'I thought you were doing rather well,' he said, and recalled that first Sunday weeks ago when he had wondered briefly if her vivacity had been nothing but an act.

'I was so scared, the only way I could stay sane was to pretend I wasn't affected. Being seen as unafraid by others gave me strength, confidence. Can you understand that? Then I met you and found someone who wasn't afraid . . .'

Maitland stifled a cry of despair. He stared around him and saw the

41

scorch mark on the concrete floor. He convinced himself he could detect, in the frozen morning air, the odour of the resident who had died here before him. He felt grief constrict his chest, fill his throat and render him speechless.

Caroline laughed. 'Do you know . . . do you know what they call us? The Islanders? Everyone else out there? They call us the "Disciples of Apollo" – '

They held each other as the snow began to fall.

Then Maitland ignited and consumed her in his flame, uniting them forever in a mutual, carbonised embrace.

SHERRY COLDSMITH

The Way to His Heart

The Blue Robin Valley executive estate was a collection of well-appointed homes, built by a large pharmaceuticals company to house its senior employees. The estate's library was a testament to the long hours worked by absentee fathers and the different kind of work done by their stay-at-home wives. Books about fishing and golf gathered dust on a corner shelf, surrounded by titles on such feminine pursuits as the cooking of fish, the sewing of quilts, doll-making and needlepoint. The cookery section alone took up an entire wall of the library.

Dr Phillip Gorman shook his head as he scanned the shelves before him. Some of the books were massive explorations of international gastronomy. Others were pocket-sized efforts, bearing such titles as *Advocating the Avocado* or *Turning out the Turnip*. Gorman's idea had seemed such a simple one: just stop by the library, check out a book or two, then go home and teach himself how to cook. Then he could get on with his work as the company's Chief Scientist and stop worrying about the greasy takeaways dulling his wits. Since Judith had left him, he'd been living on chow meins and Dial-A-Pizzas, food that made him shudder when he thought of its nutritional value.

'Would you like some advice?' a female voice behind him said.

He turned around and beheld a small, mouseish sort of woman, with streaked brown hair and buck teeth.

'Well, yes,' he said, surprised that she had left the check-out counter just to assist him. 'I want to learn how to cook – only simple things, though. I don't want a hobby. I just need a steady, healthy diet.' If he'd been alone, he would have slipped a thumb inside his waistband, to see if his trousers had got any tighter since his stodgy lunch. But the librarian might get the wrong idea, seeing a man slip a

43

hand into his pants. The fantasies of women could be very unpredictable.

'Here's a favourite of mine,' she said, pulling a frayed hardback from the shelf. 'It's very old, antiquarian almost, but it has useful tips for the beginner and it has some easy, classic dishes like *boeuf carbonnade* and French onion soup.' Her nostrils twitched in a downward motion, as if she could already smell the cooked food. 'It's ideal for the beginner.'

'Well, I guess I'll take that one. Thanks,' Gorman said, taking the book from her hands. The gold embossing of the letters had flaked away and Gorman could not make out the title. The smell of mouldy cloth made him want to gag.

A few minutes later he was starting up his BMW, glad to have the little chore over with. He'd enjoy teaching himself how to cook. He pulled out of the parking lot and realised, for perhaps the first time, that his ex-wife's absence no longer troubled him. He still missed his daughter but, if the truth were known, he was glad that the house was now comfortably his, in a way that it had never been before. Even the smell of the place had changed after Judith and Heather had moved out. Odours of perfume and a salt-something were now overlaid with the fragrance of his pipe and his takeaways. No, he was better off without a grown woman around. He'd been a competent bachelor for many years before his marriage. He could be one again.

Mrs Quinn looked out of the window of her cottage, to the modern split-level bungalow owned by Dr Gorman. Her neighbour's house was still dark. Gorman's visit to the library was taking longer than she expected, but there was no need to start worrying, not yet. In Gorman's own good time he would come home, *the* book in his hands. She could have given him the recipe outright of course, but that would have been risky. Fate abhorred an unsubtle chef. Better to let Gorman feel that onion soup was his own idea.

She took the *oeufs aux truffes* from her Aga and put the dish aside, then turned off the fluorescent light. It flickered and winked and finally gave up the ghost. Darkness in the kitchen. A bad thing, normally a sign that the woman inside had given up on life, had stopped negotiating with the Universe. But Mrs Quinn had not given up, not in the least. She was cooking up a cyclone tonight and buying time for the world.

Her culinary sense told her that the hors d'ouevre was almost cool

44

enough to serve. She waited in the gloom for a few minutes more, until she saw Gorman's car turning into the driveway between their two houses. Yes, he had a book in his hands. She bustled into the candlelit dining room, and put her masterpiece in the centre of the table. The oohs and aahs of the ecstatic diners were loud enough to rock the cosmos. But no one on the executive estate took any notice of the little stone cottage and the raucous female voices. Each double-glazed excrescence was busily collapsing, sucked inward by the force of its occupants' neuroses.

Gorman's bungalow was in a cul-de-sac, in a location coveted by the company wives since it claimed the estate's single 'period' dwelling, a listed building that had escaped demolition. Gorman was unmoved by the cottage's quaintness. Its owner was quiet and that was all he wanted in a neighbour, though there were other things about Mrs Quinn he did find objectionable. Judith and Mrs Quinn had been great friends at one time, and Mrs Quinn had taken every opportunity to overwhelm his house with her high, giggling voice. He didn't care much for her appearance, either. Though only in her late thirties, she had let herself slide into matronly decline. She had fat sausage arms, pendulous breasts and a coiffure that resembled a jam doughnut. Overall, she reminded him of a pestering Mum from some dreadful TV sitcom.

He pulled his BMW into the driveway and made a sour face at the shadows mingling behind the curtains of Mrs Quinn's house. Perhaps she was giving a cookery demonstration tonight. Or was she into rugmaking these days? Over the years, Gorman had known her to teach classes in sculpture, china painting, water colours and a half-dozen other genteel crafts. Judith had attended every class that Quinn offered, no matter what the subject, and as a consequence had not become proficient at any of her little hobbies.

Gorman dumped the cookery book in the kitchen and whistled as he brewed a cup of tea and took it up to his daugher's room. He kept the room just as it had been when Heather lived there. The single bed was covered in a patchwork quilt. The lacy pillows on top of the bed were stacked against the wall, waiting for Gorman to lean back against them, as he did every evening at this time. He listened to the howling winter wind and traced the quilt pattern with his fingers as he drank his mug of tea. He didn't know why he performed this ritual every evening; he just knew that he had to do it. Something compelled him, some hope that he would unravel memories knotted deep inside him, or perhaps decode secrets in his unconscious; secrets that might have a bearing on his work as a neuro-symbolist. Nothing ever came to mind, though.

Gorman looked up at the decorations on Heather's walls. There was a Snoopy clock next to the window and a poster of Amelia Earhart on the wall above the bed, a remnant of Judith's belief in positive role models. Next to Earhart was a poster of some female movie star, a khaki-clad woman with a little girl on her hip and a rifle-strap separating her sweaty breasts. Gorman vaguely recalled that Heather had banned him from this room on the same day she had brought home that poster – one of those pre-adolescent traumas that all girls are prone to. How many times had he carried a sleepy girl into this room, tucked her in tightly and blown good nights into her ear?

Damn Judith for moving so far away. She had said you couldn't trust men at all these days, so she had taken their ten-year-old daughter to live on some farm in the wilds of Scotland. No doubt the quilting and lacemaking and other crafts learned at the feet of Quinn were keeping her busy.

Gorman walked into the office he had set up next door to Heather's room. It had been Judith's studio. There was a desk, a halogen lamp, and a computer terminal which he used to model and test new ideas, just as if he were in a real lab. Thinking of it as a lab brought back memories of hygienic smells, of formaldehyde and alcohol. Such memories helped to focus his mind. He switched on the VDU and invoked the software he needed to begin.

As he waited for the system to find his files, he allowed himself a few moments of self-congratulation. The company was experimenting with a drug for controlling criminals, one that he had designed some years before. His employers didn't know it, but he had used early prototypes on himself, with results so intriguing that he had spent years trying to persuade his bosses to develop the drug further. The U-factor, as Gorman called it, had cured him completely of a phobia left over from childhood, a fear of onions. There were minor side-effects – that was to be expected in a prototype – but Gorman had gladly suffered them. For instance, he could not recall being present at Heather's birth, though he knew he had been there. He had stumbled across the pictures of Judith huffing away only a few days ago. He could remember holding the camera, but not a detail of what he'd actually seen.

Subsequent preparations of the U-factor were extremely promising. Even the military was interested in the drug's potential, thus vindicating Gorman's campaign to develop it. He'd spent most of his lunch that day with a gentleman from the MOD, a man who tucked into his lasagne as heartily as Gorman did.

'The convicts who have so far taken the U-factor,' Gorman had explained, 'forget the fetishes and obsessive images that compel them to commit sexual crimes.'

'And does the treatment leave them functional?' asked the officer.

'It's not like castration if that's what you're getting at. A subject treated with the U-factor simply has his chaotic unconscious "resolved" – he retains his basic habits. And he keeps the drive to do simple tasks. A four-star chef, for example, would no longer be a culinary artiste, but he would still be competent at peeling potatoes. Even better, he'd be content to peel them.' Gorman almost mentioned the prototype that he had taken, how it had done him no more harm than to make him forgetful, but he stopped himself in time. After all, it wasn't the prototype that interested his companion.

The officer had then wondered what would be the effects on normal people? Could you disperse the U-factor in a gas? The questions went on for several hours, presenting Gorman with problems he knew he could solve if he just had the time. Let the army ask for anything, anything possible, and he could deliver it, on target and within budget. He watched his screen as graphs dipped and peaked, as helices twisted and realigned. And then the doorbell went off. The interruption was as welcome as a fart in church. More raffle tickets, Gorman muttered to himself. Or yet another request for charity jumble. Did the company wives have nothing else to fill their time? He hurried down the stairs and flung the door open to the winter wind.

'Oh, I do hope I'm not disturbing you Dr Gorman.' It was Mrs Quinn standing on his doorstep, her invincible doughnut still intact despite the gale that was battering the neighbourhood. 'I've got into a terrible dilemma with my girls, and I noticed your light was on . . . '

'Please, come in,' he said, trying to keep his voice cheerful. It always pays to take your turn with the neighbours, he reminded himself. Next time she runs out of sugar, she'll remember that it was Dr Gorman who helped her before, and then she'll go off and bother someone else.

'Well, my cookery class has prepared dishes for a catering firm and

47

if the firm likes the food, they'll employ some of my students part-time.'

'But how can I be of any help?' Gorman asked. She knew perfectly well that he'd never cooked in his life. It was she who'd recommended he get a beginner's cookery book from the library.

'Oh, you could be of enormous help. We've just tasted Francesca's seafood terrine, and three of us think it needs more salt, and the other three think the opposite. Would it be an awful inconvenience if you came over to break the tie? Please? We're feeding ourselves a delightful supper tonight and you'd be more than welcome to join us.'

Now she was talking. Gorman suddenly realised that his tum was rumbling and the prospect of another Dial-A-Pizza filled him with despair. Mrs Quinn squealed her delight when he accepted her offer, saying how pleased her girls would be. He charged upstairs and terminated his session on the mainframe. He could do with a good meal.

Mrs Quinn scraped the leftovers into the cats' bowls, shaking her bouffant at the memory of Gorman's untutored palate. He had said the terrine needed more chilli, when the chef had rightly used no chilli at all. His idea of culinary discernment was the ability to tell Coke from Pepsi. He had eaten well, though, and he'd drunk a lot too. After she'd topped up his glass for the fourteenth time, he was almost sociable, pretending the keenest interest in the whys and wherefores of onion soup.

'Now there's an idea,' she had told him, her voice as beguiling as Jezebel's. 'Why don't you make an onion soup and bring it to next week's class?' Gorman had nearly choked on his brie-laden biscuit, but the chorus of affirmations persuaded him to try his hand at the dish.

The evening had been a success. In a week's time, Gorman would cook the means of his destruction and float to the Banquet of Justice on a vapour of mnemonic herbs. Oh yes, he'd remember what he'd done, so clearly and keenly he'd beg the diners to punish him. Then Heather could drink the wine of forgetting, and be free of her father's past crimes.

Mrs Quinn did not smile at the thought of this tiny victory. 'When you get very old,' she murmured as she covered fish bones with water, 'you find you are so contrary you'd contradict anyone, even God.' Gorman's crimes were small potatoes to Mrs Quinn, and the currency of agelessness in which she was paid reinforced her sense of detachment. The petty sins of humankind, incest, matricide, sororicide: these crimes of passion seemed frivolous when compared to the work of unfeeling professionals. A pinstripped gent signs a memo and a village blazes; a draughtsman sits down with his pencil and draws a concrete block equipped with fittings for gas-filled hoses. Where was Lady Justice after the dozens, the hundreds, the millions died? She was punishing some bad Daddy because he'd spoiled his kid's memories of teddy bears.

But her job specification was exact. She could only punish family crimes and the recipes she had to follow were carved in slabs of marble. The odd victory that Mrs Quinn won for humanity was just so much spare change according to the Boss. Save Heather – that was the imperative. Anything else had to be done in her own spare time.

It was late but she did not feel sleepy, only weary. She poured melted chocolate over a chilled sheet of marble. Justice was as delicate as a good dessert. One flavour out of balance and the pudding was ruined. Though Gorman was sure never to abuse another child, justice had still not been done. The victim could not be healed until the perpetrator was made to suffer. If she did not convene the Banquet, Heather's future could be grim indeed: years of self-hate that the girl would try to assuage with men who despised her. But if Quinn kept a steady hand on the sauce, then Heather would forget her past and Gorman would never have a chance to wreck humanity. That was not a tiny victory. That was a gift to the world that had nourished her for a thousand years. She had to stop Gorman before he helped grey-suited grafters win their bloody campaigns.

Mrs Quinn arranged the curls to look like chocolate carnations, a beautiful confection she'd use the next day to decorate a wedding cake. She'd shown Judith this trick, the first of many, until she'd realised, much too late in the day, that Judith was a moral lightweight, unready to face the rigours of Cuisine. Walking out on Gorman had taken every inch of backbone that Judith possessed, and now she had nothing but guilt to sustain her. Judith blamed herself for Heather's abuse, and that made her unpredictable, possibly dangerous. Mrs Quinn had long ago observed that a human would do anything to relieve herself of guilt. Judith might defend her husband just to restore her own peace of mind.

There was no sense in feeling guilty, Mrs Quinn had told Judith, carelessness was no crime. But Judith kept whining about mercy and forgiveness – ingredients that could spoil the broth of justice if used in too great a measure. Training Judith in the craft was Mrs Quinn's biggest mistake in a thousand years, and now that po-faced, reedy girl was the beloved of the Mother. Mrs Quinn tried to calm her fears as she turned out one chocolate carnation after another, but it was no use. Judith had the power to save her husband; she was the wild card. All of a criminal's relations, as well as his victims, must censure him. Surely Judith would stay away from the Banquet if she could not condemn? Mrs Quinn shook her head again, a gesture of denial that had become more and more frequent over the years. It was a mad Universe that demanded all the cooks agree on the broth, and the earth was ruled by the maddest chef of all.

Mrs Quinn finished the chocolate flowers and took one last look around the kitchen. The massive oak beams, the Welsh dresser and Victorian plates, the pine furniture now golden with age: these things, collected over centuries, delighted her eyes and steeled her nerves. If she had one really lasting success in her career, then she could retire happily, maybe have a child herself after centuries of watching other women have them. That would restore her humanity.

Gorman ran around the kitchen like a blue-tailed fly. He was looking for a garlic press, which he was sure he'd seen somewhere, and trying to locate the Sabatier knife. Surely Judith didn't take *all* the cooking implements, he told himself. And where was the chicken neck he'd bought for the stock? And all those weird herbs that had astonished the aged hippies at One Earth Wholefoods? He should never have agreed to this project, but they had caught him at a weak moment, just as he was savouring the monkfish. Or had he been lingering over the sorbet? Or had Quinn waylaid him while she passed him the cheese platter? It would take a mainframe to count the courses he'd eaten that night. He'd never felt so agreeably bloated.

But loose lips sink ships and now he was struggling over a dish that far exceeded his two skills of grilling bacon and frying eggs. The boy at the hippie shop had painstakingly labelled each packet of herbs. Gorman got them out and checked them against the recipe. 'Let's see: rosemary, bay, rue, queen-of-the-meadows, tansy . . . tansy?' He must have left it in the shop or failed to put it on his list altogether. He ran outside and hunted in his car for the missing packet, but no luck. Anyway, there was no point in panicking. He'd just better go over and borrow the herb from Mrs Quinn. He wasn't going to cock up this dish in front of those know-it-all girls.

He put on his jacket and hurried over to the little cottage, now gaudy with Christmas lights. He was looking forward to another night of feasting and drinking. Judith had never mentioned what a good time she was having at old Quinn's. She had just left him to look after Heather, something he resented. He supposed he'd played a bit rough with the girl on those nights. Perhaps that was why Judith had taken her away? God, that woman had had an evil mind.

But all women were like that. One of Quinn's cookery students, a daughter of one of his colleagues, told him that she worked in a rape crisis centre; another, an exceedingly plain young girl, whined about her 'incest survivors group'. He wanted to tell her that most such hysterias were founded in the girl infant's desire for her father but he thought better of it. What would happen, he wondered for the fortieth time, when the female unconscious was scrubbed by the U-factor? What habits would women retain? They'd still be satisfactory cooks he hoped, though it was certain they'd never be great cooks again.

Mrs Quinn answered the doorbell on the third ring. Her face was streaked with flour down one side and her apron was spattered with some kind of blood. 'Oh, Dr Gorman! You're not backing out on us, are you?' She looked positively alarmed at the prospect.

'Why no, not at all,' he said, flattered. 'I've lost the packet of tansy I brought for the soup. I was hoping I could borrow some from you, if you've got it to spare?'

Mrs Quinn assured him that it would be no problem. She returned with a dried herb, a dull green-red in colour. When he got back to his own kitchen he resumed his marathon assault on the cupboards: wrenching out drawers in the search for a grater; pulling one pot out of the cabinet and ending up with ten on the floor. After collecting all the hardware he needed, he rammed the chicken neck in a saucepan and brought the stock and herbs to a steady simmer. 'Just stay calm,' he told himself, 'there's no sense in hurrying over things.' At least he'd started the stock. Now, why not identify the rest of the sub-processes, do them, and then conclude with the main process, whatever that turns out to be? Rational. Logical.

'Let's see,' he said, running his finger down the yellowed page. 'First, take some onions.'

51

He threw the cookbook against the kitchen wall and kicked the refrigerator for good measure. He'd forgotten the fucking onions. He chewed his finger for a while. The shops were already shut and there was no way he was going to pester Mrs Quinn again. He was remembering something about onions; if only it would come back to him. Didn't Judith keep some foodstuffs in the cellar? She swore it was so cool down there, she could keep some foods fresh for months. Gorman cautiously opened the cellar door. There was an oniony smell, all right. He flicked on the light. Of course it wasn't working. He spent five minutes looking for the torch and eventually made his way down into the black pit.

It wasn't as cold as he'd expected. In fact he'd swear it was a trifle warm, almost humid. The smell of onions was overwhelming, like the heat of a body too close, an exhausted body at that. He waved the torch around, until he knocked his hand against a pillar and lost his grip. The beam of light zigzagged in the dark and then winked out. He fell to his knees and began feeling around the dirt floor, hoping to find the torch. It's black as the tomb in here, he thought. He felt opened and emptied. They'd removed his backbone, that's what Quinn's women had done. They'd plunged a needle into his bones and sucked out his marrow, filling the hollows with wet salt.

As he fumbled around for the torch, his hands brushed against the texture of coarse cloth. It was a sack of some kind. He nearly giggled out loud when he realised that this was where the smell of onions came from. He picked up the sack and heard the thud of solid objects as they hit the dirt floor of the cellar. He scratched in the soil for his onions. Oy vey, he thought, I'm a peasant digging in vile earth.

He climbed the stairs, panting more than usual, and hoisted his swag to the counter. The onions looked like enormous pearls from some mutant oyster. Imagine prizing such treasures from wavy razor-coral jaws! Imagine. The white onions were lustrous, like the little necklace of pearls he had fastened around Heather's pink, slender neck. She had hated the present, though, and torn the gift from her throat, in one easy motion. He had been so astonished by her strength that he didn't notice her ingratitude. Instead of paddling her as she deserved, he had reached down and patted her head, very tenderly.

'I don't like it when you touch me,' she had said.

'But why?' he had asked. 'Daddies are very fond of their little girls.'

'Then why do you stop smiling when you touch me? Why do you look like this?' And she had made a face at him, setting her jaw as if she were biting down on something, her eyes wide and unblinking.

'Now stop being ridiculous,' he had ordered, grabbing her by the shoulders and shaking. 'I'm losing my patience.'

The girl had blubbered some more and cried that she remembered everything, everything he had forgotten. Gorman swore as he nicked his finger with the knife. He bandaged the cut and continued slicing the onions with his Sabatier. 'My Wilkinson Sword,' he sniggered, 'my cutlass supreme.' He felt like Errol Flynn charging into a sack of flour. He did a dance with the long knife, gay that the cooking was going well and sure that he would dazzle Mrs Quinn's girls with his skills. They had been so unimpressed by his status as a scientist, saying that Cuisine was La Science. But the man who can master the atoms of the brain can master anything.

Tears rolled down his eyes as he sliced and fried the onions, but it was a good pain. He enjoyed a good pain, he realised, and then blinked at the knife curiously. What had made him think that? He poured the stock over the onions. Steam rose from the soup and lifted in the air, it swirled around the kitchen and misted the windows. He was walking over to the back door, intending to open it when he began to feel dizzy. He decided to take the soup off the boil but he could do no more than hang his head over the broth. There was something wrong with this liquor, it was making him ill. He lifted his head and staggered against the fridge. The clean white surface was cracking and blackness was sucking him down. He fingered his wedding ring, and sank to his knees. He started into a yawning pit where the black night of woman waited for him. He wanted to scream out for Judith but he was too overwhelmed by the rank odours. The stench of onions rotting in Jark, fetid earth, tore at his mind.

He was drifting, feeling light as angel's hair. Gorman saw himself bathed in white linen, laid in a hygienic manger at the edge of a starry swirl. The elements toasted him there. Three men came forward, knelt and poured a perfumed unguent on his brow to banish the smell of woman. He welcomed their ministrations. A fourth man approached him, wearing an enormous headdress made of three haloes that intersected to form a globe of pure light. A huge pearl was held captive in the white centre of those haloes. Gorman revelled in the headdress, basked in the pure liquid thought of the priest, as elegant and simple as the model for an atom. Was he ill, dreaming, or gone to heaven? He floated in the starry abyss, glad that his unconscious could create such a rational symbol.

His idyll shimmered and faded in a vapour. He was standing in a soggy field, weeping for his loss of empyreal bliss. Furrows stretched away from him into infinity. The grey earth looked like a massive sheet of corrugated iron. The wind was wet and seemed to blow in from a green ribbon in the distance – the sea? There were fat peasants trowelling the earth. He ran towards them, determined to know how he came to be in this nightmare place where rich smells coiled in his nostrils; smells of garlic and silage and rotting vegetables.

As he approached, he saw that the farmers were not peasants, not quite. They were men in suits and lab coats but they all wore babushkas around their heads and they had the fleshy faces of commoners. The first man he came to was familiar despite his corpulence; he was a scientist named Koenig whom Gorman had met at a conference years before. Gorman shrieked at the man, demanding an explanation for this wretched dream, but the man simply kept his head down and dug at the field. Gorman seized Koenig's lapels and looked into his bovine eyes. Gorman ran to one man after another, hoping someone could tell him the way out. Each man was known to Gorman, either personally or by repute. They were scientists, cut down before some major discovery or campaign by a crippling disease. Koenig had suffered from Alzheimer's disease, and two other men Gorman recognised had retired after massive strokes. He calmed himself, glad that he saw his colleagues here, digging turnips. That meant it was still a dream.

He ran towards the green sea, jumping across the furrows, stumbling often, falling occasionally. When he got close to the ocean shore, he could tell it was not the sea he had been running towards, but hundreds of dining tables each spread with a blue-green tablecloth. Dozens of little girls and a few women walked from the edge of his vision to a group of tables. They took their seats and stared at him, their faces hostile. The food before them could have matched the most glorious description. He could smell the good smells and the rank smell of woman, blowing in from the steppe behind them.

'Heather!' he heard himself cry. She was sitting next to Quinn. He halted a few feet from the table and stared down at the incomparable feast. He recognised roast pigeons, quails' eggs, smoked salmon in dill fronds; but there were dozens of other dishes he'd never seen before. A cauldron sat on the table and next to it there was a large block of ice with a bowl of something like caviar embedded in the top. Gorman looked closer and saw that the ice was carved in the shape of his own head.

Mrs Quinn felt as if she'd just catered an eight-course meal for five thousand. The Mother is almost immovable, she thought. You have to wine her, dine her, and cater for her multitudes before she will yield a single thing in favour of humankind. Judith was not present among the diners so Mrs Quinn allowed herself to hope that her efforts would not be in vain. Stay away, she mentally pleaded, don't let all this go to waste.

Gorman was stumbling in front of her table, an animal fear in his eyes. But Mrs Quinn felt no pity, still another sign that it was time to retire. When Heather had blurted out her father's shame, Mrs Quinn had felt gladness instead of sympathy. Here was a chance to remove a man who, if allowed to carry on with his experiments, wouldn't even have the decency to wish he'd been a locksmith. She couldn't touch most of the men responsible for this century's mega-deaths for they were family-loving men, eager to do a good job on target and within budget. They committed no crime that she was allowed to punish. So she used her talent in devious ways, as a self-appointed *Chef de Guerre*.

She would have liked to pour the venerable Bourgogne resting on the table before her, but she daren't let Gorman see her trembling hands; he might realise that her power was not absolute. Instead she turned her attention to Heather, who was tapping the crystal champagne flute before her. The diners stopped their chatting and fidgeting. The only sound that could be heard was the wind and the flapping of the tablecloth.

'Daddy,' she heard Heather say in a low, sibilant voice, 'are you ready to face our judgement?'

Good for Heather. As long as that girl had anything to say about it, there was no question of a trial.

The carved ice-eyes mocked Gorman's onion tears, and the red caviar pulsed in the cranium. Heather was speaking, but he could not bear the mature alto that her voice had become since her mother took her away. She was no longer his little girl.

'Why am I here?' he cried. He was unsteady on his feet and he found himself sinking to his knees before Mrs Quinn.

'Stop looking so pathetic,' Quinn scolded. 'Go on now. Face your daughter.' Quinn looked like the mould from which every school-marm in history had been cast. He rose to his feet and turned towards Heather. He could have sworn he heard Mrs Quinn say: 'There's a good fellow.'

'You're here,' Heather said, addressing her father, 'because of what you've done to me. Some of these others,' she waved her arms at the diners, 'are here because you've hurt them, too. But most are friends of mine who have suffered as much as I have. They will celebrate with me when I have wiped away all memory of you.'

The diners closest to Quinn and Heather were girls he recognised from the estate. He couldn't remember any of their names but he knew their fathers moderately well. There were some young boys present, and a few men he recognised as prisoners he had used in his experiments. The criminals were people he had helped and the little girls were scarcely known to him. How had he harmed any of them?

He worked nervously at his wedding ring, wondering why Judith wasn't with his daughter. Stroking the ring, he could feel his wife's presence and smell her natural odour. He closed his eyes and concentrated on her image, certain that she could feel his need. He could picture every line, every curve of her. He had loved her. He turned and turned the ring, certain that Judith must know his anguish, that she would descend from the heavens in a shower of light, down to this sordid plain.

He yelped as he felt something grab his ankle. He looked down and saw two hands reaching out of the soil, dirt under their encarmined nails. Judith emerged from the loose earth, like a corpse that had clawed its way out of the grave.

Gorman was giddy with relief. His wife looked so beautiful, but she did not say a word to him nor even look at him. She walked around the table and stood between her daughter and Mrs Quinn.

'Tell them,' he shouted, 'tell them I've done nothing wrong.' Judith finally looked at him, her huge brown eyes were moist with pity.

'Yeah, go on Judith, get on with it,' Quinn said. She was sloshing red wine into a huge goblet. 'Fuck humanity. You'll always be safe in your little farm.' She drained the glass in one and was pouring again. 'Great entrance by the way. Meant to show us all how tight you are with Magna Mater?'

Judith wore a look of hangdog guilt. 'I am only here,' she said, clearing her throat, 'to demand that Heather calls a real trial. Phil deserves the same chance as the others.' She pointed in the direction of the fields. Gorman turned around and saw his colleagues in the distance, still scratching in the earth.

'Mother, if you don't want to condemn him, then get out of here,' Heather said. Her words were calm but Gorman saw the fury in her face. 'How can you think of defending him after what he's done?'

Judith was here to defend him! What silly game was Heather playing? 'Now Heather,' he said, 'I want you to tell me, right now, what it is you think I've done to you.'

Judith interrupted before Heather could speak. 'You must take a vote, Heather,' she said. Her eyes flashed angrily at Mrs Quinn. 'Emma cannot be allowed to punish someone just because it suits her plans. She's got away with that too many times. This time, she will have to get full agreement.'

Mrs Quinn got up from her chair, slamming her meat-cleaver fists on the table as she rose. 'Stop bullshitting Judith. We did all agree until you showed up. Are you going to defend this bastard or not?'

Well, he'd certainly never been called that before. Gorman looked over at his wife, eager to hear her defence, but Judith was shaking her head. 'No. The fathers of these children here could find it in their hearts to forgive him. I can't. The closer I get to replacing you, Emma, the closer I come to wanting justice as much as mercy. If it pleases you, I will serve Phil's concoction.'

Mrs Quinn poured a glass of red wine and handed it to Judith. 'Well here, girl, drink to my retirement. But let me serve his crimes. Your husband's punishment will be bad enough without having to know that you condemned him.'

Condemned. They said it as if they really believed it. What would they do? Take an ice pick to his head? 'Heather,' he said, 'Don't listen to these spiteful cows. I'm sorry if I've ever done anything to upset you, but you must know that I'd never hurt my own flesh and blood.'

Heather's scream could have shattered an iceberg. Judith put her arms around his daughter. After a few minutes, Heather pushed Judith away. 'Here is your last course, Daddy, made by your own hand.' She swirled a ladle around in the steaming cauldron, and inhaled deeply. 'Ah, Rosemary, for remembrance.' Heather handed the ladle to Mrs Quinn who scooped up some of the broth and lifted it to her nose. She tasted the soup and made a sour face, but started serving it. She ladled the soup into an enormous two-handled tureen.

The tureen was passed from hand to hand. Each diner took a sip straight from the massive bowl and then looked at him with blazing eyes.

When the last diner had tasted the soup, Mrs Quinn began sucking in air without exhaling. Her chest expanded mightily so that her Himalayan bosom looked even larger. He thought he could feel air rushing past his ears.

'IF IT IS NOT JUST, SPEAK NOW.' The words were released in a gale-force wind. She held another ladle, poised above the ice head. No one said a word. There was not a whisper or a murmur on anyone's lips.

'Remember well, Daddy,' Heather said.

Mrs Quinn dribbled soup onto the ice. The cavier lost its brilliant, throbbing quality as the ice melted around it. Gorman found himself tumbling to the ground like a bowling pin, spending an eternity at each point along the curve of his fall. He saw Heather asleep, looking so perfect and vulnerable. Then he saw the bruises on her pink flesh and the howling of her foul mouth. He heard his voice making threats and entreaties, and he saw the years of abstinent longing, punctuated by explosions he could not control. 'Judith!' he cried out in his heart, but she did nothing to comfort him. As the memories crowded into his mind, he felt both shame and passion; one emotion teasing and exciting the other. It was a familiar tug of war, and he would have felt almost nostalgic had it not been for the diners glowering at him, from somewhere beyond the penumbra of his mind. He was getting weaker. He saw their hateful stares give way to triumphant smiles. They were only here in the dozens but they seemed like thousands, their faces as numerous as grains of salt. There were so many of them.

Mrs Quinn put her garden gloves away and scrubbed her hands at the kitchen sink, staring at the beautiful spring flowers outside her window. She'd have to get someone to do the gardening for her in the summer. Only five months pregnant and she was already finding it difficult to move around. Still, she shouldn't complain. She was having a wonderful retirement in a world that was no longer quite as threatening as it once was.

It was time to take the potatoes from the oven. While a pork chop cooked in the microwave, she dished out the gratin; a few marjoram flowers added colour. It didn't matter to Mrs Quinn that the diner would not notice the extra care she took over his every meal. When

58

the chop was ready, she moved it to the plate and then covered the dish. A glance at the clock on the wall told her she had to hurry. Students would be arriving soon and there was still her own lunch to cook and eat.

She took the meal over to Dr Gorman's as she always did at this time of day. She pushed the doorbell several times. It was becoming more and more difficult to tear him away from the sitcoms and game shows that he spent his days watching. Mrs Quinn wished that he had learnt rudimentary skills before he'd been called to the Banquet. Cooking was one habit he could do with now.

IAN McDONALD

Rainmaker Cometh

Seven dry years lie like seven white scars scrawled across the shoulders of the dying town. On the downhill side long years before ever the rains failed, it crouches in the desert, a tangle of tracks and trailways and transcontinentals; always on the way to somewhere else. Only in the heat of the night does it uncurl to bare the neon tattoos along its belly: the bus depot, the motel, the barbershop, the gas-station; sweating, shocking blues and pinks you can feel hot on your face. Down at the end of the bar, where the dreams collect thickest because no one ever goes there to dust them away, Kelly By the Window watches neon fingers stroking the flanks of the Greyhounds and Trailways; people change direction here like they change their shorts. Blue Highways; abandoned luncheonettes; all she will ever see of the refuge of the roads is the reflection of her face in the eldorado bus windows, slipping past, out there lost in the heart of Saturday night. Up on the roof Desert Rose announces the best hot dogs in town in blushing cerises and 'lectric blues you can read all the way out at Havapai Point. And it's true, as long as you understand that 'best' means 'only'. She's smiling. She's always smiling. She makes the law, you see. Graven into every sixty-watt rhinestone on her boots. Nobody gets off who doesn't get on again.

If he likes the tilt of your hat or the colour of your luggage, if the smell of the cologne you've splashed on in the washroom reminds him of all those Oldsmobile days hung up with his jacket on the peg by the door, Sam My Man will solicit you with his magic never-ending cup of coffee. He's a dealer in biography, paid for by the minute, the hour, however long it takes until the driver calls you on into the night. Sam My Man has whole lifetimes racked away under the bar where he keeps the empty bottles. He can tell a good vintage just by looking: given the choice between the kid in tractor hat, knee-high tubes and

61

cut-off Tee-shirt, the bus-lagged pair of English Camp-Americas propping their eyelids open with their backpacks and coffee the strength of bitumen, and the old man with the precise half inch of white beard and the leather bag like no one's carried since the tornado whisked Professor Marvel off to the Emerald City, Kelly By the Window knows which one he'll solicit with his little fill-'er-ups of complimentary coffee.

Sam My Man always leaves the airco off. He claims it makes the chili dogs taste better, but Kelly By the Window knows that he does it because someone's bound to comment that it's hot as the proverbial, and that's his cue. 'It's the drought,' he'll say. 'Rained everywhere else, but never here. You believe a town can be cursed?' Never failed yet.

'I surely could.' says this old man. 'Just how long is it since it last rained here?'

'Seven years,' says Kelly By the Window. The last drop fell two days after her eleventh birthday.

'You headed anyplace special?' asks Sam My Man, all chummy and pally-wally, like he's known this old man years not seconds. He's good, you got to give him that. Someone should have made him a lawyer long ago. Or a chat-show host.

'Had planned on heading up north, over the dam, got a woman and a boy I want to see,' says this old man, 'But then again, I may just stay around a couple of days or so. I think you may have need of my services.' He puts his bag on the counter, the Professor Marvel etc. etc., and *something* about it, *something* no one can ever call by name, makes Sam My Man step back; just a little. Even Kelly By the Window feels the *something* brush the fine downy hair along her spine. He opens the bag, takes out a thing that looks a little like a lightning rod and a little like a satellite dish and a little like a piece of Gothic wrought iron and not a whole lot like any. Afterwards, Sam My Man will swear by all the saints in Guadeloupe Cathedral he saw blue lightning running up and down the shaft, but Sam My Man, he's never let the truth get in the way of a good story.

'You want it to rain?' says the old man. 'I can make it rain. I'll bring the Rainmaker, if it's what you really want.'

And all those questions that have to be asked are stopped, suspended, because out of the night come six wheels and big blue silver: seventy more souls on the way from somewhere, to somewhere. Wiping night-sweat from his brow on the sleeve of his jacket, the driver is shouting: 'Thirty minutes refreshment stop!' Better get hopping, Sam My Man. Get that coffee brewing. Time to stop dreaming and get on the beam, Kelly By the Window. There's eggs to fry.

Beyond the Blood of Christ Mountains rumours of dawn threaten Desert Rose's sovereignty of the night, but she's still smiling. She who makes the law is she who breaks the law, on those nights when the stars are low and close and intimate and the wind smells of something best forgotten before it leaves a scar of the heart, when her flashing golden rope may lasso a stranger.

You brothers of the blacktop, you sisters of the all-nite diners, think, you refugees of the highways; think, have you seen him before, this old man-of-the-rain with his Professor Marvel bag and his precise half-inch of beard? Think, did you meet him, on a hard plastic chair in the corner of some three a.m. Burger King, rattling a chocolate machine in a bus station, by the hot-air hand drier in the gents toilet, wrestling with that one problem key in a wall of left-luggage lockers? Did you glimpse him over the top of your foam-styrene coffee cup, your copy of *Newsweek*? What did you think? Did you think nothing of him, just another life briefly parallelling your own, or did he intrigue you enough for you to abandon your attempts to sleep in the coffin-straight seats of a Greyhound or Trailway and let yourself be bound by the social compact of night-talk; in those wee wee hours did he open his Professor Marvel bag and show you the things inside running with blue lightning, did he tell you that he could bring the rain? Did he tell you he was the Herald of the Rainmaker? Did you believe him? Did you say, '*Crazy old man, lying old man, head full of crazy notions.*' Or did you think of those times, those places, when the sky was blue as a razor, did you remember how it felt when your prayers were answered and out of nowhere the clouds gathered, at first only a shadow on the horizon, then a patch the size of a man's hand, then a great anvil of darkness bearing down on your town. Then as the sky turned black from horizon to horizon, how you went into your garden and turned off your lawn sprinklers because this time you knew it really was going to rain . . . Did you lift up your eyes to the sky and whisper the word *Rainmaker* to yourself, did you turn it over and over on your tongue until every last drop of cool mystery was drawn out of it: *Rainmaker* . . .

Last person to actually spend a night at Wanda's Motel was a location scout for a Levis ad. Anticipating coke-snorting directors and overmuscled men in startlingly white boxer shorts, Wanda built a cocktail bar and installed cable TV in all her 'deluxe' chalets. Joes-on-the-go in the 'economy' rooms had to provide their own entertainment but then that's the whole idea, isn't it? Films crews chose a Jimmy Dean gas station at the end of an air force bombing range two hundred miles away. The bar's still popular but the only one who watches the cable is Wanda. She feels she has to justify the expense. She gets all the soaps.

She's not too sure about this one. It's not him. It's the things he carries in that bag of his. She sees them when she valets the room; weird things, odd things, not proper things. Things that don't look like *things* in themselves but bits of other things stuck together. Things that don't *do* anything, that are just for the sake of being *things*. She hasn't a clue what he does with the *things*, but folk coming in for the odd cocktail say he's been all around the town, holding those *things* of his up to his eye and pointing them at his feet, the sun, the Blood of Christ Mountains. Some say they've heard them make funny whining noises. Others say they've seen little grey numbers flashing up on them.

Sounds to Wanda like the location scout all over again. She's hoping she isn't going to miss out this time on the overmuscled men in the startlingly white boxer shorts. Then the stories come back about *things* even weirder, *things* like television aerials stuck into the ground all around the town, *things* like luminous kites flying in the dead of night, *things* like a cross between a boom-box and a very large cockroach left by the side of the road or clamped to a hoarding with a G-clamp, and she knows things can't go on like this any more.

'What are they *for*?' (With all the incredulity of a man who's been asked what a video remote control is for, or the little lamp in a refrigerator.) 'Why, they're my surveying equipment. I have to do a thorough geomantic survey of the location before Rainmaker can commit itself. Upper mantle standing wave diffraction patterns, earth, water and wind octaves, geomantic flux line nodes and anomalies: there's an awful lot I have to do and not much time to do it in. Can't read the flux density without this one here, the octave interface analyser. That one there, like the tripod with the black shutters on the top, that's the node localiser. Without that, I might as well pack up and go home. It's tough work. Fiddly, pernickety. You got to be inch perfect. Any chance of a beer?'

The location scout's beginning to look mighty good again to Wanda.

Again: that word: *Rainmaker*. Try it out for size on your tongue, does it sit easy in your imagination? No? Then tell me: what do you think of when you hear that word: 'Rainmaker?' Is it Tyrone Power in a bible-black hat? Is it a squadron of cloud-storming biplanes flown by leather-cat-suited blondes? Is it the ghost-dancing feet of your forefathers; is it something altogether more arcane and wonderful, some steam-driven wonder-worker all whirling vanes and blarting trumpet-mouths? If so, then think again. Rainmaker; *the* Rainmaker, is not a person, or a thing. Rainmaker is a place. A city.

How it came to be cast loose upon the sky, this city-state of two hundred souls, is a mystery. As with most mysteries, hypotheses abound: as in form it most resembles a tremendous kite (or then again, an aerial manta ray, or then again a great glass ornament, or then again . . .) it seems reasonable to assume it was launched into the air by some means; though the imagination balks at envisioning the kind of tug necessary to launch a glider one mile across. But a second image haunts you, of a city of soaring glass needles atop which the citizens have built graceful, winged habitats that hum and sway, like reed-grass, in the jetstream, and it is not hard for you to imagine how one such building might, in its pride to outreach all the others, grow so fine, so slender as to one day sever its connection with the earth altogether and cast itself out upon the sky.

The Bureau of Endangered Indigenes has granted Chief Blumberg, last of the Nohopés, a reservation the exact size of one rocking chair on the barbershop porch. Any time of day you will find him there, snapping the necks off beer bottles under one of the chair rockers, but on those nights when the first stars shine like notes from a National guitar, he is especially present. On those nights when the air smells of burnt dust and used-up time, he and his cat, midnight Mineloushe, sit watching the meteors that come down way beyond the Blood of Christ Mountains.

No one, not even Sheriff Middleton, knows what he does. It looks suspiciously close to nothing, but Chief Blumberg has the most important job in town. He prays for the town. Never despise the

65

contemplative, the intercessor. You don't know how much worse things would be without him. Town may be a long time throwing the dirt over itself, but while one soul remains to remember it to the Spirit in the Sky, it will not slip forgotten from the mind of God.

Some men when they meet have no need to speak. Some men, when they meet, know that they can better communicate by silence. St Dominic crossed the Appenines on foot to visit Francis of Assisi and neither spoke a single word throughout the entire meeting.

Chief Blumberg rocks and rolls in his portable reservation. The man who has come to meet him sits on a bench just below the barbershop window. The cat's Mineloushe-eyes shine with the light of meteors. Behind them, another Burma Shave lathers up while the radio announces fatstock prices.

Had St Francis offered St Dominic a bottle of beer neatly decapitated with one lunge of the rocking chair, history might have spoken differently. Silence expresses our similarities. For our differences, we must use words.

'So Raindog, you've come. Seven years I've been praying for rain, seven years arm-wrestling with God, and at last a verdict is announced. Seven years is a lot of praying, especially if God wants this place to go paws up, but you know something, prayer's never wasted. Prayer's got to go somewhere, like the rain; rain goes into the land and it gets bigger and bigger and bigger until the land can't hold it any more. So the land forces it out, and it changes, and becomes something else, but it always remembers what it was, and it always wants to be what it once was again. Something like you. You got a name, Raindog?'

'Elijah seems as good a name as any other.'

Whoosh! Big one! Little slitty-eyes, Mineloushe-cattie, dazzled and blinking. A white cockade in Desert Rose's hat . . . and it's gone.

' "And Elijah prayed that it would not rain, and there was no rain in the land for three and a half years. Again, he prayed and behold, the heavens gave forth rain." '

'It gratifies me, sir, to find a man knows his Bible these corrupt days.'

'Mission music rocked my cradle, Raindog.'

'So what is it you believe about me, sir?'

'I believe I prayed for seven years and up there on the edge of heaven all my prayers came together and created you.' Under the enormous sky, Kelly By the Window comes out to stand in Sam My

Man's doorway and watch the moon rise. She shakes the heat and dust out of her hair and the two men and the cat can hear the treble beat of her Walkman. 'I tell you something, Raindog, you better make the rain come soon, while she still has a chance. The drought's too deep in us, but she still has dreams.'

'I have the octave markers in position and the beacons are calling. The Rainmaker is coming, sir.'

Little Mineloushe blinks; the moon has been obscured by a sudden small cloud, not much larger than the size of a man's hand.

Time of the Tower, Time of the Tug, for generations beyond remembering Rainmaker has been a denizen of pressure gradients and barometric boundaries, flexing and curving itself to the hills and valleys of the air. Only once a year does it approach the earth, on the summer solstice it descends over some obscure map reference in a forgotten part of the ocean to consign its dead to the receiving waters and replenish its vapour tanks. This day of approach is foremost among the city's festivals; as it unfolds its tail from its belly and descends from the perpetual cloud of mystery, the rigging wires flutter with tinsel streamers and spars and ribs bristle a thousand silver prayer kites. Fireworks punctuate the sky and all citizens celebrate Jubilee. Flatlanders find it paradoxical that those who chose to live in the sky should celebrate their closest approach to earth, but those of you who have been a dragonfly snared by the surface tension of a pond will understand: it is not the closeness of the approach they celebrate, but the slenderness of the escape.

Sheriff Middleton and his stomach have enjoyed each other's company for so long now they are best friends. A satisfyingly mutual relationship: he keeps his stomach warm, full and prominent in the community behind straining mother of pearl buttons and silver belt buckles; it supplies him with public emimence and respect, a rich emotional life of belly laughs and gut feelings; even a modicum of protection, the stomach totes a .44 Magnum and has seen several Dirty Harry movies.

This stranger, stepping off one bus and not stepping on another, bag full of *weird thangs*, head full of weirder stories; stomach's got this gut feeling about him. Stomach's heard all about them on the evening news, these folk from the coast, there's *nothing* they won't do, and People are beginning to talk, (the ones whose talk matters, the ones with the capital P) and once People start talking, time you started listening to your good old buddy, Sheriff Middleton, that's been giving you nothing but heartburn and flatus all week, and Do Something.

Stomach never walks anywhere, so Sheriff Middleton drives him out to the edge of town where the man who calls himself Elijah is taping something that looks a little like a CB aerial and a little like a chromium Bay Prawn and not a whole lot like either to the side of a Pastor Drew McDowell Ministries hoarding.

There's never any way of making this sweet and easy, so don't even bother trying.

'Could you tell me what you're doing, sir?'

'I'm just positioning the last geomantic enhancer in the matrix so Rainmaker can follow it straight in. They won't have any visual guidance because of the cloud, so the Navigators will have to follow the geomantic beacons as they come in over the desert.'

Stomach may be an Eastwood fan, but Sheriff Middleton, he's seen *In the Heat of the Night* twelve times. Best Rod Steiger roll of the jowls. Slide of the mirror shades *up* the nose with the baby finger. Great banks of black clouds reflected in the shades, like a black iron anvil out there over the Blood of Christ Mountains.

'I think maybe you should take it down sir.'

'Why should I do that? Is it offending anyone?'

'No sir. As far as I know, it is not an offence to be in possession of peculiar-looking objects. However, I would surely appreciate it if you would take it, and all the rest of your geowhatchamacallit squoodiddlies down. Right now. If you please.'

'You don't quite seem to understand – '

'Correction. You don't quite seem to understand, sir. I want you, and all your micro-climatological doofuses and whatever the hell else you got in that bag of yours, on a bus out of here by eight tonight. Heard say you were headed north. Up over the dam, Neonville way, why don't you just take yourself and your Rainmaker away out of here up there?'

'Sir, with or without me, the Rainmaker is coming. No one can stop it now. Day and night the Flight Guild has been out on the high wires, rigging the sails to catch the wind the Weatherworkers are summoning, the wind that brings the Rainmaker.'

Clouds race across the twin mirrors over Sheriff Middleton's eyes, and the crazy wind from an unseasonable quarter strokes his skin. It is strong on his cheek like old whiskey tears. It tastes like jalapeños roasting on a charcoal fire, it sounds like a lone guitar bending fifths under a grapefruit moon. He can see it, the crazy wind, suddenly superimposed on his shades like the stress patterns in pick-up windows, wheeling round out there somewhere off the coast of Mexico carrying before it a great raft of warm, wet clouds. And there at the centre, something glittering and delicate and transparent as an angel's soul. He sees it all . . . and then he takes his glasses off to wipe them, and it's gone, wiped away, a smear on finger and thumb tip.

'If you'd just get in the car, sir, I'll take you back to the bus station and have someone pick up your things from the Motel. Word of advice sir, don't even think of setting foot out of there 'cept you setting it on a bus.' Rainmakers . . . flying cities . . . Soon as you get back behind your desk, Sheriff, you push buttons on that computer of yours and see if any freak hospitals are missing anyone.

A bus pants past, blue silver, dust and diesel. Chain lightning crawls along the edge of the world where the Blood of Christ Mountains meet the sky.

Weatherworkers? Flight Guilds? Is this some medieval city state set adrift in the stratosphere, complete with guilds and mysteries? Is there a vagrant Prince-Bishop lurking somewhere, or a wandering Blondin? Each man has his mystery, Guilds there certainly are, Guilds to tend the hydroponic gardens in the main residential bubble, Guilds to maintain the wind rotors that generate the electricity for Rainmaker's lights and hairdryers, guilds of teachers and doctors and lawyers and undertakers and sanitation engineers; does their very mundaneness make the airborne city state seem more credible? Listen, there is more.

Highest of the ten Guilds Major and Minor are the Rainmakers themselves, the weather-workers, a caste confined by a dominant vertigo gene to the central levels of the administrative spindle. Second to them are the Navigation and Flight Guilds, ancient rivals; the one redoubtable mappers of the topology of the sky who steer Rainmaker through the titanic chasms of air, the others daredevils of the silk-thin rigging wires (oblivious miles above ground zero) who tune the rippling acres of transparent mylar sail. Least of all the Guilds is the Guild of Heralds, for it is the only one to defile itself by walking upon the face of the earth. Yet the least of the guilds is also

69

the greatest, for without a herald walking upon the earth Rainmaker would sail the sky purposeless as a child's bubble.

Why the Rainmaker took its name and its sacred task; this is the Essential Mystery. You will find no answer in the Great Log in Flight Control at the centre of the administrative spindle. Nor will you find it in the memories of the guildpersons, even as they weave the clouds and shape the winds and spread their wings across the dry places. You will find no answer because the question is never asked. 'Why' is a wild, untamed word. It leads, one sure foot after another, toward the edge of the void. The people of Rainmaker do not ask 'why' questions because they know that the answer might be that there is no answer. Rainmaker makes rain because it makes rain.

But for you, dry-souled one, chili-dogger, dance-hall sweetheart, with the dust blowing in your bones, for you that is reason enough; Rainmaker makes rain and the rain falls on the just and the unjust alike, watering the earth, like the word of God that does not return to him empty. .

Seven-thirty, black as a preacher's hat. Hot as his Hell. Atmosphere tense as a mid-period Hitchcock. You've either got a migraine or murder in mind. Say, maybe those little men in the hats with the tracts are right, maybe this is the Apocalypse, right now, maybe, right in the middle of the prime-time soaps Jehovah the Ancient of Days is coming in clouds and lightning to judge the souls of all men.

Judgement punching up from the mountains is reflected in Kelly By the Window's shades as she drives to work. It's less than two blocks but she won't walk, not even on the day when God comes to judge her soul; that little red convertible is all the salvation she needs. The *heat*; even with the top down the sweat's dripping down her sides.

She sees him sitting on the bench by the door, backlit by the fluttering butterfly of the Budweiser sign. Bag at his feet, looks like the wind's about to blow Professor Marvel away again, high over the desert with the lights of desert towns and buses far below his rippling, flapping coat-tails.

'Sheriff Middleton throw you out?'

'He did.'

'Sheriff Middleton, he's the same as the rest of them. He's afraid of anything that isn't exactly the way it's always been.'

'There are many like him, sister. But things change, with or without Sheriff Middleton.'

'Thought where you're going, Rainmaker?'

'Up north. I have to see a woman and a boy. My boy. My successor. There is only ever one Herald, and he walks the earth alone, until he finds a woman of the earth who loves him enough to perpetuate the Guild. We serve the Rainmaker, but we may never set foot upon it. After that, I don't know. Wherever I am needed. Wherever things need to change.'

'I'm going there too. Get in.' He smiles and his bag of geowhatchamacallit squoodiddlies and micro-climatological doofuses goes in the back and he goes in the front, and off they drive, right down the street, past the blue and silver buses and the sign that says *population*: *elevation*:

'What's your name, sister?' the old man says.

'Kelly. I hate it. It's so undignified. Can you imagine an eighty-year-old grandmother called Kelly?'

'Can't say I've met that many.'

She shakes her hair free to blow back in the hot wind. Carmine polished nails search the airwaves; throbbing to major sevenths the little red convertible is swallowed by the night. Beneath a sky crazy with lightning, he asks,

'Tell me, why did you take me?'

'Because you made my mind up. Right there, in the street outside Desert Rose's. At last, you decided me. Without you, I'd have stayed behind that bar looking out the window at all the people coming from someplace, going to someplace until I grew old like the rest of them, with no destination, no direction, no kind of movement or change.'

Lightning stabs up from the horizon; for a hundred miles in every direction the desert is flashlit vampire blue. Battened down tight, a bus runs for town. Like a startled fox, a roadsign catches the light of the headlamps: *Havapai Point, two miles*.

'Could you stop the car?' says the old man. Radio powerchords go bouncing down the highway, headlamps slew round illuminating one hundred miles of old Diet Coke cans. 'I'd like to go up there. I know I can never be there, but I'd like to see it, when it comes. Would it be possible?'

She's already clawing for reverse.

Cochise came up here, to read the future of the red man, and saw Jeff Chandler. Jeff Chandler came up here, plus film crew, best boy, key grip and catering caravan, to play Cochise looking into a Panaflex. Chief Blumberg, last of Nohopés came up here and saw a chair on the barbershop porch. And now Kelly By the Window and the Herald of the Rainmaker stand here, the land cowering at their feet under a sky like the Hammer of God.

'Sunday nights when Sam didn't need me, I'd come up here with Mario from the garage. Some nights, when I just couldn't stand any more, when it felt like my skull was going to explode, it was so full of nothing, we'd take the car and drive and drive and drive but however far we drove we'd always end up here, up at the Point. We were scared, like the rest of them, you see. Mario, he'd turn on the radio and flick on the headlights and we'd dance, like the headlights were spotlights. They used to have this great Golden Oldies show on Sunday nights, Motown and the Doobie Brothers and sometimes Nat King Cole, and we'd dance real close, real slow, and pretend we'd won a million on a game show and we were whooping it up in a fancy nightclub in Neonville. Sometimes we'd say we were going to drive all night and wake up in Mexico.' A solid column of ion-blue plasma flickers between earth and heaven. 'Whoo!' yells Kelly By the Window. 'That was a big one!' She likes to shout at the storm.

'Close,' says Elijah, listening to the sky. 'I can feel it, up there, somewhere. Rainmaker is here.' Thunder tears like ten thousand miles of ripping grave-cloth. 'She's shorting out the storm, channelling the lightning down the mainframe to the discharge capacitors in the tail. One hundred million volts!'

She shivers, hugs herself.

'You're crazy, old man. Crazy crazy crazy, and you know something? It's good to be crazy!'

And then they hear it.

And the buses in the depot and Sam My Man brewing up the bribes for another night's heavy dealin' and Wanda the manageress with her ever-circling television families and Chief Blumberg with bottle in hand and Sheriff Middleton, treating his good good buddy to a few chili dogs, and all the dust-dry, bone-dry faces and places of a desert town, even Desert Rose herself, whip-crackin' away in neon spangles and boots: they all hear it. And stop. And look at the sky in wonder.

The clouds open. The rain comes down on the town. Old, hard rain, rain that has been locked up for seven years and now is free; mean rain, driving down upon a desert town. Thunder bawls, lightning flashes; Wanda's *deluxe* cables burn out in a blare of static. In the diner faces press to the glass, mouths open in amazement at the drops streaming down the windows. On the barbershop porch

Chief Blumberg rocks forward and back, forward and back, laughing like a crazy old Indian.

Up on Havapai Point the young woman and the old man are soaked to the bones in an instant. They do not care. Kelly By the Window, she dances in the headlights of her little red convertible, hair sodden snarls and tangles, print dress plastered over small, flat breasts. She throws back her head to taste the good, hard rain, it tastes like kisses, it tastes like iced Mexican beer.

'Look,' says the Herald of the Rainmaker, in a voice she has never heard before. And she looks where he is pointing, and, in a lightning bolt of illumination, she sees. She will never be certain what. *Something*. Half hidden by clouds, delicate as a dragonfly wing, strong as diamond, *something* that lives in the storm, *something* that overshadows desert and town like the wings of the Thunderbird. *Something* she knows she will never be free from again, because what she has seen is not just a *something* that might have been a Rainmaker, but a something that might have been a world that should have been, where cities can fly, and sail, and walk, and dive, where cities can be birds, and flowers, and crystals, and smoke, and dreams.

As she sees it, she knows that it is for this moment only. She will never see it again, though she will gladly spend the rest of her life searching for it.

There are tears behind her shades as she drives away from Havapai Point, into the rain, into the welcoming night.

They find the car in a ditch three miles out of Neonville city limits. It has gone clear through the hoarding; big hole right where the Republican candidate's heart used to be. The paramedic team admire her accuracy. The radio is on. Her dress is soaking wet, when they pull her from the wreck, she still has on her shades. They lay her by the side of the road while they try to decide what to do with her. Someone suggests they call Sheriff Middleton. They think they've seen this little red convertible before, cruising the boulevard of abandoned dreams with the top down.

Someone says they think maybe there was another passenger; little things; half-clues, semi-evidences. He (or she) must just have walked away.

Someone says they heard it rained down south of the dam last night. First time in seven years.

73

SIMON D. INGS

Blessed Fields

'He was born dumb and blind. They had merely to snap the drums of his ears,' my sister whispered in the night silence of our room.

'I thought a shumi player had to be born in his perfect state.'

'Our priests decided to give Mother a helping hand.'

'Clirosa!' I could never feel easy about such languid irreverence.

'Phrase it how you like,' she replied. 'It all comes down to the same thing in the end; the same plays, the same legends, the same lessons.'

I did not reply. I was too tired to argue. Anyway, the climax of the shumi cycle would soon be upon us; my sister would not be blasphemous then.

I changed the subject. 'Do you like him?'

'Who?'

'The shumi player.'

Clirosa shrugged. 'I don't know.' She pulled the sheets farther up around me and entwined her arm round my shoulders. 'He's just a set of gestures and trained responses, like every other shumi player.'

I turned and cupped my sister's shoulder in my hand. 'I don't mean as a player, I mean – as a man.'

Clirosa stifled a giggle.

'Please.'

'I'm sorry,' she whispered, 'but how can you feel anything for someone who's only half alive?'

'I just mean he's pretty is all. And he's not just "half-alive" – he's our shumi player: Ilya the Sun-Prince.'

'He's the backstairs work of a scullery maid. Let's not pretty him up.'

'I wish you wouldn't talk like that.'

She laughed, and tightened our embrace.

After a moment's silence she explained: 'The play cycle bores me. Always the same thing, year after year. What's the point to it?'

At length I replied: 'The shumi cycle has no point – not in the way you mean, not a point you can just spell out. It's like an old song. It's pleasing simply because we know it so well.'

'The trouble is,' Clirosa said, 'I don't think the plays are that good. There's no depth to them. It's different when the bards and troupes perform – they act out all sorts of new and different stories, and everybody enjoys them. But the cycle's just the same bald framework over and over again.'

'You know,' I said, 'there are things I don't like about the shumi cycle.'

'Oh?'

'It seems silly, the way it ends,' I admitted.

'I know.'

'How do you think they get the player to do it?'

'Does it excite you?'

Embarrased, I replied, 'In a way, it's – I don't know. I never thought of it that way before. But how do they do it?'

'It's all touch.'

'Well, of course; I know the figures as well as you,' I replied, scornful. 'But how do they teach him *that* by touch, is what I'm asking. And to keep so *still* . . .'

My sister sighed. 'Oh, I don't know.' She put her mouth to mine and kissed me goodnight.

It was the day of the Strawberry Harvest. Clirosa was two years older and had already reached the age of exemption. I had still to dress in a festive smock and work with the other children in the village's Blessed Fields.

The day was fine and bright. A few wisps of high cloud broke up the oppressive blue-green sky. I walked out of the village. I timed my departure so I escaped the worst of the elders' hail of stale corn; an indignity with which I was by now overfamiliar.

The climb was wearying and I arrived late at the fields. My mother scolded me. I took up a wicker basket and went across to the stall to have it blessed. Pesia, a novitiate, stood stirring a bowl of incense. He was a few years older than I, but our parents were acquainted so we had been friends off and on for some time.

He took my basket and anointed its handle. I bowed, took it back.

He said, 'Under the table you'll find a box with some packets inside. Can you get me one?'

I did so, tore open the paper and shook its contents into the incense bowl. Pesia stirred with greater vigour. A pungent stench arose – I inhaled. The heady concoction swelled in me, and the weight drained from my limbs. My eyes swam.

Pesia laughed. 'Are you all right?'

I nodded dreamily, picked up the basket and glided, as it seemed, to my appointed field. I looked back; Pesia stood with his face over the bowl. There are compensations for a religious life.

I found myself among the youngest of our clan. Strawberry picking was chore enough without their peevish gabbling, and I was unable to work my way across the field to anyone my own age. At length, therefore, I gave up in disgust. I deposited my pickings into a wattle bin and walked off through the undergrowth which surrounded this tilled land. More or less out of sight, I sat down beneath a tree and fell to dreaming.

'Above your dignity?'

I jumped. 'I was tired. I'll go back.' I made to move.

'Tired?' my mother echoed. My heart beat a little faster. 'Talking with your sister until late, no doubt.' She led me back to the fields.

'Yes,' I admitted. 'We were having an argument.'

My mother smiled, sour. 'You and your sister share some exhausting conversations. Just try not to disturb your father these last days of the cycle. He's tense, and doesn't sleep well.'

'I see,' I murmured weakly.

'Well, what were you talking about last night?' she asked as we reached the fields.

'About the play cycle.'

'What about it?' Mother's tone was easy now, with no trace of her initial harshness.

'I was saying I like the shumi player.'

'Ah.'

'That's what Clirosa said.'

'Do you like the look of him?'

Her directness surprised me. 'Yes, very much,' I replied.

'I can understand that. Though for myself, I long ago ceased to look at shumi players as men. Now it's like when I was a child – I see only the figure they represent: Ilya.'

Then she took my shoulder in her hand and turned me to face her. She said, 'There's always a short time in a young woman's life when she tries to find entertainment and spectacle in the shumi plays. But they aren't supposed to intrigue us that way.' With that my mother made to leave me to my strawberry picking, then turned back to me and said, 'They've brought him here. Have you seen him?'

'Who?'

'The shumi player.'

I went back to harvesting. In spite of myself I found the work less tedious than before. Two more panniers would complete my quota and then the day was my own.

They had brought him to the strawberry fields, my mother said. I was surprised at that. There would be churchmen around to keep him safe, of course, and my father would almost certainly be among them. Still . . .

I hurried my work and finished soon after midday. Then I went to find the shumi player.

He crouched by a wagon. His ankle was tied by a long rope to its rear axle. He squatted naked in the long grass, his hands held out in limp, senseless supplication. The heels of his palms were stained green. Flecks of grass stuck to his arms. His expression was firm, blank and unmoving. He had been trained from birth always to bear himself this way and it lent him a certain vacant nobility. His unseeing eyes were wide and blue.

I knelt down and looked deep into his eyes. As I brought my face closer to his, so my shadow touched him. His eyelids dropped shut. I drew away from him and looked around, uneasy. No one observed us.

I turned back to find him lying on the grass.

He breathed deep. The muscles of his stomach swelled. If he could, I believe he would have smiled to have the sun on his amber skin and the rough, damp grass beneath him. What animal pleasure must he get from touch, I wondered, deprived of all other senses by Mother and the surgeon?

Then it struck me: was touch his only remaining sense, or could he still taste? If he was born with the ability there was no easy way to deprive him of it, as a delicate lance into the ears had deprived him of hearing. Perhaps they had given him potions to drink, or filled his cell with strong incense. But to what end? There was clear sense to his blindness and deafness; it rendered him unable to learn or develop except as the Tutor directed him, through the ingenious language of touch. But taste, smell – these were animal senses, delicious and instinctive, and could not, I supposed, seriously disturb the shumi player's state of mind or muddle his education.

To see if this was so, I walked over to the edge of the nearest field. After some searching (for this part of the clearing had already been harvested) I found a ripe strawberry. I picked it, went over and pressed the fruit to his lips. He remained still and did not open his mouth. I was puzzled. I laid down beside him so my face was on a level with his, and pressed the fruit to his lips again, harder. His lips parted slackly and the strawberry crushed a little on his teeth. I drew it down, easing his lips apart, then withdrew my hand. I remembered the conversation of the previous night, and how I had boasted that I knew some of the Tutor's touch-figures.

On his way up the clerical ladder my father had at one time been appointed Tutor, and when I was young he had practised the figures on me. I still retained vague memories of some codes.

I slid my hand down him; the softer fat and muscle of his breast dipped to the hard ripple of rib and the smooth curve of abdomen. I reached down to hip and thigh. He stirred, uncomfortable. I withdrew my hand. I had simply been touching good flesh, but I realised that to him I had actually spoken nonsense and confused signs. It disturbed him, and one should not toy with the afflicted.

So I first practised on myself the few figures I had picked up, and only after this did I touch him, 'speak' to him.

I laid my hand on the shumi player's breast and tried a figure my father had often used upon me in my more innocent years; the code for food.

Eventually I pressed home the perfect figure. He relaxed. I took up the strawberry and pressed it into his mouth.

He licked down the sweetmeat, bit once through it, swallowed.

There was no smile of thanks.

I smiled weakly with disappointment and turned to go.

The Tutor barred my way.

Without a word he took me by the arm to my father. He described my actions to him in decidedly colourful terms and when he left my father privately admonished me.

'Just what do you think you were doing?' he said. 'Don't you have enough sense to know you *never* touch a shumi player? You know the touch-figures are dangerous. What if you had pressed home a shumi-play code? What would have happened then? Months of teaching wasted, and Mother knows what else. The touches are *important* to him – they're all he has.'

Eventually we came to the matter of punishment.

'Your acts were childish and indecent,' he said. 'Since you acted like a child, you'll be treated like one. To make good this day you will act it over, and act it properly, at the next Harvest.'

'But my age of exempt –'

'Has nothing to do with it.'

The next day my sister and I went to bathe in the South River. We reached the jetty by mid-morning. A dozen or so villagers had already arrived. Some were swimming; others lay on the river bank, made drowsy by the heat.

Clirosa thrust her lunch pail into my hand and rushed to the water's edge. She shrugged off her clothes and waded into the river.

I walked onto the jetty and came to sit by Pesia, who lay face down on the dry boards. He looked up at me, smiled recognition, and settled to sleep again. I slipped off my blouse to let the air cool me and gazed across the river. 'Do you want to go to Chancaton with me this summer?' I asked him.

'Are your parents going?'

'No.'

'Who'd go with us?'

'We'd go alone.'

'You're under age.'

'Until next month,' I admitted. 'After then . . .'

Just then my sister bobbed up beside us, heaved herself naked and dripping from the water. She lay back exhausted on the hot wood of the pier.

'They prefer novitiates to stay at home, their first year,' Pesia said to me. 'If a cleric was visiting perhaps we could go with him. Alone with you . . .'

'Well, I *am* the daughter of Mother's Vicar,' I complained. 'That must be good for something.'

'Perhaps, but will Mother's Vicar let you go?'

'Why ever not?'

'Because of yesterday.'

'Oh. That. That's sorted out now.'

'Ah.'

My sister laughed.

'There's no need for that,' I said. And then, abashed: 'I'm not proud of what I did.'

'I was surprised you showed such nerve,' Clirosa said. 'About time.'

'But Father was right. I *could* have started a shumi sequence. Not clever.'

'I don't know. The sowing of the Hemp-Seed would have been fun. Or the Purgation of Ciel-Lesch.'

'Or Mother's Cup,' Pesia put in.

'Don't be melodramatic,' Clirosa replied testily. 'Anyway, in a couple of days it'll be for real anyway, so what difference does it make?'

'At least in two days' time we'll all be in the Ring to watch him,' Pesia said. 'Something of a waste, having him act it out in a strawberry field.'

'Something of a waste, period, to have him do that – it seems so senseless.'

'But that's the legend,' Pesia explained in his best patronising manner. 'Ilya tears his flesh so Mother may drink his spirit . . .'

'But the shumi player isn't Ilya,' I replied with equal condescension. 'He . . . he's just the backstairs work of some scullery maid.'

Pesia shook his head, appalled. 'Since the legends tell us Ilya did these things, the shumi player must do them. He's been taught to believe he is Ilya, and so he must do the things Ilya did. There's nothing wrong with that.'

'There's something wrong with lying to him,' I said.

'We teach him lies,' Pesia admitted, 'but he believes them, so they become the truth.'

'I must try that on father,' Clirosa mused. 'Can I say you said that?'

'No. I'm not sure it's right. I don't know. You've got me confused.'

We laughed at him.

The day of the performance arrived. I was manhandled into my best gown and had my hair tugged roughly into a Gorgon's Knot, and my mother had a screaming argument with Clirosa over who was to wear the family's totem lace. At last we boarded the carriage which took us to the Ring.

81

The sun had set. We got down from the coach. I looked across to the scaffold, silhouetted against a purple horizon. It consisted of a simple platform on which were fixed a number of rough wooden pillars. These symbolised the various locations of legend. Upon each pillar was suspended a totem or article of mythic importance.

We sought out our seats in the Ring, and awaited the re-enactment of Mother's Cup.

Torches were lit around the platform, illuminating the stage. After a few seconds – counted off in deaf-blind isolation – the shumi player ascended the scaffold and began the re-enactment.

The last book of the Base Tale tells us that, once Ciel-Lesch had been purged of the Dragon-Tail, Ilya fell victim to the wiles of the Sybil of the Blessed City, and while she lay imprisoned in his keeping he seeded her.

In reparation for this transgression Mother demanded from Ilya a gift of Spirit. After many struggles in his search for Spirit's source Ilya despaired and spilled his own spirit into Mother's cup. Mother brought the cup to her lips but found the taste displeasing. She poured Ilya's spirit upon the Earth. Thereupon, the first grasses bloomed, and other legends begin.

Trapped in blackness, silence and touch-figure memories the shumi player played out the Tale.

In gestures he portrayed Ilya's triumph at the Purgation, his seduction at the hands of the Sybil, and his subsequent trials at the hands of Mother.

The play neared its end. He stepped back two paces. Though blind he had been taught to hold within his mind every detail of the scaffold. He reached out to his right, and took a decorated knife from its hook on the pillar beside him.

I closed my eyes.

Hand in hand, Clirosa and I trod behind the funeral wagon as it wound its way up the track to the Blessed Fields. There the shumi player's body would be burnt, and his ashes ploughed into the blessed earth. Our parents and the other clerical families followed us.

We reached the clearing. The horses were unharnessed and led away to fallow land on the other side of the fields. The cart itself was left unattended for a time while we went to gather material for the pyre.

My sister went on ahead with friends.

I lingered at the edge of the clearing till I lost sight of them. Then, alone and unnoticed, I wandered back to the cart.

I unfastened its rear panel, let it swing down.

His corpse was covered by a cotton sheet. I took it in my hand and pulled it gently aside. I uncovered his face. It was expressionless, even in death: ashen, waxen – beautiful. I ran my fingers through his hair, then cradled his head in my arm.

I gazed at him a long while, then leaned down and put my mouth to his lips. But they were cold and shrunk with death and I found no pleasure in the kiss.

'No matter,' I murmured and I thought: Next harvest, I will pick the fruit from your field, taste the juice of your ashes, and remember you.

I drew the sheet back to cover his face.

GILL ALDERMAN

Country Matters

It is said that both William Rufus and Edward the Martyr worshipped the God of the Witches.

The village, my village, is a place of inclines and angles, steep stone roofs, rough paths, the green climb of the hill into whose crown the castle has fallen, a maze of slouching towers and dead window-holes; down below, the sharp corners of grey houses and, everywhere, flights of steps leading to the monuments with which the Christians set their petrifying mark upon the ancient settlement. A cross, they believe, has sanctified the market square and the church stands high above the The Badger, the pub the city people never visit; even in the heated days of Midsummer the church casts a cold, cruciform shadow over the windows, and the steps that lead up to it are a new Via Dolorosa for mourners and the penitent.

We sat in the front parlour of The Badger: he, the landlord Nim, and I, discussing the merits of lurchers. Nim and I are old friends, and the friendship had been seasoned by the new man. He was my latest husband, a little over six feet tall, a little overweight, a trim beard; and willing. For me, the beard was a reminder of other, past, times. He had a job in the city, money; he was a young man and steady enough to be a good father to my child, when it had been conceived. Yet his sort were common enough and his urban precision was muted, at least in the country, by new pretensions to be one of us. He believed that it was wrong to eat the flesh of chickens reared under lamps and slaughtered at eight weeks, but that the putrid meat of a pheasant shot full of lead and hung for ten days was healthy food, lean meat. His waxed cotton jacket hung on the back of the door. He drank only 'real' ale.

I looked at my two dogs, lying where they had composed their long

85

bodies for the idle time which would end only when Nim blew his hunting horn for last orders. Angles, in the dogs, were elegant attitudes, all world-weariness and submission. Their speaking eyes were closed against the tedium. The brindle bitch, Syr, lay on her side, her four feet stretched towards, the fire. To me she was an aberration, a rough-coated lamping-man's dog, quick on the turn and a clean killer. I tolerated her because of her gentleness and her ability, when the time was ripe and the black mood on me, to soothe me with her sleeping body warm against my own desolation. But Pan, my best and dearest, only dog: he was and is the father, grandfather and emperor of my line of running dogs, white as snow with dark red ears pricked up, even now in sleep, his shape the expression of his swiftness, long muscle, longer limbs and a tail like a whiplash. Despite his colour, which made him visible to a keeper in the dark, the old men loved him on sight. He was 'a good strong dog', and that is high praise from a lurcher man. The young men called on me from time to time 'for a loan of your dog'; in this way I earned many fine pups and the young men earned my favour. I thought of Luke and his lean brown body, of Phil's hair like old unravelled rope, of Piers who had been so fleet of foot; and I blushed for he, the husband, was looking at me, and I like to keep up appearances.

Nim's bitch lay a little apart from my dog, Pan, the same rufous ears upstanding, the same leucous coat covering her beautiful body. She was old now and had lost some of her speed, but none of her keenness.

'Any more in here?' Patty's yellow head appeared in the hatchway which does duty as a bar in the front parlour of The Badger. I hate her. She clings to Nim and will weaken him with her misty, misplaced, tolerance, her soft femininity and her frilly, pastel-hued clothing. So many work against us. Her blood would be thin and watery like bad beer: useless. Besides, she was barren. She had refused to try the old remedies – the hawthorn tree, a votive pilgrimage to the Giant – and had adopted a child, a pallid little thing which was supposed to be male and which she kissed and cosseted as if it were one of the cade lambs which littered her kitchen every Spring and caused such anguish to the dog, disturbed from her place by the fire.

My husband pulled out his wallet and moved towards her.

Nim and I sat on, together within each other's minds, and the chatter in the bar fell about us. A group of adolescents sat in the window, three girls and two boys who talked callowly of the city. Their wheyfaces only came alive when they spoke of music. They were dressed in the dusty black clothing popular at the time, shod in scruffy canvas shoes and topped by ragged hairstyles of varying colours. My husband could have told them they were out of fashion, that neat heads were the thing in the city. They were young, so very young; I hoped they each had a purpose. I noticed that the boy nearest me, the red-haired one, was consumed by real flames. His dull coat was decorated with the badges of many lost causes, CND, Nuclear Power No Thanks, Keep Britian Multiracial, Tolerate, and he wore an earring in his left ear, its single bead a virulent green speck against the bonfire of his hair. My husband could have told him the significance, in the city, of a single beaded earring but, out here, beyond the pale, we are all innocents.

The boy stared intently at one of the girls, listening to her tumbling words; some tale of adolescent depression without apparent end – and then her words dropped into the dark pool of my thoughts. 'The nights,' she said, 'are the worst, when I can't sleep and the moon, the full, bright moon, shines in across me. I have to get up then, and I go and sit on Granny's grave in the churchyard.' She looked away from him, away from the intensity of his blue gaze, and caught me staring at her. She looked at me, slowly, deliberately, across the room. Her skin was clear and white, her hair dyed deep black. With the experimental abandon of an adolescent, she had put on a bright red lipstick too strong for her moonfaced pallor. She looked annoyed, caught out by an adult eavesdropper; and then she smiled and she and I shared the knowledge that her use of the bright lipstick was deliberate, an unsprung snare, and the tip of her tongue came out, a soft pink lozenge between her teeth. She pointed a toe and caressed the boy's leg with its grubby canvas covering.

I stroked Pan's smooth neck. He had risen from his station on the floor and pushed his long nose underneath my arm.

I looked out of the window. Barty was coming down the church-yard steps, hippity-hop, one leg and two crutches, demonstrating his stability by choosing the most difficult route. He had probably been to the vicarage. He swung up to the window and sidled against it until he felt me hissing. He leered and was gone. A cripple who is also one of God's apes is hard to deceive.

My husband came back with brimming glasses.

I drank the silken liquid through its head of foam. 'Who is she?' I thought, 'What is her name?' She was neither a Hooper nor a Ballard; she was not a Coffin. I remembered the Days, who farm near the perimeter and are seldom seen in the village; I tried to remember the dead in the churchyard, both the young who die regularly without issue and the old, the ones who had starved and frozen last Winter without pensions, food, or fire, without electricity or hot water, without timber for coffins at the end, sacrifical suicides, martyrs of a cause they never voted for.

Three pints of Nim's bitter and the warmth from his fire of turves must have taken my wits. Outside again, in the brisk March air, I stretched up and kissed my husband on the cheek.

'I want to walk the dogs,' I said, 'You go on, my dear, and set the table. I sha'n't be long.'

I turned away from him and went up the steps into the churchyard. The dogs pressed against me and drew in their tails until these were taut curves between their hocks. We dislike churchyards, the three of us, but I can reason where their untutored instincts must endure. Sulis' spring ran cold from the earth and disappeared into the stone channel where they confined it in their Year 900.

Four graves had been dug that Winter. The first was that of the girl they found drowned, out at Ower; the second was that of John Coffin, whose portrait in The Badger was his true memorial, blue-eyed, knowing, the old rogue; the third was fresh, the long mound still covered by one of those false swards of cloth with which Christian gravediggers try to mask the face of death. Over the fourth, a black marble slab had been laid, a weight to hold the old woman down. Already, spikes of grass pushed out around it and Pan sniffed them. I read the golden letters on the slab, the guilt-offering of a family which had let is beldame starve.

Freda Day
Beloved Wife of Henry
Mother of Sara and James
Dear Grandmother of Fancy

'His judgements are in all the earth.' Ps. 105,7.

Fancy Day: a tribute, or someone's idea of a pretty jest. Fancy, whose name was published by her God-fearing family, carved and blazoned in gold for all to read and for me and my kind to possess. How careless Christians are. I whispered her name in the soft ears of my dogs.

88

His name: that was harder, but the colour of his hair gave him away. The Brochets over to Hays have red hair; he was Sam, Samuel John Martin, and he was working up at Dragon's, learning to be a dairyman. I whispered his name and made it the thread of my song as I spun, moving the treadle softly, back and forth, to and fro, and letting the twist run smoothly out between my finger and thumb. I sang all that week, all day and every day, pleased by the pattern I was helping to weave and pleased by the memory of his red hair, which William had, and Aelfrida's choice who had known and loved these bare hills and the castle in the gap between them.

My husband returned from the city at the end of the week. They had given him a pass for me, his wife, but I laughed at him and it and gave the wafer quickly back, for I was tempted to throw it in the fire. I will never set foot in the city, where death is accidental and birth technological artifice, and when its bony fingers reach us here at last I shall go, further West, deeper in, and be a hound for one year and a hawk for another. I drew back the curtains to let the moonlight in. We made the beast with two backs then, on the floor where fire and moonlight met. Afterwards I looked for the blood which should have flowed with the moon, but there was none and so I was doubly satisfied and must have him again, and again, until he was exhausted. I had neglected to give him Sparrow-grass with the hen pheasant Syr had brought me. I let him sleep, rose, and put on my clothes; in March I cannot rest. Pan got up from the ashes to follow me but the bitch hung her head and crept over to the man. She lay down close to him.

My longdog went before me, knowing the way as well as I. A fox crossed the lane in front of us and the dog pricked up his ears and would bound forward, but I forbade him; nor would I permit him to course the hare which listened in the furrows when we crossed Home Field. The moon made shrouds of the shadows and in the village her pale light broke up the familiar solids of roof and wall, balestack and barn, and built new shapes from them. In the churchyard the gravestones were lonely sentinels and I avoided the shadow underneath the tower.

I had imagined her perched on the rail which surrounds the grave, a newly fledged bird chirruping to the old raven under the soil, but she was lying down upon it, curled up in the centre of the black and gold stone.

'I sit in her lap,' she said, 'She was as soft and comfortable as an old cushion, but the stone is cold and hard.'

'The stone is marble,' I told her, 'Stone from hereabouts which was once living creatures in the sea. Put out your hand, Fancy dear, and feel the young grass which is growing from your grandmother's body.'

I watched her stroke it; so, when the time came, would she caress the red-haired boy, Sam, whom I called Rufus as a charm. I helped her to rise, held her in my arms and embraced her, before I gave her the drink I had prepared and sealed in a beer bottle.

'He must drink it all,' I said. 'Give it him after a glass of Nim's Winter Ale. He won't know the difference.'

'What's in it?' she said, fearful now, and shy. 'Is it poison?'

'Would your Gran have poisoned anyone?' I asked her. 'This is a good brew. It is an ale of life brewed from Barleycorn and the Hop. The herbs of venery were steeped in it until it drew out their essences. There's Spearmint, the herb of Venus; Black and White Mustard to stir up lust and guard against lethargy; Snakeflower picked here, beside the grave of Freda Day, and Onion to increase seed; last, not least, two drops of a decoction of Lady's Tresses which soothes aching limbs.'

'Teach me,' said Fancy then.

'You have enough to do. Later, when Summer comes, I'll show you when and where to find your herbs and the signs to brew and bake under. I will give you recipes for juleps, syrups and infusions; I will teach you how to make plasters and pills and lohocks, and how to fashion a troche; I will bring you to the houses of the Lord of the Tenth and the Lord of the Ascendant – for physic without astrology is a lamp without oil.

'Now go and seek out him who loves you; but mind, he must not touch you yet. My brew will keep him devoted and hot.'

Pan pressed his trembling body against my legs. The girl looked down at him.

'Mine's a cat,' she said, 'A little tabby cat. I call her Sib.'

'This is Pan. Now kiss me and go. Later, you shall know my name.'

The musty smell of Barty hung about the steps as I went down them, and my dog growled. I sent him on, but the idiot had gone or carried a piece of care-tree, for we did not see him.

In March, the woods used to be choked with primroses and the steep fields behind my house were lavender and white with cuckoo flowers. The ladysmock still blooms, but the primroses went with the trees when we had to fell and uproot them to burn and keep us warm.

Hearth and need fires are made from turf now, or dry seaweed, or dung.

In March, I must wander and am constantly abroad; night and day, both have their separate natures. The moon speaks to me and the sun, waxing ever stronger, dances with me.

Sometimes I went as far as the sea and watched the water toss weed ashore; sometimes I climbed to Ninebarrows and walked among the old graves there, between dreams and memory. The white horse which lived there, up on the bald face of the hill, always greeted me with a kiss and, in the village, the cats came up to purr and accost my legs with their furry, twining bodies. When I passed Nim in the street, his greeting was a cheerful one and we paused in our conversation to watch my dogs sniff Bel.

As the month went on, Syr grew sullen and I often left her at home, curled up on the sofa awaiting my husband's return. A dog has only the master she chooses; I could not blame her. One night I lay down beside her and looked into her sorrowful eyes. I stroked her ears, pulling them gently through my fingers, and I bade her farewell.

Pan brought me the hare and I gave him Puss's heart and lungs for courage and her wind and her kidneys for strength; of her body I made a fragrant stew which nourished me and the new life within me which was yet too small to be thought of as a babe; the blood of the hare I mixed with flying medicine and I put it in a gallipot and preserved its savour with vinegar, aloes, and cayenne. Kitty Lander had a pass to travel North and by her I sent a greeting to my youngest daughter who is fostered by a wise one under Pendle Hill. We share the good things: Joan is old and can bear no more daughers. Also, the city is greedy, and devours seven-tenths of our milk, our sons and daughters, our wheat and barley and beer. Last year it reached and surrounded the Rufus Stone.

I did not see Fancy, but I knew she had been to have her finger pricked between Wisdom and Death.

I took down the bronze loving cup and polished it. My windows look out and down across the valley to the castle and the grey roofs below it. The pattern of furrows cut last Winter were a naked and barren body waiting to be veiled in green and the new grass grew thinly, struggling in the pastures with nettle and dock. Home Field lay waiting, a neat brown square. Be sure: too often, the crop had failed; too soon and too weak were many babies born. Beyond the castle, the waters of the Harbour sparkled but, by night, I saw a different glimmer, city lights encroaching across the heath.

I spoke the words and caused a mist to rise. It floated between me and the alien lights as I went down the hill, my feet sure in the old way. Nell was calling a fret in from the sea and as I went the vapours mingled, mine and hers, swirled and blanketed the earth and sky except – for Nell is a skilful conjuror – over Home Field where the earth was moist and yielded under my feet and where my waxing, crescent Lady rode in a clear circle of sky. Giles had sown the last seed that afternoon. I stooped and scratched for a grain of it, taking the tiny, pale oval up and placing it in the palm of my hand so that I could bless it before replacing it tenderly in the soil. Pan, waiting while I made my prayer, looked out across the plough.

We met in the centre of the field where the land rises slightly and there is a shallow pond, and Fancy, coming last, led on the red-haired boy. He gazed at her as if he were one of those lapdogs fed on titbits and cupboard love; imitating us, he raised his hands and looked up into the sky. Poor, brave Rufus; poor, noble goat.

When we looked down again, focusing on the dark field and the water in which Her sickle floated, we saw that the Hunter had come. The steeds of time stopped racing. We, the silent earth, the moon and the boy were still. The Hunter faced us. His horns of seven branches stood erect on his head and his red-eared hounds were gathered about him, the old bitch to the fore. Pan left my side and went among them; I could not distinguish him from his brothers and sisters of the Wild Hunt.

We made their bed in the ninth furrow, scraping aside the loam to expose the seed. They were both eager, hot to our hands as we undressed them. We joined hands in a circle about them and were still as we watched their pale bodies work hard upon the earth; there was silence, but for their harsh breathing and old Alison, who cried out suddenly as if she were giving birth. While they lay together in the warm wet aftermath, we danced. Then Nell led the girl aside and covered her eyes. Tenderly, she wiped the soil from her white skin.

The Hunter stepped forward and blew his horn. Like a hare frightened from its bed in the furrows the boy rose warily, and saw the Wild Hunt, the dogs which would bring his body to check and the Hunter who would take his soul. He took to his heels, swift and white across the rough plough and the dogs coursed him up and down, across the field and round the mirror of still water until he tired and faltered close by its brink. I filled the loving cup and held it to his lips. He drank his draught greedily, gulping down the spices and bitter herbs and the fresh, raw blood. He came eagerly forward to meet the Hunter's knife and while he died we each took our sip from the cup. The ground receded, we rose, we flew, and watched the boy's blood soak into the earth below. Nell held Fancy firmly by the hand.

'He bleeds,' she whispered. 'He has gone home.' She wept and, afterwards, while Nell dried her tears, she smiled.

'Now we're safe,' said Alison, 'Safe and sound for nine times nine. And pretty boys are safe from us.'

We took up his warm body and floated with it over earth, stone, and wood leaving Herne and his hounds – all but one. Pan came with us, loping over the ground below, his long labouring shape that of a swimmer over dark rock. There were roofs below us, cold chimneys and the dank smell of turf ash. The broken castle rose out of the night. We crossed the moat – running water is no barrier when you fly – and came to earth by the Martyr's Gate. Near it, under a stone cover, is the deepest well.

I poured a drop of the potion on the stone; Nell spoke the words, and we raised it. The square mass of limestone hung in the air, someone's nightmare and our salvation. Did you know that stones drink? You have been told of Rollright? Well remembered!

Over the years, the water level had fallen, so that the boy's last plunge was a slack dive into an abyss. Perhaps we should have given his earthly body to the sea whose once-bright margins were soiled with the black leavings of the oilmen who had set up their obscene metal spiders in the sea herself, sucked the liquid heart from my country and left it hollow and wanting; my country which had once been a green and magic island in which all manner of flowers bloomed, bee-orchis, angel's pincushions as blue as the sky, dull purple drummer boys, heather and ling laid like scarves across the heath; my country where fox and badger, kestrel and buzzard were free, where fish and anemones, crabs, lobsters and squid lived not in dilute poison but in a clean ocean; my country, where the gulls which now scavenged the dumps outside the city were white emblems on which poets could pin words or just birds miraculously afloat on the air. We should have buried poor Sam deep in the hungry soil where his body would rot and nourish the fields. He was the city's victim, not ours. We, seeking to escape the tarmac tentacles and the eyes which are open all night lighting up the landscape when it should sleep, had become the agents of the new civilisation. We should have laid Sam's ruined body in a shopping mall amongst the dirty paper wrappings and the plastic cups, a witness for reality beside the gaudy dreams of the window displays. As it is, his flesh and bones will dissolve in the lime-laden water; slowly, eventually, he will be returned to his mother, the earth.

The wise stone descended slowly and covered his sepulchre: these bones would not be recovered, nor would there be Christian miracles. If light flowed from Edward's body, it was because of his sacrifice: he was our martyr not theirs. As for the story of the horse which refused to carry Aelfrida, that is a priest's lie and a blatant one at that. Do you know nothing of the sacred duty of the horse?

My companions drifted away with the last of their waning power. The moon had set and the mist gone. I passed over the vandalised barrier at the gatehouse and felt the stony path rise up to support my feet. I staggered a little, for the ground has a great deal more substance than the air, and Pan ran up to me and wagged his tail. His entire body bowed, he squirmed his joy, leapt up and pointed down the lane.

There were two human figures, and the dog which led them. My dog did not know whether to greet her or growl. The heavy smell came from Barty and my husband was at his side. I ran to greet him. 'My dear,' I said, 'You know how badly I sleep: there's no need to – ' but he interrupted, throwing me and my words aside with a gesture of impatience.

'This poor fellow,' he said, 'This wise idiot, tells me he saw you with a man, a strange young man. What country matter is this? Why Morgan, why? And where is he?'

I had grown careless. I had set no charm, being tired of him, the weasel which had fastened on my way of life.

'He went by another way,' I said, 'You're too late.'

Barty swung on his crutches, jubilant, self-important and confused; but even he had avoided the truth. He, too, was country-born and bred.

Pan stood close to me and the bitch, Syr, hung her body from its bony legs in a consummate gesture of appeasement. If a dog could be said to crawl in the dirt, she did. She cowered in front of me.

'Well Syr,' I said, and knelt to be close to her, 'This is what happens when a dog loves one from the city. What will you do now?'

Her answer came after several days, during which she kept herself away, out of the house, and fed herself on what she caught. I came into the kitchen and found her curled up with Pan. She raised her head and looked at me without cringing.

After the divorce, the man who had been my husband wrote me a long letter.

'I hope you will find happiness,' it ended. 'In the city reason rules; whatever the future held for us, I could not have endured the self-indulgent interludes and crude emotions of the country for much longer. I consider myself lucky to have escaped.'

There he was unjust. We witches never hurt our toys. Finding a new husband will be simple; finding the next scapegoat: that is always a bitter task.

As for Fancy, she has many admirers; one of them is sure to prevail soon. She came to live with me and my new babe before the birth of her son. When I was sure I could trust her, I gave her my true name to add to the secrets she will never tell.

Listen, my dear, there's her hand on the latch. When you have earned them, I've secrets for you . . . '

S. M. BAXTER

The Droplet

'You're Mr Jakes. Peter, isn't it? Your brother's in the collider hall. He won't see you, I'm afraid.' He strode into the TLC reception office. He was taller and leaner than me; Paul Newman eyes fixed me from nests of tanned wrinkles.

A bit overwhelmed, I dropped my eyes to the lapel badge he wore. It was a little pyramid of emeralds. The girl behind the desk – Tracy, luminously beautiful – smiled at me. Feeling a bit stronger, I said, 'I didn't know I was so easy to recognise.'

His hand squeezed mine, bronzed calluses pressing into my pasty flesh. 'Well, I guess you do look a little, ah, Englishman lost in California. And maybe the jacket's kind of quiet. My name's Reaney. Mike. Hi.'

'Hello.'

'I work with your brother George; I took Tracy's call. George's wife told me she'd asked you to come over from England. Look . . . can I buy you a coffee?'

The corridors glowed in the sunlight, suffused with a new-carpet smell. I peered into offices that seemed full of healthy people. I couldn't help comparing it with my memories of shabby English universities.

We came to a lounge, large and comfortable, where Reaney bought me a machine-made cup of coffee. 'You know we're under threat of closure here, at the TLC,' he said.

'Yes, Mary told me about it. She said it was the cause of George's . . . troubles.'

With a rangy grace, Reaney crunched up his cup and lobbed it into a bin. 'Well, it's no picnic for any of us.' He laughed. 'Of course, most of us try to be rational . . . we're not all quite so loony-tune as

97

George. I've always thought it was the loss of their kid. Something like that leaves a hole in a guy.'

I stared up at this grinning Californian who stood in such easy judgement over my brother, and tried to think of some response. Then he said disarmingly, 'I'm sorry. I guess I shouldn't talk about him like that. To us, he's just loopy old George . . .'

'I'm grateful to you for meeting me,' I said. 'There's no reason why you should be spending time with me like this.'

He shrugged. His eyes roamed the lounge's pastel walls. 'Well, I know Mary. And I felt you came a long way to be turned away.'

'Why won't he let me see him?'

'There's nothing I can do about that, I'm afraid. In the collider hall, if it's your experiment, your say goes. George has got a deadline to beat. He says.' He pulled his face into a mock frown. 'Listen, I've a half hour free. Why don't I show you round the site? If we wait long enough maybe our hero will take a coffee break . . .'

The TLC was separated from the rest of the Stanford Linear Accelerator Center by a high, close-meshed wire fence. We followed a gravel drive out through the fence, then walked about half a mile to the east, climbing a gentle hill. At the summit I felt a lot closer to the sun. I draped my jacket over one arm, loosened my tie and felt sweat soak into my shirt collar.

Reaney, of course, merely blossomed a little. I judged he was about thirty – a decade or so younger than George and Mary.

A clay-coloured sprawl to the south was the campus of Stanford University. Incredibly healthy students cycled beneath palm trees; it seemed quite idyllic to me. Reaney pointed, the sun catching the mat of hair on his forearm. A structure like a long shed ran north from the campus and disappeared into the collider hall complex. 'See that? One of the TLC's twin linacs. Over two miles long.'

'I'm sorry . . . linac?'

'Linear accelerator. It's a huge cathode-ray tube, like in your home TV . . . it produces pulses of electrons that travel in towards the collider hall at nearly the speed of light.' A second linac came out of the hills to the north and swept into the collider complex, opposite the first. 'The second linac produces a beam of positrons,' Reaney explained. 'You know what a positron is? It's an anti-electron. Anti-matter, you know?

'The two beams shoot inwards and impact in the collider hall,

98

annihilating each other. The collision's kind of tricky to manage. It's like shooting two pistols a hundred miles apart, and getting the bullets to meet. There's also a ten per cent gradient in those hills to the north . . . We have a computer system actively controlling the whole shooting match.' He spoke with a studied languor. 'Tell me, Peter, what do you do for a living?'

'I'm an accountant,' I said. 'I work in the City. London, I mean.' I laughed. 'I feel a little shy to admit to being so boring, after all your glamorous talk of anti-matter and the speed of light. George always made me feel the same . . .'

'Nothing glamorous about it,' he said restlessly. 'Ninety-nine per cent of any job is crap. Am I right?

'Anyway, that's the TLC. The TeV Linear Collider. A TeV is a tera-electronvolt. Which means very high energy particles, and exotic physics. Although nothing as exotic as what's going on in your brother's head.' He laughed easily at his joke. 'He doesn't publish his results, you know. And that's bad for all of us. An establishment is judged on its output. But old George doesn't care about that. No, sir . . .' A breeze ruffled his corn-like hair.

If this is one of my brother's closest colleagues, I thought, how utterly alone he must be.

The phone woke me to darkness. 'Hello?'

'You shouldn't have come, you know. I'm perfectly all right.'

'George? You pick the damnedest times to phone . . .' I fumbled for a light switch. My mouth was dry; I wondered if I had enough loose change to get a Coke from the vending machine outside my motel chalet.

'Listen, Peter, go home,' said George. 'I mean, don't go, have a great holiday, see the Bay, ride the cable cars. But I'm okay. She shouldn't have rung you.' The seam of Yorkshire in his voice was refreshingly untainted by California.

With one hand I searched for a cigarette. 'Mary is worried. She thinks you're working too hard.'

'Rubbish. She thinks I'm going crackers. Right?'

'Well . . .'

'Sure I'm working hard. I've got a deadline to meet.'

'Yes, that's what Mike Reaney told me this afternoon.'

'Reaney? That dick-head?'

'He showed me round the site. When you refused to see me. Your own brother,' I added theatrically.

He laughed again.

'George, I know your TCL is under threat of closure.'

'TLC, for Christ's sake, and it's not just a threat. But that's not the only problem . . . ' His voice had an edge now. 'If I don't finish this work, now, I don't think it'll get repeated. Ever.'

'Why? What's going to happen?'

He said nothing. Then: 'How's . . . ah . . . '

'Jane?' I asked heavily. 'Fine. And the kids, Bobby age eleven and Geoff age nine – '

'All right, funny man.'

I switched off the light and sat in the darkness, smoking and savouring his voice. 'Tell me about your work,' I said.

I heard him sigh. 'All right. I guess you deserve that much. You know our machine, the TLC, is a high energy electron collider. Lovely clean physics.' His voice grew dreamy.

'So what's the point all this beautiful colliding?'

'The collisions produce packets of high energy density – like bits of the early universe, right after the Big Bang. You know what the Big –'

'Of course I do.'

'Back then physics was different. There are four fundamental forces – gravity, electromagnetic, weak and strong nuclear. According to theory, when the energy density is high enough the four unify into a single superforce. There are particles called Higgs bosons which mediate the superforce. That's what I started off looking for.'

He was losing me. I rubbed my gritty eyes. I couldn't remember the last time I'd spoken to my brother . . . and now here he was at three in the morning telling me about Higgs bosons. Well, that was George. 'Did you find them?'

'We got some evidence. I don't know. I started noticing something much more interesting.'

'So you never wrote up the boson stuff? Dick-head was complaining about that.'

'Really? I'm not surprised.' He hesitated. 'Oh, Christ, look at the time. So why are you staying at a Hyatt's? Do you know what they charge?'

'I'm looking forward to finding out,' I said drily. 'I . . . didn't feel comfortable about asking Mary for a room. I got the impression I wouldn't have been all that welcome.'

'You probably wouldn't. Even though she asked you over in the first place. And she calls me crazy.'

Again we laughed together. He agreed to let me see him, in a couple of days' time.

And, just like that, he hung up. Well, I reflected, at least I'd made contact. After Mary's rather disturbing phone calls, I was relieved to find nothing more worrying than the same old George.

My body refused to believe it was the small hours. I lay in the darkness and missed my family.

The next day I got the motel girl to hire me a Hertz car, and I drove out to Palo Alto to visit Mary.

I cruised down a broad, double-parked avenue. The crumpled car doors and wings, casually unrepaired, made me feel a long way from England and its salted roads.

Outside George's house was an old Jaguar XJ6. The house itself was a neat bungalow set in an expanse of glowing lawn.

'Oh. It's you.' Mary was a small, dark woman, looking too old for the pink jumpsuit she wore. 'You'd better come in.'

The house was open-plan and wood-panelled. The morning sun evoked a smell of jasmine and orange.

Mary made me coffee and we sat on opposite sides of a glass table. She wore a pyramidal brooch of emeralds set in gold, rather like Reaney's. 'I'm sorry. I drag you all this way, across the Atlantic, and now we can't think of a damn thing to say to each other.' She sipped her coffee and pulled at her mass of frizzed hair.

'You seem settled here,' I said.

'Oh, I am,' she breezed. 'It's a terrific lifestyle.'

I felt like puncturing her. 'It's helped you forget, then?'

She gave me a hard look. 'Philip's death, you mean? Don't flinch like that, Peter. You referred to it. Why not say it? It doesn't hurt any more.'

'They never found the cause, did they?'

'It was a cot death,' she said witheringly. 'Although the Americans have a few theories . . . Little Philip was a textbook example. Eleven weeks old, just the time when his growth was at its fastest.'

'Does that have something to do with it?'

'How should I know?' Her voice had become a little shrill. 'Anyway. To return to the point . . . the reason I asked you to come over.' She looked away, seeming embarrassed. 'I didn't know who else to turn to. George has always put a lot into his work –'

'I know.'

' – and the announcement of the closure of the TLC was utterly shattering for him. He worked even harder. He made up some sort of cot, a sleeping place, at the lab. He'd stay over one night, two. When he did show up here he'd be overtired, wound up, twitching to get back to it. You know? And finally, he stopped coming home at all.'

Her skin was tanned but dry-looking; I found myself studying the lines of her skull. On impulse, I asked: 'Do you still care about him?' – and regretted it immediately. 'I'm sorry. I don't want to sound as if I'm judging –'

She laughed lightly. 'Why not? Everyone else does. I . . . don't know what I feel,' she said. 'That's the honest truth. I've had six months of this, for Christ's sake. I'm not sure what I feel any more. When I asked you to help – I cared then, I suppose. The closure's in a few days, you know. No more high energy collisions. I was scared there'd be a crisis.'

'Surely he could get another job.'

'Evidently the TLC is unique; the only place George can do the sort of work he's gotten into.'

'I've visited the TLC. I met Mike Reaney . . . You know him, don't you?'

She met my eyes and nodded. 'What's it all about, Mary?'

'Ask him.' She averted her eyes and would say no more.

On my way out, she handed me a carrier bag. It was from some store called the Crystal Market, and was covered with Eastern-style religious symbols, rust brown on yellow. 'A change of clothes for him.'

I weighed the bag, as if weighing up Mary's feelings. 'I'll tell him I saw you,' I said, but the door was already closing.

'What's so important about my work?' George ran a huge hand back over his widow's peak. He was a big-boned man, very unlike me, and his wrists stuck out of his cuffs. 'It's only about the birth pangs of the universe, Pete. That's all. Here, give me that damn bag.' He grabbed the Crystal Market carrier from me and stalked out of the TLC reception area on his whippy legs.

Tracy gave me a sympathetic smile as I passed, but I ignored her. George was no clown.

We reached a door plastered with security notices and combination locks. 'The collider hall,' George said, slowing down. 'Where the action is.'

102

Through a glass partition I peered into a tall, gloomy space constructed of bare breeze blocks. A pipe a few inches across ran at waist height through the centre of the hall; instrument packages snuggled around its midpoint. 'What's that?' I asked. 'The central heating?'

George laughed. 'That's the particle beam guide. Lined with focusing magnets. The collisions take place right there, at the heart of those arrays . . . '

We moved on. A metal door let us into a boxy, windowless room. It looked like a storage cupboard, with unvarnished shelves piled high with dirty shirts and underwear. 'Jesus, George, how do you live like this?'

George threw the carrier onto an unmade camp bed. 'Peter, you're a bloody old woman, and I love you. Let me tell you about my work. That's what counts, not socks. Now, we're only a fraction of a second after the Big Bang. Everything's compressed into less than the width of a proton . . . '

Automatically I dumped out the clean clothes and began stuffing the carrier with laundry. George swivelled as I walked around him, a gaunt container of energy. 'The universe is filled with a sort of fluid. A quagma, a soup of quarks in radiation, bound together by the unified superforce.

'The universe goes through an inflation phase. The quagma's expanding, and cooling fast. It's like steam, supercooled below liquefying point. Bubbles form in the quagma and expand with the released latent heat. Within the bubbles, the superforce falls apart into our four fundamental forces. One of the bubbles becomes the space we live in, filled with ordinary matter.'

My carrier bag was full. I made room on the bed and sat down. 'What about the other bubbles?'

He grinned a bit wildly. 'Other universes embedded in the quagma foam. But with different physical laws, where the superforce decomposed in a different way. See? In one place gravity might be so strong the bubble would instantly collapse; in another so weak that stars could never form and the place would be full of lukewarm hydrogen . . . '

He wore a V-neck jumper with a Marks & Spencer label sticking out of the neck. I stared at him in admiration. 'My God, George, California hasn't changed you a bit, has it?'

'Bollix to California,' he said. He paced up and down, glancing at his watch. 'Droplets of quagma formed at the heart of my collisions,' he said. 'I found a way to mould the shape of the electron-positron colliding pulses to get a controlled cooling of the droplets. A supercooling.'

'Right. And you get this . . . inflation effect?'

He paced faster, kicking the leg of the cot. 'Sometimes. The droplets soon evaporate, of course, but I can tell a lot from the debris. There are bubbles in those droplets where different physical laws apply. Think of that.'

I had to smile at his enthusiasm. 'So what next, George? What are you trying to achieve now?'

'Stability,' he snapped. I could see tension in the hunch of his shoulders, the motion of his elbows – a visible impatience to get back to his work. 'A non-evaporating, self-fuelling droplet which won't need further electron collisions to sustain it.'

'And will you write up then? Or is writing up still for cissies, George?'

'I'll write up after they close me down, in a week's time. But I've got to get finished. That's all that counts. And look, Pete, I'm sorry –' Now he waved the watch in the air. 'I'll talk to you again in a day or two. Okay?'

I didn't move. 'George,' I said quietly, 'I've only just arrived. I can see you're in a state. And we've hardly talked.'

Panic crinkled his eyes. 'You've asked me about my work. I've told you.'

'Yes, but I want to hear about . . . you.' I looked away, and out of the corner of my eye I saw George shuffle with embarrassment. 'You're the reason I'm here, not the work. Come on, George. For a start, I don't understand why this particular project is driving you so.'

He grabbed the carrier off the bed. 'Then look at this,' he said, jabbing a finger at the Crystal Market logo. 'This shit.'

I stared at it. 'What –'

'Ask Mary. Or dick-head.' And he shoved the bag into my hands and opened the door.

I stood up. 'She cares about you, you know,' I said.

Astonished, he stared at me with his red-rimmed eyes.

Then he laughed once, hard, and led the way out.

I tried again a couple of days later. Reaney took the call. 'I'm sorry,' he said in an amused tone. 'You know how it is . . .'

'Yes. Look, Mike, can I ask you a couple of questions while you're there?'

'Sure . . .'

'This closure. Of the TLC. Will it really be so difficult for you all to get other jobs?'

He snickered. 'In high-energy physics, yes. The field's contracting, world-wide. But there are plenty of other options. For the realistic man.'

'What are yours?'

'Expert systems. There's one here working on a DEC Vax, controlling our colliding beams. I've had an offer from a securities firm in Frisco – an expert systems application in international dealing. Same principles, you see, just different problems. And megabucks,' he added smugly.

Well, I couldn't see that appealing to George. 'Also – the Crystal Market. George said it was the reason for his hurry. What's that all about?'

'Ah. The Market is a New Age store.'

'New Age?'

'I guess it hasn't reached England yet. It's a loose, quasi-religious movement that's taking root over here. Disappointed sixties children, a mish-mash of Eastern mysticism – homeopathy, pastel colours, pyramids – you've read the movie, seen the book . . .'

His dismissive langour was irritating. 'I notice you wear a pyramid button yourself.'

He sounded a little less easy, I noted with satisfaction. 'Yeah, well, it's the fashion . . . anyway, George takes it all very seriously. He thinks it shows the rise of anti-science in our culture.' His tone was mocking. 'No more particle accelerators. All the work of the devil.'

Sitting in that motel room, I'd suddenly had enough of this. 'Bullshit. George wouldn't use a phrase like that. Do you actually listen to what he says, or are you too busy laughing behind his back?'

'Hey, pal, no offence – '

I hung up.

'Peter, it's me.'

'George? Christ, it's after four . . .'

'I'm about to do it, Pete. I wanted you to be here. I've phoned Mary.' He sounded as if he'd been crying.

'George, are you okay?' I began searching for my shoes in the dark.

105

'Of course I am. It's just . . . I'm that close to getting one of these babies to stabilise. So many of them have failed, just at the moment of maximum growth – Peter, I have to go.'

'George?'

A sleepy caretaker at the motel desk called me a cab. Rectilinear streets slid past, dark and obscurely menacing.

The TLC was lit from end to end. It looked as if a spindle-shaped spacecraft had landed in a fold in the Californian countryside. I pulled my coat tighter around me. Somehow I doubted this display meant good news.

There was an empty police car on the gravel drive. The gate in the wire fence was closed, with a single policeman standing before it. He watched me steadily.

Floodlights suspended over the fence beat at my face; moths fried on the glass. A siren cried within the compound. 'You can't go through, buddy.' The policeman chewed gum with a practised rhythm, his eyes in shadow.

'My brother's in there somewhere. What's the problem?'

He tilted his head back and stared at me. 'Sorry, sir. It's some kind of automatic radiation alert. Hey, you from England?'

I walked away from him and followed the fence for a few feet, finishing up in a puddle of darkness between two floods. The policeman's broad head returned to its survey of the driveway.

I closed my eyes and tried to picture George in there, his jumper covered by an ill-fitting white coat. He must be alone. If what he was doing was so dangerous he would have made sure no one else was on the site.

Tyres crunched on the gravel – a Jaguar driving up the path. Somehow I wasn't surprised to see Mary and Mike Reaney climb out together. They were holding hands. I turned my face to the fence, trusting they'd miss me.

The explosion was like the fist of God slamming into the earth.

I was thrown backwards onto the shaking ground. The fence collapsed over me, bulbs popping.

Something was rising out of the ruins of the collider hall. It was hot and bright. A dry wind fled from it.

I had to crawl out from under the fence. My hands were caked with blood and dust. The officer had lost his cap. With barked questions he checked we were okay, then trotted down the drive to his car.

I stood facing Mary and Reaney. He looked at the ground, his tracksuit frame clumsy with embarrassment.

She stared into the fire and smiled.

I hit her, hard across her face. She tumbled back onto the gravel.

'Hey – ' Reaney came at me and drove his fist up into my stomach. I couldn't believe how far it penetrated. I doubled into a squat; my diaphragm seemed to cramp up and I gulped for breath.

'Leave him, Mike.'

Reaney put one mitt under my armpit and hauled me to my feet. Pain lanced through the muscles of my torso, but I stayed upright.

'You bitch,' I gasped. 'Are you so glad to be rid of him?'

She tried to talk, then spat out blood and a piece of tooth. 'You don't understand, do you?' She pointed over my shoulder. 'Look.'

I turned. Out of the collider hall's ripped-open roof had risen a colourless sphere. It was the size of a small house, and it contained a froth of bubbles that swelled and collapsed, flickering through existence almost too fast for the eye to follow.

Sirens wailed in the darkness behind us.

'He did it,' Reaney growled. 'Damn him, he did it.' He stared into the sphere. There seemed to be genuine wonder under his studied cynicism. 'That's a stabilised droplet of inflating quagma. And inside each of those bubbles is a different set of physical laws. We'll be able to study creation physics with nothing more elaborate than a freeze-frame video camera.

'This will fast forward our understanding a thousand years. No wonder he was so desperate to finish this. They'll build a statue to the silly old bastard, right here.' He laughed and scratched his scalp. He wore his green pyramid badge; now he plucked it out of his tracksuit and threw it at the droplet. 'I guess that's the end of this anti-science shit.' He turned and walked towards the Jag.

'I'm happy for him.' Mary's face was swelling a little, but the smile was returning. 'The endless deaths – I always understood it, you see. I just couldn't live with it . . . '

Her voice trailed off; she was looking at me strangely.

I found it an effort to speak. 'The door was metal,' I managed.

'What?'

Reaney turned back; I looked to him, willing him to understand. 'The room George was sleeping in. I thought it was just a store room. But the door was metal.'

'That's the safety shelter,' Reaney said softly. 'The shelter!'

The three of us ran over the ruins of the fence, ignoring the cops' shouts.

'Well, of course I'm alive,' George snapped after they dug him out. 'What kind of idiot do you think I am? . . . '

Then he saw the droplet hanging above him. His head hinged back, eyes wide, mouth hanging. His face shone in the creation light.

We pulled him to his feet. Mary grabbed his tattered sleeve, searched his face.

'My baby,' he said hoarsely, still staring upwards.

LOUISE COOPER

Cry

No.
  Yes.
  No; please. No. I can't.
  You can. You must. You know you always must.
  Please . . .
  Don't plead. You must. You will. When the times comes. You'll know
when that is.

And there was the dream, of blurred, pale faces framed against
paler walls, and the heat – an unexpected Indian summer, close and
humid and draining all life from the air. And walls that pulsed in and
out, in and out, like a heart struggling to beat against intolerable
pressure. Voices murmuring concern, the clink of something small
and metallic rattling against porcelain. One face among the blurs
looked familiar, but a name wouldn't come and focus wouldn't clear
and she couldn't remember any more, she couldn't *remember* –

'Shona?'

She blinked, and the waking world shuttered back into place. Cal
was holding her arm a little too tightly, and she wondered for a
nerve-racking instant what she'd done this time. Midway between the
embankment wall and the road with its unending stream of traffic
travelling too fast for a wet, murky night; Lambeth Bridge less than a
stone's throw away. Had she broken towards one or another,
forgetting where she was, forgetting everything but the inner images
and the memory of that voice. . . ?

'You want to watch it in those heels,' Cal said. 'Rain on top of all
that dust and grease – makes the surface treacherous.' He smiled, and
the hand transferred from her arm to her opposite shoulder, squeez-
ing, protective, proprietorial. 'All right now?'

'Yes.' Relief was an indescribable balm. She'd only slipped, nothing worse, and she closed her eyes again to savour the pleasure of the moment. Strings of lights twinkling along the river, the distant, mournful hoot of a boat's siren, the roar and smell and warm, carbon-monoxide backdraught of the cars streaming by with their headlamps cutting swathes through the rain. Their hair and clothes were soaked, her impractical shoes were full of water, his coat, when she pressed her nose against it, smelled like a warm, wet and friendly dog. And it was good, so good. Good to exist, good to be *here*, *now*, good above all else to be with him.

Here. *Now*. She pushed all other concepts of time aside with determined savagery, and thought: *Just tonight. If there's any mercy in the world, just tonight.*

Cal's arm squeezed her again, pressing her tighter against the warm-dog fabric. 'Where's it to be, then?'

'Ohh . . . I don't know. Anywhere.' She laughed, turning her face up to the rain. They'd tried on the offchance to get a table at one of the floating restaurants, the converted Clyde steamer with the white paint and swaying gangplank and tiny lights in the dining room ceiling, but the place had been full – Friday; they should have known, Cal said – and now they were footloose, hungry and with no particular direction in mind.

'McDonald's,' Shona said, and laughed again.

'God, you philistine! No, look; we'll get a taxi and find somewhere in the West End, yes?'

'Yes.' Anything. Anything that would let this night, this precious night, continue.

And so there was satay and a bottle of wine in a Thai restaurant that gradually filled up with post-theatre diners cursing the weather and discussing the shows, and intermittent ice-white flashes as a table for eight celebrated someone's birthday and an inept but determined member of the party took photographs. Shona picked at the food, practising the knack, long perfected, of appearing to eat whilst foisting most of the dishes' contents on to Cal's plate. And over coffee that looked and tasted like old engine oil, Cal said, 'You're coming back, aren't you?'

Everything within her said *yes*, *yes*; but for a moment she hesitated, waiting, alert for the inner warning signal that would mean she must shake her head and let him go through the charade of seeing her home, taking her to the hostel entrance, stealing one last kiss before the night carried him away. But the signal didn't come. This time, all was well.

110

She made the pretence, as she always did, of arguing about the bill and trying to insist that she should at least pay a share, knowing that, as he always did, Cal would utterly refuse to take a single one of the pennies she didn't possess. They left, ducking under the awning that dripped huge, wet tears on the unsuspecting, walked to the bus stop, held each other and laughed like self-conscious children until the steamy, lit-up night service bus came to bear them away to Camden and Cal's flat. And there, between the shelf of engineering textbooks and the Save the Rainforest poster, in the bed on which he'd carefully changed the sheets – and teased her yet again about the hospital corners – and under the striped duvet, there was the heat and the intimacy and the silent communion that Shona tried again and again to convince herself was not love, but which she knew could have no other name for either of them.

And when Cal slept at last, hair and skin damp, and snoring just a little, she stared into the dark, at the silhouettes of the cramped room which grew more familiar every time.

And felt the breathing, the pulsing. *In*, *out*. *In*, *out*. Walls, the cavities of a straining heart. *In*, *out*. Slowing. Reaching danger point. The bleeping of an alarm, followed by a long, indifferent, electronic note that said, *too late*. Blood somewhere, but at a great remove and no longer relevant. Stillness. Hushed voices; someone swearing softly. A swing door, hissing on pneumatic hinges as someone else went out or came in. A sigh.

And a hand, reaching out of the suddenly silent dark, to touch her brow with long, rough-edged fingernails. And the voice.

Yes, Shona.

No. Not tonight.

Not tonight. But soon. Soon.

Please –

She flung herself up like someone held struggling under water then suddenly and unexpectedly released, and the hiss of her breath was shockingly loud. Cal mumbled, snorted and turned over, flinging one arm loosely across her stomach. Wanting to grasp his hand and kiss it, she forced herself instead to push it aside, and slid out of the bed. Clothes: bra, pants, tights, dress – she'd looked good tonight; he'd told her so at least half a dozen times. The shoes with their impractical heels. Coat. Bag. Nothing in it but a hairbrush, which she flicked through her hair without the aid of a mirror. And lastly – wisdom protested, but she had to do it, *had* to – a note. Even Cal's bedroom

111

was littered with paper; technical notes, calculations, letters from his family in Inverness, half-finished letters back. She pulled a sheet from a notepad with only a few doodles of cats on it, found a Biro, hunched over the small, cluttered table.

'Couldn't bear to wake you. My shift starts early; have to be back in good time or Sister B. will have me consigned to hell as a Scarlet Woman. Tomorrow? I'll phone. Love you.'

Tomorrow? She shouldn't have said it, but she had to. She *had* to. A quick glance towards the window; just the sound of an occasional car on the main road now, and the swish of the rain. She didn't know the time, but it didn't matter. She had nothing to fear from the streets. And the lie would be perpetuated, the illusion maintained.

She closed the front door quietly, and there were no eyes to see her vanish into the night.

Shona knew the route well, the back streets, the brightly lit thoroughfares still noisy with traffic, though the cars had largely given way to delivery trucks, newspaper vans, the occasional patrolling panda with its bored occupants. No one accosted her, no one stopped her. She passed a few down-and-outs who shuffled between steel-meshed shop doorways, mumbling, rummaging through boxes and plastic sacks of refuse piled ready for the next collection, their minds half in the real world and half in another, more private hell. One old man looked up with a start as she hurried by; she glimpsed a dirty frizz of Celtic hair, eyes which might once have been sea-blue but were now rheumy and bloodshot and unable to focus, a broken-toothed mouth, dribbling, and for a moment his face registered a glimmer of shocked intelligence, as if an old racial memory had awoken. Then she was gone, unconcerned with him, and he returned to his rummaging and his mumbling as her fleeting image faded from sight and thence from memory.

More streets, more wet pavements. She was soaked through now but didn't care; barely noticed. And a last, in a dim backwater where tall, silent warehouses blocked the roar of the busy night, there were the lights of the hospital windows, chilly eyes in a high, blank wall of a face, and beyond them the gates and the weathered board at the entrance to the nurses' home.

The home was older than the hospital it served; once an almshouse, it now provided bed and board for the lay members of staff, those who hadn't taken the veil and the vows of the Quiet Sisters of Charity. She

112

didn't know what had drawn her to associate herself with this shabby but proud little privately funded maternity hospital, but it had become, insofar as the word could ever apply to her, home. And in their prayers, perhaps, the good sisters might unknowingly remember her, even though they'd never seen her face.

She passed the daunting, rusty gates of the nurses' home, passed under the cold twin lamps that glared down vigilantly throughout the night to expose the guilt of those who flouted the sisters' strict and puritanical curfew, moved on to where another warehouse, unlit, unused, its future balanced between the developer's acumen and the demolition gang's iron ball, reared against the sulphurous cloud cover. A door rocked on rust-eaten hinges behind a half-hearted barricade of slats; with the ease of long practice she slid between two of the slats and slipped through. Pitch dark and echoing emptiness that smelled of urine and mildew and dry rot waited for her beyond the door; she hovered a moment, looking out and back along the wet, silent, street, then the door shuddered back into place and only rain disturbed the stillness.

In the dream she was stretching out arms that seemed constricted by some soft, muffling substance. And though she strained with all her strength, fought with all her will, the goal she sought was always just beyond her reach. She could hear a young child crying, and thought that she cried too, that in the distorted way of dreams she and the unknown, unseen infant were one and the same. Then the hands came again, guiding her as they stroked her with their broken nails, and the voice spoke in her ear and in her mind, soothing and comforting and giving the bitter anger that burned like white metal deep inside her an outlet.

And when she woke to the greasy overcast dawn, she knew that this dawn, this day, promised more than rain. This day was malignant. This day was foretold.

It has come, Shona. It has come.

She looked up, through the ragged shadows of broken floors and treacherous rafters, and the rage came like a hurricane, screaming through her in fearsome rebuttal. *I will not answer! I will not do it! My will is my own, and I shall do what I will!* And huge, welling, the final, silent shriek of defiance: *I WILL NOT BE COMMANDED!*

But you will. You must. You know you always must.

And the rage collapsed in the face of shrivelling fear, for she knew the voice and she knew its purpose and she knew its implacable strength. Her defiance was a sham. Her path was ordained; the Quiet Sisters of Charity couldn't help her, the fictional Sister Beatrice whose wrath she pretended to fear couldn't help her. Cal couldn't help her. Above all, not Cal.

Not Cal.

She was a wraith, an urchin, huddled in her thin coat and running through the rain in search of a phone box. Plastered hair, sodden clothes, useless shoes turning her heels painfully as she stumbled, ignored by the morning crowds. *Warn him*, said a last vestige of the self-will to which she'd pretended. *Warn him. Tell him. Or there's no hope.*

Cramming into a booth at last, gasping, her breath misting the glass, she pressed the receiver to her ear. The readout flashed, asking for coins; she ignored it, stabbed the buttons, sensed the bypassing of the system and heard Cal's phone begin to ring. And ring, and ring. He'd left. A morning lecture; now she remembered; and she smashed the handset down with helpless frustration. Don't cry. *Don't* cry. *Think.*

Away. The idea was a lifeline. If she was away from Cal, far away, then she couldn't do it. She could go away, and never come back. However great the loss, however painful the knowledge that he'd never understand why she had gone, it would be better. It *must* be better.

She would go home. She couldn't remember how long it had been since she was there, but however much it had changed it was a refuge, a familiar oasis. Yes. Certainty filled her, and with it a kind of peace. She would go home.

Euston was glass and noise and an echoing concourse where the station announcements boomed unintelligibly over a susurrant background of hurrying feet. For a long time Shona stood staring up at the departure board, watching times and destinations and platform numbers turn over like a litany. Queues waiting before the folding iron gates shuffled forward and were swallowed down sloping concrete throats to their trains. She watched the travellers, watched the board, and at last saw the name she'd been waiting for. She read it three times to be certain, committing the time and the platform to memory, then turned and hurried through the zigzag of people to the travel centre.

More queues. Ahead of her, four Scandinavians struggled with backpacks and a vast canvas holdall; they bumped her, apologised in smiling, stilted English. At the ticket window they asked polite but complicated questions and had difficulty with the currency; Shona shuffled restless feet and tried not to shiver until at last, reading their tickets with intense and slightly puzzled interest, they manoeuvred their luggage out of the way and it was her turn.

She didn't know whether or not she actually asked for a single to Glasgow Central; she might have spoken the words or merely thought them. But the clerk punched the terminal without even troubling to look up, and though she put nothing on the carousel his hand moved reflexively as though to scoop up notes or a credit card. The carousel jerked again and her ticket lay on the dull metal plate before her: she took it, slid aside as a tall man in a dark coat, harassed and hurrying, breathlessly demanded Birmingham New Street.

She flexed the ticket in her palm. It felt peculiar; the wrong shape and the wrong size. Her passport out of Cal's life. She left the travel centre, looked around. Telephones. Perhaps by now he'd have returned, and would be waiting for her call. She should tell him. It was only fair. And she wanted so much to hear his voice one last time . . .

The number rang and rang without an answer. She bit her lip hard and tried again in case it was a wrong connection, though she knew it wasn't. Ringing, ringing, and still no reply. She had twenty minutes before the train left. Ten more, and she'd try again. In the event, and perhaps subconsciously aware of what she was doing and why, fifteen minutes passed before she dialled the number a third time. Four rings – then a click, and Cal's familiar, longed-for voice.

'Cal . . . ?'

'Shona. Hey, I'm sorry; have you been trying to call me? I got caught up at the college; there was – '

'Cal, I'm going home.' She cut across him baldly, bluntly. She'd tried to rehearse the things she wanted to say, but now, hearing him, speaking to him, they'd fled.

There was an instant of silence. Then: 'Wh – '

'I'm sorry.' She couldn't let him ask the questions. 'I must, Cal. I can't explain. I just . . . had to ring and say goodbye. Maybe I shouldn't have, but . . . I had to.'

'Shona!' Panic in Cal's voice. 'Shona, wait – what are you telling me? What do you mean, home? What's going on?'

'Please.' The words sounded ugly, distorted by tears. 'I have to go. I have to leave. I *have* to. But . . . ' *I love you.* She wanted to say it, but couldn't. 'Cal . . . take care. And please, try not to be angry with me.' *I love you.*

'Where are you? Tell me! I don't understand – Shona, for Christ's sake – '

I love you. 'Take good care, Cal. Goodbye.'

She stared at the replaced handset for a long time. Long enough to know instinctively that the train had gone without her. It didn't matter. There'd be another.

And later, much later, on the platform at last and climbing in through one of the open carriage doors, she knew what she'd tried to do and was thankful that she'd failed. Weakness, foolishness. She should have been stronger, and not called him. She'd known better, but she hadn't done better. But it didn't matter. Now, now that she was leaving, it didn't matter any more.

There was a creaking lurch as the train moved off, long minutes of cautious, rocking progress as it slowly negotiated its way through the spaghetti of converging lines, goods yards and overhead cables that formed the suburbs of Euston's city; and at last, at long last, they began to gather speed as the train finally escaped from London. Shona had found a place in a near-empty carriage, and sat hunched against the window, leaning away from the aisle and grateful for the three empty seats around her. Outside, wisps of smoky cloud scudded alongside the train under the bloated belly of the overcast; occasional bursts of rain spattered against the window as though someone had thrown a bucket of water at the glass. Above and below, the lines and their parallel power cables hummed mesmerically past; inside the carriage was warm and well lit, and the hypnotic thrum of power and the bogies was a familiar lullaby. Her father, Shona remembered, had worked on the railway; as a little child she had known the north-western routes well, though that was in the days before even diesel, let alone electricity, had come to rule. She'd had a record, she remembered, one she loved to play on the old gramophone. *Coronation Scot.* The rhythm of a train, running, racing, powering north into the thundering dark, carrying her home. Humming the tune silently in her mind, and trying to make it run in time with the rocking of the carriage, she closed her eyes, smiling in a half doze.

Until a presence, intruding, slid into the seat opposite hers, and her eyes flicked open.

'Shona.' His face was wild, eyes haggard and filled with a painful mixture of fear and relief.

She stared at him, and realised what she'd done.

Cal reached over the formica table and gripped her hands before she could pull them away. 'Shona, thank God I – '

'How did you know?' Her voice was a frightened whisper.

'I went to the hospital, Shona.' Now there was accusation as well as the other emotions, and she saw that he was as afraid as she was, though for a very different reason. His fingers tightened, and they hurt. 'There's no nurse there called Shona Wilson, and no such person as Sister Beatrice. Shona, why have you been lying to me? What's going *on*?'

She couldn't speak. She could only stare at him, her brain fighting between the onslaughts of horror and gladness. He'd followed her. Knowing she was playing with fire, she hadn't been able to stop herself from testing him, and he'd passed the test. He loved her enough not to let her go. And she'd thought . . .

She'd thought he wouldn't do it. She'd prayed he wouldn't, while at the same time praying that he might at least try. And now . . .

'You . . . ' Her voice caught; she licked her lips. She was shaking now. 'You shouldn't have gone there . . . '

'What did you *expect* me to do?' His fear was finding an outlet in anger. 'When you tell me out of the blue that you're going, and you won't tell me why, and – ' Heads turned further along the carriage; Cal stopped, then lowered his voice. 'Did you think I was just going to let you go, and that'd be the end of it?'

She looked away. 'I don't know.'

'Jesus *Christ*!' He pulled his hands away, running them through his hair in helpless frustration, then with an effort pulled himself together. 'Shona.' Gentle now, the anger subsided. 'I've been trying to understand, and I can't. *Why* did you lie about where you lived and what you did? Why couldn't you tell me the truth, whatever it is?'

She shook her head, mute, and he clenched his hands together on the table top, knuckles white. 'If something's wrong, something in your life, you've got to tell me about it. *Please*.'

'No.'

Another pause. 'Is it to do with your family? You're not – married, are you? Is that it?'

She laughed, harshly and without humour, shaking her head again.

'*What*, then? Shona, for Christ's sake, it's sheer chance that I got on the same train as you, but if I hadn't, I'd have gone to Glasgow anyway, I'd have followed you – '

'You don't know whereabouts I live.' She'd told him once that she was from Glasgow, but that was all.

'Then I'd have walked the streets until I found out!' Cal insisted. '*Damn* it, don't you understand what I'm trying to *say*? Don't you understand how much you *mean* to me?'

She did now; now that it was too late. 'Yes . . . '

'Then don't I mean anything to you?'

'Oh, yes.' Shona's eyes filled with tears. Her muscles tensed. 'Yes, Cal.'

'Then – '

'*No!*' And she flung herself out of the seat, lurching into the aisle, staggering and swaying towards the connecting door. Cal shouted her name and started after her, but she had a head start. She stumbled through the door that opened obligingly, turned sharply, rushed into the toilet and slammed its door at her back, locking it and leaning hard against it. She was panting, crying, trying to keep silent as she heard him outside.

'Shona.' The handle rattled. '*Shona!*'

Go away, go away.

'Shona, I know you're there. For god's sake – '

'GO AWAY!' She shouted, thumping the door with her fist. 'Get off when the train stops, go back to London and leave me alone! Cal, *please!* Just *do* it!'

There was a long pause, Then:

'Okay. I'm going to count to five, and if you haven't come out I'm going to bust the door open. All right?' His voice was sweet reason, and she knew he meant it. 'And I don't care if I do get had up in court for criminal damage. This is more important. One.'

Go away.

'Two.'

Please. For your own sake.

'Three.'

The train was slowing down. They were approaching a station. Cal wasn't going to listen to her: maybe, she thought wildly, she could break away, jump off the train, just run. *For his sake.*

'Four.'

The lock clicked. Slowly, Shona opened the door.

For a moment they stood staring at each other. Disembarking passengers were already crowding out into the gangway between the carriages; beyond the door the shapes of industrial buildings, indistinct in gathering dusk, skimmed past as the train continued to slow. People stared curiously at them, but they paid no heed. Cal was breathing hard with the adrenalin that had been building in him; now the pent energy had nowhere to go, and for one second he was unsure of himself, and vulnerable. Shona took her chance and shot out of the cramped cubbyhole like a rabbit out of a burrow. She knew she was behaving insanely, but she no longer cared; fear for him had taken her beyond reason. She pushed violently between two women, trod on a foot, heard an indignant shout of protest, and flung herself at the carriage door, clawing at the stiff and heavy catch as she tried too pull it open.

'Stop that! It's still going too fast, it – '

'Shona!'

'What's that stupid bitch doing – '

'*Shona!*' And Cal had her arm even as the heavy door swung open with a thump and a rush of cold air. Someone yelled, Shona twisted around and tried to push Cal away, collided with a heavy body, lost her balance. She felt her feet going from under her, and her legs tangled with Cal's as she struck the grimy floor –

And the shouts of horror, the shock and panic and scramble and grinding lurch of brakes as someone pulled the communication cord rose up like a tidal wave against her reeling senses, freezing into that one final image of Cal's terrified face as he lost his hold on the man who tried to save him, and fell screaming from the train.

Instinct had guided her as surely as a moth was drawn to the light of fire, and she stood in the open space in front of the main building, by an ugly, spotlit fountain that played into a tile-rimmed and sterile pool. From a place where no one would find her she'd watched the lights and the milling people in the dark, heard the ambulance and police sirens, seen the stabbing blue beams and the uniformed men and the white-coated doctor and the long vehicle that took Cal away. Then she'd turned her back on the chaos and walked, leaving the crowd and the chaos, into the city and to the place where she had to be. Now, under a sky made sulphurous by city lights she stared at the wide glass doors and the bright, separate world beyond them; not her

119

world now, but alien. Rows of lights from a hundred windows, cars parked on the forecourt, another ambulance arriving but unhurried; no emergency this time. She could smell – or imagine she smelled – that sharp hospital scent; the building seemed to exhale it. And somewhere, she knew where, she knew which window, was Cal and the people who were trying to save him.

This wasn't her hospital. Hers had been at home in Glasgow, far away in both time and distance. Tiled and antiseptic and always rushing, strip lighting and rattling trolleys, masks and gloves and fearful faces, and pain, and blood, and then a baby crying in the dark and the first touch of the hands that had reached out of the dark to claim her in death and show her what she must now become. She had seen her man's stricken face, though she couldn't now remember his name. But she had never seen her child. And that was then, and this was now, and the voice was speaking gently to her, speaking in her mind.

Yes, Shona. Yes.

The hospital's glass doors hissed open and two nurses came out, hunching their shoulders against the wind's bite and hurrying across the forecourt. Shona didn't look at them: she was staring up at one window among the many, and as she stared she pushed back the folds of the garment that covered her, letting it slide from her shoulders, down her torso, over hips and thighs, to fall in a greying, crumpled mass at her feet. Naked, she gazed at the window as the nurses passed by on the far side of the fountain. Their chattering voices were thin in the chill night; she was invisible to them now, invisible to them all. All but one.

As she bent to gather the crumpled linen, her hair fell about her face. Its long strands were like tendrils of trailing weed, dredged from ponds, from rivers, from dark water where forces older and colder than the stark, bright civilisation around her ran like blood through the arteries of the land. Like blood . . . and the stains on the shroud were old and rust-brown now as she let it fall into the pool, watched it swirl in the water like a dead woman's hair.

She might have given in, and let him follow her all the way home. Perhaps that would have been more fitting; to be in Scotland where the old beliefs were still a little closer to the surface. Or she might have stayed; she might have accepted the inevitable from the first, rather than try to change what would be. But by an indifferent quirk of chance it had ended here, in a city unfamiliar to them both, in a place where they had no roots and no memories. It didn't matter. It was all one, now.

She gazed up to the window, to the room where light and warmth and quiet voices pervaded, where the monitors and the machines were recording the failing spark of life, and her lips, clay-cold, chalk-white, formed a word.

'*Cal-um.*' Out of a dark more primal than the city night, like the cry of an owl heard on the wind, a whisper in a shunned place, a moaning from the haunted sea.

'*Cal-um.*' She called to him, cried his name in lonely mourning, summoned him home. And in the pool's cold illumination, under the tumbling stream of the fountain, her dead hands worked among the folds of linen, working at the old, old blood that could never be erased, washing, and washing, and washing.

CHRISTOPHER EVANS

The Wailing Woman

This is the fourth of five stories about an artist called Vendavo who lives in a world where invisible spirit-creatures called chimeras exist which can be fashioned into physical forms by those whose minds are attuned to them. Vendavo, a man of dubious morality but great talent, has narrowly survived a revolution and is now living in the mountains with his family.

The three-man commission arrived towards dusk, accompanied by Shubi, whom Iriyana was not expecting. Shubi had gone to Veridi-Almar two years before to study at the university, and she was now an attractive young woman of nineteen, almost a stranger to Iriyana's eyes.

Vendavo greeted her with a great display of affection, as did the ten-year-old Bila, the only one of his brood who still lived with him. Iriyana was left to usher the visitors into the reception room, where a fire blazed in the hearth and hot drinks had been provided.

She knew two of the men quite well. The eldest, Belochur, was a prominent commentator on chimera-art, while Gidrel was someone she had met at receptions in Veridi-Almar. The third, Kerkouan, was a foreigner from overseas. On their arrival, he had made a point of insisting his bags be unloaded carefully from the pack-mules. His accent was heavy but the words perfectly clear.

Belochur, renowned for his grumpiness, immediately began complaining about the chilliness of the air and the remoteness of the town itself. It was a four-day journey from the capital to the mountains, and he did not spare her any details of the indignities he had suffered while having to negotiate precipitous mountain tracks on a mule.

Presently Vendavo and his two daughters joined them for dinner.

123

The commission had been sent to interview Vendavo about his art and to enquire about the chimeras, whose nature they were charged to elucidate. Vendavo had not wanted to come, Iriyana knew, but he managed to deflect most of their questions by concentrating on Shubi. When the meal was over, he took both daughters away again, promising that he would submit to an interview in due course. He was contemplating a new creation, he added, and might conceivably allow them to be present at its birth.

This parting shot left Belochur both disgruntled and intrigued. While Gidrel and Kerkouan were shown to their rooms, he lingered.

'Is this true?' he said to Iriyana. 'I understood he'd abandoned his own work and was concentrating on developing the talents of his apprentices.'

'He's never stopped creating,' Iriyana replied. 'If only as an example to his students.'

'What exactly is he contemplating?'

'That's not for me to say. Even if I could. He seldom talks about his work before it's done.'

Inwardly she was angry. Vendavo constantly talked of new projects, but they never materialised. The boast was almost certainly an empty one.

'As his agent you must be pleased he's working again.'

Iriyana shrugged. 'As I explained, he's never really stopped.'

'I can't say I cared greatly for his monument on the Raimus Bridge. Of course the craftsmanship is first-rate, as one would expect, but it has some rather vulgar elements.'

'I don't agree,' Iriyana said bluntly. 'I think it's quite remarkable.'

The monument was Vendavo's last major work in the capital, completed ten years before to celebrate the overthrow of the Hierarchy. It showed figures of every shape and variety in a pyramidal mass, clambering over one another, each striving to reach the apex of the pyramid but at the same time seeming to help one another upwards. And at the apex itself a naked figure rose out of a circle of flames, its arms beckoning to those below it. Executed as a still life in full colour, the monument was grandiose, sentimental, even naive – but still magnificent. It dominated the centre of the bridge, and at night the flames shone with their own inner light, illuminating the androgynous figure above, a symbol of the new order, visible from almost anywhere in Veridi-Almar.

'He understands exactly why we've come?' Belochur asked.

'Vendavo? Of course.'

'You've had ample notice of our visit. The journey was most inconvenient. Especially when Vendavo regularly visits Veridi-Almar.'

'He hasn't been to the city for over a year.'

Belochur made a dismissive sound.

'We have other artists to interview in the city,' he said with all the pomposity he could muster. 'We can stay no more than three days.'

In the depths of the night, Iriyana surfaced from a dream of being called across a lake of moonlit water. Even as she rose out of sleep the cries transformed themselves into a series of plaintive wails which she continued to hear distantly.

She sat up. The sounds continued, growing louder. They were coming from somewhere outside, at the rear of the house.

She rose and went along the landing to a window which looked down over the orchard. A thick fog had descended and nothing could be seen. The sobbing sounds grew fainter, faded.

Iriyana turned and saw that the door to Vendavo's bedroom was open. She crossed to the doorway, peered inside. The bed had not been slept in, and there was no sign of Vendavo.

A flood of outrage enveloped her. She rushed to Shubi's bedroom, flung open the door.

'What is it?' came a sleepy voice.

Shubi was alone in the bed. She sat up drowsily, the blankets slipping down to reveal her nakedness. Her skin was eggshell pale in the dimness.

'I'm sorry,' Iriyana began, realising her mistake. Then she heard the wailing again – long mournful sobs, drawing closer now.

'Can you hear it?'

Shubi nodded. The crease of a blanket marked her cheek like a scar.

'Perhaps it's a wolf,' she said. 'Or a bear.'

Iriyana shook her head. It was true that animals from the mountains sometimes prowled the gardens of the house by night, but this was no ordinary nocturnal cry. It sounded human.

Shubi reached for her night robe. The two of them went to the landing window. But the sounds were fading again, and the fog blanketed everything.

Shubi slipped away and returned moments later.

'Bila didn't wake,' she remarked.

All was quiet now. No one in the house had stirred apart from the two of them.

'Where's your father?' Iriyana asked.

'I don't know. I thought he'd gone to bed.'

Iriyana was annoyed with herself for acting so impetuously by rushing into Shubi's room. She had always suspected Vendavo of sleeping with his daughter after she reached puberty, but she was never able to broach the subject with Shubi. Though Iriyana had effectively acted as her stepmother for five years, there had always been a certain reticence between them.

'I had no idea you were coming,' Iriyana blurted.

'Father wrote, asking me to visit.'

'Oh? And did he specify a date?'

'He told me about the commission and suggested I accompany them from Veridi-Almar.'

She might have guessed as much. Shubi's visit gave Vendavo the perfect excuse for distracting himself from the attentions of Belochur and the others.

'Well,' Iriyana said more softly, 'I'm pleased you're home. You were still a girl when I said goodbye to you, but look at you now – quite the fine young woman.'

Shubi smiled. A silence fell between them – a silence which Iriyana abruptly felt was at once tense and intimate, like that between lovers.

'I'd better find your father,' she said hastily.

Next morning Iriyana found Gidrel sitting alone at the breakfast table. Through the window, she saw Shubi and Bila walking together in the orchard.

'Breakfast's in the pot,' Gidrel said.

A pan of rice was simmering on the stove; it had been flavoured with nutmeg and raisins.

'Where's Vendavo?' Gidrel asked.

'I haven't seen him this morning,' Iriyana replied. She had not seen him, in fact, since the previous evening. His bed had remained empty and, as far as she knew, he had left the house.

'Can we expect to see him today?'

Iriyana spooned rice into her bowl. 'I would hope so. Mayor Laaphre is giving a reception to welcome you this afternoon. Half the town should be there.'

She sat down opposite Gidrel with her breakfast. He let her eat in silence for a while, then said, 'How long have you been his agent?'

She was certain he knew full well. She said, 'Six years.' Vendavo had appointed her almost on a whim when the regulation of artists was introduced. But she had served him well.

'What sort of man would you say he was?'

She had expected the question. 'He's wayward, careless in his dealings with others, generous, self-absorbed, a libertine. A genius at what he does.'

Gidrel lit a pipe, blue smoke shrouding his head. Tobacco was one of the many new fashions in Veridi-Almar.

'I gather his wife died soon after you arrived.'

'Two years after,' she corrected him.

'In labour wasn't it? Her and the child.'

Iriyana nodded. She had only warm memories of Nyssa, who had shown her nothing but kindness. She had given her all to the family, to bearing and raising her children, and in the end exhausted herself beyond the point of recovery.

'How did he take it?'

She swallowed a mouthful of rice, eyeing him. He seemed an odd choice for the commission because he was no authority on chimera-art. Doubtless he had been appointed because of his talent for probing the personal lives of prominent individuals. Under the Hierarchy he had been a composer of hagiographies for the recently departed ancestors of wealthy families; after its overthrow he proved himself equally adept at producing denunciations of many of his former patrons. There was no reason to think he would be well-disposed towards Vendavo.

'He was heartbroken,' Iriyana said. 'He mourned her deeply, did no work at all for at least a year afterwards.'

'You surprise me, given that he's always had mistresses.'

She wasn't going to let him anger her. 'No one could replace Nyssa in his eyes. He loved her with all his soul.'

Gidrel made a sceptical noise. 'From what I gather, you amply filled her role in the household.'

She took her empty bowl to the basin and began rinsing it out.

'If you're suggesting I became his mistress,' she said evenly, 'you're quite wrong.'

'Oh, no, I'm not suggesting that.' A placatory smile. 'Though I'm surprised you never married.' He allowed a pause. 'The daughter, Shubi, is a pretty young thing, isn't she?'

Her cheeks flushed. She turned her back to him, ignoring the comment.

'Someone had to keep the household going while the family was in mourning,' she said. 'I was here, so I did it.'

'I wonder if his powers have failed him. He's created nothing significant for several years, isn't that true? Not since his wife's death.'

She couldn't deny it.

'It's been years since he performed for the people as he used to.'

She had to defend him. 'Public performances are very demanding. He has his family here to think of.'

'Rumour has it he spent his last visit to Veridi-Almar in the city's whorehouses.'

Straight-faced she said, 'I thought the new Arbiter had ordered all such establishments to be closed down.'

'Rumour has it he's suffering from a degenerative mental disease brought on by an overindulgence in carnal pursuits.'

How he dressed up his smears in fancy words! She laughed, thinking how loathsome he was.

'I can assure you the rumours are false. He's in full command of all his powers.'

This was said as much in hope as certainty. The truth was that since Nyssa's death Vendavo seemed to lack the capacity for solitude which was a necessary part of his art. Most of his income came from the revenues of his earlier creations.

At this point Belochur entered, grumbling that he had slept badly on a bed that was far too soft. Iriyana had never been more pleased to see him.

Mayor Laaphre had given an impressive welcoming speech and afterwards insisted on taking his guests down into the spacious vaults of the old temple opposite his residence. The temple itself had been razed after a fire the previous summer, but the vaults survived intact and were presently home for Vendavo's thirty students. Laaphre announced that he was gathering finance for a new temple which would incorporate galleries to display the works of artists with studios below ground where they could work.

Belochur, Gidrel and Kerkouan greeted this news with polite

disinterest, and Iriyana, whose patience was wearing thin, welcomed their return to Laaphre's mansion for the formal banquet. The dining hall was filled with all the township's notables, including every one of Vendavo's students. The only person missing was Vendavo himself. He had not been seen all day. Iriyana questioned his students and several of his children, but none knew where he was.

'Do you think it's going well?' Laaphre whispered across the table.

He was a relatively young man, eager to promote his township as the home of Vendavo the master and a centre of artistic excellence. The town itself was growing rapidly as an increasing flow of visitors stimulated trade, but a new temple on the scale he envisaged was certainly beyond its means at present.

'Very well,' she whispered back.

'Will Vendavo be coming?'

She shrugged, though inside she bristled. It was so typical of Vendavo to absent himself from situations he disliked and leave all the work to others.

'Are there difficulties?' Laaphre persisted.

'None that I know of.' She glanced along the table. 'Don't worry – I think our guests are being kept happy for the moment.'

Gidrel was in close conversation with Leshtu, Vendavo's eldest son, while Belochur was talking to Kumash, one of Vendavo's more promising students. They were discussing a fashionable theory that chimeras were sometimes created spontaneously, unknown to the artist, from vivid dreams or reveries; Belochur, a traditionalist, would have none of it, Kerkouan, meanwhile, was pointing at objects on the table and speaking their names in his native tongue to an attentive audience of young women.

As the meal drew to its close, various students took the floor to perform for the rest of the diners. They conjured jewelled dogs, flowers with human faces, curved mirrors that warped the diners' reflections. Finally a small volcano spewed forth all manner of fabulous creatures which promptly scuttled up on to the tables before ossifying into stony mementoes of the feast.

The hall was hectic with flurries and rustlings, the invisible movement of unformed chimeras. Iriyana had been able to sense them from an early age, though she never had any desire to create herself.

Kerkouan had brought along one of his large travelling bags, and he now proceeded to unpack a variety of rods and small porcelain dishes. He assembled the rods into tall stands from which he suspended the dishes. Then he poured water into each.

While Vendavo's students continued their performance, he scrutinised each dish carefully, paying the artists themselves scarcely any attention. In response to questions, he explained that he was attempting to detect the presence of chimeras by looking for ripples in the water. He believed their manifestation should create disturbances in a liquid medium, as a wind created waves on a lake.

Belochur and Gidrel greeted the notion with derision. Iriyana herself was intrigued but sceptical. Like everyone else, she often wondered about the true nature of unformed chimeras. Were they distinct creatures inhabiting some ethereal realm or simply a mysterious aspect of the human imagination? This was one of the fundamental questions which the commission had been set up to answer, but she doubted that Kerkouan's instruments were equal to the task. While it was true that chimeras did indeed seem to cause movement in the air to those who were sensitive to them, it was never a movement that could be seen or felt in a material way. The whisperings could only be heard by not listening; the emotions that sometimes went with them could only be felt in unguarded moments.

There was a brief moment of levity when Laaphre accidentally bumped one of the dishes and Gidrel remarked that he had seen a chimera dip its toe in the water. Kerkouan finally had to admit a temporary defeat.

'The elemental presences are too weak,' he informed them, his faith in his instruments unshaken. 'I shall need Vendavo's services. They say his emanations are the most powerful, is that not so?'

By now it was growing late and even Laaphre had given up hope that Vendavo would appear.

'Do you think it was successful?' he asked Iriyana as they said farewell on the doorstep. 'I hope Kerkouan wasn't offended when I jarred his equipment.'

He was an unlikely mayor: gauche, earnest in his ambition, good-natured to a fault. She smiled.

'I think you've made an excellent impression.'

'Belochur looked annoyed that Vendavo didn't turn up.'

'Belochur will always find something that dissatisfies him. It's no reflection on you. Let me worry about Vendavo.'

'Perhaps something's happened to him.'

'Perhaps,' she said softly, thinking that something certainly *would* happen to him when she caught up with him.

Under a sky that blazed with stars, she climbed the hill to the house with Belochur and the others. In the city, where she had been born, the skies were never as dark or the stars as bright. She was the daughter of a minor lord, and before the uprising had organised exhibitions in public parks and squares. Chimeras always manifested themselves in a way which reflected the character of their creator, however, obliquely, and her sensitivity to the creatures greatly helped her in her dealings with the artists themselves. After the uprising, which she had been lucky to survive, she decided to pursue her ambition of meeting Vendavo, the greatest artist of them all. She knew his work intimately but knew little about the man himself; she had come to the mountains with the vague intention of writing his life story. Soon after her arrival, he seduced her – or rather, she let him have her because she admired him. It was a passionless coupling, her first and last with a man. He never touched her again, and afterwards treated her with a suspicion bordering on hostility. Then Nyssa died in childbirth, and everything changed.

'I think the great Vendavo is avoiding us.'

Gidrel had come up beside her. She was in no mood to tolerate him, so she increased her pace. Gidrel, overweight and already puffing, could not keep up.

Shubi had stayed home with Bila rather than attend the feast, but it occurred to Iriyana that Bila would now be in bed. What if Vendavo had returned in the meantime?

With even greater haste, she ascended the path.

There was a light burning in the kitchen window. Iriyana hurried through the garden and into the house.

Shubi was in the kitchen, Bila sitting on her lap, both of them in their night robes. Bila was sipping warm milk from a cup.

'She couldn't sleep,' Shubi explained.

'Is your father back?' Iriyana asked.

'I haven't seen him all day. I thought he was going to the banquet.'

Iriyana felt a disproportionate relief; at the same time, her anger towards Vendavo redoubled.

Without another word, she turned and left, bustling past Gidrel and the others.

She went back down through the town, then up the other side of

131

the valley. A half-moon had risen, lighting the stone-walled olive groves.

An old hut stood on a rocky outcrop halfway up the mountainside. Long before she reached it, Iriyana knew that Vendavo was there; she could sense the swarming chimeras which always surrounded him.

The hut had once been derelict, but it now had a new roof. Lantern light leaked out through the shutters on the window, and a thread of smoke rose up from a squat chimney.

Without announcing herself, she threw open the door.

Vendavo was in bed with Zulya, a farmer's daughter who was his current mistress. Both had been sleeping and were startled by her sudden appearance.

Iriyana did not attempt to hide her irritation.

'Is this where you've been skulking all day?'

He tried a smile: broad and generous, warm enough to melt the frostiest heart; but she was inured to it.

'I needed some time alone,' he told her.

'Alone?' she said scathingly. 'Are my eyes playing tricks with me, or isn't that a woman in bed with you?'.

He made soothing motions with his hands, then reached for his robe and hastily put it on. Iriyana let him lead her outside because she did not care to conduct an argument in front of the woman.

'She's been warming my bed, that's all,' Vendavo said to her. 'Surely you'll allow me a little intimacy?'

She was actually relieved that Zulya was the object of his lust rather than Shubi, but she wouldn't let him know that.

'You disappoint me. Everyone was waiting for you at the banquet. It was disgraceful of you not to attend.'

He moved away from her, shrugged his broad back. 'I had other things to concern me.'

'Oh? Things like farmers' daughters, I presume.'

He shook his head. 'A new creation.'

She gave an exasperated sigh. But before she could speak, Vendavo reached into the pocket of his robe and thrust an object at her.

It was a brass tube, or rather two brass tubes, one inside the other, with discs of glass set into each end.

'Point it at the sky,' he said. 'Look through it.'

'What is it?'

'Look through it.'

She knew he was trying to divert her, but she was intrigued

nevertheless. She raised the instrument towards her eye, but he said, 'No, the other way around.'

Under his instructions she put the narrower end to her eye and squinted. In the tiny circle of darkness at the far end there shone an uncountable number of stars.

She moved the tube, peered again, then returned it to her eye. With the instrument she could see a hundred times more stars than by her eyes alone.

'Isn't it remarkable?' Vendavo said. 'It magnifies distant things.'

He spoke with all the enthusiasm of a child. Ever since the new Arbiter in Veridi-Almar had allowed trading vessels from other lands into their ports, ships had been sailing up the Raimus and disgorging strangers from a variety of nations bearing all manner of new devices – harnesses and ploughs, eyeglasses which rectified poor vision, missiles which spat fire and rushed through the air at great speed, tiny carts and toys which could be made to move by turning a wooden key. Though his visits to the city were now infrequent, Vendavo regularly had the latest wonders transported to the mountains: lenses which concentrated the sun's light, prisms which transformed it into rainbow colours, nuggets of iron which drew nails to them without human intervention.

He took the instrument from her and pointed it at the moon.

'Look,' he said.

He moved his head aside so that she could put her eye to it. The moon filled the far end, and its surface was covered with markings: rugged disks and crescents, streaks and whorls, light and shade, everywhere pitted and pockmarked like a ravaged face. And yet it was beautiful, breathtaking.

Vendavo withdrew the instrument. The moon shrank to its familiar aspect, its butter-coloured surface blotched only with vague shadows.

'We live in an age of wonders,' Vendavo said grandly as the chimeras intensified their presence. 'Did you know that the sun is also marked? You can't look at it directly through the device because it blinds the eye. But the image can be displayed on a white sheet and there –'

'I take it you never had any intention of attending Laaphre's banquet?'

Vendavo was a stocky man, Iriyana only half his size. But he was in awe of her temper, and she knew it.

'I've been busy,' he said. 'Readying myself for a new creation.'

'And just what sort of creation are you proposing? Or is it simply another of your evasions?'

At last he seemed to shrivel and wilt. She was constantly having to bully him, to remind him of his duties.

'Listen,' she said in a more moderate tone, 'you've been asked to assist the commission in every way you can. I know you've never liked Belochur, or Gidrel for that matter –'

'I despise them both,' he said vehemently. 'Belochur's a leech, feeding off the sweat of others. There can never be any common ground between us. As for Gidrel, he's only interested in scandal of the nastiest kind. Why should I pretend a cordiality I don't feel?'

Belochur had been regarded as the most eminent commentator on chimera-art years before Vendavo had risen to prominence. He had subsequently made many pronouncements on Vendavo's work, few of which were to the artist's liking. His consistant view was that while Vendavo's talent was undeniable, his creations lacked a serious sense of artistic purpose and a suitable moral tone.

Such judgements infuriated Vendavo because he considered them utterly irrelevant, as indeed he did the whole business of evaluation. 'The commentators are incapable of *liking* anything,' he had once complained to Iriyana. 'All they can do is *admire*, and always with reservations. They swallow up art whole as soon as its produced, then spit out its bloodied bones. To them, all the sweat, all the agony of creation stands for nothing, is not even taken into account. They smother it and deaden it with their words, then move on to their next victim. Without us, they'd be nothing.'

It was rare for Vendavo to speak passionately about his art – rare, indeed, for him to discuss it in the abstract at all. Although demanding, to him it was a thoroughly natural process, something stifled by the very idea of analysis.

He squatted on the edge of the rock, pointing the instrument down at the township, which nestled in the blind end of the valley with mountains rising around it on three sides. He seemed immune to the cold.

'So,' Iriyana said, 'are you intending to hide here for the duration of their visit?'

'I'll see them tomorrow,' he said without looking up. 'I give you my word.'

She began to rage at him, to bring all her anger at his shortcomings to bear. But this time it was no use: she couldn't shame him or appeal to his fickle sense of responsibility. The overwhelming presence of the chimeras was like a cloak which shielded him from any urgency other than his own. Finally Iriyana stalked off in a huff, leaving him alone on the outcrop under the moonlight night.

Iriyana lay awake in the darkness, wondering whether Vendavo would indeed honour his promise to meet with Belochur and the others. If he did not, there would almost certainly be repercussions. In the interests of encouraging trade, the new Arbiter was eager to promote the works of chimera artists, who were unknown elsewhere, and he had appointed the commission under pressure from overseas. It was required to use the rigorous methods of investigation and analysis favoured by the foreigners, but Iriyana was beginning to doubt whether it would have any success in penetrating the mystery of the chimeras. Philosophers, priests and leaders in her own land had already spent uncounted centuries pondering their essence, building religions and empires out of them, slaughtering and sanctifying in their name. And still they remained elusive to human understanding.

Marooned in her bed, deserted by sleep, she felt like a sailor becalmed on a soft raft in a dark ocean. Time passed. Then she heard the sounds again.

As before, she was not at first certain she was really hearing them. But soon there was no doubt. They were the same pitiful wails which she knew no animal could produce. This time they came from the front of the house.

She slipped from bed and went to her window. Fog cloaked the garden, but lamps had been lit in the downstairs rooms, casting pools of murky light into the orchard

The sounds grew louder – a rhythmical sobbing, sounds only a woman could make. Her breath misted the pane. She smoothed a hole in the glass, peered again.

A figure appeared.

It was a woman in a ragged stained dress. Iriyana gasped at the sight of her.

She had two heads. The second was that of a wide-eyed and hairless child. It hung on her right shoulder.

The woman sank to her knees on the sodden grass. She began rocking on her haunches, all the while sobbing so desolately it seemed that she had gone beyond hope and even self-pity. She appeared hunchbacked, and only then did Iriyana realise that the second head was attached to a body strapped to her back.

The woman was not old, but her gauntness made her look withered. Her eyes were shadowed in her thin face. The child lolled on her shoulder as she rocked; it was alive and conscious but utterly inert.

Iriyana threw on her robe and hurried downstairs. Shubi was already up, along with several of the servants.

'Fetch lanterns,' she told them, leading for the door. She heard Shubi say, 'I'm coming with you.'

Outside, everything was dank and shrouded in mist. There was no sign of the woman. Iriyana could still hear her sobbing, but distantly now, and diminishing. She hurried through the garden, the wet grass soaking into her slippers.

The sounds grew fainter. She continued to pursue them. The grounds of the house were large, bordered by dry-stone walls which were tumbledown in many places. Escaping the garden would be as easy as entering it.

The cries were lost to the night.

Iriyana reached a stretch of wall. Breathless, she leaned over, putting her hands on her knees and listening while she gasped in air.

Nothing. The woman was gone.

Shubi emerged out of the mist. She, too, was panting, and there seemed to be something frantic and desperate in her expression. Iriyana reached out and hugged her.

'Did you see her?' she asked.

'No,' Shubi replied.

She leaned against Iriyana, each exhalation hot on her neck. Iriyana felt a welling of emotion which she knew was not maternal protectiveness but desire. It thrilled and shocked her all at once. Then Shubi raised her head, peering into her face with a fearless candour.

A hazy ball of light penetrated the gloom – a servant with a lantern. Shubi instantly drew back.

'Any sign of her?' Iriyana asked the servant.

He shook his head.

'Have the grounds searched thoroughly,' she told him.

She and Shubi made their way back to the house without speaking. Bila, Belochur, Gidrel and Kerkouan were all up. Every one of them had seen the woman from the windows of their rooms. Iriyana expected questions, demands, accusations, but none came.

136

Bila rushed to Shubi, who cuddled her. Everyone waited until the servants returned. They had found no trace of the woman.

'Was it a ghost?' Bila asked.

'No ghost,' Kerkouan said unexpectedly. 'In my room, my instruments were disturbed. It was a chimera.'

Iriyana did not sleep that night. As dawn began to break, she left the house and retraced her steps to the hut.

It was empty, the fire dead in the hearth. She stood on the outcrop, looking over the town, wondering where Vendavo might be. The sun had not yet risen over the mountain-tops, and most of the townsfolk still slept. But Vendavo was an early riser.

The fog had lifted overnight, and she could see Eswarema the priestess making her portly way along the river bank to the grain barn which was now being used as a temple. Its broad doors already hung open.

Unhurriedly, Iriyana descended the path and crossed the wooden footbridge. The barn was square, built with an arching roof which somewhat mimicked a temple's dome. Chimeras made their gentle presence felt. Iriyana slipped inside.

Benches were laid in rows on either side of the central aisle, and an altar built on trestles stood at its far end. Eswarema was burning incense and murmuring prayers. On a bench in front of her sat Vendavo, his head bowed.

Iriyana waited, listening to Eswarema's lilting, effortless drone. The priesthood had a knack of making their prayers sound hypnotic by only half-speaking the words. But Iriyana was listening carefully, and she heard Nyssa's name being called several times.

At length Eswarema stepped down from the altar. She embraced Vendavo formally and kissed his forehead.

Iriyana crept outside and sat down on the stump on an old pine until Vendavo emerged.

'I thought I might find you here,' she said gently.

Since Nyssa's death he had turned increasingly to the temple, incorporating many of its rituals into the training of his apprentices since he claimed they improved the powers of concentration and imagination. Nyssa's ashes and those of her stillborn son had been cast into the river, and Vendavo had summoned a troupe of golden angels to accompany them on their way. It was vulgar, but heartfelt. Afterwards he had come alone to Iriyana's room and wept in her arms.

137

A flock of chimeras attended him, and she could sense a great nervousness in them, a tense, unstable energy.

'Last night we had a visitor,' she said, and then she told him about the wailing woman.

He listened in silence, gazing over her shoulder towards the river. His eyes looked red with lack of sleep, and he had a distracted air.

'Kerkouan thinks it was a chimera,' she concluded.

He peered at her.

'Did you create it?' she asked.

'What did the woman look like?'

'It was hard to see, because of the fog. But it wasn't Nyssa. I thought perhaps you might have made her to give Belochur and Gidrel a fright.'

He smiled at that, but did not confirm or deny it. Something told her it would be unwise to press him in his present state of mind. When she had first come to the mountains to meet him, she had imagined he would be an extraordinary person in all manner of ways. It had taken her some years to realise that he was only extraordinary with respect to his art, and there were times when even that gift seemed imposed on him, a thing given rather than earned or deserved. In every other respect he was all too fallible.

'Today,' she said, 'you promised you'd meet with Belochur and the others.'

'Later,' he said, absorbed in his thoughts. 'I'll see them later. For now, I have work to do.'

With this, he strode off towards the footbridge, pursued by his attendant host.

Iriyana sat in the reception room while a steady rain fell outside. She had arranged for Vendavo's students to visit, and Kerkouan was busy testing various contraptions while they performed for him – assemblages of springs, pulleys, levers, liquids of every variety from hot candlewax to quicksilver. The air, which stank of vapours, was busy with the movement of chimeras, while the floor gradually became more cluttered with ossifying works of art, few of which had any merit whatsoever.

Despite all the activity, an air of aimlessness prevailed. Belochur could scarcely contain his impatience, while Gidrel spent his time mocking Kerkouan's continued failure to detect the chimeras' presence. Iriyana had told them of Vendavo's promise to meet them, but the evening was drawing on, and still he had not appeared.

In the kitchen, Shubi was supervising Bila in her chopping of parsnips. She had kept the younger girl by her side all day, and Iriyana had not had any opportunity to speak with her alone. She did not know what she would say, but there was far more than words unexpressed between them.

At the moment, however, she was preoccupied with the quiet fury which was building in her towards Vendavo. He was not only avoiding the commission but also being neglectful of his family. This had not been one of his failings before; though he often expressed disappointment that none of his children had inherited his talents, there was still a closeness between them and they would do anything for him. Leshtu had even taken the younger children into his own household after Nyssa's death.

In the reception room, Kerkouan had abandoned his experiments and was engaged in an argument with Belochur. Iriyana quickly grasped the radical essence of it. Kerkouan believed that the chimeras themselves were solely responsible for a creation, instilling into the mind of the artist the conceit that the human imagination dictated its form, whereas in fact that form was *imposed* on the imagination by the chimeras themselves. She now understood why Kerkouan had little interest in the artists themselves; to him, they were simply vessels, conduits through which the creative powers flowed.

To Belochur this was both an anathema and an absurdity. Though he personally disliked most artists, he was only too ready to credit them with full responsibility for their works. Kerkouan's standpoint made the whole emphasis of his critiques meaningless, given that they were always intimately connected with the perceived strengths and weaknesses of the artists themselves.

Gidrel and most of the students had abandoned even a pretence of interest in the debate and were engaged in a game of dice. Belochur grew more irate, while Kerkouan maintained the dispassionate air of rationality for which his countrymen were renowned. At this point Kumash arrived.

The young man's dark hair was plastered to his head, and his cloak was sodden. His late arrival surprised Iriyana, because he was a serious-minded student who relished every opportunity to discuss the theory and practice of his art.

'I've come from Vendavo,' he said breathlessly. 'He's waiting for us at Laaphre's.'

*

The rain petered out, and presently the moon became visible through tattered cloud. Huddled under their hooded cloaks, Iriyana and the others waited outside Laaphre's mansion while Vendavo paced the expanse of waste ground where the temple had once stood.

Kerkouan had set up his stands in front of the crowd, each dish containing a different liquid. Half the town seemed to have turned out, and everyone waited with an air of expectancy. On their arrival, Vendavo had announced that he intended to undertake a major creation for their benefit. Then he instructed them to assemble outside.

Belochur muttered loudly that soon it would be too dark to see anything. But the twilight was vibrant with massed chimeras – Iriyana had never felt their presence more powerfully, more overwhelmingly. She stole a glance at Shubi, who had helped Bila up on to a wall so that she could see better. Then she felt the elemental rush of the creatures.

Where Vendavo was standing, a massive white shape began to shimmer into existence above and around him. It flickered, stabilised, flickered again, then finally settled into solidity.

Many of the watchers gave a collective gasp as the enormity of Vendavo's undertaking became apparent. It was nothing less than a great temple, fashioned of something that might have been ivory or white marble. Towers, spires and vaulted walls supported a central dome which gleamed like a diamond.

It was as big as the High Temple in Veridi-Almar, but its design owed little to any building that had preceded it. The white substance of its fabric was seamless and luminescent, the dome a many-surfaced crystal reflecting the moonlight. White steps fanned out like a river from the cavernous entranceway. In front of them stood a pyre-dish shaped like a giant flower.

Iriyana had never seen anything like it. It was magnificent.

For long moments no one moved, as if fearful the whole structure might suddenly topple. Then a few people came tentatively forward, and others began to follow. Soon almost everyone was swarming up the steps.

The interior was equally breathtaking. In his central dome of faceted crystal, Vendavo had contrived to mimic the effect of the magnifying instrument: the whole sky was drawn closer, stars multiplied, the clouds and moon made larger. It was a dizzying effect, as if the entire dome had been thrust into the heavens.

Elsewhere, things were more placid. Curving beams and pillars

140

created a variety of sinuous perspectives, while the high altar rose up from the floor like a wave. There were no windows; the luminous walls filled the temple with so much light that none were needed. Iriyana was astonished. Though she had always appreciated the magnitude of Vendavo's talent, she had never considered him capable of creation on such a scale, and by a single effort of will.

Outside, Vendavo was receiving everyone's congratulations. He looked both elated and drained. Even Belochur and Gidrel appeared impressed, though Belochur could not resist remarking that the artist had not seen fit to furnish the temple with seats for its congregation. Across the street, Kerkouan scrambled in the mud, gathering up the stands and dishes which had been overturned in the rush to inspect the temple.

Iriyana realised that for once no chimeras flocked around Vendavo. The temple had swallowed up most of the townsfolk, and a moment of silence fell. Vendavo was embracing Shubi and Bila, and Iriyana awaited her turn to congratulate him.

Then she heard the cries – the same doleful sobbing as before.

Everyone turned. From out of the night, the woman appeared.

Haggard and destitute, this time she was holding the child in her arms. Iriyana saw that it was an infant boy. His head rocked to and fro as she staggered forward with him.

Her legs were covered with mud and scratches, and her ragged dress was sodden. She was dark-haired, quite tall, and she looked like a wild animal. She began stumbling up the steps, wailing piteously. Her gaze was fixed on Vendavo.

Vendavo went rigid. Everyone else also stood motionless, too shocked by the apparition to move. The woman scrambled upwards, the child lolling in her arms, its vacant eyes a deep blue. She thrust it forward, laying it at Vendavo's feet.

He looked down at it. It was naked under a swaddle of dirty blankets, its fair hair matted to its scalp. As Vendavo made to retreat, the woman reached out and grasped the hem of his cloak. He tried to pull away, but she would not let go. Her cries were so mournful they seemed to have induced a seizure of paralysis in everyone.

Then Shubi stepped forward and scooped up the child. Kumash and Laaphre took the woman's arms and tried to lift her to her feet. Immediately she began flailing in their grasp. She burst from them, hurling herself down the steps and racing off into the night.

*

141

In the orchard, Shubi plucked a withered pear from a bough and crouched in front of the boy to show him it. Iriyana watched from the warmth of Vendavo's study, through a thickness of glass.

The boy was pale, moon-faced, and since he answered to no name, Shubi called him Pelu, a nonsense name which she had used for her favourite doll as a child. Pelu now entirely occupied her days, even Bila being left to fend for herself. Shubi had made it plain that she had no intention of returning to the university to continue her studies.

Iriyana put the letter down in front of Vendavo.

'Who's it from?' he asked suspiciously.

'Belochur. It's about the woman.'

He said nothing, did not even pick it up. Iriyana had been hard-pressed to get him to his desk to attend to routine correspondence. He spent little time at the house now, preferring to create in the temple. The boy unnerved him, and it was not simply his stillness, his unwavering gaze. A doctor had declared the child a congenital idiot who would never be able to talk or move; but there was something else about him – an atmosphere or presence which seemed, if not malevolent, then deeply unsettling. Vendavo avoided him whenever possible.

A frost had descended overnight, and the child was bundled up with blankets in his wheelchair. Shubi was talking to him, pointing to trees, clouds, the town in the valley below. She seemed quite unconcerned by his lack of response.

Vendavo still refused to answer any questions about the boy or the wailing woman. After the woman had fled the temple, he went straight home, saying he was exhausted. Belochur and the others delayed their departure by two days in the hope of talking to him, but he would not emerge from his room. Meanwhile the woman had been found dead in an old pigsty on the outskirts of the town. A frustrated Belochur finally had the body transported to Veridi-Almar for dissection before it began to spoil

Iriyana picked up the letter. It was addressed to them both, and she had already read it.

'They still haven't identified the woman,' she said. 'But Belochur informs us that she appears perfectly human, inside as well as out.'

Vendavo rose from his desk and went over to sit by the fire. Undaunted, she continued.

'Gidrel believes the woman was a mistress of yours and the child your bastard son.'

She waited for a reaction. There was none.

'After all, the boy has your colouring. Gidrel thinks it possible the woman might have been driven mad by his idiocy and sought you out in the hope of forcing you to acknowledge his existence. He thinks she might even be someone you have no memory of seducing.'

Vendavo snorted. 'Gidrel's an idiot himself.'

He kept his back to her, squatting on the stool and staring into the flames.

'Kerkouan takes a different view. He's convinced both of them are chimeras, created quite unconsciously by you as an outpouring of grief for Nyssa's death.'

'So he's revised his opinion of artists as dumb servants of the chimeras, has he?'

'It's simply one of the possibilities he's considering, according to Belochur. And it's an interesting idea, don't you think?'

'That man is full of ideas. He's also full of nonsense.'

'So he's wrong?'

Vendavo thrust a log on the fire. 'Why should I confirm or deny anything? I owe them nothing.'

Iriyana felt renewed impatience with his evasiveness. But she had tried to browbeat him on the subject before, without success.

'Belochur would appreciate your cooperation,' she said, still scanning the letter. 'He's keeping an open mind, he says, though he's quite prepared to believe you may have deliberately created the woman and child, given that you've fashioned human specimens in the past which were perfectly lifelike. Of course, none of them were able to utter sounds, but it's conceivable to him that such an advance would not be beyond your powers.'

Vendavo laughed. 'The man's a simpleton. Does he think I'll tell him if he flatters me?'

'It's more than flattery. He needs your help so that he and the others can fully discharge their duties to the Arbiter. Only you can say which of them is right.'

The flames leapt up the dark chimney. Vendavo's lips formed a smile that was not a smile.

'Does it matter to you?' he asked, turning to face her.

'I won't pretend I'm not intrigued,' she admitted. 'Also, I don't see what's to be gained by silence. What purpose does it serve?'

He did not reply. The firelight shone in his silver hair. She could feel his chimeras growing unsettled, as though confined by the room.

'If I answer you now,' he said at last, 'will you promise never to ask me about it again?'

She wanted to tell him he had no right to impose such a condition. But instead, after hesitating, she said, 'Yes.'

'Tell them I don't know. Tell them I honestly don't know.'

Then he rose and swept out of the room.

The silence which always followed his departure was profound, because his chimeras went with him, leaving not only silence but also emptiness. Iriyana laid the letter on the desk, far from convinced he had told her the truth. She was quite sure he had not consciously created the woman and the boy because he had seemed genuinely startled by their appearance. But more than that, she could not say, except that in some sense she was equally sure the boy was his. It seemed as if the woman knew him, and whether she was a cast-off mistress or an unwitting product of his most private grief – in either case, the child Pelu was his creation.

Outside, Shubi was wheeling the boy back to the house. The chair had been imported from Veridi-Almar at considerable expense. The boy was perhaps three, and Iriyana had never seen him make the slightest movement.

She crept closer to the window. As she did so, Shubi looked up and saw her. Iriyana made to smile, but she noticed that the boy was also looking in her direction with his huge empty eyes. Though nothing registered in his face, she felt he was scolding and admonishing her for an intrusion. Shubi seemed to sense it too. She leaned forward to whisper in his ear, and it was as if they were exchanging a secret which Iriyana would never be allowed to share.

CHRISTIAN LEHMANN AND GARRY KILWORTH

When the Music Stopped

When the music stopped, he alone would remain on the record, an audience of one applauding a non-existent performance. The old 78, scratched and marked by decades of overuse, would contain only the sounds of a small boy's clapping. Unless – unless he were to die first of course, to leave Chuck to the solitude of his haunting piano playing.

He remembered the day when the first of them had died. The record was playing, but something nibbled at the edges of his mind. Something was not quite right with the playing. Something was *missing*. It took him several plays of the record to realise what it was.

At first he had put it down to weariness: the kind of mental exhaustion that came from having to live with a perception disability. He remembered thinking: *the music sounds a little hollow, a little lacking in background strength. The clarinet? No, that was there. He could hear the syncopating rhythm of Peanuts Baker quite clearly now that he was listening for it. What? What then?*

Then it had come to him. The trombone. There was no trombone.

He played the 78 through again, immediately afterwards, then looked at the sleeve. There was a blank where the trombonist's name should be on the list of players. Miles Teegarten! *Jesus, Miles Teegarten was dead!*

All the jazz musicians on that platter were personal to him. He had been present at that recorded jam session in Chicago, January 27, 1933. It had been a birthday treat from his uncle the day he had reached eight years of age. The clapping in the background: he was part of that sound. (And Uncle Pete too, until he died.)

What a night that had been for a young boy: the atmosphere full of cigarette smoke; the beer flowing, some of it onto the floor; the chatter and informality of great men. Louis Armstrong had actually spoken to him: wished him a happy birthday. There was much laughter when the trumpeter, his round face creased in smiles, announced, 'We have an old man in the audience. Eight years today. Man, that's a heavy burden, eight years. Let's all say happy birthday to Sabastian there, hiding behind that big glass of lemonade pop . . . '

Everyone had called out to him, some of the musicians trotting out a fanfare on their instruments. Then they had played it, *St James Infirmary*. Some might call it a morbid song but from that moment Sabastian was hooked on the blues and *St James Infirmary* gave him much pleasure whenever he heard it after that night. Until the musicians began to disappear, as he knew they would. *Then* the sadness and bitterness came.

He put the record on now, while he ate his breakfast, and since the vocals and most of the instruments – the players (even Satchmo himself) – had gone, he sung along with it, providing the lyrics himself.

'*Went down to St James infirmary – saw my baby there – stretched out on a long white table – so cold, so still, so fair. Let her go, Let her go, God bless her . . .*'

The tears streamed down his face as he tried to drink his coffee. All those gaps. All those fine people. Even the audience had gone. Just one lone player, Chuck Davis, on the piano. And a single, solitary clapper at the end. A childish, unrhythmic sound that he knew to be his own small eight-year-old hands – enthusiastic but lacking coordination.

The record finished and he left it, hissing round and round, on the turntable, while he finished his coffee and wiped the tears from his cheeks with a table napkin. Such pain. Such heartfelt *pain*.

He left the house and began to walk to work, along the avenue covered with a crisp layer of dry leaves. There was an autumnal nip to the air which made him turn up his coat collar and retreat into himself, like a turtle drawing its neck into its shell. Sabastian needed these small barriers between him and the world, especially on days like today. He knew his boss was going to offer him promotion again and he was not looking forward to it. The refusal, as it always did, would leave his boss looking frustrated and puzzled. Sabastian was a postal clerk.

'I like my work as a sorter,' he would explain. 'I enjoy the shift work – the varied hours. It gives me time to do things . . . things I wouldn't have time for if I worked nine to five. Really.'

The excuse was feeble but the real reason would lose him even his present job. If they promoted him to the records section he would be lost. Many of those records contained files on dead people, had been written by people who had since died, and to Sabastian they would be just blank pieces of paper. Of course, from time to time a letter came in written by a person since deceased, but these were rare and he could get away with putting the plain envelope back into one of the racks for the next shift to find. If one was addressed to someone who was dead, only the name would be missing, the destination would be there.

He passed the cinema and glanced at the billboard. Some of the names of the stars were missing. He could see the obvious spaces. He averted his eyes. So many reminders. There had been a time when, spurred by the talk of others, he turned to a classical programme on the radio but all he could hear was the scraping of chairs and some fools coughing and farting. He wondered why he could hear *St James Infirmary* when its creator, Primrose, was no doubt dead, but he guessed it was because of the spontaneous nature of jazz. Each performance was immediate and differed so much from the original that the connection was broken with its composer. Who knew, really? Sabastian's psychological disability was weird enough without searching for the reasons for aberrations from a standard.

His paranormal impediment (as he called it) was to a certain extent selective. It never entered the third dimension. Buildings did not disappear because their architects were dead, for instance. It just made him so miserable sometimes, this distorted perception. Some people might have felt special, but not Sabastian. He longed to be ordinary.

At the corner of the avenue was a newstand and he bought a daily paper.

'Mornin',' he said to the woman as he passed his money to her.

As usual she was dressed in clothes that must have belonged to a man twice her size, probably thirty years ago, judging from the stains and frayed trouser cuffs. He was better off than some people, he reminded himself. At least he wasn't down at heel. He could afford to feed and clothe himself properly. More than that poor woman could do.

He enjoyed the newspaper because most of the articles and photographs were still visible to him. Books were different. There was something shocking about picking up a book and finding it blank. All those white pages. It still took his breath away for one horrible moment if he had not prepared himself for it. It drained his soul. *Hemingway, where are you now?* Hemingway had been one of Sabastian's favourite authors until, in 1967, he had been reading *The Sun Also Rises* when the words started to blur before his eyes. He had not needed to put on the news to find out for whom the bell tolled.

All those books to which he would never have access! At school they had thought him retarded, gave up on him when he reached a certain age. But he could read, all right, though he had hidden it from his teachers. The post office had to hire a certain percentage of invalids and misfits and he had begun as a van driver, later to graduate to sorter when they had forgotten he was supposed to be semi-literate.

He opened the newspaper as he walked along. The centre pages were devoted to the J.F. Kennedy assassination, recently revived due to further evidence suggesting a Cuban-Mafia involvement. There were many blanks on the pages but a photograph of the Oswald killing held his attention. Lee Harvey was missing, but Jack Ruby was still there, in that half-crouched position, leaning forward, pointing the murder weapon at the spot where Kennedy's supposed assassin would have been to a person with a normal perception.

Jack Ruby should *not* have been in the picture.

He was supposed to have died of cancer in 1976 or thereabouts. So what was he doing here? There was a huge conspiracy at work somewhere, which Sabastian would dearly have loved to reveal to the world – but who would believe a postal clerk who announced that Jack Ruby was still alive because he had not disappeared from a photograph? They would put him away, no doubt about that whatsoever. Sabastian had a gift that was not a gift: it was an affliction, a burden.

Someone greeted him from the far side of the road – one of his fellow workers – and he waved back. The day's work had begun.

Sure enough, his boss offered him the promotion he sought to avoid, and as usual his reluctance brought the expected reaction: the shaking of the head and the resigned expression. Some of his workmates were a little jealous of his rapport with the boss. They showed it by their silence when he returned to the office. However, by lunchtime he was back in his place on the sorter's desk and they

148

realised that once again he had refused promotion. It made him, perversely, something of a hero amongst them. They bought him beers in the pub where they had their lunch.

Then one of them had to go and play a few records on the juke box, some of which he heard and some not. He recalled, morosely, the time he had reached fourteen and Herbie Lund, the sax player, had disappeared from his favourite record. It was the first time he realised the full personal scope of his disability, the first time it struck home. Uncle Pete had been there that night and had come up to his room to comfort him while he sobbed. He remembered the knock on the bedroom door, and Uncle Pete coming in, silently. He tried to recall his uncle's expression, but the man was gone now and the features had faded from Sabastian's memory. Most of the conversation too, was forgotten, but he recalled the sentence, ' . . . Herbie's gone, but his music's still there, Seb. His music hasn't gone with him. It goes on.'

But for Sabastian the music did not go on, and he had nearly blurted out the whole of his secret to Uncle Pete – the secret that was to cause so much emotional pain throughout his life. He had held back, letting his uncle think he had read of the death in the newspaper, not wanting to hurt the old man of whom he was so fond. Sabastian was the only member of the family to share Uncle Pete's love of jazz and if his disability were known it would have caused his uncle a lot of sorrow. To be without jazz was death itself to Pete.

At four o'clock the shift finished and the evening sorters came on duty. Sabastian was on evening shift the next day, so he had quite a few hours to fill until then. He kicked at the leaves as he strolled home, feeling just a little better than he had done on leaving the house that morning. The autumn sun was a huge ball of orange behind the changing street trees. A woman passed him with two laughing children. He wondered what it would be like to live a family life with loved ones filling the silence of the rooms with happy talk and warm feelings. He had always been too shy to approach girls and now that time was long past. Who wants a man in his late fifties with nothing to offer but a bizarre viewpoint on death?

He often thought of phoning one of the marriage bureaux to see if he could find a companion with whom to spend his last few years of life. At least he didn't drink heavily, or smoke, or anything like that. *Boring*, he thought, suddenly. I live a boring life. Tomorrow. Tomorrow he would contact one of the agencies – find someone who

149

needed him. There, the decision was made. He *would* go through with it. There was surely a woman understanding enough to allow him his deviant perception without becoming frightened of it?

He picked up a bunch of leaves and threw them into the air like confetti, watching them float slowly to the ground. Suddenly, he was aware he was being observed and saw a woman hastily turn the key in the lock of her door, then disappear with a quick glance over her shoulder. He felt uncomfortable for a moment, then laughed it off. Hell, she was probably one of those old crones who peeked from behind curtains at the world outside and found it all a bit distasteful, a despicable place inhabited by odd men who threw leaves into the air and allowed them to settle on their shoulders and hair while wearing silly smiles. He wasn't going to let a woman like that put him off. It was people like her that took all the romance, all the magic out of the air, and left a dry insipid place with no hope for the future. Let her grumble into her cup of coffee and reduce her own world to ashes and dust. She wasn't going to affect *his*.

He came to his own house, entered, made himself a cup of hot milk then had a bath. Filling the time was a bit of a problem, but of course all that would change when he found himself someone to share his life. They would be able to talk, well into the night, exchanging experiences. Maybe he could find a woman with a disability of some kind, so they had something in common? It would not be like *his* problem of course, he was pretty sure he was unique, but something, some missing thing with which he could sympathise. That would make a change: to feel sorry for someone else, instead of feeling sorry for himself.

He started.

This won't do at all, he thought. No, no. He shook his head sadly. Instead of thinking about sharing happiness, he had been indulging in thoughts of exchanging feelings of *pity*. Perhaps he had lost the ability for happiness?

As the evening wore on he became a little morose again. Finally, he switched on the TV for the late night movie. It was the wrong thing to do. Late night films are almost always old ones and it turned out to be an umpteenth reshowing of *Casablanca*.

Like *St James Infirmary* the movie *Casablanca* had got to him from the first time he had seen it in 1945. There was a powerful haunting quality to the film. It spoke to him of almost-forgotten memories, good times that had gone by, friends now lost. Maybe it was the way the theme song 'As time goes by' had triggered the opening of old wounds.

He sat and watched the film, waiting for *her*.

She was all he had left now. Bogart had gone early, around '57, and so had Peter Lorre and Claude Rains. The German heavy, Conrad something or other, had died just after the film's release, and Sabastian had never seen him, which hadn't helped his comprehension any. Up until three years previously, every time he watched *Casablanca* he would make bets with himself whether the refugee would still be there; the old guy who had been the only surviving character in the film's first twenty minutes, who turned to an invisible actor to deliver that incredible line, 'We hear very little and we understand even less.' Every time he saw him, Sabastian cheered the old geezer's appearance on the screen. *Hang on in there, buddy*, he would say. Then one evening . . . he sighed, remembering . . .

He watched the empty background streets, scenes, waiting for her: his beloved survivor.

Ingrid Bergman glided into Rick's Café Américain, moving around the screen like a beautiful ghost in the silent empty room. There were drinks on the tables smouldering cigarettes in the ashtrays, and not a single person in sight. Doors opened and closed for her, chairs were pushed back as she moved along, lovely and remote, warm and mysterious, the unattainable woman in an impossible romance.

She roamed through the dead marketplace, where Persian rugs and embroidered curtains rippled and displayed themselves, craving attention. His heart went out to her, wherever she was on this earth. If he had been a poet he would have imagined her as an angel, walking with courage amongst the ruins of this dying, forgotten world. But he was a simple man, one of the strays of life, and when she spoke her lines into thin air he filled in the blanks, as she waited for the non-existent replies from the unseen Bogart.

'We'll leave Casablanca together, Ingrid,' he said out loud.

'You're the only woman I have ever loved,' he murmured, as she embraced empty space.

They were lovers in an ancient game, far from the prying eyes of the crowd. It was the only time his disability became a boon. To be alone with her, Ingrid-Ilsa, in the moonlight sequences in Paris, to kiss her one last time . . . no, there wasn't any need for that . . . he wasn't Bogey, he didn't have to be left behind. Every time he boarded

151

the plane with her on that rain-swept airfield, just before the car's doors opened of their own volition for dead German soldiers who would never, now, stop the lovers. In fact it even seemed to him once that the slamming car doors was an applause for their escape.

The image of that plane leaving Casablanca, carrying his lover with him, would keep him company well into the night. He anticipated it eagerly as, luminous, she turned towards him (Bogey?) and, with that heartbreakingly beautiful look on her face, told him, 'I said I would never leave you.'

Something was wrong with the television set . . .

Ingrid smiled faintly and then her face began to blur.

Sabastian sat upright on the sofa. Christ! That damn TV set. Not now!

She came back, one last time, a solitary tear running down her cheek. Then she was gone. She had disappeared from the film. There was nothing wrong with the set. Ilsa had gone. Ingrid Bergman was dead.

It was such a shock that Sabastian sank back into the sofa, his heart like a crumpled paper bag. She was gone, dead, forever. His Ingrid.

Bogart, the real Bogart, had her now. Had taken her away from Sabastian in the end, as if he had been mocking him from the grave, all along. *When I want her, I'll just click my fingers, sweetheart.* No, that wasn't Bogey. Bogey was hard on the outside but tender underneath. Death was the one to blame.

Such a feeling of sorrow choked him, coming out like the sound of a baby's gargle. His head developed a pain which threatened to split it from brow to the base of his neck. Death. Was it a nothingness? Was he privy to the afterworld, where there were not even shadows of the living? Just blank spaces where people had once been? Someone once glowing with animation? Was this the promise of the hereafter?

He switched off the set and sat staring at the grey screen, nursing his aching head in his hands. Tomorrow. He had to do something tomorrow. He couldn't live with this horrible knowledge alone any longer. He had to have someone to share the terrible secret with him.

He pulled open a drawer which had been closed for years and wrenched out a photo album, tearing through the pages in a kind of frenzied excitment. His father, his mother? Uncle Pete? Where? Cards with background scenes, but no people. Portrait photographs with no faces, just studio background curtains. Where was Uncle

Pete? He wanted to see him again. Study those kind old features. Nothing. An old school photo was there. Rows of chairs, only half of them occupied. All those empty seats. Nothing people who had led nothing lives and now blanks in the nothingness of death. He ripped the picture to pieces, ranting at the same time, scattering the shreds. He snarled and turned on the frame with the white card which, before 1973, had been a print of Picasso's *Bathers Playing Ball*. He took hold of it and smashed it over the back of a chair.

The shards of glass crunched under his feet as he moved around the room destroying things. His head was a ball of raging pain. It spurred him on to greater demolition. He wrenched the wires of the TV out of the socket with a savage yell of rage and sorrow.

When he had worked himself into a state of exhaustion, he crawled up the stairs. In the bathroom cabinet was a bottle of painkillers. Sabastian swallowed two, then three, then began cramming them into his mouth, washing them down with water, until he had finished the whole bottle. For a while he just leant against the white tiles, feeling their coolness behind his agony, then the pain began to recede.

He stumbled, almost fell downstairs, and moved over to the record player, putting on his favourite disc. Then over to the sofa, in front of the blank television screen.

. . . *she can look this whole wide world all over – she'll never find another man like me*. Drifting. Drifting. . . . *a boxback coat and a stetson hat*. Into the night. Long into the night. Sleep. *And the boys will know I died, standing pat*.

The piano. He could hear nothing but the piano. No clapping. At first it was faint, but then it built in volume, until Satchmo's voice growled from the platter and all the instruments began to come in, one by one.

The television was right in front of his eyes. Misty pictures began to appear on the grey screen. They seemed muddled at first, slightly distorted, coming from far away, then near. People.

What's happening? he wanted to say, but had difficulty in even just thinking the words.

The man in the white smoking jacket and bow tie turned towards the black man. He spoke with a faint lisp.

'He hasn't got it yet. Look at him,' and he nodded out at Sabastian from the screen, smiling that lopsided smile.

'You know what he wants to hear,' said the beautiful woman,

153

coming up behind the two men. 'You played it for me, now play it for him. Play it again. It's his day . . .'

The black man's face fractured into a grin, as lifting his trumpet to his lips, he said, 'Man, all those years. That's a heavy burden.'

The sounds of the trumpet filled the air and suddenly the screen began to get very crowded. Then the man in the white jacket turned and leaned out of the group. He cocked his thumb and pointed his finger.

There was a tremendous final bolt of pain in Sabastian's chest.

Playing to an empty room, the piano was the last survivor.

CHRISTINA LAKE

Wintertime Beauty

The small boy wriggled underneath the wire surrounding the building where they kept his sister and crept across to the window. He couldn't see much, so he climbed up on the ledge and pressed his nose against the hard panels of glass. The small room was very crowded, but none of the figures crawling around on the floor looked like anything that could be his sister. Through the air vent he could hear them talking to each other in what sounded like squeaks and grunts. He thought that it must be some kind of code. He watched in fascination, and was still watching when the door to the room opened. A basket was pushed inside, tipped on its edge and the door quickly closed again. Vegetables and crusts of bread rolled over the floor. The creatures in the room were quiet for a while, then gradually they resumed their former activities. One or two even began to pick at the scraps of food.

'Justin. Come down from there at once!'

He was off the sill in a second and diving for shelter, but he wasn't fast enough. His mother caught him by the belt of his coat, pulled him back to her, and slapped him hard across the face.

'I was only looking for my sister . . . ' he tried to explain.

'Never,' she said, her face contorted with fury, 'Never, let me catch you here again. These people are no concern of yours. You don't have a sister, do you understand? You don't have a sister.'

When Justin first asked if he could come and work for her at Miradoc, Helena had had her doubts. She and Meredith, Justin's mother, had been girls together at the Emergency Centre, learning what they could to live in a world where over seventy per cent of children were born unteachable, and the old technology was dying. Meredith had been a nervy, quick-tempered, difficult girl who offered little in

155

return for the friendship and attention she expected. Helena wasn't sure if she had the energy to provide a similar service for Meredith's son.

Luckily, Justin was quite different to his mother. He worked hard and was willing to take on any aspect of the tough, unglamorous life of the community, from the long hours of repair and maintenance work, to the sometimes hazardous journeys to find vital components. He was also prepared to help with those who couldn't take care of themselves – the patients in the hospice who had never grown up, only grown old, waiting for the ever more elusive cure to be found.

Miradoc meant a lot to Helena. Her grandfather had made it over to her when she spoke her first coherent sentence: thus she inherited the crumbling buildings, the underground heating plant and the care of her less able siblings and cousins. Justin had fitted in well and was happy here. So that, two years ago, when Meredith wrote demanding that her son be sent home, Helena had replied that Justin was old enough to live his own life, and had not put any pressure on the boy to return to his mother.

Now Helena's doubts returned as she switched channels on her viewing screen to look for Justin. As she had expected, he was in the hospice building. A tall figure with untidy brown hair, he was passing round spoons, whistles and other trinkets for the patients to smell and touch, never getting angry when they let things fall to the floor or lost interest in what was happening. He simply picked the objects up and started all over again, talking as he did so, as if he thought they might understand. Helena sighed for the futility of it all, then cut in to transmit her message.

'Justin, we've just had a new arrival. It's your mother.'

Justin looked up briefly towards the camera, his expression quizzical. A child, lying on the floor, began to kick chubby legs up and down, monotonously, against the carpet. Justin shrugged his shoulders and turned back to his work. Helena took this to mean he was not going to rush out and greet his mother.

She switched off the screen and hurried outside into the dark rainy courtyard where the car was still being examined by security. It was a late model rechargeable automatic-programme Mercedes: a valuable vehicle that many people would murder for. Meredith was lucky that she hadn't met any of them on the way.

Next to the car stood two women, dressed oddly for the time of year

156

in light jackets and skirts that trailed round their ankles in the mud. Helena recognised Meredith instantly. Her hair was a copper-red where it used to be brown, but her face showed the same old mixture of impatience and mistrust. She chewed on the corner of her lips, glaring at the men examining her car.

'Meredith, why didn't you say you were coming?' said Helena, crossing over to her quickly.

'Oh there you are. I was beginning to think we would have to stand out here all night.'

Helena ignored her cutting tone. 'Who's this beauty then?' she asked, turning to Meredith's companion. The girl looked like a figure from a Pre-Raphaelite painting, standing there so still, letting the wind whip through her long wavy hair and stir the folds of her skirt.

Meredith smiled with pleasure. 'This,' she said portentously, 'is my ward and special companion, Lucy Tremgloris.'

The girl looked up briefly out of strange blue eyes. Helena saw with a pang that she was indeed a beauty. As her own lost daughters might have been, perhaps. She pushed the thought aside; her daughters would have grown up big-boned and clumsy like her. 'Let's get in to Miradoc before we all perish of cold.'

She took her guests straight to the winter community building. Her husband Hugh had been drinking again; she could hear his laughter above the other voices in the room, but at least he was still sufficiently sober to greet the new guests.

'What have we here?' he asked, looking with undisguised pleasure at the beautiful girl.

'Hugh,' Helena cut in. 'This is my old friend Meredith. Justin's mother.'

Indoors, Lucy looked even less real, Helena thought. A girl made out of cloth and ivory.

'Ah yes,' said Meredith, the impatient look back on her face. 'Where *is* my son?'

'Off negotiating with some farmers, I shouldn't wonder,' said Hugh. 'He's quite an organiser, that boy of yours.'

'I wouldn't know,' remarked Meredith icily.

At dinner time, trestle tables were drawn out from cupboards and benches carried in to the big heated room where most of them ate in the winter. Helena sat at the top table, next to her husband, like the lady of some medieval castle. When she was younger she had fought against the rigid family hierarchies imposed by her grandfather. Later she had come to see the sense of it. There had to be some kind of structure if you were going to keep the community together. Helena glanced at her own son, Rowen, sitting on the other side of her husband. He looked just like Hugh had at eighteen, with the same open face, brushed-back hair and athletic body. He would be all Hugh had failed to be and more, she thought, listening to him make sensible conversation with Meredith while her husband boasted on about their horses to Lucy.

Lucy, Helena noticed, never said a word.

Meredith had her back to the rest of the room, so she didn't see when her son came in. 'Hello Justin,' said Helena, wondering what would happen next. Meredith's hand tightened around her wineglass, but she betrayed no other sign of emotion.

Justin came forward with only the slightest hesitation to the place laid out for him, near his mother. He did not seem unduly perturbed, and let his gaze pass over Meredith and on to the beautiful Lucy Tremgloris before coming back at last to his mother.

'Hello, Meredith,' he said, sitting himself down. There was no welcome or gladness in his tone.

'I see they've not fattened you up here,' remarked Meredith, casual in her turn. 'You look less healthy than you did back in Truro, and you looked unhealthy enough then I always thought.'

Justin didn't bother to answer, but started to scoop half-warm food from the serving bowls onto his plate, while normal conversation resumed all around them.

Helena breathed a sigh of relief, because there wasn't going to be a scene after all, and went back to her study of Lucy. The girl had said nothing during the meal, simply smiling when anyone spoke to her. She ate very slowly too, her movements careful and precise. Helena sensed that she was nervous, as if she thought everyone around would be watching her and passing judgement. She wondered why Meredith had come, and what she planned to do with this beautiful protégé of hers.

In the room they shared, Lucy Tremgloris shook out Meredith's clothes and hung them in the wardrobe. Meredith was bathing as she did every day in her own home, but now there was only Lucy to fetch the water. 'You might as well get some practice,' said Meredith tartly. 'You're not in care now. Here you'll act like a civilised human being AT ALL TIMES.'

This, it transpired, meant that Lucy too must bathe every day.

'I've arranged for Rowen to take you round Miradoc tomorrow,' Meredith told the girl when she emerged, still dripping, from the bath. 'Why didn't you use the towel, child?'

But Meredith wasn't really angry, and plaited Lucy's thick golden hair for her so it would be wavy in the morning.

'Don't let that drunkard husband of Helena's get you alone,' Meredith continued, putting a cap over the wet hair. 'You're not for him, you understand. There'd be no gain in snaring him.'

As Meredith talked, Lucy stared at the figure in the mirror, the pretty girl in the white cap, fascinated because she did not recognise herself.

The open air was Rowen's element. As was Miradoc where he had lived all his life. He strode joyously along its paths, telling Lucy what all the old buildings had been used for. Once it had been a university campus, but most of that had fallen down. Only the older parts remained; people had forgotten how to build later. The shell of the supermarket had survived, but the lecture theatres and the libraries and the swimming pools had all gone.

Lucy shivered, not liking to think of the times Rowen described. Also she was cold and her shoes pinched, and only the fear of Meredith's wrath stopped her taking them off and walking barefooted.

They came out by the second winter building – a mirror image of their own. Inside were those who could not take care of themselves. Lucy was glad when Rowen did not offer to show her inside.

'Most of them are old now,' he said. 'It's not that my mother's cruel. She's realistic. Every damaged child we let grow up is a burden on the next generation, and it's hard enough to support ourselves. Sometimes they have children of their own and that's even worse. My great grandfather wouldn't let any of his children be sterilised. He thought they'd breed true in the end. But we're still waiting.'

Lucy looked at the group of boys playing by the stream. Could you tell at that age which would grow up normal? she wondered. They all looked like wild animals to her.

'My mother says we can't spend all our time caring for them, or there won't be any future,' concluded Rowen.

'And I say the opposite.' It was Meredith's son Justin. He had come up to join them while Lucy was watching the children. 'They *are* the future. We might as well accept it. Three in every four births and rising. Your mother's a good woman but we can't stem the tide forever.'

'I don't want to stem it,' said Rowen. 'I only want to live.' He smiled impishly at Lucy and she smiled back, but all the time she was conscious of Justin's gaze on her.

'Lucy Tremgloris,' Justin said reflectively. 'I never heard of a Lucy Tremgloris.'

Meredith announced her intention to stay for the winter. The snows had come early and the roads to Cornwall were either unsafe or blocked off completely. Besides it was a bad time of year to travel – there were desperate people on the roads. Helena gave Meredith the spacious room that had once been the vice-chancellor's office and watched amused as her former schoolfriend turned it into an audience chamber. There Meredith held court with Lucy Tremgloris as prize exhibit, drawing to herself like-minded souls, bored by the long winter evenings, the frequent power cuts and the rowdy behaviour of those men like Hugh who found nothing better to do than drink to excess. Rowen was a frequent visitor to the rooms, as was Helena herself, who would drop in for a chat over old times, when pressure of work allowed.

Not that the old times had been so good. The air of incipient drama reminded Helena of when Meredith's second child had been certified unteachable, and Meredith had spent several weeks alternately railing against fate and pretending that the child had been perfect. She seemed to feel she had some divine right to escape the scourge; in reality anyone who made the decision to have children had to learn to live with it. Helena should know, she had lost enough children of her own this way. Meredith, though, had thrown a tantrum, divorced her husband, and had her defective daughter locked away where she need never see her again.

One of the few people who never came near Meredith's rooms was Justin. He spent more and more time at the hospice where, the joke went, he was trying to teach arithmetic, or was it astrophysics, to the three remaining children there. But there were rare encounters between mother and son, and Helena had the dubious privilege of overhearing one of them.

'I wish you wouldn't associate with those children,' Meredith was saying, clearly audible from the end of the corridor. 'People are talking.'

'So what?' asked Justin, in a tone of voice Helena had never heard from him before. 'Are you afraid it will damage Lucy's prospects?'

'Don't be obtuse, Justin. It's you I care about. I don't want people making fun of you behind your back.'

'Mother, you're the only one who's doing so,' he replied, turning on his heel and walking off in the opposite direction.

Helena hurried over to talk to Meredith, pretending she had seen and heard nothing.

It was around this time that Lucy detected a change in the drift of Meredith's plans. The hours previously spent being prepared and put on display by Meredith were shortened, and she was encouraged to get outside and walk around those parts of Miradoc where Justin might be.

'You'll make my son see reason, won't you?' said Meredith. She tipped Lucy's blemishless face up towards the light and kissed her on the cheek. 'You're a lovely girl; he won't hold it against you for long that you come from me. Not if you smile at him a few times.'

Lucy smiled obediently into the mirror, looking at the perfect white teeth of the girl who sat there so frail and delicate in the giant hands of her mistress.

'That's right. But don't forget, it's Helena's son I'm saving you for.'

Justin sat on the grassy bank of the stream while the children played by the water below him. It was a while before he noticed Lucy, and then his greeting was hardly friendly.

'Miss Lucy Tremgloris. So, you've been allowed out of my mother's keeping.'

He was wearing plain thick trousers and seemed not in the least disturbed by the mud. Lucy, on the other hand, hesitated to climb down, knowing how dirty her long pale dress would get.

'I'm taking a walk.' She wondered what excuse she could find to stay.

Justin, she saw, was plainly wondering the same thing.

'All alone? Without your escort?'

'You talk as if I can't do anything by myself.'

'Can you?'

A child screamed as it slipped in the mud, opening its mouth and letting out a mindless wail. Lucy took a step back.

161

'Of course.'

Justin went to pick up the child, whisked it around and set it back down on its feet laughing.

'Why do you spend so much time with these children?' The words came out without her meaning them to, tinged with disgust. How could he bear to touch them, to listen to their idiotic shouting, to look in their animal eyes?

Justin laughed. 'These are the normal children, Lucy. But of course in my mother's household, they don't let *those* children run wild. They don't let *those* children get dirty. They don't let them do anything that might risk their precious lives.'

'But . . . ' said Lucy. If these were normal children, what could the ones hidden away in the hospice be like?

'People are scared to let them play, because then they see there's really not so much difference. There's not much difference between the ones who will never speak, never dress themselves, never learn to read and the children they are bringing up so carefully.'

'And you want to drag them all down to the same level?' Lucy could still hardly bear to look at the children by the stream. 'You want them all dirty, all stupid, all disgusting animals?'

'Who's been telling you that, Lucy? Our less fortunate brothers and sisters are born without the ability to learn, but in the end they can be much cleaner, and certainly much nicer than the dregs of the human race we see assembled here around us. Tell that to my mother if you want.' He looked angry. 'Tell her they're not animals unless they're kept like animals.'

The fires from the old towns were alight in the hills again. Not for the first time, Helena felt like the general of a besieged army, or an explorer watching hostile natives close in on her. Her mother had been right, she shouldn't have read so indiscriminately as a child. It only made reality that much harder to bear when you knew what you had lost.

'Mother,' said Rowen, who had been waiting patiently for Helena to turn away from the window. 'I want to marry Lucy Tremgloris.'

It was not precisely a shock. Helena had seen it coming almost as soon as she had set eyes on Lucy standing in the mud, looking fragile and beautiful, and Meredith behind her with that scheming look on her sharp, ageless face. Ah, Meredith, I can read you like all those books I shouldn't have read in my youth. But what is the girl's secret?

162

'I'm thinking,' said Helena, 'we don't know much about Lucy Tremgloris. Don't rush things, Rowen. We have a whole winter ahead of us.'

'What is there to know that we can't see already?'

'Nothing, I expect. I'm just getting overcautious in my old age. Will you do this for me, Rowen? Don't say anything till the winter's over?'

'But supposing someone else . . . ' The boy floundered, his face turning a rosy pink.

'Someone else claims her first? I daresay Lucy has a mind of her own.' – A fact which Helena privately doubted – 'She probably guesses what you feel so let her use her judgement. I don't think you'll be disappointed.'

Lucy wandered into the library. Restless and curious, she took out book after book, leafed through one, put it down and tried another. Some had strange shiny pictures of things she had never seen, but most of them were just words, endless lines of black characters, telling of matters people had once thought important and now no one cared about. She began reshelving her pile.

'Let me.' Justin padded up to her on his soft indoor shoes. '*A Tale of Two Cities*. Miradoc and Truro, do you think?'

She said nothing. Meredith made her recite poetry to her friends and talk about the latest Cornish writers, but she had never said anything about *A Tale of Two Cities*.

'Very eclectic,' he said, reading the other titles. 'My mother's toy is now taking an interest in palaeontology.'

'Not so,' she said, goaded at last by his rudeness. 'I only wanted to see how much stupidity people could write. And now I know. Nothing in these books could possibly interest me.'

'So I should imagine. Because you can't read, can you?'

It was a guess, Lucy thought. It had to be. Unless there was something people who read books did that she'd forgotten.

Justin was looking at her strangely, as if surprised himself at what he had just said. 'No, that doesn't make sense. My mother's very thorough. She would at least have taught you to read before she brought you here.'

So that's what he thought, Lucy realised. That she was some rough, travelling child adopted by his mother out of spite, to trick her friends.

'Unless,' Justin continued, 'Unless there was too much else she had to teach you . . . '

'No,' said Lucy, turning away. 'No. Of course I can read. Everybody can read.'

'Good,' said Justin. 'Then come with with me to read to the children in the hospice.'

But Lucy went on staring out of the window, and would not turn round till Justin was safely out of the room.

'Rowen has asked me to marry him,' Lucy told Meredith. 'But he wants me to keep it a secret till the spring.'

'Word will get out. It always does.'

'I. I'd rather it didn't,' said Lucy. It had begun to occur to her that she did not want to marry Rowen. He bored her.

'*You'd* rather. Who do you think you are? Marry before spring, and Rowen will look after you for life, one way or another. Wait for the thaw and it may be too late. Besides Helena will make enquiries about you all through Cornwall, and then see if she will let you anywhere near her precious son.'

And what of your son? thought Lucy.

But Justin only seemed to despise her. She saw him striding off towards the hospice, but still could not bring herself to join him, to let herself be dragged into that dark, insane world. Instead she concentrated on preparing for New Year, helping Rowen and the few other people of their age build the great bonfire in the courtyard.

When the time came to light it, Lucy was scared. She stood watching Rowen and his father bending to insert flame into the heart of the pyre, fussing around with matches and wood until at last they were satisfied it would take. She did not smile like the others as the flames crept across the wood, rising upwards to hiss and spit at them. She knew why she didn't like it. The fire created shadows. She tried to keep her attention on the warm, moving bodies around her in the bright circle of the fire's light, but every now and then her eyes were drawn away beyond the fire.

There was something out there. She could see it move. Not a person. Not an animal. A shadow within the shadow, lumbering in the darkness.

'Take a sausage, Lucy. Rowen's waiting for you.'

She turned back to the light. Meredith thrust a toasting fork into her hands, and Lucy used it to spear a pink shiny tube of meat.

It was worse standing by Rowen, her arm stretched out, the fire hot on her face. Now the thing was behind her, advancing at her out of the darkness. She wanted to run away, but when she glanced sideways, looking for an escape route, all she could see was Justin watching her with his sarcastic eyes. She tried to concentrate on toasting the sausage, but on the edge of her vision she caught the movement again – something hitching itself along in the darkness. Coming towards her, as if it knew . . .

She watched mesmerised as it crawled into the circle, seeing a white face inhumanly smooth caught in the firelight, and baby-blue eyes, gazing up at her, completely innocent, completely mad.

She didn't realise she had screamed out till she felt Justin's hand on her arm. 'It's all right. It's only one of Helena's cousins. Attracted by the light. They're taking her back now.'

Rowen had moved in to help, and already they had lifted the mad woman out of the circle.

'No,' said Lucy. 'She was coming for me.'

Justin took Lucy back to her room. She lay on the bed and stared at the ceiling.

'Are these what you take?' He had found the drugs in a cupboard. Lucy nodded. She didn't know what was in them. Only that she had to take them twice a day or she stopped understanding things, started to slip back into the darkness.

'I knew there was something wrong about you from the start,' said Justin, still wandering restlessly around his mother's room. 'There weren't so many girls of your age in Truro – I would have remembered you. I thought my mother might have bought you, except you were too pretty and she wouldn't have been able to afford the price. None of it added up. Why supply Rowen with a beautiful wife? Why couldn't you recognise normal children when you saw them? Why mess up the library? It took me a long time to believe, but it's true, isn't it? You were born one of them.'

Lucy didn't have the strength to deny it any more. She and the creature with the staring eyes had the same inheritance, the same defect that had cursed the human race for almost a century now: the inability to learn and the insanity that drew them further and further away from normal life as they grew older.

Justin came and sat on the edge of the bed.

'I know so little,' she told him, feeling she owed him whatever

165

explanation she could give. 'There was just darkness and warmth and food to eat. Then people started making me do things. They bullied me. It was like waking up from a long sleep, and not wanting to be awake.'

But now I'm awake, she thought, I don't want to go back to sleep again.

'You shouldn't be ashamed. You shouldn't be pretending. What's happened to you is good. It's good for everyone.'

Yes, Lucy thought. It certainly felt good to her: having Justin's approval at last. Then she looked up and saw Meredith.

'So you think we've found a miracle cure?' Meredith stepped into the room, a half-eaten sausage still in her hand. 'I know Miradoc is a backwater compared to Truro, but don't you think you'd have heard something, Justin?'

'What are you saying? That Lucy was born normal after all?'

'I'm saying that it won't last. Lucy will forget. She will require higher and higher doses of the drugs, until it will be a choice between her mind and her body, because they will be destroying her liver.'

'And you started this, knowing what it would do? Just to see Rowen married to a mad woman? Helena's your friend.'

'Yes, she's my friend, and she took my son.'

'Nobody took your son.' Justin had forgotten about Lucy; he'd forgotten everything except his old feud with his mother. 'I left of my own accord. Nobody took me, it was you, you and your cruel experiments that drove me away. And if Helena hadn't taken me in I'd have gone somewhere else, that's all. Because I'd have never gone back to you. Never. And I never will.'

Lucy put a pillow over her head and began to cry. If the darkness was going to come, she hoped it would come quickly. She felt Justin's hand on her shoulder, and she cried all the more, because it was too late now. The only hands that she'd know in the future would be those that fed and dressed her.

Helena stood in the dining hall on her son's wedding day, and smiled at the guests like any mother would. Only she could not quite bring herself to smile at Meredith. Not just for what she had done to Rowen, though that hurt every time she thought of it. Rowen had made a difficult decision, and she was proud of the decision he had made, but at the same time she knew it would cost him more than he realised. More than he could possibly know just now.

166

But it was the thought of what Meredith had done to Lucy, and why, that would stop them ever being friends again.

Lucy looked beautiful in white lace; only her face gave her away. She wasn't the perfect doll that Meredith had brought with her any more. She looked more like a lost bewildered child. One more daughter Helena would have to let go.

'At least she's had the chance to live,' said Justin from her side. 'She's luckier than most.'

He went up to give the couple their present. Helena could see that it was a book, and thought that she could guess Justin's words to the bride.

'I'm going to teach you to read,' was what he said.

It was a futile gesture in a day of futile gestures, but for the first time since the night of the bonfire, Lucy smiled.

KEITH N. BROOKE

Passion Play

The rabbit had been dead for some time and its body was furred with a poisonous-looking mould. Blackbird wanted to eat it but was mindful of what she had been taught. The mould could be dangerous, it might be *imbuto*: its invasive hyphae might penetrate and infest her own crusty mycelium, drawing the life slowly from her body.

Unable to decide, she lay down and spread her wing-like underarm membranes in the hot spring sun. She closed her eyes and crooned softly in her wattled throat. The warmth felt good, penetrating her microflora, soaking through the fungal outer layers of her skin. With long fingers she groomed the matted surface of her arms and legs and as she did so she watched the unmoving rabbit. She needed the energy for the approaching display but still she was wary.

The sun was aiding her preparation, anyway. It helped her relax, eased the tension that had been dogging her. She had displayed many times before, and had never suffered from nerves. But now she was a star.

Gradually the more experienced women had secured their partners and most were now back with their mother groups, proudly bearing their children in love-humps. Blackbird and her sister, Streak, were now at the top of the heap; the others were too young and inexperienced to mount a serious challenge. Streak was the oldest and should have expected to find a partner first, but Blackbird's voice was sweeter, more alluring; that was why Blackbird had been named for her soft tones and Streak only for the silver strip that ran down the centre of her otherwise plain green back.

As children, Blackbird and Streak had lived with their mother group in the skeleton of an old pink-stoned house. There had been no roof and no windows and the children had all been scared by late-night stories of what might live beyond their walls. That house

169

had been secure and Blackbird's vague memory-images of it made her feel good. The fears had been forgotten. But she did remember the lessons the mothers had drilled into her, time and again. *Never go into a strange house alone. Keep away from the Old Town.*

The dangers of the countryside were subtle and insidious, like the rabbit with the possibly invasive fungal coating that Blackbird so wanted to eat. But the dangers of the Old Town were more direct. Animals lurked in the buildings and the old underground tunnels. Beasts that could walk faster than Blackbird could even run, with her slow, shambling gait.

But she had needed something that would help her perform better than Streak, so on the morning of the display she had gone to the Old Town, shuffling along over an asphalt strip that was pitted with holes and tufted with clumps of spring flowers.

The houses were square and made of red bricks, not the rounded pink stone she associated with security. She had visited the Old Town as a girl, but then she had been one of a group; the mothers had been scavenging and, at the same time, teaching the children the dangers of the world. Then it had been an adventure. Alone it was terrifying. There were strange noises, strange creatures scurrying away through the fallen masonry, strange scents of decay and – more frighteningly – smells of vibrant, active life.

She had chosen a house more or less at random. Leaving the road, she had advanced cautiously, skirting a high pile of bricks that was topped by a pungent, writhing crown of moss. A puppy had snapped at her feet but its roots were planted firmly in the rubble so she ignored it.

Once inside the building, smells of animate life diminished and Blackbird managed to relax a little. She pulled at a cupboard door and a cube fell out and landed at her feet. Immediately a curious pink head, fringed with brown hair, appeared in the air above the cube. Despite its strange colour the head looked almost human. Its eyes looked straight at Blackbird and its mouth opened. 'Darling,' it said. 'I still love you but it's bad for us both. I'm sorry.' The head vanished.

Its words were strangely formed, like the words of the songs Blackbird was seeking. She nudged the cube with one foot and the head re-appeared. 'Darling. I still love you but it's bad for us both. I'm sorry.'

Blackbird turned away and began to search through the cupboard.

170

Eventually, in another room, she found what she was looking for. It was a cube, much like the first, but this one didn't cast up a ghostly face when it was moved; instead, it played a song. It was beautiful, a tune she had never heard before. Mentally, she shaped her tongue to the words and committed it all to her memory. When the final notes had left the cube Blackbird struck it against a wall. It broke in two, then crumbled and finally the pieces vanished into the air. Blackbird's new song was her own.

The tune had played through her mind many times but she would not sing it out loud until she was on the display ground with a male to hear it. The sun had reached its highest point and Blackbird rose from where she had been lying. It was nearly time to sing her song.

She eyed the rabbit again. One of the girls from the mother group had eaten food coated in a fungal layer that had been *imbuto*. It had invaded her body, taken it over, and she had been driven away to die in the wilderness. The poisonous spores from her corpse could have killed the entire group. Blackbird still had nightmares where all she could recall were the pain-filled screams of her *imbuto* friend.

Eventually there always came a time of commitment: eat it or leave it. In the end you have to fall back on instinct. She left the rabbit.

On her way to the display ground, she scooped up some berries and folded them into one of her false wings. Instantly tiny nerve-filled hyphae penetrated the fruit, like eager babies' fingers. As the nutrients began to pass into her body she knew that the fruit was good. Slowly she walked on, the refrain of her new song filling her head.

Girls on the fringe were faltering in mid-song and Blackbird knew that something was happening. She hoped desperately that the disturbance was due to the arrival of a man. There had been occasions recently when they had performed for most of a day without a man appearing on the scene.

There were at least thirty women gathered for the display. The senior performers held territories in a central patch of flattened vegetation, raised slightly and edged with kerbstones. The less experienced women performed on the surrounding circular road and in the openings of other roads that radiated from the circle.

Blackbird had been one of the last to arrive; she knew that nothing ever happened in the early stages. A young pretender had been in her space, crooning and flashing her false wings at anyone who cared to look. The girl had fled when Blackbird approached.

171

Streak had arrived a short time later, crossing Blackbird's patch to reach her own. Blackbird had cursed and sung a threatening cascade of notes at her sister but Streak had only waggled her throat wattles in mock apology. They both knew that this was the big showdown.

Striving for calm, Blackbird continued her warm-up and tried to ignore the disturbance. She would not look until her sister had done so first.

One by one, the experienced women glanced towards the fringes and then stepped up their displays.

By now Blackbird was sure that a male was on the display ground and the need to look diminished. As if struck by the same realisation, Streak spread her false wings and sent darts of colour sparking across her fungal outer skin from the silver stripe that ran down her spine. Notes rose from her throat, bubbling indecisively, finding no tune.

Blackbird tried to match her sister's chameleon display. She made her skin phosphoresce in waves of pastel colours, her mind full of the spring flowers she had seen in the Old Town. She sang an old song, one that demonstrated the delicacy of her tones.

Some of the others were singing raucously, excitement tainting their judgement. One of the women near to Streak faltered and then tried to start again.

Then Blackbird saw the approaching man and she felt her own throat tighten and her notes almost faded from the air.

He was small, even for a man. He barely reached the bottom of Blackbird's rib-cage. His head was big, his body thin and malnourished; he would not provide a woman with much of a love-hump but there was little choice these days. Any man was better than none at all.

His movements seemed to flow disjointedly and his head lolled from side to side. His hand was between his legs, holding his penis out, waving it at the women. *This is my gift*, his mad grin seemed to be saying. He waved it at Blackbird and she felt herself go weak. Then he waved it at Streak and the battle was on.

Streak turned her back to the man and flashed violent colours across her wing-membranes. She bent over and displayed her genitals, waves of colour drawing even Blackbird's eyes down to what was on offer.

The man jumped up and down and grunted.

Streak's song was one she had sung many times, a tune learnt in the mother group. Her false wings wrapped protectively around herself, Blackbird joined her sister's song. She made her voice grate mockingly, allowed the tune to waver. She drew no response from her sister but the man looked curiously between the two of them.

Breaking from her sister, Blackbird burst into the song she had found in the Old Town. '*Leaves, disks, Lap-top twists,*' she sang, the words meaning nothing to her, merely sounds she had memorised. '*Slowing on the highway, low.*' Many of the performers stopped just to listen. They could have heard nothing like it before. It might have been a song written specially for Blackbird's triumph.

Not content to let her song do all the work, Blackbird slowly allowed her self-embrace to relax. Delicate quivers passed through her body, in curious counterpoint to the music. '*Slice, cut, Lap-top slut.*' She let one arm drop away from her phosphorescing torso. '*Rising on the blackout, white.*' She let her body sway and hummed an orchestral interlude.

The man appeared hypnotised by her performance. She knew that victory was close, her sister would have to wait for another day.

Then he looked back at Streak. She was dancing to Blackbird's song, miming to her sister's music, humming out of key. She was mocking her, trying to echo the way Blackbird had stolen her limelight.

Streak's song began to wander from Blackbird's; perhaps she had realised that her voice could not compete with that of her sister.

Blackbird thought she recognised the song her sister was moving into, but then she caught the words, blurred by her sister's poor diction, and knew that this was something altogether different. Streak must have found a new music box too.

The man had been standing between the two of them but now he took a step towards Streak. Blackbird put even more into her song and drew him back to the centre. The other women were nothing to Blackbird; some just watched but most were driven to continue their displays by the presence of the man.

Looking from sister to sister, he waved his penis about and jumped up and down. He grunted eagerly as if trying to join the music, his noises unintelligible due to his excitement. Blackbird knew they could actually speak when they were calmer, or at least they could before puberty, when they were still part of their mother group.

Streak seemed to be winning. Desperately, Blackbird decided to try her sister's crude tactics. She had never been this close to winning a mate before. She lay on her back and spread her legs, writhing about as she sang, trying to tempt him with her body.

He stepped towards her. Then he took another step and another. They could almost touch.

Streak began to cry aloud, flapping her wings slowly as if she could fly. Colours seemed to flow off her body and there was a curious musical quality to her cries.

The man turned, distracted from Blackbird, drawn again to her sister.

Blackbird stood up and grabbed him. He was surprisingly light. She lifted him and tucked him under her arm, turned and shambled away as fast as she could.

There was an outraged scream from behind, but Blackbird didn't slow. The other women looked on in disbelief, nothing like this had ever happened before and they were not going to interfere. The man seemed content in Blackbird's arms and she moved as fast as she was able.

Streak was bigger and slower. Her wide underarm membranes – so useful on the display ground – slowed her and Blackbird began to widen the gap between the two of them.

When she had finally left her sister behind, Blackbird put the man down in front of her and looked him up and down.

A man.

He waved his penis at her and she smiled. She was falling in love with him already.

Their courtship lasted until the sun began to redden in the cloudless sky. Throughout, Blackbird could not understand why such a ritual should be insisted upon but she managed to cope. After all, she had a *man*. She had never known an adult man before and had only seen them as they were seduced by the older women at the display grounds. Now she could touch him, smell him, even talk with him in a stilted manner.

She had wanted to consummate their relationship straightaway, but instead she had held back. The mothers had always insisted that courtship should not be hurried. *You must know the man*, they had said. *You must be sure of him. You must* love *him.*

They had been such strange, frightening words. Yet now she felt both strange and just a little bit frightened.

It was almost impossible for her to communicate with her prospective mate. 'Mother group where?' she had asked him. 'Me-mine in pink-stone.'

174

Her question was clear but all he had done was grunted and rubbed his penis. 'Cock sex,' he had said, his first intelligible words. '*Sex.*'

The boys from the mother group had been just as bright as the girls. They could talk, they could read their surroundings, there was nothing different about them. But men – if this could be regarded as a typical man – appeared stupid, unaware of the world around them.

Despite the communication barrier, Blackbird rapidly grew fond of him. Close up, she could see the ritual scarring on his face, she could see how strange his fungal skin looked, so unlike any she had seen before. He so obviously wanted her as his mate – he had chosen her instead of all the others – and there was the way his eyes kept darting nervously about, independent of his movements. Once, his passion became so great that all he could do was stand shivering, saying, 'Cock sex cock sex cock sex,' over and over. Blackbird had been tempted but, remembering her teachings, she had kept her distance until he calmed down. She felt that she knew him, now, but she had been taught that she must *love* him, too.

Later, he gave her flowers. He picked them with his own hands, rubbed them along his penis and then thrust them eagerly into her face. They had tasted good.

Finally, she felt that she loved the strange little man. She had been cautious, she had taken her time, but – as the mothers had also taught her – there comes a moment when you have to suck and see. In the end, you have to fall back on instinct. As they stood by a quiet little stream, she reached for him and turned him to face her. 'Cock sex *now*', she said, hoping he would understand.

A look of fear flashed across his face. He clearly understood. 'Sex eat *die*. No!'

Blackbird had a firm grip on his wrists. His reaction was unsettling but she felt that she could understand it. But this was the way of things. She leaned back in a bed of grey grass and pulled him down with her. As their bodies pressed together he gave in to the inevitable and began to cooperate.

They moved together for a time, then Blackbird knew it was drawing to a close. The man curled up against her and his head pressed into her rib cage. Her arms had been spread out by her side but now she raised them and wrapped them around her lover. His body heaved and she held him in her wings, felt the strange writhing of her hyphae melding with those of the man, gripping, penetrating, binding. She lay back and let it happen.

175

Lying by the hurrying stream, Blackbird's world gradually settled back around her. She unfurled her arms and looked down at her new love-hump. Already its features were fading, the outline of the man was melting away. Already it was impossible to tell where he had finished and she began. The hyphae of her fungal skin were still writhing, growing accustomed to the new presence. Now she could think of finding a mother group, either her old one or a new one, she wasn't sure which yet.

Just then, vague thoughts began to flow through her head. She had expected this: the man in his final act of penetration, shreds of his persona trying to lodge in her own. It would pass soon.

But this was more disturbing than she had been told. Suddenly Blackbird knew what it was to be eaten slowly alive, what it was to fade slowly from the world, what it was to be dead yet horribly aware.

Blackbird tried to shut her mind to the thoughts but it was impossible. The only image of her own she could draw upon was the rejected meal, the rabbit covered with mould that may or may not have been *imbuto*.

Like the fungal skin of her lover.

Another image invaded her mind. She was lying dormant yet alive. She could feel poisonous spores bubbling up from her own mouldering body.

She looked down at herself, at her new love-hump. Relieved, she saw that she was not mouldering as the image had had it. But there, amongst the writhing hyphae, she could see the man's fungal flesh merging with her own, flowing into her. His crusty skin was gradually moving down and spreading over her body.

Suddenly, she realised why the man had been so reluctant at the last moment. Why he had struggled, trying to protect *her*, not himself. And she knew why the mothers had been so careful. *You must know him*, they had said. *You must love him*.

He might be *imbuto*, they should have said.

Frightened now, she felt alien hyphae digging into her flesh and then, finally, she felt the first pains.

CHRIS MORGAN

Losing Control

Ellis Tateosian got married at nine in the morning – or at least, about three hours after the blue-white sun crawled above the horizon.

This marriage was a milestone. Not so much for being his eleventh as because Wanda was the first of his granddaughters to achieve puberty. She seemed to be doing fine and enjoying the arrangement, if the tiny gasps she was making now – at maybe nine thirty a.m. with Tateosian on top of her – were anything to go by. He had kept the ceremony brief as usual, conducting it himself. After all, he was still captain, wasn't he? And now he was enjoying what he thought of as the first course of the wedding breakfast.

'Ah-hum! Sir?' said a voice from the cave entrance.

Without losing rhythm, Tateosian turned his head. Silhouetted against the furious daylight was Jay, his second son, standing to attention, waiting for permission to speak. He was naked, as they all were. None of the indestructible uniforms had lasted past the tenth year and now, after twenty-nine years of the colony, scarcely any of the tools or artifacts were usable either.

Tateosian said equably, 'Get out . . . Go see . . . Scott . . . Let him make . . . a decision . . . for a change.' Scott was his eldest son, frighteningly unimaginative but efficient at obeying orders.

'Sorry to disturb you, sir. Scott sent me. It's Hopalong – looks like it's giving birth!'

Realising that the interruption was unassailable, Tateosian sighed and allowed himself to slip out of Wanda. He patted one of her small breasts unselfconsciously. 'Stay here. I'll be back as soon as I can.'

He stood up slowly in case dizziness should strike. When it didn't he stepped from the niche and moved briskly to the back of the cave, rinsing his hands and face in the streamlet that trickled down the wall there. Drops hung in his full beard, making the white streaks gleam.

177

He walked round Crab, which occupied the middle of the cave, touching its flank with no less gentleness or love than Wanda's breast. Stooping, he picked up a nugget of food from the floor beneath the creature's mandibles. He bit into it as he led the way out of Crab Cave; today it was pale yellow and smelt of cream cheese but the texture was more crunchy.

The short tunnel merged with the rocky overhang which fronted all the caves and kept the worst of the heat and light at bay. Tateosian hurried along the strip of relative shade to the far end – to Hopalong Cave – shielding his eyes with his hand and trying to breathe only through his nose. Even through the haze of volcanic dust it was a scene too bright and ferocious for human eye: better to view its shadow at the back of the cave, he always thought.

What surprised him most when he arrived was the hubbub. About thirty people – almost the whole colony – were grouped around the alien. The adults argued while children ran about, laughing and shouting, their pink and brown forms darting through the gloom, their voices combining to fill the lofty hemisphere with a jungle of sound.

'Quiet!' he said, raising his voice only slightly, his deeper tones sharpening as echoes. He had never needed to shout in order to impose his authority. 'Listen to me! I want this cave clear in two minutes except for Scott, Jay and Crystal. Food and cleaning details disperse to the other caves. Diane, you can teach school in Big Spider today. Meg, I want you to go and keep Wanda company. Tell her everything is under control but I may be delayed for a while. Anybody else who's usually in Hopalong can use Maple-leaf. Carry out your normal duties as far as possible. Understood? Now, children first, move!' Giving orders was second nature to him. It was a lonely business, maintaining discipline, holding himself apart from the rest of them, yet it had to be done. For the good of them all, it had to be done.

As they streamed out quietly he approached Hopalong. Unlike the others it was named for its motility rather than its shape. Resembling an outsize pear some ten feet tall, it could bounce along on the globular base, pointing the upper spindle in the direction of travel. It seemed to be the least specialised or most adaptable of the five aliens, and even after almost three decades of watching it Tateosian found himself still surprised by its ability to produce a mouth or manipulative or sensory organs at any part of its surface. Normally its waxy skin pulsed with faint purple and yellow patterns, though now it was a uniform dull lime.

Hopalong was leaning against the cave wall, its base split open and a soft pearly ovoid, eighteen inches across, oozing slowly out. It was new in the humans' experience.

For a moment Tateosian was shocked. Was the creature ill, dying maybe? There was something obscene about that ovoid. Then he recalled what Jay had said.

'What d'you think, Crys?' he asked. Apart from being his first wife she had, once upon a time, served as medic and senior biologist of an interstellar expedition.

'Almost certainly parturition,' she said.

Already understanding, but, as usual, irked by her insistence on using scientific jargon, he pressed her. 'You mean it's having a baby?'

'Funny looking baby,' said Scott with a snort of laughter.

Tateosian silenced him with a glance.

Crystal shook her head and the white hair swirled. 'You know it's dangerous to think in human or even in Earth terms.' She was speaking to her son, Scott, but Tateosian knew that she was chiding him.

'Do we know how long Hopalong's been like this?'

Jay said, 'Since dawn, sir. It – she? – was leaning over when I woke up. I told Crystal and Scott before the ceremony but we didn't want to worry you.'

'Sure.' Tateosian was trying to think on his feet. It was funny how he'd come to take the strange and unexplained for granted because it was the same strange and unexplained as yesterday and the day before. But Hopalong's condition was the first wholly new thing the planet had provided in maybe twenty years or more.

His authority had grown as the size of the colony had grown – from nine to thirty-two – but the situations had all been much the same after the first traumatic year or so. He'd been able to maintain his command with relative ease, drifting through a haze of nubile flesh without making any difficult decisions. At the back of his mind he'd always thought of this place as an abnormal situation which would correct itself, or as a kind of dream from which he would someday awake. Meanwhile he'd done his best – hadn't he? – to ensure that a little bit of America survived on this alien soil, with most of the traditions he'd grown up with still proudly intact. Or – he corrected himself – with some of the traditions intact. Many things were

179

different for reasons of expediency, but at least he'd kept the inadvertent colony going. They were still united, healthy and well-fed after almost thirty years. He'd done his duty as a leader and father; could anybody have done more? In many respects it was an idyllic life he'd achieved for them all.

He decided to consult the nearest thing to an expert. 'So what would you recommend?' he asked Crystal. 'Try to help or leave it in peace?'

'Probably the latter. If it's not a natural function there's little we could do to help.'

So they could do nothing and he could do nothing, but to prevent himself feeling powerless Tateosian issued a string of orders. 'Okay, Jay, I want you to stay in the tunnel and keep Hopalong under observation. You can have somebody with you if you want. But stay back and report any changes. The rest of us will leave now. If anybody wants me urgently, I'll –'

'Excuse me.' It was Diane. 'Big Spider's gone quiescent and I think it's splitting just like Hopalong.'

Over the years Tateosian had established a strict rota system for sleeping individually with his wives. (He never thought it odd that at the age of sixty-two he still retained the capacity and the enthusiasm for nightly lovemaking.) That night he spent with Wanda, properly consummating their marriage. After all, it was his duty to help enlarge the colony, wasn't it?

And in the morning, by the first pale light of dawn, he could see that Crab, too, was giving birth. Like the rest its offspring was soft and almost shapeless – a jelly egg which flattened under its own weight. It gleamed with a pearly whiteness. That similarity of offspring, and the fact that all were giving birth together, was the first proof that the five dissimilar aliens were related. He rested a hand on Crab's back and wished – not for the first time – it could answer when he talked to it. He could think of nothing constructive to do about the situation.

In the early years he had often asked Crystal, 'Are they intelligent?'

Her answer had always been the same: 'There are no universal parameters for intelligence. It's a function of cultural patterns, communication and awareness. If a life-form is too different from us we may never recognise its intelligence – and vice versa. Of course, commensalism does not require intelligence or even awareness to operate perfectly.'

Now Tateosian knelt down to inspect the ovoid. He touched it gingerly. It felt slimy and seemed to quiver very slightly. He snatched his hand away and went to perform his morning rituals as if all were normal. He washed at the back of the cave, drank two handfuls of water and combed his long hair – now mostly white – back with his fingers, tying it at the nape of his neck. His breakfast was a handful of food dropped by Crab: this time it was brown in colour, smelling of carrots but tasting almost like chocolate.

The first duty of the new day was to mark the calendar. He took up his scriber (one of the few usable pieces of metal remaining) and added another short scratch to the regimented thousands. The days on this world were within three per cent of Earth normal duration, but the length of the years was unknown. There seemed to be no axial tilt or procession of seasons, and the stars were rarely visible through the dense atmosphere. He ascertained that it was Saturday and crossed off another week. Elsewhere on the walls of Crab Cave were his carvings: animals and flowers chipped out from memory, representing years of patient work.

Wanda came up behind and hugged him. He smiled and led her outside – properly outside, a few paces beyond the overhang, into the quietest part of the day.

'After doing the calendar,' he said, 'I always look across at the city to see if I can learn anything new.'

'The city?'

'Over there. Follow my finger. Just to the left of that bluish rock.'

'It's all a blur,' she said.

'Ahh.' He had forgotten her myopia, which never normally mattered. 'It's my optimistic name for a regular formation of some kind, the other side of the valley. Could be ten or fifteen miles away. I don't suppose anybody else thinks about it these days – I know you young ones have got your own mythologies. Anyway, it's unattainable and unknowable but I've never given up hope. I always watch it for a couple of minutes just before sun-up, when the seeing's best.' He didn't need to mention that this was also the safest time to be out. In theory the night predators had sought shelter while the daytime horrors had not warmed up sufficiently to move.

Yet he'd never forgotten what happened to Darrell and Jase, the first week after the crash. Two good men. He could still see them, in

181

green fatigues and armed with laser pistols, running through the dawn the quarter mile downhill to the ship. A lot of smallish creatures had swarmed over them. They hadn't screamed for long. And a little later Tateosian had seen something large fly overhead with a human leg in its mouth. Of course, the wreck had disintegrated over the years. Storm, acid rain, vegetation and animal life had all taken their toll, and only a jagged brown patch showed where it had been. Meanwhile the colony had survived, even prospered, without those vital items – what were they? – that he'd sent them to fetch. Could it have been that he'd known the dangers and sent out the only other men to their deaths deliberately?

'Did I want all six women so badly?'

'Pardon, Ellis?'

'Nothing.' He looked towards the city, unchanged by its exposure to the harsh environment. A time or two he'd seen rocket exhausts there, or aircraft coming in to land, though they could just as easily have been volcanic activity or giant birds. Today it looked no different. Probably it was just rocks, and the aliens were no more than dumb animals.

'If Crab and the others were intelligent,' he said, 'they wouldn't live here in bare caves without possessions.'

'Why not?' asked Wanda. 'We do.'

Tateosian could find no answer to that. He shook his head and escorted her back to safety.

Soon after sun-up he made his rounds of the five caves.

The situation was not good. Each of the aliens had given birth or was giving birth to a jelly blob: that was okay. But Hopalong and Big Spider – who were a day ahead of the others – had stopped producing food: that was potentially disastrous.

Tateosian spoke with Bea, who was in charge of food stocks. She was also the only first-generation female who'd turned him down. That didn't bother him so much any more, though it still rankled that he'd never been able to beat her at chess or go (she was the colony champion at both). He just accepted her for what she was and they had a reasonable working relationship. Which means we still disapprove of each other, he thought, but most of the time we try not to show it. Though he couldn't resist winding her up now and then, knowing it to be an expression of his feelings of inadequacy at being unable to impose his will on her through games or sex.

'So how long can we last out?' he asked her.

'We have five days of normal rations. And we seem to be gathering three-fifths of normal today. Nutritionally it wouldn't hurt too much to go onto half rations, so we'll be all right for eleven days including today.'

'Could we reduce rations even further?'

'No, it'd be self-defeating. Some variants are already deteriorating after a week. Ten or twelve days is about the maximum most of it'll keep.'

'Okay,' he said. 'And what about the types that last almost indefinitely – the stuff you must've been squirrelling away over the years for your own use?'

'I've been doing no such thing!'

He noted the flush on her cheeks and on her thin, floppy breasts. 'I believe you, Bea. Keep calm.'

'But what happens if they don't start producing food again within eleven days?'

'We cut open an alien.' He smiled at her aghast expression. 'They'll feed us one way or another. See you later, Bea.' He dismissed her and she left him in Crab Cave.

He was more worried than he was prepared to admit. Like all the others, showing so much flesh whether he liked it or not had made him learn to conceal his emotions.

All the colony's food came from the five aliens, but in a peculiarly enigmatic fashion. Every thirty-ninth day – plus or minus three – Hopalong, Crab, Big Spider, Little Spider and Maple-leaf bounced, crawled or oozed out of their respective caves and took a constitutional in the great outdoors. For some reason they were mostly ignored by predators. On the unusual occasions when they were attacked they came to no apparent harm but their attackers were either repulsed or splattered against the rocks. (Whatever their defence mechanism, the aliens had never employed it against a human.) The five moved out of sight into a ground depression about six hundred yards away. They reappeared ten hours later and ten to fifteen per cent bulkier.

It was so infuriating not to know exactly what they did out there, and the only attempt to find out – back in the second year – had been a terrible failure. Suzie had tied herself securely beneath Big Spider, but she hadn't returned.

Crystal had theorised that the aliens loaded up with a proto-food, probably dried, which they could store for long periods, making up small amounts each day into edible form by the addition of enzymes and water. But for some reason the finished food – infinitely variable in taste and consistency – was not directly assimilated. It was always passed out of the body and manipulated by tentacles, claws or mandibles before being taken into the mouth and digested. In the process some forty per cent of the food fell to the floor – a terrible waste unless it was necessary to fertilise the ground or to feed a commensal species.

Tateosian sat down on the floor and leaned against Crab, hugging its flank, watching it eat and contemplating the blob that rested beside it. He knew that he could never bring himself to harm one of the aliens, despite his contrary assertions to Bea. Oh, he'd never openly worshipped the aliens, not even in the mild cargo-cult way that Bea and a few of the others did. To him the aliens were more like friends – as solid and unchanging down the years as he felt himself to be. He would no more cut one of them up for food than slice a meal from his own arm. So many times he'd felt himself to be on the verge of communication with one of them – especially Crab. Nor would he risk hurting a blob: there was no telling how an alien parent would react.

With a jolt he realised that he was no longer in command of the colony.

The aliens were. Perhaps they had been all along, intelligent or not, but now it was out in the open. They could provide food for the colony or not. They held the cards, the power of life and death. It was their play. He could only wait, reacting when they moved, acquiescing to his loss of power. But the responsibility was his. He should have thought of this, made contingency plans, done more to ensure the continued wellbeing of the thirty-one people whom he had – perhaps arrogantly – presumed to lead.

Feet were almost silent on the smooth rock but his ears caught the quick padding and he looked up at Wanda as she hurried in.

'What's happened?' he asked her. 'What's Hopalong doing?' It was more than just a guess.

'I'm not sure. But it could be eating its baby.'

'No!' He pulled himself upright against Crab, paused for a second and followed her out.

Hopalong had sprouted new appendages. With a pair of stubby tentacles it held its offspring steady, three feet off the floor. A large, wet-looking mouth had opened up near the base of its spindle, from which a long flexible organ extended.

In a half whisper for fear of disturbing something, Tateosian asked, 'What's it doing?'

Crystal hardly glanced at him. 'In anthropomorphic terms,' she said, 'it's licking its embryonic child into shape, like the bears of legend. See, the blob is already much longer and thinner, and notice the colour.'

'But you can't mould a live animal as if it's clay!'

'It's probably fine enzymic control over whatever passes for DNA and RNA on this planet,' said Crystal. 'There's nothing quite so sophisticated back home, though insects do something similar inside a chrysalis. It takes them at least a week, but I think Hopalong's going to do a slightly faster job.'

'And what was that about bears?'

'Never mind, Ellis. Just watch.'

He watched as Hopalong's tongue moved swiftly over the blob, spreading and patting, pulling and crimping. The material was being coaxed into a five-pointed star.

It was the brightest time of the day now, and white-hot light surged up the tunnel, ricocheting off rock to illuminate the scene in the cave. The light glistened on chains of mucus which seemed to attach the tongue to its work in progress. Five humans stood around the alien. To Tateosian's right were Crystal and Wanda; to his left were Jay and the teenaged Holly (whom he might have married instead of Wanda, but who seemed likely to become Jay's second wife).

Now four of the star-points were being lengthened, stretched into limbs, the limbs further divided into fingers and toes. Unable to look away even for a moment, Tateosian saw muscle shapes adjusted, fingerprints impressed, pale hairs inserted. With a deft flick the clamping tentacles turned the new creation round so that the back and buttocks could be finished. Round again, and small nipples were extruded, chest hair was established, a penis and scrotum added. Then Hopalong began to fashion the head, its tongue still working quickly and surely, never pausing for more than an instant, like some complex computer printer. It was as silent in its work now as it had been in the half-lifetime Tateosian had known it, making barely a rustle or a slurp.

He watched it, uncomprehending, as it put flesh on the bones, wrinkles in the flesh, white hair on top of the wrinkles. By now the other four could understand what Hopalong had done.

'Urgh!' said Jay, shaking himself in a pantomime of disgust.

Crystal said, 'Wasn't that wonderful! If only I could write a paper . . .'

'It's so strange,' said Wanda, while Holly would not even look, keeping her face pressed tightly against Jay's chest.

Tateosian felt there was something distasteful about an alien creating a human likeness. Then sudden recognition forced him to gasp. He could feel his heart beginning to pound. A trickle of sweat ran down his temple.

After pausing for a few seconds, Hopalong finished and released its creation. Hopalong junior was a four-foot manikin of Tateosian, apparently complete in every detail.

As Tateosian watched, simultaneously enthralled and appalled, the manikin opened brown eyes and stood, swaying slightly, looking around. There was human intelligence in those eyes, but not human emotion.

'Ho-ha,' said the manikin, as if trying out its larynx. 'Ho-ha, ho-ha!' It looked around at them all, seemed to notice Wanda and said, 'Ho-ha!' a bit louder. As they all watched, its penis thickened and rose to attention. (Jay sniggered.) It stepped towards Wanda.

She gave a little cry of horror and moved back a pace, trying to get behind Tateosian and clutching at his arm for protection.

Hopalong junior stepped up close and Tateosian said, 'Keep your distance.' He shoved it away from him.

Crystal said, 'Don't hurt it, Ellis!'

It staggered but came straight back towards him (or maybe towards Wanda), saying, 'Ho-ha.'

Puppies and children, he thought, have got to be made to know. His grandmother had told him that and he'd always found it true. He hit junior hard with a back-handed slap across the face and it went down. Its joints bent oddly and it seemed to bounce more than a human.

'That's the way to do it,' said Jay enthusiastically.

Tateosian said, 'Now get out, all of you. Leave me alone in here.'

Crystal touched his arm. 'Ellis, you won't injure it – '

'Do I look that much of a fool?'

'Don't you want me to stay and help you, sir?'

'I'll manage. Now, go on!'

As soon as they'd left he threw his arms around Hopalong and hugged it to show there was no ill-will. Acutely aware of his action, he thought, 'A man only hugs women and dogs, or perhaps a favourite horse.' And he wondered how the aliens classified him.

'I didn't ask you to make your child in my image,' he said, and he sobbed into its waxy skin.

After a while he felt something nuzzling against his arm. It was Hopalong junior. He couldn't bring himself to hug a naked four-foot image of himself, but he shook it by the hand, hoping that would be all right.

Big Spider's jelly egg ended up identical to Hopalong's.

While the adults – except for Crystal – viewed the manikins with varying degrees of repugnance, the children loved them. Tateosian watched, envious, as two eight-year-olds taught Hopalong junior a hand-slapping game. They accepted it without question; it learned from them, becoming integrated into their play activities with an instant rapport which Tateosian found remarkable. He had never been able to play with the children – his own children – like that. Had it been merely his greater size which had put them off, or his attitude? Perhaps he had been wrong all these years to delegate the raising of children, to hold himself apart, to play the grim authoritarian so as to reinforce his shaky control over them all.

Could he, even at his late stage in his life, change his spots enough to sit down on the floor and indulge in play? The children were adaptable, so why shouldn't he be?

He watched the game closely, but had no worries for the children's safety. He still found it very strange – a little spooky – to see miniature versions of himself moving freely about, but he was getting used to it, as they all were, and the manikins had quickly demonstrated intelligence – an ability to learn and to fit in without causing trouble. They hadn't learned to speak words yet, but in the few hours of their existence their progress had been remarkable.

Tateosian shook his head in wonder and strolled along to the next cave, where Crystal was testing Big Spider junior as best she could without scientific instruments.

'Oh, Ellis,' she said, 'it's fascinating! Their appearance is not much more than a facade. I'm almost certain of internal differences so major, so radical –'

' – that they could almost be humans designed by an alien?'

'Well, yes. By an intelligent alien capable of making improvements. It's so frustrating not to be able to take tissue samples and analyse them. And how about their behaviour! Did you notice how the two of them touched hands for a few seconds just after this one was fully finished by its parent? I'm sure that was communication. This one hasn't made any of the behavioural goofs that Hopalong junior made.'

'Do you think the other three offspring are going to end up looking like me, too?'

'Probably.'

'And will they stay this size or grow to my size?'

'Logically – and this is human logic, Ellis – they should grow to the same sort of mass as their parents, which would mean a fairly bulky human being, maybe seven or eight feet tall. That would fit in with their size at parturition, which is a likely optimum for creatures the aliens' size. But of course, we can't apply human logic. They may restrict their imitations of us to the human size range. We don't even know why these manikins were produced. It may be too anthropocentric to consider them as offspring, even. They could be auxiliary bodies under the control of their parents' minds. They could be another species which uses the original aliens as hosts. They might have been produced for no other reason than to please us – but don't ask me why!'

Tateosian nodded as he tried to understand the implications of each possibility. He wanted to know why the manikins should resemble him, why they should be produced now after almost three decades of alien inactivity, and how such apparent biological sophistication could possibly exist here in the midst of a dangerous wilderness.

'I don't suppose we'll ever know,' he said.

'Oh, look on the bright side, Ellis. There've been more exciting developments in the last two days than over the previous twenty years. It's such a fluid situation that anything could happen. Don't you find that prospect exhilarating?'

He couldn't reply. Exciting developments may be fine for you, he thought, but don't you realise how each one strips me of power and shows up my inadequacies as a leader!

The ship arrived the afternoon of the following day. It settled on the ground in front of the caves with hardly a whisper. The humans knew it was there because its enormous bulk blocked out the light. The aliens knew it was coming, because they had all begun moving towards the cave entrances a couple of minutes earlier.

188

By now the five alien offspring were miniatures of Tateosian – all of them faithful copies between four and five feet tall.

A shallow ramp slid out from the ship and several aliens emerged to stand at the side of it. Most resembled Maple-leaf, though one was similar to Big Spider. They remained motionless as Hopalong, Crab, Big Spider, Little Spider and Maple-leaf moved into the ship.

Their offspring, chorusing, 'Ho-ha, ho-ha,' stood at the bottom of the ramp, beckoning the humans aboard with expansive arm gestures. Most of the colonists stood outside the caves, in the shadow of the ship, milling about in some confusion, asking unanswerable questions. They would follow the aliens anywhere but were, in some cases, still distrustful of the manikins.

'We must go with them,' said Crystal, cheeks alight, eyes gleaming with anticipation.

Tateosian felt his world collapsing about him. He had always anticipated rescue, though never by aliens. 'But where?' he asked. 'The city or another planet?'

'It doesn't matter.' Crystal was half-way up the ramp. 'We'll starve if we don't go. But I wouldn't miss this opportunity for anything!' She disappeared inside. Scott and Bea followed. Diane shepherded the children up the ramp, some of them holding hands with the manikins.

Jay came up to Tateosian. 'Is this what you want, sir? For everybody to go on board?'

'It's out of my hands.'

Jay looked puzzled for a moment, then nodded and turned away. He called to Holly and to Meg, his first wife, and together they entered the alien craft.

One of the few people still standing in front of the caves was Wanda. 'You are coming on board soon, aren't you?' she said, holding his arm.

He forced himself to smile at her. 'You go on ahead,' he said noncommittally. And he watched as she ran lightly up the ramp – she was still so young and delightfully childlike.

Then, shaking his head, Tatesosian wandered off to inspect each of the caves in turn. All were empty.

Finally, in Crab Cave, he sat alone in the middle of the floor, feeling rejected, superfluous. 'Whatever I did,' he said aloud to the echoing walls, 'I did for all of them, for humanity, for civilisation. Not just for myself. I never expected thanks.'

A captain, he thought, should know when to go down with his ship. Guilt for the original crash-landing returned now, to haunt him, though he knew it had not been his fault. His wives and children had left with such alacrity that it was clear they didn't want or need him any more. Twenty-nine years of command had come to a sudden end. He had always tried to do his best to maintain control and hold things together. But now his authority was totally gone. The aliens could reproduce copies of him if anyone cared to have a figurehead leader. His purpose in life was finished.

He would stay here, with his carvings. There was food left – perhaps eight days' food for thirty-two people. Even if some went bad he could survive for months. The solitude would not bother him, though he would miss . . . yes, he would miss the enigmatic aliens, especially his favourite, in whose cave he had chosen to live.

A sound fainter than a breath roused him. Crab was there in the doorway. Slowly and with great gentleness it lifted him up and carried him out to the waiting ship. He didn't resist. He lay in its arms like a child as traitorous tears of joy – or relief – misted his eyes. Like it or not it seemed he was to be borne off to a marriage of species more complex than his eleven-fold experience and to a future strange beyond comtemplation.

LISA TUTTLE

Heart's Desire

I don't know how it happened, or even what. I try to remember, and
when I can't remember, I tell myself stories, to try to understand.

There was a yellow plastic cup. I couldn't have been more than two
years old; I may have been less. I have forgotten so much from that
time, but I remember this. I remember the cup. It was mine. Now it
was somewhere I had not put it, on the seat of a ladder-backed chair,
one of a set my mother had rescued from some junk shop, stripped,
and painted a glossy white. Paintbrush in her hand, she was decorat-
ing the chair, painting a circle of tiny red roses in the centre of the top
slat. She was close enough to touch, but she wasn't looking at me. I
reached for the cup and drank.

I don't remember the taste. I remember the yellow plastic cup. I
remember how my hand closed on it, and then the feel of the ridged
rim against my lower lip as I poured the liquid into my mouth and
swallowed automatically. Then: the gasping noise my mother made,
sucking in hard, as she stared, as if seeing me for the first time. Then a
barely controlled flurry of activity. She was holding me tight, talking
desperately into the telephone. She was giving me something to
drink, horrible yuck. She was holding me over the sink, pushing my
head down, telling me to throw up. She was pleading with me, and
coaxing, and calming me – although I don't remember feeling
alarmed – and asking me, again and again, the question I could not
answer, then or ever: 'Why? Why did you drink? What made you
swallow?'

Jill went, one warm, wet summer's evening, with her friend Harriet
on the Northern Line from Clapham to Leicester Square, and from
there on the Piccadilly Line to Finsbury Park. Simon lived there;

Simon, whom Harriet had loved. Jill had not met him, although she'd had an affair with him, vicariously, through Harriet.

'Why, why, why are they all like that? He's the same age I am – a year older – and he's never been married. Why doesn't that bother him? Why doesn't he want to settle down? How can men and women be so different? It doesn't make sense. They're like children. Short attention span. Constantly wanting to be amused. Unwilling to give, terrified of commitment . . . He actually talked about *himself* in those terms. "Afraid of love" he said; "unable to commit" – God, it was like one of those books: *Women Who Love Men Who Won't* or whatever. I mean, who *isn't* afraid, and so what? Is he going to stay a lonely, single coward all his life?'

'Probably,' said Jill.

Harriet slumped a little in her seat. 'You're supposed to be providing moral support.'

'I am. You know you're doing the right thing. Simon's not going to change. You're better off without him.'

'I know.' She sounded unconvinced. 'But maybe, this evening, when we see each other . . .'

'Same song, second verse?'

They looked at each other and both sighed. 'I know it's not enough, but when he looks at me, when he touches me . . .?'

'Then I won't leave you alone with him. Unless you really, really want me to.'

It was both relief and disappointment to discover that Simon was not at home. He'd left a note taped to the door saying that if he hadn't returned by the time Harriet was ready to leave, would she please push the keys back in through the letter-slot.

'Coward,' said Harriet wistfully.

'Let's not hang about,' said Jill. 'Need a hand with the packing? Tell me what to do.'

'I didn't leave much here. A few clothes. I'll get them. You can, well, why don't you just have a look around?' She vanished into the bedroom. Licensed to prowl, Jill wandered into the sitting room. It was decorated in shades of brown and beige and sparsely furnished, but each piece was a good one. Jill was attracted particularly to a many-drawered apothecary's chest. She touched the smooth, reddish wood, feeling the tug of material desire, and pulled out one of the drawers. It was empty. She pushed it shut and tried another. Empty, too. Then a third. In its depths, something rattled.

Reaching inside, her fingers closed on something small and round. A wooden box, no more than an inch in diameter. As she admired it, the top came off in her hand. Inside was lined with black satin, and within that dark nest something gleamed. A jewel? With forefinger and thumb she plucked it out and held it aloft. It glowed dark red in the light, like a ruby or a garnet, but it was warm and soft, lacking the hardness of stone.

Without thinking, Jill popped it into her mouth, and it had slipped down her throat before she could decide otherwise.

Harriet was coming down the hall, saying something. Hot and confused, heart pounding hard enough to choke her, Jill dropped the little box into the drawer and closed it.

In the pub on the corner, Simon suddenly lost all appetite for his pint. He felt quite queasy, in fact. Inexplicably nervous. He wondered if Harriet had come and gone yet. Maybe he should have acted on his first impulse, to stay in and talk to her, to try to rescue their relationship. When he had thought, a few days before, that he would never see Harriet again he had felt so miserable that he'd known it was love. This morning, though, the thought of what he would have to do to win her back – the apologies, the explanations, the evasions, the effort – had filled him with such paralysing, suffocating boredom that he simply had to escape. He reminded himself that just because the sex was good, and she was smart and pretty, that didn't mean he had to tie himself down to her for the rest of his life. Which was what she wanted. Of course he wanted to settle down eventually, but meanwhile what he wanted was . . . freedom. Freedom to take chances, to follow his heart, to act on his desires instead of hers. Freedom to go out when he chose, where he chose, with whom he chose. Freedom to sit right here and finish his drink, instead of rushing back to her. He picked up the drink he no longer wanted, and raised it to his lips.

That night Jill dreamed. This was no ordinary dream; it felt more like waking. And she was not alone. There was someone very close to her, so close she could feel the breath moving his lungs, could feel the rhythm of his heart and blood, different and somehow more real than her own. He was closer than if he was in her bed; closer than any lover had ever been. It was as if she was inside him, her own body miraculously slimmed and stretched to mere filaments of being, around which his bone and flesh and blood and skin wrapped like layers of clothing. She was still conscious, still herself, but not separate from him. When he breathed, so did she; what she felt, he did. Perfect harmony; perfect happiness.

Then she woke to the electronic beeping of her alarm, to the grey light and emptiness of morning, and she was alone. And aware of her solitary state – although she had lived by herself fairly contentedly for almost eight years – in a new and painful way. It was a bereavement, and a fiercely physical one. Going out into the crowded street was worse; there, her senses were constantly assaulted by the world, abraded by the incomprehensible otherness of other people. Everything was at the same time remote and unbearably close. She would go mad or die, she thought, but of course she did not. As the unbearable day wore on, she learned to bear it; gradually she built up defences until sensation dulled to the level she recognised as 'normal'. The pain she felt ceased to be agony. It was merely discomfort; merely life.

But she had lost something, and she knew it, even if it was only her innocence. She knew now what she had never fully realised before, that she was alone. The knowledge had made her lonely. But life didn't have to be like this. She knew, from her dream, that something else was possible.

Jill was travelling on the Piccadilly Line to Finsbury Park again. She hadn't thought about why. Even when she found herself outside Simon's door, pressing the buzzer, she didn't know what she would say. Maybe she wouldn't have to say anything, she thought. Maybe he would simply look at her, and he would know, and they would be together.

But he wasn't in. At least, he didn't answer his bell. She tried pressing the other two in turn, but there was no response. She had to go on standing on the doorstep, exposed to what was turning into a chilly drizzle. It couldn't be long; surely it wouldn't be long before he came home. She wondered what he looked like, and tried without success to imagine his face. She couldn't even remember what colour Harriet had said his eyes were.

Finally – it was raining now – she retreated to the pub on the corner. If she stood near the door and kept an eye on the street, she would be sure to see him when he passed. That she had never seen Simon before did not worry her. She would know him.

There was a drunken woman on his doorstep.

'Simon? Simon, I'm Jill. A friend of Harriet's? She must have mentioned me . . . Anyway, I came with her yesterday. When you weren't here. Look, could I come inside? I could explain it to you. I'm not drunk, not actually, I just had a few drinks while I was waiting – you were ever such a long time coming! – Well, maybe I am a bit pissed. Coffee would . . . Would you make me a cup of coffee? And then we can talk.'

He didn't want to let her in. Harriet's friend! Harriet wasn't the sort to send her friends around to plead her case . . . besides, he had never sent Harriet away; it had been her decision to leave him.

'What do you want?'

'I can explain, if you'll let me in.'

She was so close that, short of physically pushing her away, he would hardly be able to keep her out once he opened the door. He did not want to let her in, but could see no real alternative.

Under the bright kitchen light she was not unattractive. She might, under other circumstances, have been someone he fancied – but the way she stared at him! As if she would eat him up with her eyes. He felt uneasy turning his back on her to plug in the kettle, and was glad the knives were in the drawer he blocked with his body. 'It'll have to be instant, I'm afraid. And I don't mean to be inhospitable, but I am quite tired, and it is quite late . . .' Looking up, he caught her hungry gaze straight on, like a blow. 'What *is* this?'

She had seemed about to smile, but now her expression flickered uncertainly. 'I'm sorry . . . I . . . don't quite know how to explain . . . I had hoped you would know.'

'Know? Know what? I never even heard of you until a few minutes ago.'

'I thought . . . Harriet might have said something.'

'Harriet and I are finished. If you're her friend, you should know that.'

'Yes, I was here with her, yesterday. That's when I . . . lost something. At least, I think I did.'

'What sort of something?' She was lying, he was sure of it. But why? What was she hiding?

'A little . . . a ring. My grandmother's ring. I mean it's mine, she gave it to me, but I've lost it. I thought I might have dropped it . . . I might have left it here.'

'I haven't seen anything like that.' He remembered coming home from the pub, how empty his flat had felt. As if something vital had been taken away. Harriet, of course. Not her things – they'd been few enough – but her presence, even her anticipated presence, and even, somehow, the memories of her presence in the past. Simon wasn't one for irrational feelings or metaphysical speculation, but there was a quality to his solitude he'd never felt before. It was almost as if by going, Harriet had taken away something more than herself – something he couldn't name, but could ill afford to lose. He almost phoned her, to call her back, but he had stopped with his hand on the telephone, knowing that she wouldn't be home yet. She was out there somewhere, crossing London, unreachable. And then the moment had passed.

'I didn't see a ring, nothing new. Things were missing, that's all,' he said.

'Missing?' She looked at him. It made his skin crawl, the way she looked at him. He didn't lack self-confidence; strangers had found him attractive before now – but why her? Why like this? Her interest seemed a threat.

'Here's your coffee,' he said. 'We'll take it through to the sitting room, and you can look for your ring.'

Still she stared at him. 'What did you mean when you said things were missing?'

'Harriet's things were gone. Nothing of mine.' Briefly, he wondered if she had lifted something, maybe a record or a videotape, something he wouldn't notice right away. He wasn't going to ask. He didn't want her confession. If she was a kleptomaniac, he didn't want to know. Let her keep it, whatever it was. 'The sitting room is just through here.'

'And there's the chest,' she said. 'It's a beautiful piece. I was admiring it, and . . . I'm afraid I took the liberty of opening a few drawers . . . I didn't mean to pry, you know, I wasn't thinking what I was doing, just pulling out a few drawers . . .' She gave him a look heavy with meaning.

'That's all right,' he said. 'I don't keep anything in it, as I'm sure you found out.'

'Yes you did.'

She spoke so certainly he could hardly contradict her. Besides, he wasn't sure. Maybe he had dropped something in there once, a spare set of keys or something small, unimportant, quickly forgotten. 'Well, nothing valuable.'

'You don't mind if I . . .?'

'Have another look? No, by all means. Go ahead. Pull out every drawer. See what you can find.' A yawn racked him, and he sank down on the couch.

She was clumsy, fumbling with the tiny knobs, first too rough and then too gentle, plunging a hand into each empty drawer in turn, as if she couldn't believe the evidence of her eyes. And when she had been through them all and found nothing, she turned to him, looking so despairing that, even though he neither knew nor trusted her, he pitied her.

'There was something,' she said. 'There was something in one of the drawers . . . where is it? What was it?'

'I don't know. You tell me.'

'It was a little, round, wooden box, very carefully made and lined with black satin. And there was something in it. I never saw it very well. It looked like a ruby – it gleamed red – but when I felt it, it was more rubbery, something like a wine gum or a cough sweet.'

He laughed.

'You know what I'm talking about! It was yours!'

He swore. 'You're drunk. Or crazy. I don't know what you're talking about.'

'You *do*. You must.'

He struggled for calm, but that was no longer possible. She made him angry. 'So what if I do? That chest is mine, and whatever's in it is mine, and it has nothing to do with you. If I want to keep cough sweets in my apothecary's chest I don't have to tell you; it's not your business.'

'But it is. It is now. Because I swallowed it, you see. I didn't mean to. I don't know why – I was just going to feel it with my lips, it looked so smooth, and then it was in my mouth and I was swallowing before I'd had time to think. If I'd thought about it, I wouldn't have. But I couldn't help myself.'

There were tears in her eyes, and he felt sorry for her again. 'It's all right,' he said wearily. He traced a cross in the air. 'I forgive you, God forgives you. Bless you, my child. Now, go, and steal no more wine gums.'

'It wasn't a wine gum!'

'Cough sweets, then. Look –'

'No, you look! I've told you the truth. I don't know what it means, but it's real, it's important. I dreamed about you last night. I'd never met you before, but I knew you, as soon as you came near. You know what I'm talking about. You must feel it too. I didn't ask for it any more than you did. All right, I know it was my fault, but . . . I didn't mean it; I didn't know what I was doing. And now it's done. You can't deny it. It affects both of us.'

How easy it would be, he thought, to let it happen. To let go, and let her entangle him in her madness. All he had to do was open his arms. All he had to do was take her to bed. That was what she wanted . . . why shouldn't he want what she wanted, just for once? Except that it wouldn't be for once. It would go on and on, and she'd want more and more. He remembered the way she had looked at him in the kitchen. She wanted to consume him utterly; she wouldn't be satisfied with anything less.

Fear turned to anger, and he held it like a shield. 'What do you want from me?' His tone said that whatever it was, he would not give it to her.

The slump of her shoulders said she understood. 'Please . . . let me stay.'

'No.'

'Please. Just for tonight . . . it's late; the tube's closed now.'

.'I'll call a minicab for you.' He got up and went to the phone. He felt, as he moved and spoke, that he was playing a part, echoing something done by an earlier self. He remembered a quarrel with Harriet.

'Hello. Could you send a car . . .'

Behind him, motion, displacement of air. He heard his door open and shut, and then the muffled slam of the street door.

'Oh, never mind, cancel that order. I'm sorry to have troubled you.' His heart raced. As he hung up, his body tensed, ready to run. Not to run away, he realised, but to run after her. But why? He'd made his decision. He knew what he wanted – or, at least, he knew what he didn't want.

Only, the flat seemed so empty now. He looked at the apothecary's chest. He had grown up with it. His grandmother had made hats, and used the little drawers to hold her trimmings. The chest was so familiar, he'd almost stopped seeing it. His mother had made him a gift of it when he bought this flat and, although he was very fond of it, he'd never actually found a use for it. And yet, from time to time, hadn't he deposited odds and ends in the little drawers? The image of something red and gleaming like a gem teased his memory. Had he hidden something away for safekeeping only to forget all about it?

198

He stopped himself, hand outstretched. No. There was nothing. She hadn't stolen anything from him. He hadn't lost anything. How could he lose something he'd never had? She was crazy, that woman, but it was nothing to do with him. Nothing at all.

He sat down again, feeling hollow and so light the merest breeze could have blown him away.

Once I thought desire had an object; thought that I wanted someone or something missing from my life, whether it was a pair of lapis lazuli earrings or my own baby; I thought I wanted back something that had been lost, whether my yellow plastic cup or a man who had left me. But desire is not so simple as a wish. Desire *is*. It possesses you, or it does not. It's a feeling, a force, a natural disaster like an earthquake or gravity, and there's no denying it. There's no satisfying it, either. *I want* is a sentence which can never be finished.

Jill was in despair. She'd blown it. She had frightened him, and ruined everything. Her best chance. But she must have another. She could try again. After much thought, and agonising over the choice of both words and picture (Gwen John's *The Convalescent* was surely sufficiently cool and unthreatening?) she sent him a postcard apologising for her behaviour while 'under the influence', and suggesting he could show his forgiveness by letting her take him to dinner. But although she gave him her address and her work and home telephone numbers, Simon did not get in touch with her.

She couldn't understand it. Why didn't he feel as drawn to her as she was to him? She had his heart, after all: she could feel it beating slowly and steadily between the beats of her own. For most of the time she was not consciously aware of it, any more than she had ever been aware of her own, but late at night, lying awake in the quiet dark of her lonely bed, she felt the two hearts beating together, and the tears ran down her face as the pain of his absence became almost more than she could bear. She wanted to go to him, to cast herself, body and soul, at his feet. But she didn't dare. She remembered too well how he had looked at her, and drawn back. If he looked at her like that again, she thought, she would die. Better that he should not see her at all. But she had to see him.

She could hardly think of anything else. Work, and even the most ordinary business of day-to-day existence, became steadily more difficult. She found herself going to Finsbury Park at all hours – she would start off intending to go to work, or to lunch, or to do some shopping, and she would find herself, once again, on the Piccadilly Line going north. With no idea of whether or not he was in it, she would watch his house like a faithful hound, bargaining with herself each time for the right to stay just a little longer . . . until, finally, one day she was rewarded by the sight of him coming out of the house.

He didn't notice her, and she did not draw attention to herself. She kept a safe distance as she followed him down the street to the Underground station, and she was careful to enter a different carriage. She went with him all the way to Leicester Square, and watched him go into a pub. She waited on the street for a few minutes, plotting a 'chance' meeting. He would be wary at first, of course, not pleased to meet her again, but she would be as light and charming as she knew how to be, and he would gradually relax, suggest they continue this enjoyable conversation over dinner . . .

But when she entered the pub she saw him at once, and knew her plan was doomed. For he was sitting at a table near the far wall, already in conversation – light and charming – with an attractive young woman.

Her heart thudded so hard she thought he should feel it, and she ran out into the street, cursing her, cursing him, cursing the passion that had driven her mad.

She knew it was madness, but the next evening found her again in front of his house.

Following him became her routine. It was more than just a habit; it was her life. She found out where he worked, and she saw him shopping. She knew what he ate and where he drank. She saw the women he met from time to time, and they meant no more, no less, to her than they did to him; no less, no more, than anything else that impinged upon his life, the life she longed to share. She memorised the way he moved, his own particular walk, his small gestures when talking, the width of his back and the way his hair grew. In her dreams she was with him, so close no one could see her, and in her waking hours she got as close to him as she dared.

Until, one day, she went too close, and he turned at the sound of her breath at his back, and she saw him see her, saw him see the unspeakable, unacceptable hunger in her eyes.

And in his eyes, that look that she had never wanted to see again; the fear she had never meant to inspire. In that moment of mutual shock and recognition she saw herself through his eyes: saw herself and was repelled.

Jill turned and ran as if she could outrun her own madness.

How did desire ever come to be confused with love? It has nothing to do with the human connections and needs and emotions that lead to marriages, families, children . . . Desire is an affliction. Madness. No, not madness. Because whatever else it is and does, it is *real*.

Jill went to stay with relatives in Yorkshire. Things had gone too far, and she understood that if she did not make some radical change in her life things would go further still. Where the end might be she could not, would not let herself, imagine. Staying in London was obviously not on, when from one day to the next she couldn't control her own movements. Maybe, if she took herself far enough away from him, she would no longer feel the pull. At any rate, situating herself miles from the nearest railway station would at the very least slow her down. She no longer had a job to quit, so there was no problem about that. All her relatives needed or wanted to know was that she'd been disappointed in love; a man had let her down. When she was with them, she talked and thought as they did, about normal, ordinary things: dinner, the weather, and the people and the world as seen on television. She ate large meals, slept long hours, watched television, helped about the house, went for walks. This was her convalescence, and also her cure.

Always, of course, her thoughts were drawn to Simon: distance made no difference. But just as she would not allow herself to see him, so she tried to forbid the very thought of him. She cut off all fantasies and reminiscences sharply, as soon as they began. She used relaxation techniques and methods of behaviour modification, learned from books. She had decided to treat her feelings about Simon as she would any addiction. Habits can be changed, even habits of thought.

But she could not control the dreams she had while sleeping. And awake, while thinking of something utterly removed from Simon – advising a friend of her aunt on a new wallpaper pattern, or playing bridge – she would suddenly realise that she had, quite unconsciously, made one of Simon's gestures, or feel his slightly lopsided smile on her lips. Walking to the shops she sometimes stopped dead, sensing that her stride was absurdly masculine for someone wearing a skirt but unable to remember how she usually walked. She heard his laugh coming from her mouth, and when she swore, it was with his scowl and tightened shoulders. And regardless of whether she allowed herself to think about it, his heart went on beating inside her breast.

Desire must eventually wither away for lack of nourishment, Jill thought. She concentrated on other things, becoming a better cook, sewing, building her physical endurance with long, hard walks, and reading a great many books. As the days and the weeks passed she felt better and stronger, and she knew she was healing. Perhaps she dreamed of Simon, but she woke from her dreams without anguish. She had not forgotten him – she knew now that she never would – but she no longer felt that horrible empty aching loneliness that meant she needed him. She didn't need him to make her whole; she *was* whole. It was time to go back to London and take up her life again.

Simon shrank back against the doors of the train. Christ! There she was, that woman, Harriet's friend!

Months without a sight of her, and now – was it starting up again?

Then he realised that she couldn't have been following him. She was already in the carriage, already seated, when he got on. So it had to be coincidence.

He eyed her cautiously. Absorbed in her book, she didn't seem to have noticed him. Even so, he thought he'd better get off at the next stop, move to another car. He was afraid of attracting her attention, but he could not stop staring at her with hungry, curious eyes.

Since she had run away from him, Jill's absence had haunted Simon far more than her unsuspected presence ever had. That last time, when he had seen her on the street, he knew at once that this was no coincidence; that she must have been trailing him for days. But it had taken a very long time for him to believe that his discovery of her had really frightened her off for good. For weeks he had been on edge, sleeping badly, checking the locks on his door obsessively – he even had them changed, just in case – jumping at unexpected sounds, glimpsing her in every crowd. Finally, he had decided to confront her. He was glad, then, that he had never thrown away the postcard she had sent him (in fact, he had tucked it away in one of the drawers of the apothecary's chest). But when he called her office they told him she had left the company, and no matter when or how often he tried her home number there was never a reply. He had been forced to accept that she had left his life just as abruptly and inexplicably as she had entered it. He had thought about her from time to time, wondering if he would ever see her again. And now, here she was. He could confront her, if he wanted to.

He had looked away from her for a moment, to recollect his thoughts, not wanting to be caught staring until he knew what he meant to do – whether or not to show he recognised her. Now, looking back, he thought he was ready for anything. But he was not ready for what he saw.

She was gone, and in her place – in the same seat, reading the same book – was a man. Except that she *hadn't* gone; she was still there, somehow within the man – it could have been done on film, a simple overlay of images, a double exposure – inside the man like his living soul. And the man was himself.

Simon's hands were like ice, and his muscles had seized up. He couldn't move, not even his eyes. He had to go on looking at this impossible sight, terrified that he/she would look up and see him, and yet wanting it. Whether or not he'd ever heard the legend that to meet your double is to meet your death, he sensed danger. Surely, once their eyes met, something would end? How could they both continue to exist?

The train was pulling into the station. Passengers were standing up and moving towards the doors. The figure that was Jill/Simon shimmered. Boundaries flowed and lost definition, and then the body redefined itself, closing the book it held, and standing up. When Jill got off the train she was herself again.

BRIAN ALDISS

A Tupolev Too Far

I know you want fiction for this anthology, but perhaps for once you would consider a true story. I offer a thought in extenuation for what is to follow: that this story is so fantastic and unbelievable it might as well be science fiction.

Well, it would be sf except for the fact that there is no scientific explanation for the bizarre central occurrence – or none beyond the way bizarre events occur with regularity, as vouched for by Charles Fort, Arthur Koestler, Carl Jung, Jesus Christ, and other historic figures.

Unfortunately, the story is not only bizarre but raunchy. It is the sort of tale men tell each other late at night, in a bar in Helsinki or somewhere similar. It has no moral and precious little morality.

Sex and lust come into it. And murder and incest and brigandage of the worst sort. There are some insights to be gleaned regarding the different natures of men and women, if that is any consolation.

Another thing I have to add. This is not my story. I heard it from a friend. One of those friends you know off and on throughout life. He always enjoyed talking about the bad times.

We'll call him Ron Wallace.

And this is what he told me.

This helping of agony took place in 1989, which had turned out to be a better year for Ron than he had expected. He had been unemployed for a while. Now he had a good job with a West Country firm who made safes and security equipment employing the latest electronic devices. Ron was their Overseas Salesman. The Russians approached his company, who were sending Ron out to Moscow as a result. The managing director, who was a good guy, briefed Ron before he left, and he set off on the flight from Penge Airport in good fettle. His wife Stephanie saw him off.

Ron flew Royal Russian Airlines. Which, after TransAm, is regarded as the world's best airline. Plenty of leg room, little engine noise, pretty hostesses.

It was a brief flight. On the way, he picked up an in-flight magazine which had an illustrated article on the Russian Commonwealth and on modern Moscow in particular. There were photographs of Czar Nicholas III with the Czarina opening the grand new Governance of Nations building, designed by Richard Rogers, on White Square, and of the redecorated Metro in St Petersburg. Ron dozed off while leafing through such commonplaces and was woken by a terrific bang.

The aircraft was passing through a ferocious storm, or so it seemed. Lightning flashed outside and the airliner began to fall. It shook violently as it fell.

Ron sat tight. He remembered his grandfather's account of the terrible firestorm which had partially destroyed Berlin in July 1914. His grandfather had been working in Berlin at the time and always talked about the experience. The old man claimed that was the first occasion on which all Europe had united in a major rescue operation; it had changed history, he claimed.

These thoughts and less pleasant ones ran through Ron's mind as the plane fell earthwards.

'I'll never screw Steff again – or any other woman,' he said aloud. To his mind, that was the biggest bugbear regarding death: no screwing.

For an instant the plane was bathed in unnatural light. Then all became calm, as if nothing had happened.

The plane pulled out of its dive. Cabin staff in their white uniforms moved down the aisles, soothing the passengers and bringing them drinks.

Everyone started talking to each other. But only for a few minutes. After which, a silence fell over them; they became uncannily quiet as they tried to digest their narrow escape from disaster.

Twenty minutes later, they landed at Sheremeteivo Airport.

Ron was surprised to find how drab and small everything was. He was suprised, too, to see how many men were in uniform – unfamiliar uniforms, too, with mysterious red stars on their caps. He had no idea what the stars stood for, unless for Mars, on which planet the Russians had just landed.

Of course, Ron had got down as much whisky as he could following the alarming incident on the plane. His perceptions were possibly a little awry. All the same, he could not help noticing that most of the planes on the ground belonged to an airline called Aeroflot, of which he had never heard. There were no Royal Russian Airline planes to be seen.

When, at the luggage carousel, he asked a fellow passenger about Aeroflot, the man replied, 'You ask too many questions round here, you find yourself in the gulag.'

Ron began to feel rather cold and shaky. Something had happened. He did not know what.

The whole airport, the reception area, the customs area, gave no sign of the hightech sheen for which Russia was renowned. He felt a sense of disorientation, which was calmed slightly when he was met by his Russian contact, Vassili Rugorsky, who made him welcome.

As they passed out through the foyer of the building, Ron observed a large framed portrait dominating the exits where he might have expected to see a picture of the graceful young Czar. Instead, the portrait showed a thick-set almost neckless man with glittering eyes, a mottled complexion, and an unpleasant expression.

'Who's that?' he asked.

Vassili looked curiously at Ron, as if expecting him to be joking.

'Comrade Leonid Brezhnev, of course,' he said.

Ron dared ask nothing more, but his sense of unease deepened. Who was Brezhnev?

He was shown to a black car. Soon they were driving through the city. Ron could hardly believe what he saw. Moscow was always billed as one of Europe's great pleasure cities, with smart people, and a vivid nightlife staged amid elegant buildings – fruit of Russia's great renaissance in the early forties, when the Czarina Elizabeta Ship Canal had linked Baltic with Black Sea. Here Parisian panache thrived among Parisian-type boulevards. Or so the legend had it. As they wound through a dreary suburb, he saw lines of dowdy people queuing at shops hardly worthy of the name. The buildings themselves were grey and grubby.

Red flags and banners flew everywhere. He could not understand. It was as if the whole place had been hit by revolution.

But the men he dealt with were agreeable enough. Ron prided himself on his powers of negotiation; his opposite numbers were cautious but amiable. He gathered to his mild astonishment that they regarded British technology to be in advance of their own.

'Of course, the KGB have all the latest Western equipment,' one man said jokingly as the contracts were signed. Ron did not like to ask what KGB stood for; he was clearly expected to know. It was all peculiar. He wondered if the electric storm he had flown through had affected his mind in some way.

It was on his second day that the contracts were signed. The first day was given over to discussion, when Ron often felt that the Russians were pumping him. At one point, when he had occasion to mention the Czarina Elizabeta Ship Canal, they all looked blank.

Even more disconcertingly, the Russians asked him how he liked being in the Soviet Union, and similar remarks. Ron belonged to an electronics union himself, but had never heard of a Soviet Union. He could almost fancy he had arrived in the wrong country.

Nevertheless, the contracts were signed on the second day, on terms favourable to Ron's company. They were witnessed in the ministry at three in the afternoon, following which the parties involved got down to some serious drinking. As well as Russian champagne there were vodka, wine, and a good Georgian brandy. Ron was an experienced drinker. He arrived back at the Hotel Moskva, contract in briefcase, just after 6.30, still more or less in control of his wits.

I'm trying to tell you this story as Ron Wallace told it to me. When he came to describe the Hotel Moskva I had to interupt him. I've stayed in that hotel a couple of times. Once I took the Camberwell–Moscow Trans-Continent Express on a package tour which included three nights in that very hotel. It was the pleasantest place in which I have ever stayed, light and airy, full of elegant people. In fact, a few too many of the Russian aristocracy for my simple tastes.

It was not the dowdiness and gloom of the hotel about which Ron chiefly complained, or the uninteresting food, but the lack of beautiful women. Ron was always rather a ladies' man.

An old-fashioned band was playing old-fashioned music in the hotel restaurant. It was a period piece, like the hotel itself. He could not credit it. The dining room was cavernous, with stained glass windows at one end, and a faded style of furnishing. The band lurched from Beatles hits to the 'Destiny' waltz. The place, he said, was a cross between the Café Royal in the nineteen-twenties and Salisbury Cathedral in the fourteen-twenties.

As Ron told his tale, I kept thinking about the concept of alternative worlds. Although the idea is at first fantastic, there is, after all, a well-attested theory which says that whatever is imagined moves nearer to reality. Edmund Husserl, in his pioneering work on phenomenology, *Investigations in Logic*, shows how little the psychological nature of historical processes are understood. Turning points in history – generatives, in Husserl's term – occur in greater or lesser modes related to quantal thought impulses which are themselves subject to random factors. The logical structures on which such points depend exist independently of their psychological correlates, so that we can expect subjective experiences to generate a multiplicity of effects, each of which bears equivalent objective reality; thus, whether or not signatures are appended to a treaty, for example, is dependent on various epistemological assumptions of transient nature, while the results of signing or non-signing may be multiplex generatives, giving rise to a spectrum of alternative objectivities, varying from slight to immense, affecting lives of many people over considerable areas of space and time. I know this to be so because I read it in a book.

So it seemed clear to me – though not to Ron, who is no intellectual and consequently does not believe in variant subjective realities – that the electric storm which hit the Tupolev had been a Husserl's generative, causing Ron to switch objectivities, and materialise in a parallel version of objectivity along the spectrum, where history had at some point taken a decided turn for the worst.

Feeling a little weary, Ron decided not to go up to his room immediately, but to eat and then retreat to bed, in preparation for his early flight home the following morning.

Diners were few. They could scarcely be distinguished from the diners in a provincial Pan-European town, Belgrade, say, or Boheim-kirchen, or Bergen. There was none of the glitter he had expected. And the service was terribly slow.

The maître d' had shown Ron to a small table, rather distant from the nearest light globe. From this vantage point, he looked the clientele over while awaiting his soup.

At the table nearest to him, two orientals sat drinking champagne. Their mood was subdued. He judged them to be Korean. Ron spared hardly a glance for the man. As he told me, 'I could hardly take my eyes off the woman. Mainly I saw her in half-profile. A real beauty, clear-cut features, hawkish nose, dark eyes, red lips . . . Terrific.'

When she smiled at her partner and raised her glass to her lips she was a vision of seduction. Ron dropped his napkin on the floor in order to take a look at her legs. She was wearing a long black evening dress.

He said his one thought was, 'If only her husband would get lost . . .'

His desires turned naturally to sex. But he had sworn an oath to his wife, Steff, on the subject of fidelity. As he was averting his eyes from the Korean couple, the woman turned to look at him. Even across the space between their tables, the stare was strong and disturbing. Ron could not tell what was in that stare. It made him curious, while at the same time repelling him.

He took a paperback book of crossword puzzles from his briefcase and tried to study a puzzle he had already started, but could not concentrate.

A memory came back. Of his first love. How innocent had been that girl's gaze. He could recall it perfectly. It had been a gaze of love and trust; all the sweetness of youth, of innocence, was in it. It could not be recovered. No one would ever look at him in that fashion again.

The Korean couple had decided something between them. The Korean man rose from the table, laid down his napkin, and came across to Ron.

'My god,' Ron thought, 'the little bugger's going to tell me not to ogle his wife . . .'

The Korean was short and sturdy. Perhaps he was in his mid-thirties. His face was solemn, his eyes dark, his whole body held rigidly, and it was a rigid bow he made to Ron Wallace.

'You are English?' he asked, speaking in English with a heavy accent. 'We saw you dining here last night and made enquiries. I am on official duties in the Soviet Union, a diplomat from the Democratic People's Republic of North Korea.' He gave his name.

'What do you want? I'm having dinner.'

'Meals are a source of fear to me. I can never rid my mind of one dinner in particular when I was a child of five. Someone from political motives poisoned my father. A servant was held responsible, but we never found out who was paying the servant. The servant did not tell, despite severe torture. My father rose from his place, screamed like a wounded horse, spun about, and fell head first into a dish – well, in our dialect it's *pruang hai*, I suppose a sort of a kedgeree, though with little green chillies. He struggled a moment, sending rice all over us frightened children. Then he was still, and naturally the meal was ruined.'

210

Ron Wallace took a sip of mineral water. Although the Korean was white and trembling, Ron would not ask him to sit down.

The Korean continued. 'I should explain that there were four of us children. Three of us were triplets, and there was a younger sibling. My mother was demoralised by my father's death. I have to confess she was of the bourgeois class. Never a very stable personality, for she was an actress, she suffered illusions. One starry night, she jumped from a tall window through the glass roof of the conservatory to the ground. A theory was that she had seen the stars reflected in the glass and thought the conservatory was the Yalu river. This was never proved.

'We children were handed over into the care of an uncle and aunt who ran a rather poor pig and sorghum farm in the mountainous area of our land. My uncle was a bully, given to drink and criminality. He committed sexual atrocities on us poor defenceless children, and even on his farm animals. You can imagine how we suffered.'

He looked fixedly at Ron, but Ron made no reply. Ron was aware of the avid gaze of the Korean's partner, back at the table, smiling yet not smiling in his direction.

'Our one consolation was the school to which we were sent. It was a long walk away, down the mountain, a cruel trial for us in winter months when the snow was deep. But the school was run by a remarkable Englishman, a Mr Holmberg. I have been told that Holmberg is not an English name. I cannot explain how that came about. In the world struggle, there are many anomalies.

'Mr Holmberg had many skills and was unfailingly kind. He taught us something of the world. He also explained to us the mysteries of sex, and kindly drew pictures of the female sexual organs on the blackboard, with the fallopian tubes in red, despite a shortage of chalk.

'The day came when the ninth birthday approached for us three poor orphans. There we sat in the little classroom, stinking of sorghum and pigs, and this wonderful Englishman presented us with a marvellous gift, a kite he had made himself. It was such a kite as Koreans made in dynastic times to carry the spirits of the dead, very strong, very large, and well decorated. It was for us, the first gift we had received since our father was poisoned. You can imagine our delight.'

He paused.

'Where's my bloody boeuf stroganoff?' asked Ron, looking round for a waitress.

211

Greatly though he desired something to eat, he desired much more the absence of this little man who stood by his table, telling his awful life story unbidden. Ron had never heard of the Democratic People's Republic of North Korea, and did not much want to. It was another department of the terrible world into which he had fallen.

He tried to think of pleasant English things – Ovaltine, Bob Monkhouse, cream teas, Southend, the National Anthem, Agatha Christie, *The Sun*, Saxby's pork pies, Kylie Minogue – but they were drowned out by the Korean's doomed narrative.

'We had a problem. We feared that our cruel uncle would steal the kite from us. We resolved to fly it on the way home from school, to enjoy that pleasure at least once. Halfway up the mountain was a good eminence, with a view of the distant ocean and a strong updraught. The three of us hung on to the string and up went the grand kite, sailing into the sky. How we cheered. Just for a moment, we had no cares.

'Our little brother begged to be allowed to hold the kite. As we handed him the string, we heard the sound of shots being fired farther up the mountain. Our anxieties were easily awoken. In those lawless times, bandits were everywhere. Alas, one can pay for one moment's carelessness with a lifetime's regret. We turned to find that the kite was carrying away our little brother. His hand was caught in the loop in the string and he was going. He cried. We cried. We waved.

'Helpless, we watched him about to be dashed against the rocks. Fortunately, he cleared them as the kite gained height. It drifted towards the north-east, and the ocean and the south-eastern coast of the Soviet Union. That was the last we saw of him. It is not impossible that even now he lives, and speaks and thinks in the Russian language.'

The Korean bowed his head for a moment, while Ron tried to attract the attention of a distant waitress who had lapsed into immobililty, as if also overcome by the tragic tale.

'We were upset by this incident. We had lost our valued gift, and a rather annoying little brother as well. We fell to punching each other, each claiming the other two were to blame. Then we went home, up the rest of the mountain track.

'My uncle was in his favourite apple tree, quiet for once and not swearing at us. He hung head down, a rope round his ankles securing

212

him to one of the branches of the tree. His hands were tied and he was fiercely gagged. His face was so red that we burst out laughing.

'Since he was still alive, we had a splendid time spinning him round. He could not cry out but he looked pretty funny. Then we got rakes and spades from the shed and battered him to death.

'Our aunt had been thrown in the pond. Many and dreadful were the atrocities committed on her body. We dragged her from the water but, so near to death was she, we put her back where we had found her.

'The house had been looted by the bandits whose firing we had heard. Those were lawless days before our great leader, Kim Il-sung, took over control of our destinies. We were happy to have the place to ourselves, especially since my uncle's two huge sons had been shot, bayoneted, and beheaded by the bandits.

'Unfortunately, the bandits returned in the night, since it had begun to rain. They came for shelter. They found us asleep, tied the three of us up, put us in a foul dung cart, and promised to sell us for slaves to a foreign power in the market of Yuman-dong. Next morning, down the mountain we bumped. More rain fell. The monsoon came on in full force. We were crossing a wooden bridge over a river when a great rush of water struck the bridge.

'The bandits were thrown into confusion or drowned. We were better off in the cart, which floated, and we managed to get free.

'We ran to Yuman-dong for safety, since we had another uncle there. He took us in with protestations of affection, and his elder daughter fed us. Unfortunately, the town was the headquarters of the brigands, as we soon discovered. My uncle was the biggest brigand. The three of us children were made to work at the degrading business of carting night soil from the village and spreading it on the fields. You can imagine our humiliation.'

The Korean shook his head sadly and searched Ron's face for signs of compassion.

'Where's my bloody food?' Ron asked.

'But fortune was as ever on our side. It was then that our great leader, Kim Il-sung, became President of our people's republic. My uncle was awarded the post of local commissar, since in his career of bandit he had harassed rich oppressor landlords such as my late uncle and aunt up in the mountain. Much celebration followed this event and everyone in the village remained totally drunk for twenty-one days, including the dogs. Three died. Maybe four. It was

213

during this period of joy that a dog bit off the left ear of one of my brothers.

'Those were happy times. Under my uncle we marched from farm to farm along the valley, beating up the farmers, threatening and exhorting the workers. There was nothing we would not do for the Cause. Unfortunately, much misery was to follow.'

'Don't tell me – let me guess,' murmured Ron Wallace.

'But you cannot guess what befell us triplets. It was discovered after many years that the brother who had lost an ear was a capitalist running dog and had been associating secretly with the enemies of the state, who varied from time to time. Sometimes the enemies were Chinese, sometimes Russians. My brother had associated with all of them. I felt bound to denounce him myself, and his wife. A terrible vendetta of blood then started – '

In desperation Ron stood up, waving his book of crossword puzzles.

'Sorry,' he said. 'I have to finish this page. It is a secret code. I am employed by MI5.'

'I appreciate your feelings,' said the Korean, standing rigid. 'We must all exercise our duties. However, I tell you something of my history for a reason. The remarkable Englishman, Mr Holmberg, who taught me at school, stays ever in my mind as an example of decency, morality, fairness, and liberalism. It is no less than the truth to say that I have modelled my life on him.

'Unfortunately, however, during the revolutionary times of the Flying Horse movement, it was necessary to have Mr Holmberg shot. A tribunal convicted him of being a foreigner in wartime. To me befell the honour of carrying out the execution with my own hands. I have a small souvenir for his family back in England which I wish you to carry home to present to them. Please come to my table and I shall give it to you, concealed in a copy of *Pravda*.'

Ron Wallace hesitated only for a moment. All he wanted was his dinner. But if he went over to this madman's table, he would be able to snatch a closer look at his companion. He rose.

At the Korean table sat the remarkable person with the bright red lips and shoulder-length black hair. The full-length gown swept to the floor. Diamonds sparkled at the smooth neck. A cigarette in a holder sent a trail of smoke ceilingwards from a bejewelled right hand. A look of black intensity was fixed on Ron. He bowed.

'I'm pleased to meet your wife,' he said to the North Korean.

214

'My brother.' The Korean corrected him. 'My sole surviving brother. Here is the souvenir for the Holmberg family – in fact for the small daughter of the son of the man I knew, who was convicted of the crime against the state. Her address is enclosed. Please take it, deliver it faithfully.'

Ron had been expecting to receive the head of the late Mr Holmberg, but it was a smaller object which the Korean passed over, easily rolled inside a copy of *Pravda*. He bowed again, shook hands with the Korean, smiled at his brother, who gave him a winning smile in return, and returned to his table. A waitress was delivering a boeuf stroganoff to his place.

'Thank you,' he said. 'Bring me another bottle of wine and a bottle of mineral water.'

'Immediately,' she said. But she paused for a second before leaving the table.

Setting the newspaper between his stomach and the table, Ron unrolled it. Inside lay a wooden doll with plaits, a savage grin painted on its wooden face. It wore traditional dress of red and white. Tied round its neck was a label on which was written the name Doreen Holmberg and an address in Surrey. He rolled it up in the paper again and shut it in his briefcase.

He began to eat without appetite the dish the waitress had brought, forking mouthfuls slowly between his lips, staring over the bleak reaches of the restaurant permeated by the strains of 'Yesterday', and avoiding any glance towards the Korean table. He sighed. It would be a relief to get home to his wife, although he had some problems there.

The waitress returned with the two bottles of wine and mineral water on a tray. She could be sighted first behind a carved wooden screen which partly hid the entrance to the kitchens. Then she was observed behind a large aspidistra. Then she hove into full view, walking towards Ron's table, a thin middle-aged woman with straggling dyed hair.

He had been too preoccupied with the Koreans to pay the waitress any attention. As he scrutinised her in the way he scrutinised anything female, he saw that her gaze was fixed on him, not with the usual weary indifference characteristic of a waitress towards diners, but in a curious and not unfriendly fashion. He straightened slightly in his chair.

She set the bottles down on the table. Was there something suggestive in the way she fingered the neck of the wine bottle before uncorking it? She poured him a glass of wine and a glass of the mineral water in slow motion. He caught a whiff of her underarm odour as she came near. Her hip brushed against his arm.

'You're imagining things,' he said to himself.

He raised the wineglass to his lips and looked at her.

'Enjoy it please,' she said in English, and turned away.

She was tired and in her late thirties, he judged. Not much of a bottom. Not really an attractive proposition. Besides, a waitress in a Russian hotel restaurant . . .

However, after a few more mouthfuls of the stroganoff he summoned her across the room on the pretext of ordering a bread roll. She came readily enough, but he saw in the language of her angular body an independence of mind not yet eroded of all geniality. A spark of intent lit in his brain. He knew that spark. It could so easily be fanned into flame.

She did look worn. Her face was weathered, the flesh lifeless and dry, with strong lines moving downwards on either side of thin lips. Nothing to recommend her. Yet the expression on her face, the light grey eyes – somehow, he liked what he saw. Out of that ugly dress, those hideous shoes, she would be more attractive. His imagination ran ahead of him. He felt an erection stirring in his trousers.

Her breasts were not very noticeable as she bent to place the bread by Ron's side. No doubt she ate scraps in the kitchen off people's plates. A fatty diet. No doubt she had taken orders all her life. It was a matter of speculation as to what her private life could be.

He asked her if she ever did crosswords.

The shake of her head was contemptuous. Again the whiff of body odour. Possibly she did not understand what he said. She smiled a little. Her teeth were irregular, but it was an appealing smile.

Watching her hips, her legs, her ugly shoes, as she retreated, he told himself to relax and to think of something that a candle did in a low place, in six letters.

But a long dull evening stretched before him. He hated his own company.

Over the sweet, he extracted a few words from the waitress. She spoke a little German, a little English. She had worked in this hotel for five years. No, she cared nothing about the work. The lipstick she wore was not expertly applied. But there was no doubt that in some measure she was interested in him.

When she brought him a cup of bitter coffee, he said, 'Will you come up to my room?'

The waitress shook her head, almost regretfully, as if she had anticipated the question. It did not surprise her; probably she had often been asked the same question by drunken clients.

Her glance went to where the impassive maître d'hôtel stood, guardian of his underlings' Soviet morality. No doubt he had awful powers over them. She left Ron's table, to disappear into the kitchens.

Ron looked down at his puzzle.

When she came to pour him a second cup of coffee, he suggested that they went back to her place.

The waitress gave him a long hard look, weighing him up. The look disconcerted him, inasmuch as he felt himself judged. He saw himself sitting there, secure and decently dressed, possessor of foreign currency, about to return to the strange capitalist world from which he had come. Not bad looking. And yet – yet another man out of thousands, with a vacant evening before him, just wanting a bit of fun.

'There is difficulties,' she said.

The words told him he was halfway to his desire.

Elation ran through him, not unmixed with a tinge of apprehension. Again, the stirrings of an erection. He told her she was wonderful. He would do anything. He smiled. She frowned. She made a small gesture with her hand: Be quiet. Or, Be patient.

As if she already had her regrets, she left the table hastily, clutching the coffeepot to her chest. Ron observed that she said something to an older waitress as they passed on the way to the kitchens.

Now he had to wait. He tried to think of an uncomplicated curative plant in six letters.

The waitress had disappeared. Perhaps he had, after all, been mistaken. When his impatience got the better of him, he rose to his feet. She appeared and came over. He had a sterling note ready – of a modest domination, so as not to offend her.

'Where and when?'

Their faces were close. Her foreignness excited him, nor was he repelled by her body odour. She barely responded, barely moved her lips.

'Rear door by the wood hut. Midnight.'

'I'll be there.'

'Will you?'

He nodded a curt goodnight to the North Koreans, and retreated with his case to the bar. He sat alone, apart from a group of what he guessed were Swedes, getting heavily drunk in one corner. He had three hours to wait.

Idly, he picked up a newspaper printed in English and started to glance through it. It bewildered him utterly. For a while he entertained the thought that his company was playing an elaborate joke on him.

According to the newspaper, there was no Liberal government in power in Britain. Nor was there any mention of Bernard Mattingly. The Prime Minister, it was said, was a Mrs Thatcher, head of a Conservative government. This piece of information disturbed him more than anything he had encountered so far. It seemed that the President of the United States was not Alan Stevenson but someone called George Bush.

In a medical columun, he read that the whole world was being ravaged by a sexually transmitted disease called AIDS. Ron had never heard of it. Yet the column claimed that thousands of people were dying of it, in Africa, Europe, and the United States. No cure had been found.

Just as disturbingly, an editorial on disarmament moves appeared to be saying that there had been two wars involving the whole world during the twentieth century.

Ron knew this could not have happened. There was no way in which Albania and Italy or England and Germany – to take two instances – could possibly attempt to destroy each other. What it all meant he did not know.

With a sudden uneasy inspiration, he checked on the date of the newspaper. It read September 1989 clearly enough. The idea had entered his head that he had been caught in a time warp and was back in the early years of the twentieth century, before the days of the reforming Czars. Such was not the case.

He hid the newspaper under the table and clutched his head.

He was going mad. The sooner he got home the better.

After an hour, the Korean couple entered the bar. They ignored him and sat with their backs to him.

He thought of his wife. Their marriage had been a good one. Both had ruined it by their infidelity. Both nourished hurt feelings and a desire to get their own back. One of them was always an infidelity

218

ahead of the other. Yet Steff had remained with him, had put up with all his drunkenness and bullying and failures. Now they had a little place of their own, heavily mortgaged, it was true, and were trying to build a better relationship. Ron had vowed never to hit her again.

The best advice he could give himself was to forget about that slut of a waitress and enjoy a good night's sleep in his comfortless single room. He had to catch the early flight from Moscow's Sheremeteivo Airport, to be in time for an important meeting with Bob Butler, his boss, tomorrow afternoon in Slough. He might get promoted. Steff would be pleased about that. She would also ask if he had been fucking other women.

He could lie his way out of this one, particularly if the promotion to sales manager came through.

Besides, this creature might give him some insight into what was happening. Perhaps she could tell him who Brezhnev was and what KGB stood for.

By this time, Ron – not an imaginative man – began to realise he had somehow got on an alternative possibility track. The shabby city that surrounded him felt heavy with sin – no, with sinfulness. It was as if some terrible crime had been committed which everyone had conspired not to discuss. And this secret had weighed the population down, so that the cheerful Moscow of his own time had sunk down into the earth from human view.

God knows what weird versions of clap the waitress might be carrying round with her. He had no idea what he was getting into.

Still, the thought of a woman's company in this miserable place was greatly attractive.

He tried to look at it all as a great stunt, a caper. How his pals would laugh when he told them. If he ever got back to them.

He smoked cigarettes and eked out a beer. The Swedes grew louder.

Came eleven-thirty, Ron put on his coat, grabbed his case, and went out into the streets. Everywhere seemed dark and depressing. It was as if he had somehow crossed a border between day and night, between yin and yang, between positive and negative.

As he walked along by the Moskva he observed there were none of the cheerful riverside restaurants, no floating pleasure-boats, which he had heard were the centre of the city's nightlife. No music, no wine, no women. The river flowed dark between high concrete banks, unloved, neglected, isolated from the life of Moscow, rushing on its secretive dark way. What if I am stuck here alone for ever, he asked himself. Isn't there a science of Chaos, and haven't I fallen into it?

It was impossible to know whether the waitress was an escape from or an embodiment of the unreason into which he had fallen.

He turned on his heel and made his way warily down a back alley to the rear of the hotel. A rat scampered, but there were no humans about. He came to an area of broken pavements covered with litter, which he waded through in the dark, cursing as he trod in something soft and deep. He could not see. From a small barred window came an orange fragment of light. Spreading a hand out before him, he arrived against a barrier. Searching carefully with his fingers, he found he was touching wood. Most probably this was the hut the waitress had designated.

Feeling his way, staggering and tripping, he finally reassured himself that he was waiting in the right place. He located the back door of the hotel, tried it, found it locked.

He stood in the dark, cold and uneasy. No stars shone overhead.

Following the sound of tumblers turning in a lock, the hotel door opened. A man emerged and walked off briskly into the night. The door was locked again from the inside; he heard the sound of a bolt being shot. The Russians had a mania for secrecy. So did Ron. He understood.

Several staff emerged from the door in pairs or alone. Worried in case his waitress missed him, Ron stood out from the sheltering hut. Nobody looked in his direction.

A lorry with one headlight jolted along the alley and wheezed to a halt. Two men got out. As Ron shrank back, he saw that one of the men was old and bent, moving painfully as he climbed from the cab. They both began to sort among the rubbish outside the hotel, occasionally throwing something into the back of their vehicle.

The door of the building opened again. Ron's waitress came out. It was ten minutes past midnight. She paused to get her night vision and then walked over to him. He pressed himself against her, feeling her hard body. Neither of them spoke.

With a gesture of caution to Ron, she went over and talked to the men by the lorry. The old man gave a wheezing laugh. There was a brief conversation, during which all three lit cigarettes the waitress distributed. Ron waited impatiently until she returned to his side.

'What's going on?' he asked.

220

She did not reply, puffing at her cigarette.

After a while, the men were finished with the rubbish. The younger one gave a whistle. The waitress returned the whistle and went forward. Ron followed as she climbed into the back of the lorry. He had misgivings but he went. They settled themselves down among the trash as the lorry started forward with a lurch.

Once through the maze of back streets, they were driving along a wide thoroughfare lit by sodium street lamps. Ron and the waitress stared at each other, their faces made anonymous in the orange glow. Her face was a mask, centuries old, her hair hung streakily over her temples. He felt in her a life of hard work, without pride. The perception warmed him towards her and he put an arm round her shoulders. He had always loved the downtrodden more than the proud and beautiful. It accorded with his poor image of himself.

She was slow to return his gesture of affection. Languidly, she moved a leg against his. He stared down the vanishing street, as once more they turned into a dark quarter. The excitement of the adventure on which he was now embarked dulled his apprehension, although he wondered about her relationship with the two lorry men, speculating whether they would beat him up and rob him at journey's end. He clutched his briefcase between his knees; it was metal and would be a useful weapon in a fight.

Here at least he was on familiar ground. Ron was no stranger to fights over women, and was used to giving a good account of himself. Whatever else had gone wrong with the universe, some constants remained: the art of getting the leg over, the swift knee in a rival's goolies. He sang a familiar little song in her ear:

> *With moonlight and romance*
> *If you don't seize the chance*
> *To get it on the sly*
> *Your archetype will be awry*
> *As Time Goes By.*

The waitress gave every appearance of not knowing the words, and silenced him with a hand over his mouth. They bumped on in silence and discomfort for a while.

'How far to go?'

'Ein kilometre.' Holding up one finger.

He tried to observe the route in case he had to walk back. Where

221

would he turn for help in case of trouble? He did not want to end up in the Moskva. He had a mad pal in Leeds who had been beaten up and thrown into the canal.

The depressing suburbs through which they passed, where hardly a light showed, were without visible feature. Flat, closed, bleak, Asiatic facades. At one point, on a corner, they passed a fight, where half-a-dozen men were hitting each other with what might have been pick-helves.

The rumpus vanished into the night. Moscow slept like an ill-fed gourmet, full of undigested secrets. The lorry stopped abruptly, sending its passengers sliding among the filfth. Ron climbed out fast, ready for trouble, the waitress following. They stood on a broken road surface. Immediately, the lorry bucked and moved off.

They were isolated in an area of desolation. It was possible to make out an immense pile of splintered wood, crowned by a bulldozer, where some rough-looking men sat by the machine, perhaps guarding it, warming themselves round a wood fire. To Ron's other hand, where a solitary lamp shone, a row of small concrete houses stood, ending in a shuttered box of a shop which advertised beer. Farther away, black against the night sky, silhouettes of tall apartment blocks could be seen. It was towards these blocks that the waitress now led Ron.

The heap of wood and beams was more extensive than he had thought. There were figures standing in it at intervals. It seemed to him that a complete old-fashioned village had been bulldozed to make way for Moscow's sprawl. Homes had been reduced to matchwood.

Someone called out to them, but the waitress made no answer. She led down a side lane, where the way underfoot was unpaved.

To encourage Ron, she pointed ahead to a looming block of jagged outline.

They skirted a low wall and reached the building. She went to a side door, knocked, and waited. Ron stood there, staring about him, clutching his case and feeling that he needed a drink.

After a long delay, the door was unbolted, unlocked, and dragged open. They went in, and the waitress passed a small package from her coat to a dumpy matron in black. Without changing her expression, the dumpy woman locked and bolted the door behind them and retreated into a small fortified office.

The smell of the place hit Ron as soon as he stepped into the passage. It reminded him of his term in jail. Here was a similar institution to prison. The smell was a compound of underprivilege, mixing disinfectant, polish, urine, dirt, fatty foods, and general staleness, bred by too many people being confined in an old building.

The waitress led him past notice boards, battered lockers, and a broken armchair to another corridor, and on to a stairwell. The odours became sharper. They ascended the stairs.

The steps were of precast concrete, the rail of cold metal, and the staircase cared nothing for human frailty. It was carpeted only as far as the first floor. As the waitress ascended beside him, Ron saw the weariness of her step. 'Some night this is going to be,' he told himself. He placed a hand encouragingly in the small of her back. She grimaced a smile without turning her head.

Smells of laundry, damp sheets, overworked heating appliances, came and went. On the upper floors, he listened to a low stratum of noise issuing from behind locked doors. Despite the late hour, several women were wandering about the corridors. None took any notice of Ron and the waitress.

In a side passage the waitress pulled a large key from her coat pocket, unlocked a door, and motioned Ron to go in. As he entered, he saw how scratched and bruised the panels of the door were, almost as if it had been attacked by animals.

The same sense of something under duress was apparent in her room. The furnishings crowded together as if for protection. Every surface was fingered and stained, their overused appearance reinforced by the dim luminance of a forty-watt bulb shining overhead. The murkiest corner was filled by a cupboard on which stood a tin basin; this was the washing alcove. Close by was a one-ring electric stove, much rusted. The greater part of the room was occupied by a bed, covered with a patchwork peasant quilt which provided the one note of colour in the room. A crucifix hung by a chain from one of the bedposts. Beside the bed, encroaching on it for lack of space, was a cupboard on top of which cardboard boxes were piled. The only other furniture – there was scarcely room for more – consisted of a table standing under a narrow and grimy window letting in the dark of the night.

The waitress locked her door and bolted it before crossing to the window and dragging a heavy curtain over it. By the window and under the bed were piled old cigarette cartons, all foreign, from Germany, France, England, China, and the States. He knew instinctively they were empty – probably saved from the hotel refuse bins.

Perhaps she liked the foreign names, Philip Morris and the rest. Well. He was up to his neck in the unknown now, and no mistake. Still. Nothing was ever going to be a greater shock than his first day at the orphanage, when he was four . . .

He was beginning to enjoy the adventure. He said to himself, 'Now then, Ronnie, if you can't fight your way out of trouble, you'd better fuck your way out.'

He set his case down and pulled off his coat. She hung the coat with hers on a hook behind the door, then went to the cupboard and brought out an unlabelled bottle with two small glasses. She poured clear liquid and passed him a glass. He sniffed. Vodka.

They toasted each other and drank.

He offered her an English cigarette, then handed her the pack. As they lit up, she gave him a smile, looking rather timid. Turning abruptly as if to hide weakness, she recorked her bottle and put it back in the cupboard. That was all he was getting in the way of alcohol.

'An instinctive liking,' he said. 'I mean, this is how it should be, eh? Friends on sight, right?' They sat side-by-side on the bed, puffing at their cigarettes; he laid a hand on her meagre thigh.

Two cheap reproductions hung on the walls facing them, one of birch forests deep in mist, one of a woman looking out of a deep-set window into a well-lit street. He pointed to it, saying he liked it.

'Frank-land,' she said. 'Franzosisch.'

She threw down her vodka, rose, pulled out a stained and tattered nightdress from under her bolster. It was or had been blue. She smoothed the wrinkles with one hand, while looking at him interrogatively.

'You won't need that,' he said, and laughed.

She paused, then threw the garment down on the end of the bed.

Suddenly, in her hesitation, he saw that she considered saying no to him and throwing him out. He dropped his gaze. The decision was hers. He never forced a woman.

Thoughts of Steff came back to him. He remembered the bitterness they went through after his trip a few weeks ago to Lyons in France. Steff had discovered that he had gone with a prostitute. A row had followed, which rumbled on for days. She had poured out hatred, had made the house almost unliveable. In the first throes of her fury, she had coshed him with a frying pan when he was asleep on the sofa. He had become terrified of her and of what she might do next. Finally, he swore that he would never go with other women again.

Yet here he was, settling in with this strange creature with the disgusting nightdress. The little whore in Lyons had been pernickety clean, a beauty in every way. Steff was always clean, always having a shower, washing her hair. This poor bitch had no shower. Her hair looked as if it had never seen shampoo.

Stubbing out her cigarette, the waitress paused by the light, then switched it off. The room was plunged into darkness. She had made up her mind to let him stay. He heard the sounds of her getting undressed and began to do the same.

As his eyes accustomed themselves to the dark, he saw her clearly by the corridor light shining under the bottom of the door. She pulled off soiled undergarments and threw them on the table. Fanning out, the light shone most strongly on her feet. They were grey and heavily veined, the toes splayed, their nails curved and long like bird claws. He saw they were filthy. They disappeared from view as she threw herself naked on the bed and pulled the quilt over herself.

An icy draught blew under the door. Ron put his clothes neatly on the table, trying to avoid her dirty undergarments, and climbed under the quilt beside her. She lifted her arms and wrapped them round his neck.

A rank odour assailed him, ancient and indecent. It caught in his throat. He almost gagged. It wafted from her, from all parts. She was settling back, opening her legs. He could scarcely breathe.

He sat up. 'You'll have to wash yourself,' he said. 'I can't bear it.'

He climbed off the bed again, fanning the air, rather than have her climb over him.

'You not like?' she asked.

When he did not reply, she got up and went on her grey feet over to the basin. Her toenails clicked on the floor covering. She poured water in the basin and commenced washing. He pulled open her cupboard, to drink from her vodka bottle, tipping the stuff down his throat. The waitress made no comment.

She rinsed her armpits and her sexual quarters with a dripping rag, drying herself on a square of towel.

'And the feet,' he ordered, pointing.

Meekly, she washed her feet, dragging each up in turn to reach nearer the basin.

*

225

This is Ron's story, not mine. But I had to ask myself if there wasn't, in this sordid lie he was telling me, something I deeply envied. I mean, not just the tacky woman, the foul room, the filthy fantasy world of 'Brezhnev's Russia', whatever that meant, but the whole desperate situation, something that took a man up wholly. This wish to be consumed. The whole romantic and absurd involvement. A hell. Oh yes, a hell all right.

And yet – we work away to build our security, to get a little roof and pay the rates. Still there's that thing unappeased. Don't we all secretly long, in our safe Britain, to take a Tupolev too far, to some godforsaken somewhere, where everything's to play for. . . ?

I only ask it.

At length she came back to the bed, standing looking at Ron in the deep gloom, as if asking permission to re-enter.

At this point in the proceedings, he was again tempted to call the whole thing off. As he struggled with his feelings, to his reluctance to pass by any willing woman was added his kind of perpetual good humour with the other sex, quite different from his aggressive manner with men, which urged him not to disappoint this unlucky creature who had so far exhibited nothing but good will.

The waitress had started all this by encouraging him at the dinner table. He did not know if there was danger involved in this escapade but, if so, then she probably had more to lose than he. Men might not be allowed in this – lodging house, or whatever it was. He would hardly be sent to the gulag if he was caught, but no one could say what might happen to the waitress. He supposed that at the least she might lose her job; which would bring with it a whole train of difficulties in Brezhnev's Russia.

I should explain where I was when my friend Ron was telling me this story, just to give you a little background.

We met by accident on Paddington station. We had not seen each other for about a year. I had come up on the train from Bournemouth to consult my parent company in Islington, and was crossing the forecourt when someone called my name.

There was Ron Wallace, grinning. He looked much as usual in a rather shabby grey suit with a cream shirt and a floppy tie – the picture, you might say, of an unprofessional professional man working for some down-at-heel outfit.

We were pleased to see each other, and went into the station bar for a pint or two of beer and a chat. I asked him where he was off to. This is what he said:

'I'm off to Glastonbury to see a wise old man who will tell me where my life's going. With any luck.'

It was an answer I liked. Of course I had some knowledge of how his life had been, and the hard times he had seen. I asked after his wife, Stephanie, and it was then that he started telling me this story I repeat to you. Just don't let it go any further.

So there he was stuck in this pokey little room with the waitress. Torn between compassion, lust, boredom, and exasperation. The way one always is, really.

He lay in the bed. She stood naked before him in the half-light, appearing helpless.

'You ought to look after yourself better,' he said, raising the quilt to let her in.

A sickly smell still pursued him. Concluding it came from the bed itself, he ignored it. She laid her head beside him on the patterned bolster. She smoothed dull hair back to gaze at him through the dim curdled light.

He stroked her cheek. When she buried her face suddenly in his chest, in a gesture of dependence, he caught the aroma of greasy kitchens, but he snuggled against her, feeling her still damp body. The waitress sniffed at him and sighed, rubbing against his thighs, perhaps excited by talc and deodorant scents, stigmata of the prosperous capitalist class. Prosperous! If only she knew! Ron and Steff had all manner of debts.

She opened her legs. As Ron groped in her moist pubic hair, he thought – a flash of humour – that he had his hand on the one thing that made life in the Soviet Union endurable. The Soviet Union and elsewhere . . . He penetrated her and she went almost immediately into orgasm, clutching him fiercely, bringing out a cry from the back of her throat. He thrust into her with savage glee.

Only afterwards, as they lay against each other, she clutching his limp penis, did her story start. She began to tell it in a low voice. He was idle, not really listening, comfortable with her against him, half-wanting a cigarette.

What she was saying became more important. She sat up, clutching a corner of the quilt over her naked breasts, addressing him fiercely.

227

Her supply of English and German words was running out. He gathered this was something about her childhood. Yet maybe it wasn't. A horse was dying. It had to be shot. Or it had been shot. This was somewhere on a farm. The name Vladimir was repeated, but he was not sure if she referred to the town or a man. He tried to question her, to make things clear, but she was intent on pouring out her misery.

Now it was about an infant – 'eine kleine kind', and the waitress was acting out her drama, dropping the quilt to gesticulate. The baby had been seized and banged against a wall – this demonstrated by a violent banging of her own head against the wall behind her. He could not understand if she was talking about herself or about a baby of hers. But the pain came through.

The waitress was sobbing and crying aloud, waving her arms, frequently calling the word 'smert', which he knew meant 'death'. Her body shook with the grief of it all.

It reached a melancholy conclusion. The story, incomprehensible and disturbing, ended with her coming alone to Moscow to work.

'To work here in this place. Arbeit. Nur Arbeit. Work alone. Abschliessen.'

'There, there.' He comforted her as he once used to comfort Steff's and his only child, wrapping her in his arms, rocking her. He was shaken by the agony of her outburst, angry with himself for failing to understand.

Of course there was no misunderstanding her misery. He felt it in his stomach, having known misery himself. Even in the pretty comfortable world he had left – to which he hoped to return on the morrow – personal tragedy was no rarity; some people always held the wrong cards. But he had fallen by accident into a shadow world, the world labelled 'Brezhnev's Russia', or 'Soviet Union', a world racked by terrible world wars and diseases. It was safe to say that whatever woes the poor waitress suffered, she represented millions who laboured under similar burdens.

He gave her a cigarette. A simple human gesture. He could think of nothing else to do.

She cried a little in a resigned fashion and wiped her tears on the quilt. Then she began to make love to him in a tender and provocative way. For a while paradise existed in the squalid room.

Ron Wallace woke. A full bladder had roused him. The waitress lay beside him, asleep and breathing softly. In the dim light, her face was young, even childlike.

Disengaging his arm from under her neck, Ron sat up and looked at his watch. Next moment, he was out of bed. The time was 5.50 a.m. A suspicion of daylight showed round the curtains, and his flight was due to leave at 9.30. His check-in time at Sheremeteivo Airport was 8.00 a.m. He had two hours in which to get to the airport, and no idea of where he was.

He listened at the door. All was quiet in the building. He had to return to the hotel and collect his suitcase. And first he had to have a pee.

His impulse was to awaken the waitress. Capable though she had shown herself to be, she might be less reliable this morning. She would find herself in a difficult situation to which perhaps she had given no thought on the previous evening; the entertaining of foreigners in one's apartment was surely a crime in Brezhnev's Russia.

Since she did not stir, he decided to leave her sleeping. Keeping his gaze on her face, he dressed fast and quietly. He stood for a moment looking down at her, then unstrapped his watch from his wrist and laid it by the bedside as a parting present.

As noiselessly as possible, he slipped into his coat and unbolted and unlocked the door. In the corridor, he closed the door behind him. Thought of the tragic life he left behind came to him; damn it, that was none of his business. It was urgent that he got to a toilet. There must be one on this floor.

All the doors were locked. He ran from one to another in increasing agony. There seemed to be no toilet. He was sweating. He must piss outside, fast.

He went quickly down the stairs, alert for other people. He heard voices but saw no one.

His penis tingled. 'Oh god,' he thought, 'have I caught a dose off that bitch? I must have been mad. How can I tell Steff? She'll leave me this time. Steff, I love you, I'm sorry, I'm a right bastard, I know it.'

He rushed to the front door, which had a narrow fanlight above it, admitting wan signs of dawn. The door was double-locked, with a mortice lock and a large padlocked bar across it. Next to the door stood a cramped concierge's office, firmly closed. Everyone had been locked in for the night.

229

He ran about the ground floor rather haphazardly, gasping, and came on the side door by which, he believed, he had entered the previous evening. That too was securely locked. He gasped a prayer. At any moment his bladder would burst.

At this point in Ron's story, I broke into heartless laughter.

He stared at me halfway between anger and amusement.

'It's no fun, going off your head for want of a piss,' he said.

I controlled my laughter. Ron is not a guy you like to offend. What amused me was the thought of a man who had been inside for GBH and done a stretch for breaking and entering in a situation where he was attempting breaking and exiting.

After trying and failing to kick in a panel on the side door, Ron ran about almost at random, looking for a way of escape.

Two steps at the end of the main corridor led down to another locked door, a boiler room in all probability. Next to the door was a broom cupboard and an alcove containing a mop, a brass tap, and a drain.

With a groan of relief, Ron unzipped his trousers and pissed violently into the drain. The relief nearly made him faint.

By now it must be almost half-past six.

As the urine drained from his body, he heard a door open along the corridor and a woman coughing. Her footsteps led away from where he stood. He heard her mount the stairs. Other doors were opening, female voices sounded, a snatch of song floated down; the noise level in the building was rising.

At last he was finished. He zipped his trouser, wondering what he should do to escape.

Two men were coming towards him. Although he saw them only in silhouette along the dark corridor, he recognised that they were old. They walked slowly, slack-kneed, and one jangled a bunch of keys. Ron sank back into the alcove.

The men passed within eighteen inches of him, talking to each other, not noticing him in the gloom. They unlocked the boiler room door and went in.

Immediately they were gone, Ron came out of his hiding place and hurried back to the main door. As he went, he tried each handle in the corridor in turn. All were locked.

At the front door, he was looking up at the narrow fanlight, wondering if it would open, when he heard faint sounds from the concierge's nook. Impelled by urgency, he pushed the office door open and looked in.

A plump old woman with her hair in a bun was just leaving the main room to enter a cubbyhole which served as a kitchen. She began to rattle a coffeepot.

In the room lay three men, sleeping in ungainly attitudes. Two were huddled on a sturdy table pushed against the far wall, the third lay under the table, his head resting peacefully on a pair of boots. A cluster of empty bottles and full ashtrays suggested that they had had a good night of it.

The room, in considerable disarray, had five sides. It served regularly as a bedroom as well as an office; against the left-hand wall a bed stood under a shelf bulging with files. Timetables and keys hung from the walls.

The loud and laboured breathing of the men reinforced the stuffy atmosphere. Where two of the walls came to a point was a window which the old woman had evidently opened to let air into the room.

Without hesitation, Ron crossed over to the window. In doing so, he kicked one of the empty vodka bottles. It rattled against its companions. He did not look round to see if the woman had caught sight of him.

One pane of the window had been repaired with brown paper. Taking little care not to injure himself, he forced himself through the opening feet first. The ground was further down than he had expected. He landed on concrete with a painful bump. Above him, an angry old woman stuck her head out and yelled at him. Ron got up and ran round the corner. At least he was free of that damned prison, where women were locked in every night.

Then came the thought.

'My bloody briefcase!'

He had left it standing by the waitress's bed.

Cursing furiously, he marched round the outside of the fortress. It was built of grey stone. All of its windows were barred.

A pile of rubbish, including the burnt-out carcass of a vehicle, stood against one wall. Even if he climbed up that way, it led only to a barred window. He prowled about, searching for the window of the boiler room, assuming there was one; he might be able to bribe the two old men to let him in that way.

He was frantic, and mad to know how the time was slipping away –

what a fool to leave his watch with that bitch. He had to catch his plane, otherwise there would be trouble with his company and with Steff, not to mention all the difficulties with the airline – whatever it was called now . . . Aeroflot. And he could not leave without the briefcase. In it were his precious contracts.

Struggling to deal with his anxiety levels, he kept from his mind the more dreadful and nebulous fear: that the airliner would deliver him not to his lovely Steff and the England he knew but to some other England ruled over not by Queen Margaret and P.M. Bernard Mattingly but by – whoever the lady was as mentioned in the newspaper – he had forgotten her name. He would perish if he was trapped forever in a dreadful shadow world where history had taken a wrong turn.

Despite his frenzy, he remembered something else. The damned doll the North Korean had given him. He was convinced it was packed with heroin or some other illegal substance. He had not believed the Korean's unlikely story about Mr Holmberg for one moment, and had intended to throw away the doll as soon as he was outside the hotel. Sexual pursuit had made him forget.

Ron became really frightened.

Running round the building, isolated on its wasteland, he could find no low boiler room window. He stood back, frustrated, when a stocky female figure in a black coat emerged from the building and walked off rapidly in the direction of the gigantic piles of broken wood Ron recalled from the previous night.

She had emerged from a side door. He ran to it, only to find it already locked. But even as he stood against it cursing, he heard the key turn from within, and it opened again. As another woman emerged, Ron dashed in. When an old man standing inside, key in hand, moved to stop him Ron pushed him brutally in the chest. Other women were pressing to leave the building for the day's work, stern of face, burly of shoulder. He ran into the main corridor and hastened upstairs.

But which floor?

Which bloody floor?

He had seen from outside there were five floors.

Which floor was the waitress on?

Not the ground or first floors. Not the top . . .

Christ!

The scene was changed from a few minutes earlier. Everyone was now up and about, and women in states of undress were wandering the corridors. They yelled at him and tried to grab him. In a few minutes, they would get themselves organised. Then he would be arrested.

He tried the second floor. He ran down the side passage. First door on right. He remembered that. As soon as he faced the door, he remembered the markings on the waitress's door, the savage scratches as if an animal had been there. This was not it.

He ran up to the third floor, causing more disturbance, and to the side passage. God, this nightmare! He was furious with himself. Now he faced the door with the deep scratch marks, and hammered on it. The door opened.

Ron took a swift look back. No one saw him, though he heard sounds of pursuit. He went in.

The waitress stood there, half-dressed, hand up to mouth in an attitude of misgiving.

One reason for that misgiving was clear. On the bed – that bed! – on top of the quilt and the dirty blue nightdress, the contents of Ron's briefcase had been spread, a dirty shirt, a pair of socks, a pair of underpants, some aspirins, the crossword book, the Korean doll, a copy of the *Daily Express* from a week ago, the precious contracts, and other belongings. The case lay with a screwdriver beside it. She had managed to prise the lock open.

'Get dressed,' he said. 'Schnell. I need you to get me out of here.'

'And to get me back to that sodding hotel,' he thought.

The waitress tried to make some apology. She had not expected him back. She thought the case was a present. He barked at her. She hurried to put on yesterday's dress and fit her grey feet into her heavy working shoes, whimpering as she did so.

He hardly looked to see what he was doing as he pushed everything into the briefcase, shouting to her to move. She was now his guarantee. She could get him out of the lodging house. She knew the way back to the Hotel Moskva.

'Schnell,' he growled, deliberately scaring her as he forced the case shut.

She offered him his watch back but he shook his head.

'Let's go. Fast. Vite. Schnell.'

'Okay, okay,' she said.

Together they hurried down the corridor and down the stone stairs, Ron with a firm grasp on her arm. Several women gathered.

They called to the waitress, but when she snapped back at them they stood aside and let her pass. A younger woman began to laugh. Others took it up. Soon there was general laughter. This was not the first time a woman had had a lodger for the night. Probably, Ron reflected, this was not the first time the waitress had had a lodger for the night.

The old man unlocked the side door and they were out with a stream of other workers into the chill air. Great was his relief. He had a chance with Steff yet.

'The hotel,' he said. 'Schnell. I must catch that bloody plane.'

Ron Wallace caught the bloody plane. He rang his office from Penge. The managing director had had to go up to Halifax, so happily he was not wanted till the following morning. The day was his. He was able to go back to Steff, preparing as he went to be innocent. After all, she meant far more to him than any of these stray bitches. He would serve another stretch for Steff. He told himself he had learnt a lesson. He would never go with another woman.

Sitting on the coach going home, he was relieved to find everything was as normal. The *Daily Express* he picked up at the airport carried a photograph of Bernard Mattingly, Britain's popular Prime Minister, opening the first stretch of a new motorway that would run between London and Birmingham. He searched for a reference to Russia. A small paragraph announced that Russia had a record wheat surplus, which they were shipping to the Third World. And the Pope had returned to Rome from his tour of Siberia.

Everything was normal. He thought again of the strange electric storm which had bathed his plane on the flight out. Perhaps that had all been subjective, a major ischemic event in the brain stem. He had been working too hard recently.

Nothing had happened. He had imagined the whole dark world, Brezhnev, the waitress, and all.

Steff was amiable and credulous and listened to all he had to say about the boredom of Moscow. While he was showering, she even went to unpack his things for him.

He stepped naked from the shower. She had opened the briefcase. She was holding up for his inspection a dirty blue nightdress.

234

Contributors

KEITH ROBERTS lives in Amesbury, Wiltshire. He trained in the visual arts and produced covers and interior illustrations for *Impulse* and *New Worlds* in the 1960s and 1970s. His books include *Pavane*, *The Chalk Giants*, *Kiteworld* and the recent *The Lordly Ones*. Through the small press Kerosina he has also published *Kaeti & Co.*, *Grainne* and, most recently, *The Road to Paradise*.

J. D. GRESHAM was born in the Midlands in 1952. She has worked as a teacher for thirteen years, two of which were spent in Italy. She now lives in London, from where she makes frequent escapes into the country to indulge her passion for walking. She is currently working on her second novel.

ERIC BROWN was born in Haworth, West Yorkshire, in 1960 and has lived in Australia, India and Greece, where he ran a youth hostel for a time on Crete. He has published stories in *Interzone* and a collection, *The Time-Lapsed Man*, is due from Pan in 1990, which will be fifteen years from when he started writing.

SHERRY COLDSMITH worked in Britain for ten years as a computer systems designer before returning to her native Texas in the summer of 1989. She has published 'Caruso' in Lewis Shiner's *When the Music's Over* and 'Ticanau's Child' in Lisa Tuttle's forthcoming anthology of horror stories by women. She now works as a full-time writer and has a novel in progress.

IAN McDONALD was born in Manchester in 1960 but has lived most of his life in Northern Ireland. His first story was published in 1982. He was nominated for a John W. Campbell Award in 1985, and his 'Unfinished Portrait of the King of Pain, by Van Gogh' was a Nebula finalist in this year's novelette category. His new novel is *Out on Blue Six*, which he describes as a 'totalitarian comedy'.

SIMON D. INGS was born in Hampshire in 1965 and lives, works and writes in London. 'Blessed Fields' is his first published story; since then he has sold a humorous fantasy to *Interzone* and has just completed his first science fiction thriller – a heady farrago of werewolves, incest and trifle.

GILL ALDERMAN was born in Dorset and lives in Northamptonshire with her husband, three cats and two lurchers. Her first novel, *The Archivist*, will be published by Unwin Hyman in October 1989.

S. M. BAXTER grew up in Liverpool, is married, and now lives in High Wycombe. He has a maths degree and has worked in academic research, teaching and a series of computing jobs. He has been writing sf for about 15 years, 'but selling for rather less, mostly to *Interzone*'.

LOUISE COOPER published her first fantasy novel, *The Book of Paradox*, in 1973; it was followed in 1985 by *The Time Master Trilogy: The Initiate, The Outcast*, and *The Master*. She is currently writing an eight book series called *Indigo*, of which *Nemesis* and *Inferno* have been published, with *Infanta* and *Nocturne*, due in 1989. 'Cry' is only her second short story published.

CHRISTOPHER EVANS has recently completed a novel, *Chimeras*, and is about to embark on another. He presently teaches full time at a secondary school in South London. His short stories have appeared in *Interzone, Dark Fantasies* and *Zenith 1*.

CHRISTIAN LEHMANN was born in Paris in 1958, of Anglo-Mauritian and French parents. His love for science fiction and fantastic literature led to many channel crossings during his adolescent years, to visit conventions, during which he met and befriended many British fans and writers, including his collaborator in *Other Edens 3*, Garry Kilworth. He is a medical doctor living near Paris, and is currently working on his second novel following the success of *La Folie Kennaway*.

GARRY KILWORTH has recently abandoned his estates in Essex to live and work in Hong Kong, from where the usual flood of stories and novels continues to issue. His recent novels are *In The Hollow of the Deep Sea Wave* and the acclaimed *Hunter's Moon*, a story of foxes. A new collection of short stories is forthcoming.

CHRISTINA LAKE lives in Bristol and works three days a week as a technical librarian in the water industry. She has also had a short story, 'Assyria', published in *Interzone* and is due to appear in Alex Stewart's *Arrows of Eros* anthology.

KEITH N. BROOKE was born in 1966 and has a degree in environmental sciences. He has been writing full time for two years, supported by his wife, Alison. He has written two novels and has stories waiting to appear in *Interzone* and the second Games Workshop 'Warhammer' anthology.

CHRIS MORGAN has had sf, fantasy and horror stories published. His most recent book is *Dark Fantasies*, an anthology of subtle horror published by Century in the summer of 1989. Born in Oxford, he now lives in Birmingham, where he writes, edits, reviews and teaches creative writing.

LISA TUTTLE was born in Texas but has lived in Britain since 1980. Her novels are *Windhaven* (co-written with George R. R. Martin), *Familiar Spirit* and *Gabriel*, while her short stories are published widely and have been collected as *A Nest of Nightmares* and *A Spaceship Made of Stone*. She wrote the *Encyclopaedia of Feminism* and *Heroines*, and most recently has edited *The Skin of the Soul*. She is currently working on a new novel.

BRIAN ALDISS's recent books include the *Helliconia* trilogy and a revised version of his landmark history of science fiction, *Trillion Year Spree*. He was born in East Anglia but now lives in Oxford. His other books include *Non-Stop, Hothouse, Report on Probability A, The Malacia Tapestry* and *Life in the West*. His most recent novel is *Forgotten Life*.

237

OTHER EDENS
Edited by Christopher Evans and Robert Holdstock

Sixteen fantasy and science fiction tales from established British-based writers including Garry Kilworth, M. John Harrison, Tanith Lee, Brian Aldiss, Michael Moorcock, Keith Roberts, Lisa Tuttle and Ian Watson.

Take a flight of the imagination to distant planets, future worlds, other Edens; through mysteries ancient and modern, dark rituals, spine-chilling hauntings and creatures made from human flesh, and travel beyond the stars, to the enigmas of science and time, and man's eternal battle for survival and for power.

'The whole collection is excellent value.'
New Statesman

'Although the theme is science fiction and fantasy the contributors to this original anthology are all imaginative story-tellers in their own right and the tales can be enjoyed by the general reader, as well as the specialist.'
Echo

'Marvellous stories . . . four of these are absolutely brilliant, the rest only very good . . . highly recommended.'   *Birmingham Science Fiction Group*

'. . . a collection of quality writing.'
Terry Greer

KAIROS
Gwyneth Jones

The streets of London: Japanese tourists in smog-masks and Work Force youths in their tagged orange overalls. It's the first decade of the new century and business as usual for UK Ltd. BREAKTHRU reps in their preposterous angel fancy-dress stalk the dissidents, making many converts with their own brand of extremism.

Slash-Hack-Burn: break down the old, make room for the new age. KAIROS is fear. KAIROS is chaos. KAIROS is opportunity. KAIROS is the ruler of change. It will break down all the walls – even that sacred and infinitely necessary barrier between Mind and the World. The KAIROS has the power: BREAKTHRU have the KAIROS.

An act of surreal terrorism is about to be set in motion – and it's about to go badly wrong . . .

CLOUDROCK
Garry Kilworth

On Cloudrock the penalty for imperfection is death: death by the long fall into the void, through the poisonous mists and gases that rise from the deadlands far, far below. The two tribes who survive on the Rock, the tribes of Day and Night, keep their families tight, their bloodlines pure and true, by incest, by cannibalism and by murder. Parcelling out their tiny world in measures of light and time, they wrap themselves in ritual and taboo, each family denying the presence of the other.

Then came the Shadow.

Born to the matriarch Catrunner, the Shadow is deformed – a neuter dwarf – a natural candidate for instant death. But for this mutant, fate intervenes. The Shadow may live – on the condition that none acknowledge its presence: one word, one glance, and the Shadow will join its luckless kin in the long death-flight.

Surviving on the outskirts of the family, the Shadow's very existence creates an unspoken question that challenges the ties that bind.

This is the Shadow's tale.

TERRAPLANE
Jack Womack

On the walls of the bars and restaurants of twenty-first century Moscow Big boy grins down from the ads in twelvecolour holograph. GO NOW AND BUY. MONEY IS LIFE – SPEND IT. THRIFTY ARE TRAITORS.

But Luke and Jake are not touristing: they've got a job to do for O'Malley and Dryco: to steal Oktobriana Osipova and the experimental transferral device from under the nose of the Dream Team.

It's a bold and dangerous plan that goes fatally wrong.

Twentieth-century New York. 1939. It's a nightmare. The slave trade has only just been abolished. It's a world of identity passes, police roadblocks and imminent war. Churchill is dead. Roosevelt has been assassinated, Europe lies vulnerable. Luther, Jake and Oktobriana find themselves trapped in warped history, in an unfamiliar world racing headlong to destruction, with only a chance in a million of escape . . .

THE ICE MONKEY
M. John Harrison

The world of *The Ice Monkey* is a dangerous place, which steals over you like a dream. It is a twilight world of stark cities, doomed humanity, bizarre rites and psychic horrors. Powerful and unsettling, this collection established M. John Harrison as a distinctive and significant voice in contemporary fiction.

'Harrison's imagination is merciless. His fiction is a scalpel slicing through the skin of the world to make dissections both strange and disturbingly familiar. This collection puts him in the company of Ian McEwan and Peter Carey, but he is grittier than Carey and wittier than McEwan.'   *Times Literary Supplement*

'. . . a sharpness of detail and sureness of overall control that is wholly admirable . . . writing of remarkable resonance and power.'
London Review of Books

'M. John Harrison is the finest British writer now writing horror fiction and by far the most original.'   *Ramsey Campbell*

'Stylish, accomplished, evocative short stories, exemplary fictions of unease shot through with poetic insights and most beautifully written.'   *Angela Carter*

'Overpowering'   *Punch*

'. . . material handled with a grace that approaches the mandarin . . . A brief review can only serve to indicate the richness of this book if taken as a whole . . . Mr Harrison's progress becomes fascinating.'   Robert Nye. *The Guardian*

Welcome to the nightmare world of Paradys!

BOOK OF THE DAMNED
Secret Books of Paradys 1
Tanith Lee

Jehanine: demon or saint?

Her days spent at the Nunnery of the Angel; her nights in the vicious backstreets of Paradys, wreaking revenge on men for the wrongs she had suffered at their hands.

'How fast does a man run when the Devil is after him?' Andre St Jean is about to find out, as a young man collapses at his feet and presses into his hand a strange scarab ring, containing the secret of life . . .

The stranger pushed a note across the table: 'In a week or less I shall be dead.' In a week, he was, and most unnaturally. She found herself drawn to the house where he died, to unravel the web of mystery and horror that had been spun about him . . .

BOOK OF THE BEAST
Secret Books of Paradys 2
Tanith Lee

It was created on the fifth day of the Earth; scaled not feathered – the Beast.

From the most ancient of days, passed through the seed of generations, still it preys on the unlucky, the unwary and the unchaste. Its appetite is ravenous and eternal.

Tanith Lee weaves a chilling tale of horror through the streets of Paradys: from the times when the Legions ruled the Empire, and Centurion Retullus Vusca hoped to change his luck ...

To the wedding of an innocent maid who hoped to win the affection of a cold, but handsome lord, unaware of the consequences of her seduction ...

To a scholar, wise in the ways of magic, who was determined to end the terror ...

And all the while there were cries in the night, and blood on the stones in the morning.